Acclaim for the ...................................................
and Eve Pollard

'Spicy, sharp but sympathetic insider's view'
Celia Brayfield

'Flashy, trashy and lots of fun, this book sashays as confidently as its authors through the media circus'
*Daily Mail*

'An entertaining account of boardroom battles and family rivalries'
*Woman's Journal*

'A page turner . . . great fun'
*The Times*

'Enjoyable blockbuster'
*Sunday Times*

'Sizzling'
*Ideal Home*

'An ebullient airport novel . . . a rattling good yarn by three media high-flyers who have been there, done that and survived to tell an exciting tale'
Carmen Callil, *Telegraph*

'The three heroines are indeed a sympathetic trio, swapping love and advice and caustic banter but always caring, sharing and raising a glass to friendship'
Lesley White, *Sunday Times*

'Witty, perceptive and warm . . . should not be missed'
*Daily Express*

'Sex and shopping with a touch of class'
Maureen Freely, *Options*

Val Corbett, Joyce Hopkirk and Eve Pollard are also the authors of bestselling SPLASH, BEST OF ENEMIES and DOUBLE TROUBLE.

Val Corbett was a newspaper journalist in South Africa and London before switching to television. She produced several acclaimed programmes and became a director of a leading independent television production company. She is married to Robin Corbett MP and has a daughter and two stepchildren.

Joyce Hopkirk has been an editor on *Cosmopolitan*, the *Sun* newspaper, the *Sunday Times*, the *Daily Mirror* and the magazines *She* and *Chic*. She has twice won the Magazine Editor of the Year Award. She is married to Bill Lear, an executive of De Beers; they have a daughter and a son.

Eve Pollard worked on newspapers and magazines before becoming editor of the *Sunday Mirror*, where she won the Editor of the Year Award. She was editor of the *Sunday Express* when it won both the Newspaper of the Year and the Sunday Newspaper of the Year awards. She is a regular broadcaster on television and radio. She is married to Sir Nicholas Lloyd and has a daughter, a son and three stepchildren.

*Also by Val Corbett, Joyce Hopkirk and Eve Pollard*

Splash
Best of Enemies
Double Trouble

# Unfinished Business

## Val Corbett, Joyce Hopkirk and Eve Pollard

**HEADLINE**

First published in 1998
by HEADLINE BOOK PUBLISHING

First published in paperback in 1999
by HEADLINE BOOK PUBLISHING

10 9 8 7 6 5 4 3 2 1

ISBN 0 7472 5639 X

Typeset by
Letterpart Limited, Reigate, Surrey

Printed and bound in Great Britain by
Clays Ltd, St Ives plc

HEADLINE BOOK PUBLISHING
A division of Hodder Headline PLC
338 Euston Road
London NW1 3BH

Dedicated to the ones we love

# ACKNOWLEDGEMENTS

Executive coach, Jinny Ditzler; financial guru, John Minshull-Beech; Jane Reed, News International; Tony de Angeli; Mary Corbett, chief executive of Marriage Care; Christine Matthews; Ben Phillips; Sue Thomas; computer doctor Peter Venes who came when called; Lee Bender; June Hutcheson and Sandy Sidman; Andy Lamont; Fionnula McDonnell; Janine Dines; Pauline Beard; Stephanie and many others who have been trying to conceive a baby and told us about it; Anne-Elisabeth Moutet; Lord Thurso, Gilly Turner, Sister Marian and the staff at Champneys health resort; Maureen Lipman; Nicholas Coleridge, publishing director, Condé Nast; Terry Mansfield, managing director, National Magazines; and in memory of Ghislaine Armitage Clairon d'Haussonville.

As always we are grateful to our editor Marion Donaldson, agent Carole Blake and thank our children and our husbands whose rock-like qualities we appreciate more every day.

# Chapter One

Helen's heartbeat was erratic as she gazed numbly at the pile of discarded papers on her husband's desk. She could picture him, spectacles on the end of his nose, frowning as he pored over his paperwork, the pen that he'd been holding only an hour before he left home discarded by the side of the silver letter opener, an anniversary present from her.

She began to feel dizzy as she tried to absorb the contents of his devastating letter.

'I can't explain why I needed another woman . . .'

Another woman? She stared aghast at her husband's portrait above the mantelpiece. His brooding eyes seemed to be gazing directly at her.

'. . . why I needed another woman when I had you.'

There was a pounding in her head. What was he talking about? Was this why he had been on his way to the Hamptons? Cheating on her until the day of his death?

By now her throat had closed up and the pain in her head was excruciating. She knew him so well. How could he have put on such an act? She corrected herself: she thought she knew him so well.

The letter slipped on to her lap. She found she could not focus on her husband's familiar handwriting and it took her a moment or two to recover before she could start reading again.

'I don't want you to be too sad about my death,' he wrote. 'It's been a great life and, Helen, you've been there every step of the way, a wonderful partner and mother to our girls. We've often said we've been married too long to have secrets from each other. That was a lie, I'm afraid, one of the many I want you to forgive me for . . .'

Helen lay back on the sofa, fighting for control.

'. . . and if you've been given this letter, it means that this other woman is still part of my life.'

Part of his life? How much of a part?

With an effort she turned to the next page. 'But for all this I need you to know that I have loved you since our wedding day and I still do. Our years together have been very happy ones and I thank you for them.'

The hypocrisy was too much to bear and Helen flung the letter angrily to the floor and shouted furiously at the portrait, 'Liar! Liar! Liar!'

Like a guilty schoolgirl the dark-haired woman sneaked up the back staircase, making for the executive cloakroom. After giving the prearranged coded knock, the door opened slightly to reveal the company's most high-profile director. He was wearing just his boxer shorts.

'You were taking a chance,' she said, her brown eyes

glinting mischievously. 'It might've been the chief.'

He caught hold of her tightly. 'I happen to know he's still in the States. Come here, you. I've a whole half an hour and I've left my mobile downstairs.'

'Then you must be serious.' She ran a hand through the unruly hair which caused her so much trouble each morning and gazed round at the ornate gold and blue furnishings.

'I bet we're first to christen this place,' he said as he moved his fingers lightly down her arm, giving the little-boy grin which had first attracted her to him. 'Our own version of the mile-high club.'

'But we'd better keep the turbulence down,' she replied, kicking off her shoes, enjoying the feeling of the deep-pile carpet beneath her stockinged feet. He took her black jacket and hung it over a dolphin-shaped hook behind the door, which he locked.

Most of the rooms in the building could not be locked from the inside, a legacy from a previous owner who suspected staff of impropriety. There was a security camera in the corridor but no sign of hidden lenses or bugging equipment inside the cloakroom. And as they were two of only five privileged key-holders, there was little risk of being interrupted.

Like many tycoons of short stature, their chairman Mark Temple-Smith favoured an over-stated Renaissance baroque style which he thought would impress outsiders. The pale blue and gold colour scheme of this executive cloakroom was his trademark; he used the same colours in his cars, his customised Lear jet, and as his racing colours. Long ago someone had apparently told him the blue matched his eyes and the gold epitomised success.

'Isn't it puzzling that such a successful man employs such duff designers? This one was given too much power,' she remarked. Her rangy frame darted into the adjoining white marble bathroom and returned with a pair of white fluffy bath sheets which she spread on the divan, one of the comforts of the executive cloakroom.

'You should see the loo in New York. Compared to that, this decorator was restrained.'

As she struggled with the zipper of her close-fitting dress, he half-lifted her into the air and moved her towards the divan. He pulled her on top of him. She was well above average height for a woman and he was five inches taller; the divan, however, was short.

'I think we'll be happier on the floor,' he grinned and pulled her down, bath sheets and all. She started to reply but he silenced her by kissing the corners of her mouth, then slowly travelled down the length of her throat to her breasts. He paused to savour each nipple, stroking, touching, nibbling. She groaned with pleasure, loving the feel of his mouth and what it was doing to her. She ran her nails up and down his back, feeling his body arch, feeling the increasing hardness of him against her.

Perhaps it was the unusual surroundings or the danger of being discovered that heightened their passion but as they lay panting side by side afterwards they agreed it had been unforgettable.

'That was so good,' she said, burying her face in his

shoulder. 'Do you think we should come here more often?'

They started to laugh. He cupped his hand over her mouth in an attempt to suppress the sound. Then he ruffled her dark wavy hair and kissed her tenderly.

'You're very necessary to my life, Mrs Drummond.'

'Thank you, Mr Drummond, smooth-talking bastard.'

He laughed and pinched his wife's arm.

When they first married four years ago, Georgina had been physically shy and Alistair had had difficulty persuading her she had a desirable body. She complained that her arms were too bony, her hands and legs too thin and took great care to cover up in public. But he had given her confidence and lately she was far less inhibited about her coltish looks.

They did not need to seek out extra sexual stimulants; that was not their motive for coming to the cloakroom. He was about to leave on a business trip and after seven months of trying for a baby they had to time their lovemaking to coincide with her most fertile days. Each month there were only three or four days when conception was likely and when he was due to be absent, like today, they had to seize their opportunities, however awkward. He was beginning to feel downcast about their chances. At forty-four he was eleven years older than she was so he was the one who heard the biological clock ticking loudest. It was he who marked the relevant days with red ink on the calendar in their oak and chrome kitchen and keyed it in to her electronic organiser. And his. Though neither had admitted it to the other, this had diminished the fun of what had been their favourite recreational activity.

Today, the adrenalin surge of knowing that only a few metres away, editors, art directors and writers were busy organising fashion shoots, writing features, sub-editing articles or choosing photographic spreads while they enjoyed secret sex might do the trick.

They were gathering up their clothes when Alistair pointed to the door handle which was moving up and down.

'Someone's trying to get in,' he whispered.

Georgie reached for a towel, while Alistair hurriedly dressed.

'Alistair? Are you in there?' called a voice.

It was Harry Ferguson, their magazine group's circulation director.

'Yes, what's up?' Alistair asked.

'I've just had Giles on the phone from New York and he needs to speak to us urgently. Where is Georgina?' Harry sounded agitated.

'I'm not sure,' said Alistair. 'But leave it to me, I'll find her. Let's meet in my office in a few minutes.'

It took Alistair very little time to finish dressing. He smoothed his wayward blond hair, a legacy, as he used to joke, of his Nordic ancestry, opened the cloakroom door and strode swiftly along the corridor towards his office. Alistair always moved at a fast pace and most of his colleagues had difficulty keeping up with him.

Conscious that eyes might be watching, Georgina

waited a few minutes before following her husband. When she reached his office he had already put a call through to their headquarters in New York.

'Giles? Georgina and Harry are with me,' he said, switching on the speaker phone. 'What's happened?'

The clipped voice of their chief executive echoed around the room. 'There's no easy way to tell you . . . Mark's had a car accident. He's been killed.'

For a moment the three stared blankly at each other. Alistair's face drained of colour, Georgie covered her mouth with her hands, and Harry sat down heavily.

At last Alistair found his voice. 'I can't believe it, I only spoke to him a couple of days ago and . . .' he broke off.

Georgie put her arm on her husband's shoulder, a rare tactile display in public.

'Was Helen with him?' she asked, bending close to the microphone.

'No, thank goodness. I've already sent her flowers on our behalf but she's not taking any calls.'

Unusually, Giles told them, the chairman had been driving himself along the freeway towards New York, having given his chauffeur time off.

Alistair studied his hands and for a moment it seemed to Georgie that he was going to break down. But he cleared his throat and said dully, 'But Mark was such a careful driver. In twenty years he's not so much as scratched a bumper. When did it happen?'

'A few hours ago. They still don't know what caused it, we're waiting to hear from the police. As you can imagine, everyone's in shock over here. You need to tell the staff as soon as possible before the news gets out.' The disembodied voice went on briskly, 'I'll keep you informed the moment I hear anything more. Goodbye.'

Alistair switched off the intercom.

'It's so cruel,' said Georgie, her voice breaking. 'Poor Helen, she'll be devastated.'

'My God, he was only fifty-six.' Alistair began to pace distractedly around the room. 'He had so much more to do. I can't imagine this company without him.'

'That's the trouble,' said Harry, speaking at last. 'I always said he should have delegated more.'

'Cut that out, Harry,' said Alistair sharply. 'Mark wasn't only my boss, he was a friend.'

'I'm sorry the chairman's dead,' said Harry defensively, 'but we have to think about what's going to happen now.'

'For God's sake, let's have some time to mourn the man before we start speculating about the future,' said Georgie indignantly.

Alistair intervened. 'Harry, could you call the staff together, say in fifteen minutes?'

It was obvious from Harry's expression that he still took umbrage at being given an order by Alistair.

Mark Temple-Smith had been deft at defining the pecking order in his organisation. Unlike other publishing companies, he had elevated the role of publishing director ahead of marketing, finance and circulation. When, a couple of years previously, he had taken over the group for whom Georgie then worked, he had divided the company into two sections: the seven women's interest magazines, headed by Georgina Luckhurst (she had retained her maiden name), and the eight news and male-orientated titles which he had put under Alistair Drummond's command. Mark had so structured the pyramid that the industry's golden couple had overall responsibility for the commercial health and creative strategies of their titles. As joint publishing directors, Georgie and Alistair enjoyed equal status and avoided being in direct competition for prestige and power because they each had their own magazines to nurture in the marketplace. They were scrupulous about not invading each other's territory.

Mark allowed his executives great freedom, but he insisted they report directly to him on any important matter and in this way he kept control of his privately-owned company. His long-serving chief executive Giles Beamish was seen merely as a figurehead, and although his top employees all had the title director, none of them owned shares.

Harry opened his mouth as if to say something but changed his mind and nodded curtly as he left the room.

Alistair rubbed his eyes wearily. 'I can't take it in. Mark was healthy, vibrant, full of plans. I can't believe I'm never going to see him again.' He took hold of Georgie's hands. 'I hope he didn't suffer.'

She was silent for a moment. 'It's probably not much comfort now but we have to think he died at the peak of his powers, happy to have achieved everything he'd set out to do . . .' Her voice cracked.

He put his arms round her. 'I used to talk to him three or four times a week. I'm going to miss him. Imagine what it's like for Helen and the girls.'

They were silent for a while, immersed in their misery. Eventually Alistair said, 'I must get myself to New York right away. I'm not sure what use I can be to Helen but I can't just sit here. We used to be friends in the old days though we've drifted apart lately. Still, maybe she can talk to me more easily than some of the others.'

Georgie nodded solemnly. 'Mark always treated you like the son he never had and you should be there.'

Alistair had gained his journalistic spurs in the provinces, mainly on the *Birmingham Post*, the influential and prosperous morning paper in the Midlands. After six months of reporting weddings by moped he progressed to social events, then court reporting and on to the giddy heights of feature writing. By then he had concluded that provincial papers were not the fast-track route to success.

His first big break came when he met Mark at a Christmas party given by a printing firm. Mark was about to start his own magazine company and Alistair sent him two unsolicited articles which, to his pleasure, Mark accepted. Alistair's love affair with magazines started from that moment. He saw how much better articles looked when printed on glossy paper. But when Mark offered him a job, he demurred at first, worried about joining such a young organisation which, as far as he could tell, had little start-up money. Besides he still enjoyed the fast world of newspapers. 'I'm not sure I want to get into the slow lane and wait a couple of months before my words are published,' he told Mark.

Mark urged him to join, Helen at his side. 'We're going to grow. We intend to turn this into an international company. Our expertise is in advertising and marketing and we need editorial skills like yours.'

Alistair was impressed by how much influence Helen had in those days. Later he ascribed his own attitude towards bolstering female talent directly to the example she set the tiny staff then. He remembered her words which clinched his decision to join their company: 'You'll have the chance to create your own magazines. You'll be the one in the driving seat. A title could be a success or failure due entirely to your efforts. Now what could be a better challenge?'

They could not afford to match the salaries paid by competing magazines and with the rapid staff turnover, Alistair found himself deputy editor within a few months. From that base he learned all he needed to know about editing and survival. His role in the new company did indeed come from his own initiative. He procured expensive art books from publishers to review in *Literary Adventures*, after which he would sell them at a second-hand bookshop. The cash he received was spent on reviewing restaurants for another of Mark's fledgling magazines.

The glorious Technicolor world of the glossies became Alistair's métier. Everything he touched turned to gold. He was fêted as the launch king, able to spot the next gap in the magazine market. As the company prospered, so did he. Before Mark decamped with his family to New York after enlarging Amalgamated's empire by incorporating several titles there, he appointed Alistair UK publishing director, the youngest in the industry, responsible for a group of highly profitable and successful magazines. Mark's faith in him had been unshakeable, and Alistair knew his death would leave a gap in his life that would be hard to fill.

He walked to the window, surveying the grey panorama of roofs stretching out below the building. 'If anything happened to either of us,' he asked dully, 'what would we leave behind?'

'I don't know,' Georgie said slowly. 'Not much, I suppose.'

'A few magazine titles, some awards, nothing really important.' Alistair's voice grew stronger as he walked towards her and again took her into his arms. 'I hope we were successful today because what I want most in the world right now is a child.'

# Chapter Two

Helen's anger was mounting as she paced the floor of the pristine white bedroom. It and the adjoining his-and-her dressing rooms, twin bathrooms and atrium gym were unrelieved by a single touch of colour. That was one damned thing she would change at once. The designer had been Mark's choice, of course. Too prone to the latest vagaries of interior fashion, one minute he veered towards the florid, the next to minimalism. Like the dutiful wife, she hardly ever voiced criticism but this time she hadn't been able to resist commenting that it was like sleeping in a clinic. Mark had laughed, saying it was entirely appropriate and would prepare them for the future. But of course he was never going to grow old with her now.

His death was difficult to grasp. Only a few hours earlier he had been having breakfast with her, then she was opening the doors to an impassive police officer who told her the stark details of the accident not far from the Hamptons, the millionaires' playground on Long Island. The police did not have many details but there was no doubt concerning the identity of the driver. He had been alone in the car. Where the hell was his chauffeur?

Mark was supposed to have been in New York, not on his way to the weekend haunt of socialites. The Magazine Society was having an all-male 'roasting' for Roger Fenton, the man Mark had bested in the takeover two years ago. This sort of occasion, during which the chief guest was subjected to a plethora of funny if vituperative jokes, remarks and anecdotes, was well-known in show-business and now journalists had adopted the idea. It would be a late night so he had said he would stay over at their duplex in Trump Tower.

Good God, he had not even allowed her to mourn his death, thrusting this confession at her via his bank manager, who had arrived soon after the police, while she was still in a state of shock. Whatever his motives, it was hard to forgive him for that.

She had been sharing him for nearly a third of her married life. Her marriage had been a sham. How could she have not known, not even suspected? And why, why, did he choose to tell her now? Did he expect her to accept all this breast-beating as compensation for having been deceived all these years? She could almost hear his voice as he sought to excuse his behaviour.

'I want you to believe that my mistress took nothing away from you. Many times she urged me to leave you and the girls but I never considered divorce. Never once.'

Relying on him, as she had totally, for emotional and practical support, she needed to believe the affectionate words he had penned, to help lessen the anger. But how was it possible? If the affair had been limited to his loins, the sexual betrayal would have been hard enough to bear. Helen had a sophisticated attitude towards infidelity. But it was apparent from the *eight years* the affair had lasted that this woman must have engaged his mind as well as his body. This was particularly hard to bear when she remembered how close they had been.

'Helen, I beg you to forgive me for the hurt I am causing you now. But as always, my dear, I am being practical.'

Practical? After dropping that bombshell? Her fury threatened to overwhelm her.

'There is a no-kiss-and-tell contract with the woman concerned but to ensure her silence I have deposited diamonds to the value of approximately five million dollars in her name in two foreign banks. The stones are divided equally into two parcels. I've arranged that she will have access to the first parcel three months after my death and the final one two years later, on condition she does not talk about our relationship. These diamonds plus the remainder of the rental package on the house in the Hamptons and the apartment on Fifth Avenue . . .'

Diamonds. An ocean-side home. An apartment in the smartest area of New York. The thought of such reward for a woman who had stolen her husband's time and affection nearly choked Helen.

'. . . should give her adequate financial provision for the rest of her life. This settlement will not affect your personal fortune. You will still have enough money left to last two lifetimes. I am as certain as I can be that she will not embarrass my memory by publishing details of our time together.'

His memory. What about hers? Why did he have to make them worthless in such a cold, calculating way?

'The diamonds are an insurance to protect you, the girls and, admittedly, my reputation, at least for two years. After that I don't suppose anyone will be interested in her story.'

The affair had been a secret for such a long time, she thought bitterly, couldn't he have paid off the woman the way they had lived, surreptitiously?

As if on cue, his letter answered her question.

'By now you are probably wondering why I needed to burden you with all this. Why didn't I leave instructions for it to be handled without involving you? Although I know you will be both deeply upset and enraged by this settlement, you cannot, and should not, contest it. It would have been impossible to withdraw such a sum of money from the company. I couldn't risk having an IRS audit so I am using our personal portfolio. Although our private estate can well afford this amount, you would, of course, have queried the disappearance of such a substantial sum, however cleverly I disguised it. That's why you needed to know my secret.'

Her husband's main concern seemed to be about the publicity and the tax man, not his wife of twenty-five years. Surely he could have found a way to keep her in ignorance and spare her feelings? He had spent more time worrying about his mistress's financial future than he had about preserving the memory of his past with his wife and daughters.

Helen felt a sudden panic. The two girls would soon be here. Instinctively she felt she should not burden them with this squalid revelation. But would she be strong enough to keep the secret from them? She persuaded herself that apart from gratifying her rage, it would do little good to destroy memories of a loving father. The girls had had a privileged and happy childhood even if she had spent it excusing their father's absences by telling them that he was working hard to earn money because he loved them and wanted them to have everything he did not have at their age.

Would she be able to act convincingly? Her daughters would expect her to be distressed but how could she keep up the pretence of being the grief-stricken widow? Would this be the start of yet another life of lies?

The letter went on to remind her how their company had started. It made painful reading for her. It was when they were young and in love, when they believed everything was possible.

'Do you remember that scruffy little office where we started our first magazine? When a working-class boy called Smith became Temple-Smith? That was a bit of cheek but it did the trick. You once asked me to write on the back of an envelope what I wanted out of life, remember? I said I wanted to be a multimillionaire, be married to you and play cricket for England. Well, two out of three ain't bad! It was hard work but together we built up a thriving company.

'It will survive me. Good people are in place, so trust them.' She could almost hear him talking. 'You've barely been involved in the business since we came to the States; keep it like that, have some fun. If at some stage you decide you want to sell your stock, Condé Nast and News International have indicated several times over the years that they would be interested. Discuss it with your advisers. I give you my blessing to do whatever you think best.

'As to the rest of it,' the handwriting was showing signs of his legendary impatience, 'I'd like to spare you the stress, not to say the expense, of shipping my body back to Britain. Anyway, as you know, I hate the idea of mouldering away in some dank cemetery. I would much prefer to be cremated but I'm going to ask you for one last favour. Remember that hill back in Yorkshire over-looking our home town where we used to go walking? That was the place we did our dreaming (and other things!). I'd like you and the girls to go to the very top and scatter my ashes to the four winds.

'Thank you, my darling, for all you've given me during our years together. Tell the girls I have always loved them and that they must take care of you. I'll be watching! And please, Helen, don't judge me too harshly. I love you.'

He signed his name with a flourish. No doubt he had been feeling pleased with himself, his life all neatly tied up in parcels. His wife, his mistress, the diamonds.

There was no mention of the woman's name. He

would not have wanted a confrontation between them. But Helen was determined to discover her identity.

She walked swiftly to the study where the bank manager was waiting and, waving the letter at him, asked edgily, 'Do you know what's in this?'

'I told you, no.'

'Are you asking me to believe that you don't know about his whore?'

Paul Wallis's face contorted. 'I don't know what you're talking about.'

Helen watched him carefully for signs of guilt. 'He rented a house in the Hamptons for her, and an apartment in New York. He must have bought her jewellery, clothes. Are you saying none of this showed up on his account?'

'If my clients are in credit, I am not in the habit of scrutinising their expenditure,' said Paul uneasily.

'Don't try and fob me off. You were more than a bank manager to him, you were a friend. You must have known about her. Her name. I want her name.' Helen was making a determined effort to appear businesslike but to her own ears she sounded shrill.

'Helen, I wish I could help.' Paul appeared embarrassed. 'I don't know anything beyond my instructions, which were simply to deliver this letter to you personally anywhere in the world immediately I heard of Mark's death.'

'I won't rest until I know who she is,' Helen said angrily.

Paul reached out as if to take her hand, but appeared

to change his mind. 'I didn't know of her existence until now.'

'You haven't met her?'

'No.'

'You're lying.'

'I assure you I am not.'

'You must have known he often wasn't where he was supposed to be.'

'Yes,' he said slowly. 'Some time ago I became aware that I couldn't always track him down but—'

'I think you'd better read this.' She handed him the letter and walked over to the window. Abstractedly she watched a flock of geese on the lawn. She had read Mark's letter only once but the words were imprinted on her brain.

Paul was silent as he read and occasionally Helen glanced at him to see his reaction. But his face was expressionless and she had to exercise great control not to interrupt. After what seemed an interminable time, he laid the pages on the desk and said, 'Helen, this is awful for you. I'm very, very sorry.'

As if in a trance she moved from the window and sat down.

'You've had a bad shock,' he said, looking wretched. 'Shall I come back another day?'

She came out of her reverie. 'I suppose he hoped I would die first, didn't he?' she said bitterly. 'And then you wouldn't have had to involve yourself in his dirty games.'

'Helen, I can only say again I had no idea—'

'I promise you I'll fight it,' she said fiercely, 'and if you refuse to help me I'll switch all my accounts to another bank, and that includes the company's.'

'You don't need to threaten in that way,' he said, his expression hurt. 'You must know that my loyalty is to you. When Mark handed me the letter, I did ask him if I needed to know what was in it, but he refused point blank to tell me anything. He said the less I knew, the better. To be honest, I assumed it was some kind of tax dodge. Believe me, if I knew the name of this woman, I would tell you.'

'Prove your loyalty.'

'How can I do that?'

'Find out which bank is dealing with her and let me have the number of the account. And the date of the first consignment.'

'I'd never be able to obtain that information.' Paul's face registered shock. 'I'd be breaking the law even if I could track down from his papers where the diamonds are lodged. Those foreign banks are paranoid about security. Even if I got the account number, they'd never reveal the name. And knowing how meticulous Mark was, he would have made the arrangements watertight.'

Helen hesitated. She would find out the name of her husband's mistress with or without Paul's help. So many millions for the bitch who stole time away from his family? Not while she had breath left in her would she allow this woman to take possession of the diamonds. If it meant that the world would see her duplicitous husband for what he really was, what did she care for scandal? But it was probably wiser not to say anything of this to Paul.

'Take my advice, don't let this destroy your memories,' said Paul gently. 'Try and remember the good things.'

She gazed at him morosely. 'What good things?'

Paul took his leave soon afterwards. Helen saw him to the door and then made her way to the living room. She stared at the framed photograph sitting on the grand piano. It showed a husband, wife and two beautiful daughters taken on the wedding day of their eldest.

All so happy. All so fake.

From now on she would question every memory, every single thing they had shared together. That last holiday in Barbados which he had joked was their third, fourth, fifth honeymoon. Had he sneaked away to make phone calls to her? When he touched her, did he yearn for younger, firmer flesh, for wilder caresses?

When Helen had first arrived in Manhattan she had quickly learned the American definition of middle age: when your age started to show around your middle. And if she did not work to remain slim, youthful-looking and clever, she would lose her husband. Well, she had taken the advice to heart. She had joined a gym a few blocks away from their apartment and worked bloody hard on every aspect of her appearance, starving sometimes to keep her weight down.

To please him, she had volunteered to assist on various committees, and when her photograph occasionally cropped up on Page Six, the *Post*'s gossip column, he would be delighted. She never demurred when the company's public relations office wanted to use her and her daughters for a spread in *Town and Country* magazine or sent their photographers to show her at some charity do. And of course she had made sure Mark's every personal need was catered for. Apart from organising a varied social life for him, she took complete charge of an increasingly complicated domestic entourage. This included combining the complex schedules of their demanding daughters with the running of two lavishly appointed homes. Nothing was left to chance. She would even pick out the right books on the *Times* bestseller list to read and then pen a précis of them so he could talk about them later with his peers.

And after all these efforts, what had happened? She had lost him anyway, only he had not bothered to tell her. For the past eight years he had been no more than a physical presence. His mind was with *her*.

Helen turned her gaze to the evidence of Mark's past triumphs, which lined the panelled walls – accolades from the advertising industry, a Publisher of the Year award and a citation from the White House honouring him as a charity fundraiser.

'Mark, you bastard,' she said out loud, 'you think I should "have some fun"? Stay out of the business? Well, stick around and watch me. And as for carrying your ashes back home to England, I'm not going to waste my time.'

# Chapter Three

Harry Ferguson hurried through the doors of the coffee shop up the street from the office and was relieved to see his colleague already there and irritated, judging by the fingers drumming on the marble-topped table.

'What's so urgent we couldn't talk in the office? It was difficult getting away, the whole place is in a state. Couldn't it wait?'

'No, it couldn't, and keep your voice down.' Harry sat down on the leather seat. 'Coffee?' he asked.

'Don't have time. What's all this about?'

Harry caught the waiter's attention and indicated one coffee then said softly, 'I've been talking to Ned Mastrianni in New York. He's got his sights firmly fixed on the big job and he reckons he's got a good chance of getting it. I've said I'll help him.'

'You haven't wasted much time mourning then?'

'The king is dead. Long live the king. That's my motto. Isn't this what we've been dreaming about? OK, I expected Mark to retire not die but the results are the same.'

'How on earth would backing Mastrianni help you?'

'I can't believe you're being this dense,' said Harry impatiently. 'Ned's only got experience as publishing director in New York but he'll have to do a stint in London before they give him Mark's job. Giles is the obvious choice to replace Mark in the short term. But then it will be Ned's turn, and when he moves up . . .' Harry tapped his chest with a finger.

'You? Ahead of Alistair? Dream on.'

'Ned doesn't agree with you,' said Harry firmly. 'And neither do I. Ned doesn't rate Alistair. Never has. Thinks he's a soft touch so he'll do anything to stop him. Ned and I would be a bloody great team, we could finally get this company moving.'

'Won't our current chief executive have something to say about this? Giles does rate Alistair, and if he becomes chairman, he'll want Alistair to succeed him as chief executive here. It's what Mark would have wanted too.'

Harry leaned back. 'But Mark is dead and Giles's opinions have never carried much weight. Ned reckons that under the new regime the thinking will change anyway. He believes money will be much more important to the widow than to the dear departed. She won't care about cover lines, she'll be interested in the wonga that'll help her hook her next millionaire, and for that she'll want Ned, not Alistair.'

His companion appeared unimpressed. The finger-drumming began again.

'I've decided to catch the first plane to New York,'

Harry went on. 'You know how our dear chief exec is liable to cave in under pressure.'

'Surely they'll wait for the funeral before talking serious business?'

'The Americans? Don't you believe it. And we don't want to get sidelined while those blood-suckers carve up the company between them,' he said grimly. 'They'll try and take over our territory and I haven't worked here for fifteen years for that to happen.' He leaned forward. 'Are you going to help us? What we need to do is shake everyone's faith in Alistair's abilities, wrong-foot him when we can. We don't want him here as the boss instead of Ned.'

'What would you want me to do?'

'For now, just be my eyes and ears. You're so well-connected, no one will suspect you, and together we'll cover most of the departments, find out what Alistair's doing, and I'll tell Ned.'

'What do I get out of it?'

Harry pursed his lips. 'Something you've wanted for a long time,' he said silkily. 'And that's a promise.'

Now the fingers were still. 'All right, count me in.'

On the way home Georgie halted the taxi in Jermyn Street to buy Alistair a black tie. As far as she could remember he had never had cause to wear one and she was certain it was not something he would think about now. She made another stop in Park Lane to pick up his favourite herbal sleeping pills. This was part of a well-ordered routine, honed since the early days of their marriage. They were an organised team, and if she was the one due to travel he would organise the same back-up for her when necessary, like valet parking at the airport and buying currency.

At work she regarded herself in every way as her husband's equal. And so did he. When they were first put on the same footing as publishing directors, the arrangement was regarded as a formula for disaster by their critics in the company but Mark had been right. Having two brains to tackle similar problems was proving an undoubted asset, as the rising profit figures showed. Having two powerful careerists co-operating was a commercial advantage that Mark, especially, had valued highly.

Georgie had been promoted to her job because of an ability to develop ideas into major campaigns and articles. She was unrivalled in the way she could pick out the one transparency from hundreds which would blow up into a magic cover, and renowned for her skill in evolving the 'big picture' from small detail. But unlike most editorial types, Alistair included, she positively revelled in maintaining tight budgetary control. And she had done this, so far, without alienating her staff, a rare quality, as her husband was fond of telling her.

The taxi edged its way through the narrow lane between the cars parked on either side of the tree-lined road where she lived. She and Alistair had traipsed around London inspecting dozens of properties before falling for the high ceilings, stoutly-built brick walls and well-maintained interior of a third-floor mansion flat in a block near Kensington High Street.

She paid the driver and walked through the doors, her mind on Mark's death and how it might affect her well-ordered life. Who would take over in New York? Would she be allowed as much autonomy as she had now? Mark had promised her freedom to run her own division, and he had kept his word. He had been Alistair's mentor, too, responsible for much that was good in their lives. Would that change under a new boss?

Georgie walked through the hall, past the collection of early originals by unknown artists subtly lit by converted gas lamps, into Alistair's dressing room. She put her purchases on a table where he was sure to spot them.

When they had first started living together Georgie had been amused to see the regimental way Alistair laid out his entire range of shoes to give them a military-style polish. Then carefully he would insert heavy wooden shoe blocks before placing them in red suede bags.

'I didn't realise I'd fallen in love with a spinney,' she had teased.

'A what?'

'A cross between a spinster and a fanny.'

He had lunged at her and dabbed her nose with boot polish.

When Alistair came back from the office late that afternoon, he was grateful but not surprised to discover that she had thought of the black tie.

'God, you're a marvel,' he said, leaning against the breakfast bar. 'It didn't occur to me.' He inspected his watch. 'I've booked the taxi, it'll be here in ten minutes. I suppose I'd better get some things together.'

When the taxi arrived, Alistair kissed her goodbye and said he would phone as soon as he landed. Georgie opened the balcony shutters to wave him off. She was sad to see him go. Since their marriage she had gradually become used to being dependent on another person. After a lifetime of keeping everyone at bay, she now enjoyed being part of a pair.

It was not something her background had prepared her for. At fourteen she had elected to move from her home in Newcastle to her grandmother's cottage some miles away to be nearer the grammar school to which she had gained a scholarship. The move caused a rift with her parents who thought she should have opted for the local school. It was the beginning of her pursuit of academic qualifications, which would take her far away from her working-class background and the memory of an unfulfilling home life. Her potential was singled out early by her teachers and she was hot-housed into university, the first member of her family to do so, gaining a two-one degree in English.

Her favourite teacher had attempted to reconcile Georgie with her parents by saying pride in her achievements might lead to a better understanding. But over the course of the scholastic process everything about her had altered. She lost her Geordie accent, she dressed differently and, more importantly, her attitudes and ambitions were altered. She set herself higher goals. Where another woman from her background would have been content to be someone's PA, Georgie wanted to be the one giving the orders.

Her parents, uneasy about the way she had changed, seemed to think that by doing well for herself she considered herself too good for them. In the event there were few family occasions she attended and when she did go home, her efforts to talk about their lives and interests did little to bridge the gulf that separated them. Both her parents were dead now, and while she grieved for their passing she could not pretend she missed them.

Georgie was convinced that adversity was often necessary to some personalities to give them an extra reason to strive for recognition and she was of the opinion that her past had made her stronger.

In London, Georgie joined the Fenton Group of magazines, considered number two to Amalgamated in the media business. She began as a trainee but was quickly promoted, first to assistant fashion editor, then features editor, then deputy editor rising to editor, and finally to publishing director. With her quick wit and patrician looks, she had had no shortage of admirers but she had held back from serious involvement. Until Alistair.

As her husband lifted his head and waved to her before disappearing into the taxi, Georgie felt sudden disquiet. Alistair was right. Mark's death had made them both aware that life was uncertain. She could understand why the death of his mentor would make Alistair ponder his own mortality. Producing a child was the obvious answer. But was it the answer for her?

She felt he had too rosy a view of parenthood. Until their marriage, they had both led an urbane, sophisticated existence in which children did not figure. But in the last few months Alistair had taken a great interest in the small son of one of their colleagues, Josephine Clarke. Since the boy had begun to talk, Alistair's affection had grown, encouraged by Josephine, a single mother. But as Josephine pointed out, Alistair only saw the toddler when he was rested, sweet, bathed and beautiful; he had never experienced what she described as the child's monster times.

Alistair had talked about the importance of having a family to such an extent that Georgie had agreed to let nature take its course and had given up taking contraceptive pills a few months earlier.

Like most women who had trouble conceiving, Georgie was initially disappointed, then disturbed that she was not up to fulfilling the most basic female function. Although tests showed Alistair's sperm count was normal and there was nothing physically wrong with her, not being fecund was beginning to make her feel a failure.

Although they had discussed the possibility of moving from the flat to a house when she became pregnant, they had not talked about what would happen to Georgie's career. It wasn't that they avoided the subject. They had difficulty in envisaging what life would be like being parents. In her mind Georgie assumed that if Josephine, as a single mother, could manage being a magazine editor, she who had the help of a loving husband would cope quite well.

Mark's death had focused Alistair's mind even more firmly on having a child. If nothing happened this time round, she would consult a fertility expert.

She wished Alistair had not had to go off so soon; she needed to talk about Mark's death with someone who understood as much about the company as she did.

She reached impulsively for the phone. If she was quick she might be able to catch Josephine on her mobile before she reached home and seduce her round with the offer of a glass of wine.

Josephine Clarke was one of Amalgamated's long-standing editors and had worked with Mark since the beginning when the small company had published only four titles. Since then Mark had built up his London stable to ten titles, three of them aimed at the coveted AB readers, the highest spenders, the opinion-formers who regularly shopped at Prada, Gucci and Ralph Lauren. Seven years later he had bought an American publishing company specialising in business and educational titles and had relocated his family to New York. But he remained proud of British editorial skills and occasionally brought editors from his London office to work with him in America.

Josephine might have climbed further up the ladder this way but some time ago she had incurred his displeasure by turning down his offer of promotion because of her young son. She was bringing Luke up on her own. She had steadfastly refused to identify the father, saying that as he did not want to participate in Luke's upbringing, there was no point.

Josephine was renowned throughout the company for her inability, or unwillingness, to play the company game. She was frank to a fault, something that the Suits in the organisation did not always appreciate. But her creative abilities were such that she was now editor-in-chief of *Woman's View*, widely regarded as the firm's cash cow.

Few would have guessed from her unlined complexion and strikingly glossy brunette bob that she was nearing her fortieth birthday, a milestone she was determined to deny. She had little difficulty attracting a certain kind of loser who admired an attractive, high-earning female, but what she was seeking was her male equivalent, until now without success.

As the longest serving editor in the group, Josephine had been the most senior female employee until Mark's takeover of the Fenton Group two years earlier, which brought with it a talented editorial team, including Georgina Luckhurst.

Soon after the acquisition, Georgie was elevated to the British subsidiary board. In the magazine fraternity her directorship had caused a stir in a male-dominated industry. Amalgamated's rivals, National Magazines and Condé Nast, had never followed suit and Georgie was the only female editorial employee in both Britain and America to be given such a senior appointment.

Instead of the expected sparks, a friendship had gradually developed between the two journalists. They had already met several years earlier on an overseas press jaunt to Grindelwald for the launch of a Swiss cheese. That had been a five-star experience and the two young editors had become allies while struggling to remain upright on the nursery ski slopes. They had been seeing more of each other outside work lately because Josephine had moved into an adjoining neighbourhood and often shared a taxi with Georgie or accepted a lift when Georgie took her Jaguar into work.

As she dialled Josephine's mobile, Georgie crossed her fingers. Thankfully her friend answered at once. She was in a taxi on her way home and swiftly agreed to make the short detour.

Josephine was breathless after running up the stairs. She was in the habit of ignoring the lift in an effort to keep fit.

'God, I'm still in a state of shock,' she said, taking off her coat. 'I'm glad you phoned. My staff hardly ever met Mark and I need to talk to somebody about him. I can't take it in, I mean he was only fifty-six. I'm sorry for his family, aren't you? I talked to him only last week when he asked me for advice about a present for Helen's birthday. He was devoted to her, she must be devastated.'

Georgie took her arm and led her into the sitting room. She poured two glasses of chilled white wine and the two women sat curled up at either end of the high-backed, tasselled sofa.

'People are crying all over the office,' Josephine said. 'It reminded me of the days after Diana's death.'

'Yes, it's the same suddenness, the same shock, not quite believing that it's happened.'

'He was a funny mixture, you know,' Josephine smiled.

'If it was a toss-up between a great feature and a saving in the editorial budget, there'd be no contest. Believe me, that's rare these days when bean counters wield such power. But he'd OK my budget to buy a set of Mario's pictures one minute, then the next he'd walk round the room picking up rubber bands so they could be re-used.'

'Yes, I remember.'

'That mean streak used to drive everyone crazy, especially Helen,' Josephine went on. 'She used to laugh it off, explaining that as they'd come from nothing he was always worried that one day someone would grab it away from him.'

'I keep on forgetting you've known him for ever,' said Georgie.

'Yes, right from the start,' said Josephine. 'No one else would have given someone like me a chance with no university education and precious little experience. I remember being so critical of all magazines on the market that he challenged me to launch one that I'd read myself. And I did.'

'And the rest, as they say, is history,' said Georgie, reaching for the bottle and watching as the amber liquid filled their glasses. 'When I married Alistair I was with the opposition but Mark never made me feel like an outsider. That's why I wasn't unhappy when he took over Fenton's. Mark suspected that some of the senior lot here would give me the frost and he was right. People like Giles and Harry starved me of information and when Alistair finally told him what was happening, Mark ordered all the department heads to give me every copy of important memos and stuff. His intervention caused a stir and they watched themselves after that.'

'Those damn dinosaurs categorise females only as readers and, occasionally, as editors but definitely not as managers,' said Josephine tartly. 'They think we have our ornamental bits in the wrong place.'

'It's a good thing Cherie Blair and Hillary Clinton don't work for our lot,' smiled Georgie.

'I bet they'd be as good at the job if not better than their husbands,' said Josephine. 'It's a shame we'll never know.'

'It's a pity that the decision makers in the industry aren't more like Alistair,' said Georgie. 'Did you see that interview with him in *Media Week*?'

'Yes, I loved his quote,' Josephine flourished a hand, ' "I choose the right man for the job, whatever the gender." Great stuff.'

Georgie picked up the half-empty bottle then set it down again, a hand to her mouth. 'I'm not supposed to have alcohol while I'm trying to get pregnant.'

'You can't be blamed for drinking in these circumstances,' said Josephine. 'But I suppose we'd better eat. Is there any food in the fridge?'

'Yes, sure. I can make us an omelette.'

'No, I'll do it,' Josephine said hastily. She had suffered the effects of Georgie's indifferent cooking before. Georgie was apt to say she had too much on her mind and was in too much of a hurry to concentrate on preparing meals.

Josephine quickly whipped up some eggs. 'You don't

have to be indiscreet if you don't want to . . . but, what do you think is likely to happen in the company now?'

Georgie walked to the fridge to find a bottle of mineral water. 'Giles is the obvious choice for a stopgap chairman because he's near to retirement and no threat to anyone. I can't see him holding the reins as tightly as Mark did even if he wasn't due to retire, so the key question is, who will replace him as chief executive in London?'

'What does Alistair think?'

'We haven't discussed it,' said Georgie. 'It seems so callous when the boss is hardly cold.'

'Yes, but you have to be realistic,' said Josephine. 'I bet the others are plotting away already. It wouldn't be smart for a big company like ours to be rudderless for long. And my money's on Alistair for chief executive. In fact the post room have already started a book on what date he'll take over.'

Georgie frowned. 'I don't think he reckons it's as certain as that.'

'Well, everyone else does so you'd better get used to the idea of having an absentee husband. They'll want the new guy visiting the territories.'

'If he does get the job it'd be difficult for everyone to treat the wife of the boss as one of their colleagues and,' Georgie gave a small sigh, 'it wouldn't be easy for me, either, having my husband in charge.'

Josephine eased a perfect omelette out of the pan and placed it carefully on to a plate. 'Surely you two can have a professional working relationship? You have until now.'

'Yes, but we're on an equal footing. I don't report to him.'

'What would happen if you got pregnant?' asked Josephine. 'Would he be generous with maternity leave?'

Georgie chewed her bottom lip. 'Who knows? In any case, that isn't an issue. I didn't know how difficult it would be to get pregnant.'

'You're overworked and stressed, how do you expect your poor body to react? Give it time.' Josephine finished cooking the second omelette and brought it to the kitchen table, together with a dish of flageolets.

'Jo, this is delicious, I'm never going to cook for you again.'

'Promise?'

'Surely I'm not as bad as all that.' When her friend raised an eyebrow she went on, 'I can be good when I have the time.' They ate appreciatively for a moment then Georgie asked, 'When did you realise you were ready for a child?'

'Nobody's ever ready,' replied Josephine, smiling. 'Listen, I was in labour and I wasn't ready.'

'If I have a baby I think I'd want to go on working.'

'What's to stop you? I work and I have a baby.'

'But I don't think I could combine having a baby with controlling seven magazines,' said Georgie.

'It'd be difficult but you could fix most things for a time that suits you.'

'That would mean a complete culture change in our company. You know how fond Giles and the rest are of having little chats in the pub after work where the real nitty-gritty gets discussed.'

Josephine nodded sympathetically. As editor, she was queen in her own world, and able to follow a more civilised timetable to fit in with Luke's schedule.

The sound of the phone made them both jump. It was Alistair from the departure lounge at the airport.

'Darling, has Harry called?'

'No.'

'He's meant to be meeting me here.'

'Harry?'

'Yes, he's . . . oh, it's OK, I've just spotted him. 'Bye, I'll be in touch as soon as I land.'

'What was that about Harry?' asked Josephine after Georgie had replaced the receiver.

'He's off to New York with Alistair,' said Georgie slowly.

'Really? Who arranged that?'

'I don't know.'

'Let me get this straight. One publishing director's going to New York. The circulation director's going to New York,' Josephine's voice began to sing-song as if she was reciting a list for a commercial voice-over, 'and where's the other publishing director? Having bought her husband a tie, like the dutiful wife who uses Brand X, she is sitting in her flat in London having a quiet drink with her friend.'

'It's not like that.'

'That's what it looks like to me.' After the shortest of pauses, Josephine said almost to herself, 'You know the problem with us women?'

'What?'

'We always think we have to massage a man's ego or the balance of the marriage will be upset.'

'I don't do that.'

'Maybe not consciously. But too many of us think we got there by luck,' said Josephine tersely. 'Men assume a self-confidence that comes with mother's milk. They just go for it, whereas we analyse, we consult, we dither.'

Impatiently Georgie stood up and put her plate in the sink. 'That's a very sweeping statement.'

'Is it? How many main board members on any magazine company in Britain or America are female? You know the answer. None, zero, zilch, not one.' Josephine clenched her fist. 'God knows, most of us are still nervous, worried that if we draw too much attention to ourselves we'll become too high profile. And that would never do, would it? That might cause too much trouble. And why?'

Georgie left the sink and sat down.

'Because being pushy is for them, not us,' Josephine went on. 'Take this situation. There's no question in my mind that you should be on your way to New York, pitching in with the rest of them. Ned Mastrianni is sure to be in the thick of it. He's got his eye on London because he knows that's the pathway to power. You need to be there.'

'Come on, be realistic. We can't all rush over and they know Helen much better than I do.'

'Georgie, extraordinary things might be decided in the

41

next few days. If you're not around, you don't have a voice.'

'I can't,' Georgie frowned. 'I've such a lot on at the moment.'

'And they haven't? Huh. That hasn't stopped them. That's the kind of action men take without thinking. But if you don't like what they get up to over there, can you influence them from here?'

'No,' said Georgie thoughtfully.

'That's exactly my point.' It was almost a growl of irritation.

'I don't believe they're excluding me deliberately.'

'Maybe not but with men it's like drawing the wagons round into a circle. You're either inside or you're outside. If you're outside, you don't count. And it's no use going in later with your hand up saying please, sir . . .'

Georgie let out a sigh.

'Watch out that you're not building your own glass ceiling. If you think it's right to be in New York, don't wait for Alistair's permission or Harry's, just go.'

'Permission? I'm *not* waiting for that.' Georgie was stung.

'Then what's stopping you? And anyway, what makes you assume Alistair wouldn't be delighted to see you? As a colleague, not as a wife.' Josephine looked at her watch. 'OK, I've had my say, I'm going to leave you to do what you think is right. I'm off to put my child to bed.'

While Georgie rinsed the dishes, she debated the options. Josephine had made a lot of sense.

If she flew off right now she could write some of her reports and memos on the plane. But what about the presentation to the advertising agency later in the week? Well, her deputy could take her place. It would be good experience for her. Georgie frowned. There were some difficult things she could not postpone. She really couldn't get away.

Then an image of the circulation director's nattily dressed figure came into her mind. What was it Mark had once said about him? No person was too boring to take out to lunch in the name of ambition.

Harry. Manipulative time-server. Not as well-regarded in New York or London as she was, according to Alistair. Yet Harry was on the plane.

Georgie made her way into the study and opened her electronic organiser. Right. She punched up the number then picked up the phone and made a reservation for the next British Airways flight to New York.

# *Chapter Four*

In the twenty-four hours since Helen had read Mark's confession, she had single-mindedly spent her time not in weeping, not in recriminations but in determining how to find out as much as she could about the other woman in her husband's life.

Her daughters and their young husbands thought that her continued pacing was a sign she was nearly mad with grief. Hiding her rage was difficult. Hour after hour through the night she lay in bed casting her mind back, trying to pinpoint the moment when the affair had started, like an archaeologist searching among the debris for the defining link.

Like so many women in her position, she blamed herself. Had she provoked Mark into deceiving her by being dull and uninteresting? Had something happened to make him feel his ego needed a surge of adrenalin? Perhaps, once she left the company, she had bored him with domestic trivia. Maybe it had been a mistake to relinquish her career at the office to stay at home to be with the children. Perhaps this woman had snared him by being on tap, in the business, up with the news and gossip.

Paul Wallis, desperate to retain the Temple-Smith personal account and the Amalgamated portfolio, and maybe for more humane reasons too, had said he was doing all he could to trace the woman and the banks holding the diamonds, but to no avail so far, though he intended to go on trying.

So many questions. How often had Mark and this woman met during the week? Who else knew about her? Were people at the office part of his subterfuge? Where did Mark meet her? And when? God forbid, had he brought her to their home on one of her rare absences? That would be too hard to bear. Where would she find the answers?

In the morning, Helen arranged for a limo to take her into Manhattan and for the next few hours, ignoring all offers of help, she locked herself in Mark's office, searching for clues among his papers, diaries, bank statements and telephone records. She checked all those special family days when his only involvement was a phone call bemoaning the urgency of the conference which made it impossible for him to be home for their wedding anniversary, a child's birthday, his own birthday . . . She sat back, drained, remembering with fury how grateful she'd been when he arranged a get-together days after the event.

Away from her he had been enjoying an alternative marriage, most certainly exchanging Christmas presents and treats on birthdays. She tortured herself with the idea that they probably had their own song, their own jokes. A special place to eat. They'd had a life together, robbing her and the girls of his company. The letter had come as such a shock because Mark had never shown any signs of being a philanderer. At functions he would never flirt and seemed to prefer the company of men. Business, business, business was all he ever talked or thought about. Or so she had believed. Maybe that had made her a touch complacent. And why not? He had never given her any cause for worry. But his treachery had been complete. He must have spent time either planning to be with her or actually being with her most days of his life. Cross-matching office diaries against the dates of the many meetings, conferences and exhibitions he had said he had to attend, Helen discovered that each one of his trips out of town had been extended by several days before or after the meeting he was attending. He could easily explain this by pretending to prepare for a heavy advertising sell before the conference or tying up loose ends afterwards. Or both. The bastard.

He always made a point of calling her when he was away. How often had his mistress been listening in? On one of the rare times when she accompanied him she recalled with distress how a school play in Connecticut had cut short her stay at that wonderful south of France hotel by three days and she had returned home before him. Now she wondered if someone else had flown out to join him.

There was no record of any hotel or travel bills for the

tart. They must have booked separately through different travel agents on a separate credit card. It showed how careful and clever they had been and what effort Mark had put into keeping his mistress away from prying eyes.

Helen had been sitting in Mark's office for hours. She pressed the intercom to order a cup of black coffee in the hope it would keep her alert.

As she drank the coffee, she thought of those lazy Sundays in Greenwich around the open fire, when she would watch her husband mark up the *New York Times* travel supplement, carefully underlining a telephone number or address. She winced as she recalled how she and Mark would smile at this habit of his on a Sunday evening. These would be the places they would visit when he eventually retired and they would add them to their wish list. She remembered feeling relaxed, lucky, chosen. Occasionally she would mention one of their chosen places when they were on holiday in the area but he would always find some excuse not to visit it, usually that he had checked it out and it was not worth the detour. She had not been at all suspicious. She had been blind while his mistress could see. That situation had not changed. And now the bitch would be rich.

Helen's rising fury at her husband and all he had done to ruin the memories of her marriage threatened to suffocate her. The double-dealing shit. Had Mark lain by her side in bed dreaming about his lover, plotting future trysts? Had he fantasised about her while they were making love?

Words from his letter came to mind, '. . . my mistress took nothing away from you.'

Liar. Liar. Liar.

Alistair and Harry were propping up the bar of the St Regent's Hotel when Georgie walked in from the airport.

In repose her husband's face gave the impression of being severe but at the sight of his wife his expression changed to one of pleasure.

'Darling, you're always surprising me. What brought you here?'

'It seemed like a good idea,' she said levelly and gave him a meaningful look. He understood immediately that she wanted to talk to him alone. She smiled at Harry and gave Alistair a swift kiss.

After his initial greeting, Harry was silent. From his expression it was clear that her arrival in New York was not wholly welcome to him.

Alistair ordered Georgie a spritzer. 'Thank God you're here,' he said. 'We certainly need a woman's touch to deal with Helen. I've phoned her twice but she's too distraught to come to the phone.'

'Poor woman,' said Georgie. 'Of course I'll do my best but don't you think it's better if we do that together.' It was more of a statement than a question.

Harry's eyes flickered and he picked up his briefcase. 'I'll see you later,' he said, and left.

Georgie waited until he was out of earshot before telling Alistair, 'I'm not really here with my wife hat on, darling. I'm here for the same reason as Harry. For the same reasons as you. For work. And I'll stay as long as it takes, don't you think?'

Alistair seemed edgy. 'It may be a good idea if you talk to the people over here, make sure they realise we're not going to sit back and let them take us over. Mark wouldn't have wanted that. He always said the European operation had more flair.'

'I don't think Ned Mastrianni agreed with Mark on that. He doesn't have such a high opinion of us over this side of the pond.'

Alistair agreed. 'Yes, he's certainly made that clear to me on a number of occasions. I was tempted to ask him how he explained to himself our infinitely superior profit ratio.'

They left the bar and went up to Alistair's room on the eighth floor, which afforded them a panoramic view over Central Park. While Georgie turned on the taps for the bath she always craved after a long flight, Alistair took a sheaf of newspapers off the coffee table to show her how well the New York media had covered the dramatic death of their chairman.

'Helen should be pleased. He comes over as a cross between Citizen Kane and Rupert Murdoch.'

'Only fitting, he was a legend in the business,' said Georgie, scanning the headlines.

'At least he left the company in good shape. But I still can't believe that he's gone.' He shook his head. 'It's so hard to accept.'

'You look tired,' she said with concern. 'Is there time for you to have forty winks?'

'Over here it's called a power nap,' he smiled.

'Does that make it more permissible?'

'I suppose so but I haven't time. Helen's called a special meeting in the boardroom in half an hour.' He rubbed his eyes. 'We went straight from Kennedy to the office. They're all shell-shocked there. Nobody can believe what's happened.'

'Has anybody discovered what he was doing in the Hamptons? Who goes to the seaside during the week?'

'That's what we all want to know. And why the hell he gave his driver the morning off. The guy says he wasn't required till the afternoon.'

Georgie walked into the bathroom and examined the array of bath salts and oils. She selected one to drop into the jacuzzi. She had taken off her clothes and was settling down tentatively into the bath when Alistair came into the bathroom and sat down on the towelling stool. He gazed at Georgie unseeingly.

'Mark was always doing deals,' he said. 'Maybe he was buying a magazine from some old guy who's out there for the summer.' He rose, peeled off his shirt and fished out another from a closet drawer.

'Do you think Helen plans to sell the company?' Georgie asked.

'Mark would turn in his grave if she did.'

'Pass me that towel,' she said. 'I'd better get a move on if I want to be at the meeting.'

Alistair frowned. 'But Helen doesn't know you're here and I'm not sure how many people are supposed to be there. If you like, I'll ask her to a nice quiet dinner with just the two of us.'

There was a pause. Georgie's chin lifted. 'Will Harry be at this meeting?'

'I think so, yes.'

'Then I ought to be there too.'

'Take it easy,' he said gently. 'You haven't been invited.'

'And who invited you?'

Alistair inserted a cufflink. 'No one. I thought it would be helpful.'

'Who invited Harry?' Georgie towelled herself so vigorously her skin was turning pink.

'I suppose he thought the same thing.'

'So why can't I operate in the same way and assume that as I'm in New York, Helen would want me at the meeting?' Seeing him hesitate she pressed on, 'Come on, this is a pivotal time for all of us. OK, decisions might not be taken today but the people there will be the architects of what's going to happen tomorrow and I don't want to be on the outside peering in. Anyway, I make more of a difference to the profits of this company than Harry ever does. Why shouldn't my voice be heard?'

'Everybody's touchy at the moment. If you're there, Ned will think I'm up to something.'

'Why would he?'

'Because you're my wife.'

'I'm also a publishing director.'

'Yes, but Mark always said Ned was suspicious of me. He thought I was after his job. As if I wanted to be publishing director of his titles. They make money but where's the challenge in the educational field? If you turn up he's certain to think I've already started to plot, that I'm getting my supporters into position.'

'Alistair,' her voice was beginning to reflect her impatience, 'you're making a quantum leap here.'

'Remember, I've dealt with Ned for years, I know how he thinks. He believes he's in line for Mark's job and so do at least three others on the New York board. And those are only the ones I know about.'

'I think I can fight my own corner,' said Georgie firmly. 'Anyway, why wouldn't they think Harry's on your side too?'

'They know Harry well.'

'Then they know what a schemer he is. He's upset that I'm edging into the boys' club.'

Alistair sighed. 'Why does this all matter so much to you, especially at this point in your life?'

'What point?'

'At the point we're trying for a baby.'

'What has that got to do with it? I've no intention of taking a back seat when we have a baby. Don't look so surprised.'

'You said you didn't want to be one of those have-it-all women and never see your child.'

'Absolutely not, but neither did we imagine I was going to become the little housewife either.'

'No, but at the level you're operating on you can't have the same power and influence when you've had the baby.'

'Why not? You will.'

'That's different.'

'How's it different?'

He gave an exasperated sigh. 'I would have thought it was quite obvious. I'm not the one giving birth, am I? I can't breast-feed the child either, can I?'

'But that doesn't mean I can't come to the meeting today. I'm not pregnant.'

'More's the pity.'

At this they smiled at each other.

'Come on then,' he said, 'we can't be late.'

It was a sombre group of eight men and one woman who gathered on the thirty-second floor in the antechamber of Amalgamated Magazines' main boardroom in New York. Georgie thought she noticed a few sideward glances and an extra buzz of conversation when she walked in. Her instincts were to stay close to Alistair and yet she despised herself for it, particularly when Harry went effortlessly from group to group, confident of his right to be there. Ned Mastrianni, publishing director in Amalgamated's head office, was talking quietly in Italian with the publishing director from Milan. Several of the overseas executives were grouped around him. He gave only the curtest of nods when the Drummonds appeared but Georgie noticed he smiled at Harry.

Harry sidled over and whispered to Alistair, 'Keep a close eye on those buzzards. They'd like nothing more than to get their hands on our titles. They think because they just about speak the same lingo they could run London.'

'Let them try,' Alistair said quietly.

'When's Helen supposed to be here?' asked Georgie.

'Ten minutes ago,' replied Harry. 'Giles isn't here yet either, but I see the Murphia are represented.'

Declan Geraghty, head of the company's Irish operations in Dublin, was moving from group to group looking fresh and assured in the knowledge that though Dublin was a small territory he had nearly doubled its profitability.

Harry moved closer and kept his voice low. 'The feeling here is that Helen's so depressed she's going to sell the whole lot. And who could blame her? It's years since she's been involved with the business and the daughters have never been interested in it. They're both married and busy with their own lives.'

Alistair raised an eyebrow at Georgie. 'Why pre-empt things? We'll know soon enough.'

At that moment their chief executive made his appearance and walked straight over to Alistair, appearing more self-important than usual. Giles Beamish was of the firm opinion that his employees all thought the trees cut down for paper had money stuck to them. Mark had been fond of commenting that he read financial proposals, bank statements and expense forms like other people scanned comic strips and often with the same relish. But Mark had implicitly trusted Giles's financial acumen, which was why, at sixty-two, he still headed the London group. It occurred to Georgie that, with his protector gone, Giles might fear that he would be pensioned off immediately. But the silver-haired executive presented his usual urbane self as he smiled at Alistair and Harry and bent his head in acknowledgement at Georgie. She was unsurprised by this lack of warmth towards her; he had never come to terms with a woman publishing director in the company. In his world, females were either in front of a computer or holding a tray. He had been gracious enough once to tell Georgie she wasn't 'making a bad fist of things' but she had gained the impression he thought this was only due to Alistair's help and guidance.

'Helen's taken it rather badly,' said Giles. 'Apparently she's been closeted in Mark's office all night. And what do you think she's been doing? Poring over his old diaries, going back years.' He shook his head sorrowfully.

'Perhaps she's trying to relive old memories,' suggested Georgie.

Giles dismissed this with a shrug. 'She's going to need all our support – of course she already knows she has mine. Ah, here she is now.'

The widow's entrance silenced the room. Ned Mastrianni swiftly took the lead and embraced her but Helen barely acknowledged his greeting. For a second Ned seemed to be disconcerted then the mask of attentive concern swiftly returned.

Ah ha, thought Georgie, all's not well in the kingdom. The Queen doesn't like her courtier and he knows it.

Helen moved round the room, acknowledging the muttered sympathy. Not for the first time, Georgie observed how badly grown men dealt with emotional situations. Most of them were shuffling awkwardly, not knowing what to say, not versed in dealing with bereaved women.

When it was her turn, she said softly, 'I'm so sorry, you and Mark were a great team.'

At those words Helen's eyes focused and she stared at Georgie. Her expression was difficult to read, but for a moment Georgie could have sworn it was hostility.

Georgie was right, it was hostility, but it wasn't directed at her.

A great team indeed, Helen was thinking bitterly. How little you know.

She moved to what had been Mark's chair, dimly aware that this seemed to come as a surprise to most of those present. Where the hell did they think she would sit? She turned and faced the room.

'Thank you for all your flowers and expressions of sympathy. They have sustained my daughters and me at this tragic time. I'm planning to have a quiet funeral next week. Mark will be buried in the churchyard close to our home in Connecticut.' She paused, savouring the thought of him decomposing in the dank earth. 'It will be a private affair for the family but of course you are all invited to the memorial services. One will be in New York and another in London.

'Because of Mark's death I've had to make certain decisions but before I announce them I want to emphasise that although they were made swiftly, they were also made in the full knowledge of what this company now needs.'

Harry raised an eyebrow in Alistair's direction.

'I want to assure you of one thing,' Helen went on. 'As the major stockholder I will not now, nor in the foreseeable future, sell this company. I thought you should be reassured of that immediately.' She let this sink in before continuing, 'I have decided to take over Mark's role and run this company myself.'

Helen had prepared herself for an adverse reaction to this announcement. She expected shock and surprise but what she had not anticipated was such complete silence.

It was obvious they thought she had no right to take on Mark's mantle. They seemed to have forgotten that she had been an equal partner in starting the business. It was only after they moved to America that she had taken a back seat. Alistair's wife was the only person to meet her gaze and show some measure of approval but that was probably because she felt solidarity for a woman, any woman. So that, thought Helen, didn't count.

When the silence became intolerable, she cleared her throat. 'My future and that of my family is intrinsically bound up in this company and from now on I aim to play an important part in it. By that I don't mean I will take the title of chairman and leave all the work to you, I mean I will be in here on a day-to-day basis and will involve myself in all aspects of the business. But not in the way Mark did.' She studied each of their faces in turn.

'As some of you might know, I had been urging him to delegate more of his responsibilities but it was not in his character to do this. I, however, am made in a different mould and I will have something to say about this in a moment.'

After an uneasy pause, Ned began hesitantly, 'Helen, we understand what you're saying, and speaking for myself I welcome your interest in the company.'

Like hell, she thought, remembering that Mark had considered him a competent but devious employee. 'Great at his job,' he'd said, 'but his views on women, gays and blacks in business are primeval and he doesn't realise that because of that he's got as far as he can with us. He's a legend only in his own imagination.' She allowed herself to savour the thought of Ned's chagrin at having to report to a woman. But Ned had spent a great deal of time with Mark. Certainly this one knew where all the bodies were buried. Did he know about *her*?

'I think it's wonderful that you're going to continue Mark's work,' Ned was saying, 'but I do feel . . .'

Here we go, she thought.

'. . . that it is my duty to the staff and to the other shareholders, small as they may be in number, to ask whether this is the right move for the company. We're playing in an international ballpark here with hard-nosed players and the person at the top—'

'I don't think you've fully understood me, Ned,' Helen interrupted. 'To make it clear I'll say it again. I have decided that as the major stockholder I am not going to put my future in someone else's hands.'

'Of course I can see your point but to take over from Mark . . .' Ned's voice trailed off.

Everybody in the room appeared ill at ease. This was

the moment to stay strong, she urged herself.

'I acknowledge that I can't run the business without all your immense talent and skills and I appreciate that my announcement has come as a shock. Many of you may not relish the idea of working for me.' She gazed directly at Ned. She had never liked the man. Ned Mastrianni was loyal only to Ned Mastrianni and if she didn't negate his influence at once he would muster his troops and plot against her. 'I want to make full use of the expertise in this room and I intend to show my appreciation of it by making the company profit-sharing. I shall arrange a system of share allocation in proportion to your duties and input.'

She allowed time for this information to permeate. Their expressions indicated how welcome this change would be.

'I will be relying on all of you here for your support,' she went on, 'and will be asking each and every one of you for recommendations as to how the company should approach the next five years, in every area of our operations.

'Now the first change I want to announce is the appointment of Giles Beamish from our London office to work with me here as chief executive.' Helen agreed with her husband's judgement that Giles had become a pedantic bean counter but she needed him as a bulwark. While Mark's editorial genius had powered the company, Giles's steady stewardship had been adequate. No longer. His appointment would be short-lived so she added, 'In view of his pending retirement, this will be a temporary position, but it will give me the opportunity I need to seek out the best permanent chief executive for New York.'

Ned's face was slowly turning puce. Giles, in contrast, seemed unruffled, thought Georgie. Helen must have squared things with him earlier.

'I want us to take a fresh look at all aspects of the company. As most of you know, Giles has been with Mark since the beginning and he will be invaluable in helping to guide me. In the discussions I have had with him I have been impressed by his financial acumen.

'Of course Giles's absence from London means we'll need to replace him there as chief executive. In the past Mark intended that the head of his European division based in London would take over from him in New York.' Helen paused then said with emphasis, 'But this is not written in tablets of stone by any means and it may be that Giles's successor in London will stay in place. We will have to see.'

That went home, she thought, studying their wary expressions. This was not the moment to encourage questions so Helen decided to bring the meeting to a swift end.

'Thank you for your attention,' she said. 'We have a great deal of work to do and I intend to start right now.'

In the silence that followed, Helen walked steadily out of the room.

Mark had written that he had been discreet about his mistress. But how could she believe a liar? How many of these men were gloating in the knowledge that their new chairman had been cuckolded for the last eight years of her married life?

Harry shifted comfortably on the king-sized bed of his Manhattan hotel room.

'So far so good,' he said into the phone. He settled his head further into the down pillow. 'Ned's furious about Giles's promotion, but he hasn't walked out. He knows it's only a short-term thing. I'm convinced the widow will give him the job, who else is there with his experience and nous? And then he'll be a valuable ally.'

The caller spoke and Harry nodded. 'Ned's convinced the widow will get bored with her new toy and Giles will get buried alive by the boys here. Then Ned will make his move.'

Harry listened intently to a stream of advice.

'Good thinking, I'm glad you're on my team. You're absolutely right about the strategy. If she's planning to put Alistair in charge of London we'll have to spike his guns so it doesn't happen, and between you, me and Ned we ought to be able to do it.

'For a start, Ned's going to suggest that I'm part of the decision-making process for the London job. She'll need people who know the way Europe works. Then I'll have some power to influence her into seeing that Ned would be the best man for the job. I'd say I've manoeuvred myself into a pretty good position.'

But the words down the line from London were not what he wanted to hear, and Harry's satisfied smile swiftly changed to a frown.

'Of course I still need you.' His mouth tightened. 'It's a little late to start being pious now. No you can't back out.' He gave an exasperated grunt. 'Because I won't let you, that's why. Otherwise some interesting information could find itself getting around and we don't want that, do we?' His voice hardened. 'Do we?' He waited then nodded. 'I'm glad we sorted this out.'

# Chapter Five

The jeweller was delighted to see her. Two or three times a year he did good business with this woman, always the best pieces. Of course the stuff looked great on her, anything would. Great neck for triple-strand pearls. Each time she walked into his Fifth Avenue shop, he came to see her as profit on two legs as well as a walking advert. She rarely haggled and she was sure of what she wanted. He had never seen her with anyone, man or woman, but once she had returned a pair of emerald earrings saying she had changed her mind. It was obvious to everyone working in the shop that whoever was paying hadn't liked them. She wore no wedding or engagement ring and he sometimes wondered if she belonged to one of the Mob or if she was a high-society hooker but she seemed too classy for that. Still, this was not a woman who clocked into an office each day. She had the air of being one of those ladies who liked lunching and lingerie.

He had never seen her in anything but restrained, classic clothes, design numbers obviously, and although she had a perfect body, she never made a feature of it by showing too much flesh. She had streaky blonde hair and the kind of skin that glowed, as if she spent most of her time diving into the blue sea of the Bahamas. Or skiing in Aspen. Unlike many of their clients, she had a soft voice, a nice way of talking and she was always polite, even to the juniors. She was a joy to serve. Most New York women who came in here were always in a rush but she would allow him to lead her from cabinet to cabinet, discussing the craftsmanship of the exhibits. Often, after she had left, her face would linger in his mind and he would wonder what kind of life this beautiful woman was leading and where she found her money.

He became less dreamlike about her when he realised that today she wanted not to buy but to sell some of his own creations, but he was not averse to taking them back. They had retained their value at the top of the price range.

They retired to his back office and from her handbag the woman pulled out a black velvet sachet which contained some well-remembered pieces from her collection.

He examined the stones through his magnifying loop. 'You bought only the best from me,' he commented.

'So you said at the time,' she smiled. 'I'm sorry to part with them but I need some capital to tide me over for the next three months.'

She proved a tough negotiator, unwilling to take his first offer, only accepting when she was satisfied he had reached the end of his bargaining.

A week later she called in to collect a substantial cheque. She seemed subdued, and when he tried to interest her in a pair of crescent-shaped pearl drop earrings which would have cost only a fraction of the cheque in her handbag, she smiled and declined. 'I've always loved coming here,' she told him, 'surrounded by beauty and perfection. But it's time to say goodbye.'

She could remember to the moment when she had first been introduced to Mark Temple-Smith. She had been standing in a small group at a party, nervous at the prospect of meeting so many new people. When he walked into the room, she immediately noticed his aura of power. His short, stocky frame had the look of a prize-fighter. His hair was greying with a noticeable widow's peak which lent a devilish air to his strong features.

He had come up to the group and stood next to her. Someone introduced her but after the briefest of eye contact, he turned to take a glass from a waiter's tray. She remembered thinking he seemed like a man who expected his decisions to be obeyed, his voice to be heard, his will to be done, someone equally equipped to charm or kill in pursuit of a goal.

There were no witty words, no seductive stares when he turned back to her. He simply took her elbow and put his mouth close to her ear in an effort to be heard above the clamour of music and conversation. 'I need to circulate, come with me. It'll stop me being bored to death.'

The touch of his hand on her bare arm burned. They moved through the crowded room with difficulty and it seemed entirely natural when he steered her towards the French windows out into the fresher air on the balcony. Despite a slight breeze, she felt her breasts, her shoulders and her upper lip begin to glow. She had never before experienced anything like this with anyone.

He stood so close to her, brushing against her body, that her nipples began to harden. What they talked about neither of them could recollect later. But the chemistry between them was overwhelming as he led her to a wrought-iron double seat in the shadows where they sat down. His finger began to trace slow circles round her nipple, and she froze for a second then relaxed, making no attempt to move away.

Mark seemed entirely unconcerned that anyone might appear and discover them, and in the sexually aroused state she was in, for a mad few moments she did not care if they did. This was unbelievable behaviour but the way he kissed her, the way he used his hands, the way his eyes were half-closed in passion was so sensuous she could not break away, regardless of the consequences. When his hands reached above her stocking tops to her inner thighs, she opened her knees, wanting more. But he withdrew his hand and leaned back.

'I don't know what you've done to me. I don't usually behave like this,' she said as he pulled her unsteadily to her feet.

'You're dangerous,' he said fiercely. 'We'd better go back.'

As they reached the French windows and moved inside, her husband of two months came over. 'Ah, there you are. I was wondering where my beautiful bride had got to.' He looked at her proudly. 'I see you've met Mark.'

Mark's face did not change but she noticed his hands clenching at his sides. 'You're a lucky man,' he said. 'I'm sorry I wasn't able to attend your wedding.' He looked at his watch. 'I'm off to Hong Kong in the morning. I'll see you in about a week.' And he made his way out of the crowded room.

From that moment Mark appropriated her thoughts and dreams but she did not hear from him for ten days. Then at four one afternoon he phoned and announced that he was outside her flat. Five minutes later they were making love in the marital bed. She never believed she had any choice but to leave her husband. It was ordained. Her divorce was uncontested and because she had not asked for alimony, very speedy.

Mark had hardly needed to lure her to New York, they were desperate for each other though she did arrive on the promise that he would end what he described as his sterile marriage. However, his excuses not to divorce multiplied. Eight years was a long time to hang around but Mark was skilful at maintaining her hopes and she did not have the willpower to walk out on him. At first he had begged her to wait until the children left school, then college. Once, an important merger meant that he could not separate from his wife who was a major stockholder in his privately-owned company. Lately it was Helen's hysterectomy operation. Still, she believed the title Mrs Mark Temple-Smith would be hers if she was patient. And the waiting was made palatable by Mark's generosity, which allowed her to live in a style that was at least equal with that of his wife.

Over the years her insecurity at being a mistress, relying on her appearance and sexual expertise to hold Mark, had meant she had taken the matter of men and lust seriously. She was forever on the outside looking in on other people's lives and this feeling of isolation had encouraged her to learn how much a woman could do to enhance her own value and mystery.

Voraciously she had read about geishas, harems and the *grandes horizontales* on the tricks of pleasing men. She had discovered that a woman could be powerful if she looked and acted the right way, being visible but not voluble. Limbs which received scant attention in the most dedicated beauty routines were constantly attended to. With vigorous discipline she exfoliated her shoulders, upper arms and décolletage every week until the skin gleamed. These were the parts of the body most discernible at a packed cocktail party or above a dining table when men were around. Her methods were old-fashioned by feminist standards, no doubt, but they worked.

Her clothes were exquisite and expensive but they were never chosen in a haphazard way; they always had a job to do. The most useful tip she had been given was from another millionaire's mistress, to buy the softest, sheerest bras then cut out the cloth around the nipples so as to make them more prominent. It was a hundred-percent successful in attracting male attention, as the woman had put it, 'like a pilot finding his landing lights'. She had been proved to be dead right.

Whenever Louise was tempted to leave Mark she thought about life without the excitement he provided – the unexpected trips by helicopter to some exotic place, the laughter-filled hours as he recounted his manoeuvrings in the business world, and the special times when they stole away together and hardly left the bedroom. She rarely admitted it to him but she had fallen in love with the energetic, mesmeric tycoon.

Only her memories of the times she was with him compensated for the inevitable loneliness when he was obliged to be with his family. Those times had come to assume more importance than the Fifth Avenue apartment, the summers in the rented house in the Hamptons, the live-in maid, the closets filled with designer clothing.

She closed her eyes, almost hearing him laugh when she thanked him, usually in bed, for a beautiful present. 'It's better to live right than die rich,' he would say. She smiled to herself, thank God he had done both.

Glancing around the empty apartment, she noticed the outlines on the hand-sponged walls where once paintings, photographs and mirrors had hung, images of an existence she must never talk about.

Most of her life here was now neatly swaddled in tissue paper or bubble-wrap and stowed in large wooden crates ready for shipment to London. Twelve of them lined the corridor of the Fifth Avenue apartment which overlooked Central Park and the Guggenheim Museum. This was it. The end.

She contemplated the white ceiling, the cornices high-lighted in white with a touch of blue, Mark's sugges-tion. God, how many hours had she spent staring at that Arctic wasteland? Waiting. For the phone to ring, for the key to turn in the lock, for his smile, for his hands, for his lips. And when he did arrive there was never enough time. The more successful he became, the more rushed their lovemaking – except when they escaped the city, on their trips out of town or to their bolt-hole in the Hamptons. Only then was he able to relax and enjoy the hours of languorous sex at which she was expert. The trouble was, the further up the ladder he went, the less he felt entitled to his pleasure. This was not guilt but a fear that his luck quotient was running out.

She was always on the lookout for signs that his interest in her was on the wane, but he continued to be possessive about time she spent away from him. She was his property and he liked to know she was around, waiting. He would ring her on his mobile at all sorts of hours to check her whereabouts. He might call from the men's room in a Greenwich restaurant while his family ate dinner close by, or from his four-acre Connecticut estate. Sometimes she could hear music and laughter behind his soft words of love or the slurp-slurp of water as he lay in the tub. He took incredible risks to keep in touch but his calls had been noticeably less frequent in the last few months before his death. That was when she had occasionally called the office, although it infuriated him.

Lately Mark had become irritable if she tried to raise the subject of when he would leave his wife. Not that she had been sitting around waiting all these years. Unknown to him there had been two liaisons in that time but they had fizzled out. Nobody could match the chemistry, the humour between her and Mark, and his generosity. But try as she might to be perfection for him, he steadfastly stayed with his wife, their daughters, the dogs, the horses, the marriage.

After the shock of seeing that brutal television news flash depicting Mark's crushed car, metal flattened by the impact, she had rushed into the bathroom to be sick and had taken to her bed for two days. As well as being her lover he had been her educator, her jester, her organiser and cheerleader.

She was at a loss to know who to telephone for details of what had happened and had to resort to reading newspapers and watching television bulletins for fragments of new information. It was then that she realised how few friends she had, certainly none in common with Mark, and none with whom she could discuss this tragedy. She did not even have the comfort of photographs of the two of them together. Mark had been paranoid about any kind of evidence of their affair, although she tried to reassure him that they were for her eyes only.

When he first mentioned that she would never have financial worries after he had gone, she took it to mean after they had split up but he had shaken his head vehemently, 'No, I can't imagine my life without you. But if anything happens to me I want you to know that you'll be well taken care of.'

When she asked him what this meant, he said he intended to give his financial advisers explicit instructions to safeguard her future. 'Everything will be watertight,' he told her. 'Watertight,' he repeated. 'You'll have no problems.'

A day after Mark's death a bulky envelope was delivered by special courier from his lawyer. It contained a loving letter in which he explained about two tranches of diamonds. She could pick up the first in three months' time from a bank in Vaduz, Liechtenstein, the second two years afterwards from a bank in Geneva. Letters of introduction to the banks were enclosed. The account numbers and authorisation they contained would unlock the safety deposit boxes holding the stones. In return she had to remain quiet about their affair and, because he'd been forced to reveal their affair to his wife, to leave America as soon as possible, she supposed for Helen's sake.

Well, she would depart from New York with few regrets. Without Mark, the city held little appeal, but she had always adored London. She would make a fresh start there. With the money realised from selling some of the jewellery Mark had given her over the years, and the fortune awaiting her, she would take control of her own destiny. She was still a young woman, her thirty-one years had barely made an imprint on her face or her body. She would always miss Mark, but she must put her grief behind her and look to the future. No more secrecy, she vowed, no more hiding, no more waiting.

From now on she was going to be on the winning side. The wife side.

# *Chapter Six*

Georgie and Alistair settled back in their seats on the London-bound Concorde and waved away the proffered champagne. Years ago they had decided it was only inexperienced travellers who indulged in alcohol on long journeys. Without it the body clock had a much quicker chance to revert to normal.

'How are you going to square the cost of these tickets with Giles?' asked Georgie. This was her first supersonic flight.

'We're only following orders,' he smiled at her. 'Return to base a.s.a.p., Helen said. There's no quicker way than this. Three hours and we'll be back in the office. It's a small price to pay.'

Giles had confided that the reason Helen was twitchy was that after a short laudatory period the media would stop writing complimentary pieces about Mark. 'Then the City pages will have a bean feast about how Amalgamated will be lost without its founder chairman. We may not be a publicly-quoted company,' Giles had gone on, 'but our rivals are and they'll take advantage of this unexpected hiatus. We need to head this off so you'd better alert your PR people to have good quotes ready to refute any bad publicity.'

Sitting in her window seat, Georgie reflected on the past few extraordinary hours, still too depressed about Mark's death to enjoy the comfort and the gourmet cuisine.

She turned to Alistair, who was leafing through his briefcase. 'Are you worried about Helen taking over?'

'Not as much as you, obviously.'

'That's because I've only met her at a couple of functions and she was very much "The Wife".'

'Don't be fooled by that, she was bloody formidable when we started. She was the tough one. And Mark took notice of who she rated. But whatever she said at the meeting, I think she might well decide to sell the company if she feels Mark's death affects its profitability. That's why I think transferring Giles to New York to be acting chief executive is a smart move.'

'I'm glad to see the back of him. He and I rub each other up the wrong way,' said Georgie, whose editorial demands had frequently brought her into conflict with the cheese-paring chief executive.

'It's a pity about that, he and I have always managed to work well together.'

'That's something to do with your gender,' laughed Georgie. 'He has an old-fashioned view about women in power.'

'Still, I think Helen's hoping his appointment will stop some of the infighting because he's seen by the guys in New York as no threat.'

'I don't think she's too fond of Ned,' said Georgie. 'Did you see her face when he was trying to smarm up to her?'

'He's a smart operator, Ned. His deputy told me how he was "hated but rated".'

'Nice description, the very opposite of your style.'

'He's a poisonous sod. The buzz in New York is that he has his eye firmly on Mark's job. He'll be gambling that Helen will be there short term then he'll take over. You sure you understood what he was saying to Roberto?'

'Definitely. He said words to the effect that Roberto shouldn't worry about the new magazine Mark wouldn't let him start, that he should go ahead and that Ned would square it with the widow.'

'Is your Italian that good?'

'*Certo sono sicura.*'

'I presume that means yes.'

'*Sì, signore.*'

'At last those language tapes we stuck on that teen mag have come in useful.' He stretched back in his seat. 'Now I understand what I'm up against. It's just as well you were there.'

She could not stop a triumphant smile.

'OK,' he grinned, 'I admit it. You were right to come.'

'I'm glad I did.' Her eyes were impish. 'Otherwise I'd never have had the chance to put Harry's nose out of joint.'

'I didn't see him at the airport. Apparently he didn't feel the need to hurry home,' said Alistair, frowning.

'Something pretty important must have cropped up for Harry to miss out on a Concorde trip.'

Trying to fathom what it could be gave way to wondering who would replace Giles in London. By tacit agreement they had avoided discussing a far more crucial topic than the one aired so hotly in New York: How a baby would affect their much prized careers.

Harry was ensconced in Ned's brownstone on the Upper East Side, mineral water in hand, doing some rapid calculations.

His mental arithmetic stopped at two million with the Hockneys in the drawing room. That figure didn't include the Bechstein baby grand. This place was a planet apart from his own townhouse in Pimlico. His home was an elegant four-bedroomed Georgian residence within the sound of the House of Commons division bell and a convenient fifteen-minute walk to his office in the West End, but it contained nothing of value apart from a grandfather clock and that paled into insignificance next to some of Ned's antique treasures.

'Right, Harry,' said his host, offering him a generous scoop of Beluga caviar on toast, 'Giles will do his damnedest to get Alistair the top job in London. And that'll be bad news for both of us. Giles doesn't like you, and Alistair and I don't rate each other. But Harry,' he leaned forward, putting his face inches away from his colleague's, 'Mark's job has my name on it. I don't think I need a spell in London with all those tight-assed know-alls, present company excepted. But the widow thinks if you haven't served your time in Limeyland you can't take over here.'

'It would be great for the company if you were at the helm. Let's face it, Mark was getting past it.'

'Yup, I plan no longer than a year, eighteen months tops, so when I'm back in charge, I'll see you have the London job after me, buddy. That's a promise.'

Mark's personal assistant had been with him for six years and during that time she had been unfailingly courteous to Helen, giving the impression of having all the virtues of a perfect office paradigm. Mark had often commented that although she was friendly, they had a somewhat impersonal relationship. She was always 'Miss Conlan', he never addressed her by her first name. She discouraged questions about her personal life and ran the office like an automaton. Only for a second did Helen toy with the idea that Miss Conlan might have been Mark's mistress. No, that was too absurd. She wouldn't have needed to stay in the job with that kind of bounty awaiting her and, besides, she didn't have the right physical assets.

Like everyone else, Margery Conlan had been shocked by the suddenness of Mark's death but she made no pretence at being overwrought. She was as expansive as Helen needed her to be on business matters but her discretion about Mark's after-hours activities was as impenetrable as her outfit, a navy suit buttoned up to the neck and walking shoes that were better suited to a weekend hike than the streets of Manhattan. Helen felt no kinship with her but she needed her on side. She wanted information about Mark's mistress and where better to start than with his trusted PA? But Miss Conlan was like a stone wall; all Helen's attempts to draw her out about Mark's activities outside working hours led nowhere.

Finally Helen said, 'Let's get out of this office and have lunch. Just you and me.'

A fleeting expression of what might have been alarm crossed Margery Conlan's face. But after a pause she said quietly, 'That would be pleasant.'

Despite blandishments Margery refused wine and while Helen dissected a char-grilled plaice, she toyed with what seemed to be the most unappetising salad on the menu. Thirty minutes of small talk at the smart eaterie failed to make any impression on her. What would break down her reserve? Trained not to impart a morsel of information to inquisitive outsiders, even if that outsider was a wife, Helen doubted whether she could call on her compassion. She had to make the conversation more personal.

'Did he ever talk to you about the early days?' she asked.

Margery shook her head.

'We started a magazine together, a small one,' said Helen with sadness in her eyes. 'It was called *Slimming For Success* and as it was the first of its kind in Britain we were overwhelmed by free publicity.'

Helen recalled with pleasure those eighteen-hour working days when she shared every aspect of the toil with Mark, from planning stage through to seeing the launch edition roll off the presses. Sitting at her desk opposite his, in that cold, shabby, attic office, matching his drive and commitment, she had spent hours on the phone persuading, coaxing, cajoling often reluctant advertisers to take a chance on such an untried idea.

'Do you know what he did at the launch of the magazine?' she continued. 'Went round displaying the waistband of his suit to show how much weight he had lost. He said it was because of an exclusive diet we printed in the first issue. Actually all he'd done was buy a suit two sizes larger.'

Margery gave her first spontaneous smile. 'That sounds like the Mark I worked for. When he had a goal in sight there was no stopping him.'

Helen judged this the moment to pretend to be the uninformed housewife.

'I used to know every dot and comma of his business at first,' she said, 'but over the last couple of years he seemed more withdrawn, more preoccupied. Did you notice that?'

'No, I don't think I did.'

'He stayed away from home more. You must have noticed that.' Helen gave a short laugh. This was getting her nowhere. What had she to lose by being direct? 'You made all the arrangements for his trips, didn't you?'

'Yes.'

'Arrangements to help him lead a double life.'

'I beg your pardon?'

Helen gave an exasperated sigh. 'You must have known my husband was keeping a mistress.'

83

Margery was silent and Helen studied her face, searching for clues, anything to indicate guilt.

'You don't have to cover up for him any more,' Helen said encouragingly.

Margery examined her sensibly short nails and avoided Helen's eye.

'You wouldn't be being disloyal. I know all about his mistress. And do you know who told me? Mark himself. That's why I was ransacking his papers, to find out more.'

At this, Margery glanced up briefly and Helen pressed on, 'Yes, he'd only been dead a few hours when I was left under no illusions about how he'd been deceiving me.' She was almost gabbling now. 'It was all detailed in a handwritten letter. He wanted me to know everything about her.'

Ah, now there was a reaction. Margery's eyes flickered uneasily and a tiny splodge of colour appeared on each cheek. After the smallest hesitation she said, 'I know nothing about that.'

Helen gritted her teeth. It was inconceivable that this woman had not even had suspicions.

'I could hire a private investigator to find out about her,' she said, trying to keep her voice emotionless, 'but I don't want an outsider asking questions about my husband and risk it leaking out.' Her gaze did not waver from Margery's face. 'That would dishonour his memory,' she said quietly, surprising herself with the thought that she still cared, 'and in spite of what's happened, I wouldn't want that – not so much for him, you understand, as for my children. I know how fond you've become of them over the years so I imagine you wouldn't like that either.'

It worked. Margery Conlan's expression softened. 'I know how desperate you must be to find out all you can, but you have to believe me, I know nothing about it. If I could help you I would.' Helen noticed she was twisting her napkin under the table and longed to shout at her how important it was that she should be frank, that she was the only one who could help. With a great effort of will she restrained herself. She must not risk frightening Margery off.

'Well,' she said eventually, 'you probably don't even realise it but there might be something, any little detail that could help.'

Margery hesitated for a moment. 'The only thing I can think of, and it doesn't amount to much, was that in the last few months his private phone occasionally rang when he was out of the office. Mark had told me not to bother with it if he wasn't there but I always did – a reflex action, I suppose. It was a woman's voice and she said she had the wrong number.'

'Did you ever mention her to Mark?'

'No, I thought it was simply a mix-up. It's only now, in view of what you've told me about his private life, that I wonder whether it was significant.'

'Was it the same voice each time?'

Margery considered this. 'The woman only said a few words but I think so. I can't tell you anything else because I don't know anything else.'

Helen felt deflated. The trouble was she believed Margery Conlan.

# Chapter Seven

Alistair walked into his empty office suite rejoicing in the fact that he felt no jet lag. If only he had a permanent pass for supersonic travel.

His secretary would not be in for half an hour. When she first started working for him he had used all his guile to try and persuade her that an eight o'clock start would suit him. But since the day often stretched to 7 p.m. she had rebelled at coming in so early and he could not blame her.

Soon after his appointment as publishing director, Alistair had initiated an open-door policy, which irritated some of his fellow executives who used their offices as shields against unscheduled intrusion. 'How do you ever get any work done if you let people barge in whenever they want?' they asked. But Alistair understood the editorial craving for instant reaction to an idea. His editors appreciated the way they could get a response to any of their problems, whether it be a staffing difficulty or a delicate negotiation with a big-name interview. Nevertheless he was startled to get a phone call this early. Journalists did not usually rouse themselves at this hour.

It was the cheeky young editor of a high-circulation men's magazine, who had been poached from a rival a few months before. He wanted to know who would be running Amalgamated now.

Alistair frowned. 'Surely you've heard. Helen's taking over.'

'Yes, yes, we all read about that in the business supplements. But she hasn't been involved with the company for years.'

'Maybe, but she's the major shareholder and she wants to become involved with it now.'

'Nah, what's the real story? The crocodiles are already circling. I had one on this morning trying to pump me about what was going to happen and all kinds of rumours are buzzing around this place?'

'What are they saying?' asked Alistair.

'Oh, that the widow's trying to sell, that we're all going to be made redundant, that the London office is going to be scaled down. Of course I'm telling them not to be ridiculous.'

'It's exactly because of this that I've asked Helen to come over here as soon as possible to talk to the staff,' said Alistair. 'Nothing's changing, no one's scaling down and Helen has investment plans. Does that sound like someone who intends putting the business up for sale?'

Rumours like these were dangerous, an indication that Amalgamated was seen as a rich cherry ready for picking. And this kind of talk would cause dissent among the troops.

All day the phone rang with endless queries about what was really happening. 'Haven't these fuckwits anything better to do with their time?' Alistair railed at his secretary. The situation was the same in New York, Paris and Sydney, and the company's PR machine worked overtime to nail the wild stories flying around and impress upon the media the support that Helen's chairmanship had among Amalgamated's executives.

Alistair was tapping away on his computer, editing an introduction to a major feature in his flagship news magazine, when Georgie walked through the door.

It was a source of intrigue to the staff that they almost acted like courteous strangers in the office, rarely leaving or arriving together. They still refused all requests from television, radio or newspapers for joint interviews, preferring to be thought of as individuals rather than part of a so-called golden couple.

Both were constantly in demand at industry events, being prized speakers who could tempt promising graduates into the business, impress advertising organisations or talk about the future of magazines in the new millennium. These requests meant they were rarely at home, being out, either together or separately, many evenings of the week.

Alistair used to say wryly to Georgie that their diaries were laid out so many months ahead they should schedule lovemaking sessions. Once they had thought this was amusing but since conception was proving more difficult than they had envisaged it had become a self-fulfilling prophecy.

'Mr Drummond, I have a giant favour to ask you,' Georgie said now, sitting in the chair opposite his desk.

'I'm really sorry, Ms Luckhurst, but the answer's no.'

'You can't say no. You don't know what it is.'

'I know that giant favours mean trouble.' He smiled at her, as always appreciating what a lovely, vibrant face she had. 'All right, what is it?'

'I need you to be at that advertising dinner tonight.' When he began shaking his head she went on, 'Alistair, my ad man's got flu. I wouldn't ask at this short notice if I wasn't desperate.'

'Do you really need me there?'

She nodded.

'OK,' he said, 'I'll fix it.'

'Thank you, I really appreciate it.'

'I'm hoping for more reward than that.'

'What had you in mind?' she asked impishly.

'What do you say to a baby-making weekend in the south of France? The weekend after the memorial service, out Friday night, back Sunday.'

'Difficult. We're due to spend that weekend with the Graingers.'

'We can't. The dates are right. It has to be that weekend.'

'Everyone will be there, including most of the legal eagles in town, possibly a couple of newspaper proprietors, and there's even a rumour the PM's coming. What excuse could we give them?'

'The truth, that we're trying to make a baby.'

'They'd say we could do it some other time and they might ask whether we really need their advertising contract when it comes up for renewal.'

'I could tell them what to do with that contract. They could—'

'OK,' she interrupted. 'I'll phone them and grovel.'

'Good thinking. Tell them that if the weekend works, we'll have a bouncing baby to bring to their party next year.'

The enmity in the room was almost tangible. Helen gave an exasperated sigh and was further maddened when she saw Giles Beamish, her newly-appointed right-hand man, raise his eyebrows slightly. Discussions had not gone well between them. He had disagreed with virtually everything she had suggested, including the hiring of a highly-regarded firm of London head-hunters in the search for a new chief executive for London as well as her proposal for an appointments board to choose the best candidate. Marginally placated when she had asked him to serve on it, he had been forthright almost to the point of rudeness about Harry's inclusion but he reserved his ire for the head-hunters. 'At least see the front runners in our own company first before you bring in these outsiders. When this gets out it will be terrible for morale.'

'I don't agree,' Helen had said firmly. 'We can't afford to waste time. I'm not ruling out our own people, of course not, but I want to measure them up against what's out there in the marketplace. This is a chance we don't often get, to survey all the fish in the sea.'

'I've worked bloody hard for this company and because I'm an elder statesman I have no axe to grind. All I want is the future prosperity of Amalgamated.' He leaned forward earnestly. 'And it's not about my pension either.'

'My mind is made up, Giles.'

'Mark wouldn't have liked this. His constant refrain was that it was important to nurture our own talent, that was the secret of our success. It was his credo.'

'Mark isn't in charge now. Do I have to keep reminding you of that?' Her voice was soft but her tone was steely. This man was getting on her nerves. If he was going to question all her decisions, perhaps she should have thought twice before blocking Ned Mastrianni.

She had understood the board's shock at her announcement that she would take over and had made allowances for it but she was damned if she would be patronised by these guys. She had more at stake than they did, after all. It was her business and her reputation.

She studied Giles as he tried to control his mutinous expression. He was a well-preserved sixty-two, lean, with a mane of thick white hair and a languid manner. She could see his attraction for some women. Was he faithful to his wife? Probably not. Perhaps Mark had set the tone for the whole office and had made infidelity acceptable. She had once watched Giles dancing with his secretary at one of the company functions and wondered now how close they were.

Well, the decision she would make – she, not anyone else – for the job of London chief executive would be based on character as well as ability. She suspected that the only choice Giles would approve of was Alistair Drummond. But the candidate would have to be someone who would empathise with her plans, who would have the capacity and imagination to achieve consensus.

'Helen, with great respect,' said Giles, 'who understands more about this business now than I do?'

'And who, Giles, understands as much as you do about Mark's future strategies for the company?' she said more resolutely than she felt. True, Mark had used her as a sounding board when he was wrestling with a problem but in the months before his death he had sought her business advice only rarely.

'This is a tough business, Helen, and not one for amateurs.'

'I am not an amateur,' said Helen, her voice dangerously quiet. 'And I would remind you that I have a mandate in the shape of my husband's,' she corrected herself, 'my own shareholding. You do not.'

'I was hired by Mark for my expertise and worked hard for the position I have. You inherited yours by marrying the right man.'

'How dare you! Have you forgotten who started this company? Whose idea it was that set us on the road? Who worked all the hours God sent to establish the first four titles? I cannot believe you're sitting there saying this to me.' She was breathing hard. The patronising shit.

Giles slapped his knee and let out a laugh. 'You passed that test.'

'What?'

'The first law in fighting your corner is not to give an inch. I'm impressed, very impressed,' his head was nodding as if it was attached by a spring. 'From now on you can count on my support.'

Helen's face reddened. She was not fooled. This was expediency. Giles had read the signs and realised he would have to concede or risk being cut out of the king-making process – anathema to someone who had been in the driving seat alongside Mark for many years.

Was Giles an enemy pretending friendship? They were always the most dangerous and she would do well to remember that.

Georgina's office was in marked contract to Alistair's. While he had piles of manuscripts all over his desk and side table, hers was tidy and uncluttered. The afternoon sun streamed through the window that overlooked a small square and heightened the scent from a display of cream roses in an elegant cut-glass vase on the window-sill.

Rosemary Drummond edged round the corner with a wooden tray bearing a floral china cup and saucer and a small cafetière and placed it carefully on the desk.

Georgie took a sip of the hot coffee. 'What a godsend. Thanks, Rosie.'

'You're welcome. When did you get back from the States?'

'Sunday night.' Georgie's hand flew to her mouth. 'How awful of me. With Mark's death I completely forgot you were supposed to be coming round for lunch. I'm sorry.' She hesitated. 'We'll make it another time. Soon.'

'You've had so much on your plate lately, please don't worry.' Rosemary wasn't fooled. It had always been obvious to her that Georgina was jealous that she and her brother were so close. That's why she tried to keep them apart.

When Alistair had become serious about Georgie, Rosemary's world had turned bleak. For an all too brief interval between his divorce from his first wife and his involvement with his second, she had enjoyed status as the woman in his life. But because of Georgina, she had lost the companionship of her beloved brother. She would never forget the last time Georgina had deigned to have her at their place. Fancy serving up shepherd's pie for Sunday lunch, especially when she knew Georgina ordered gourmet stuff for her smart friends.

That lunch with its nursery food was imprinted on Rosemary's mind. Georgie had made a point of telling her that for once she had made the pie herself and not bought it from a supermarket. Big deal. The taste would have told anyone that. Alistair did not seem to notice. The kitchen was a mess too, pans and potato peelings and the Sunday newspapers all over the place, not like her neat and tidy office. But then Georgie had staff to do everything for her in the office. When her sister-in-law had to set the table she had taken the opportunity to peek inside the fridge and the cupboards. There was hardly any food around. Poor Alistair, he'd come home tired and hungry from the office and find nothing to eat.

Everything Georgina did was a source of friction to Rosemary, even the coffee. *She* had to have it freshly ground while the rest of the staff made do with instant. And that bloody china. Rosemary had been reprimanded when she tried to use it for herself on her first day. 'That's only for Miss Luckhurst,' she was told by Georgina's snooty secretary.

She glanced up to find her boss watching her with an expression on her face Rosemary could not quite fathom. She believed she could mask the often venomous thoughts that flitted through her mind. Over the years she had learned to be agreeable when her natural feelings were to be aggressive. But lately she wondered how successful she had been. Georgina was no fool and there seemed to be more tension between them these days. As Alistair was her only family, she couldn't afford to upset his wife. She had better be more careful.

Before Rosemary's arrival at Amalgamated she had held a series of short-term jobs that had led nowhere. Georgina's offer of a job as a computer operator after she was made redundant eighteen months ago had been a lifeline at the time, but Rosemary regarded the work as boring and far below her talents, just something to tide her over while she tried to find a 'proper' job. She disliked working for Georgie and hated the fact that she was beholden to her sister-in-law for her livelihood. She was desperate to leave. She was neither on the editorial side nor on the management but stuck somewhere in between. The two men who worked in the computer department with her were pleasant enough but they were concentrating on an Internet magazine and were at least fifteen years younger. Also it was hard being the most junior Drummond in the company. Fellow employees seemed to treat her differently. They tended to guard their words in her presence, and Rosemary was rarely invited to join them for lunch or an after-hours drink. At least, that was her explanation for her lack of friendships in the office.

Rosemary had made a habit of arriving first in the mornings, mainly in the hope of finding out what she could about Georgie's activities. She justified herself by blaming her boss for being meagre with information and an inability to delegate. While the office was unattended she would wander around, testing a drawer here and there and occasionally finding one unlocked. So far this had proved unrewarding but as she gained access to more keys, her range had extended to Georgina's office.

Despite her love of high tech, Georgina still kept a leather-bound diary in her office and it did not take Rosemary long to decipher her cryptic notes. The information had not been particularly useful so far but it was comforting to have an idea of Georgina's whereabouts (and therefore, Alistair's) and their planned holiday dates. Certain days were circled, which she assumed referred to her boss's monthly cycle.

Although only eighteen months older than Alistair, a

great deal of his day-to-day care during their childhood had been left to Rosemary because their mother had complained that two babies in as many years had worn her out entirely. As a result, Rosemary had become Alistair's emotional rock. They had a loving father but more often than not he was absent from their home in Edinburgh on trips abroad for his job as a shoe buyer. The two children quickly realised that their lives were different from those of their contemporaries at school. On the rare occasions their mother was at home when they returned from school she was usually having one of her 'little naps'. They came to understand much later when she disappeared from their lives to live with 'Uncle' Frank what those afternoon naps signified.

By the time their father died, when Rosemary was twelve, Alistair had overtaken his sister in height, and he was clearly going to be the more attractive of the two. Though the siblings shared family characteristics like dark blonde hair, Alistair's was straight and gleaming, while Rosemary's was curly and frizzed in the rain. Soon Alistair became tall and strapping, with wide shoulders and long arms. His sister had inherited those same shoulders and arms but on her shorter frame they merely made her appear stocky.

Despite the lack of love and attention from their mother, Alistair thrived, basking in the admiration of his older sister. But when he moved to London, they drifted apart. She briefly met his first wife and had felt instinctively she was the wrong woman for him. But she had resisted the temptation to say so even when the marriage failed. Rosemary was the one he turned to after the break-up and she immediately sold her flat and moved south to take care of him.

'Rosemary.' Georgie laughed as Rosemary started. 'You were miles away.'

'Sorry.'

Georgie opened her diary. 'Why don't you come over this Sunday? The Harrisons will be there.'

'No, no, I won't do that. I'll wait for a Sunday when you're free.' She hadn't seen her brother socially for ages. Just this once couldn't Georgie arrange a meal for her alone and not treat her as an appendage?

'All right, but we'll make it soon.' Georgie closed her diary. 'Has Jane told you that I've put you down for that special computer course starting next month? Two nights a week.'

Rosemary frowned. 'I thought that wasn't going to happen until the end of the year.'

'You can never have too many qualifications. And the sooner the better. This is absolutely right for you,' said Georgie with that imperious air which so irritated Rosemary.

'OK, fine. Thanks. I appreciate the chance.' Rosemary felt slighted. Why did Georgie behave as if she wasn't up to the job, even though she worked her fingers to the bone for a pittance? She was being asked to gain more qualifications in her own time. Two evenings a week and she wouldn't be paid for overtime. Oh no, there was only one person well paid around here.

'That's OK, Rosie. Close the door, will you? I've some calls to make.'

Rosie. Hadn't she yet realised only Alistair was allowed to call her that? That insensitivity was another reason she disliked her sister-in-law.

# Chapter Eight

The New York memorial service had been small and intimate but the London setting was more impressive, thought Helen, and demanded a congregation of hundreds. St George's Church in Eaton Square was filled with cornflowers, gypsophila and daisies, the blue and white of Mark's racing colours.

As Helen walked to her place in the front pew, followed by her daughters, she could not avoid thinking what a charade all this was. Not only had Mark soured her past, he was forcing her to live a lie now.

The memorial ceremony had been planned as meticulously as Princess Diana's funeral. Alistair Drummond had been immensely helpful in booking the church and in the placing of notices in the court and social sections of *The Times* and the *Telegraph*. Although it had been years since she'd had any contact with him, apart from a few business dinners where they had each been singing for their supper, she felt comfortable with him and had been grateful to see a familiar face at her first board meeting. She regretted now that she had turned away his attempts to come and see her in the days after Mark's death. He was a reminder of those uncomplicated days when they worked ridiculous hours and there were more laughs than obstacles, when 'yes' was said more often than 'no' and everything seemed possible.

She had resisted asking him to make the address at the service in case it would appear as if the decision about who would head the company in London was a *fait accompli*. Helen still had an open mind about the job.

But there had been an awkwardness between them when he went over the tribute to be read by one of Mark's oldest friends. Helen had almost shown her anger when in one paragraph Alistair referred to the chairman's loyalty to his wife and daughters. Alistair, thinking she was grief-stricken, had been tiptoeing around her and it was an easy matter for her to alter the text to a comment on Mark's enjoyment of family life.

Balancing the expectations of the company employees, all of whom felt they should attend, with those of the large number of celebrities, racing folk and business colleagues who were Mark's friends, was a complicated task. Applications had streamed in once the memorial date was announced and as Canon Smith gently reminded Helen, 'Even those without invitations could hardly be refused entry into a place of worship.'

Helen would not have been able to cope with the memorial service if it had not been for Margery Conlan. Over the intervening weeks Helen had established if not a friendship then a mutually respectful and harmonious working relationship with her. Helen had thrown everything she could on to Margery's shoulders, a list of people she needed to see or phone, documents that had to be located. She had only to mention an item and Margery had either dealt with it already or the relevant paper would arrive on her desk within the hour. It was an impressive performance.

The big breakthrough in their relationship had come one evening when they were having a coffee break. Before going home Margery had said suddenly, 'I'd be pleased if you called me Margery.' Nothing had gratified Helen more than this acknowledgement that she had earned her spurs.

They had been in the middle of arrangements for Helen's protracted stay in London. She wanted to choose a new chief executive while she was there and was determined to remain until the appointment was made. Once that had been achieved, she promised herself she would concentrate on tracking down the woman who dominated her night-time thoughts. What decided Helen to suggest that Margery accompany her to London was Margery's absolute discretion. Helen was confident she would show the same standards of loyalty and trust on her behalf as she had on Mark's. It would also be good to have a familiar face working alongside her.

Margery had seemed overwhelmed at Helen's invitation but accepted gladly, saying this was her first business trip abroad since joining the company. Implicit but unsaid was that Mark would not have wanted her with him.

The congregation in St George's included politicians

from both sides of the House. Two Cabinet ministers were accompanied by their inconspicuous detectives tucked close to the ornate columns of the nave, keeping a careful watch on their charges. Helen could not help observing how much more attractive women looked wearing black than men. Make-up made a huge difference, of course. Most of them appeared washed-out and tired. She wondered how many were having anxious thoughts about which one of them would be the next to receive this treatment.

The choir began singing 'Jerusalem', a hymn Mark particularly disliked and one of the reasons Helen had chosen it. When they came to the words 'dark Satanic mills', she risked a glance at his family sitting in the pews opposite, who had travelled down from their homes in the north of England. She and Mark had drifted apart from them and it was some time since there had been a family reunion. Her two brothers-in-law were each accompanied by a new, younger wife not much older than their stepchildren. She and Mark had not attended either of the weddings but Mark had always been generous towards them financially. How much had Mark's money allowed them to ditch their responsibilities? Yes, his money had been responsible for as much unhappiness as happiness, she thought, as she tried to picture the faces of her original sisters-in-law, but the images stubbornly refused to appear.

The familiar words of the Twenty-Third Psalm began next and as the words washed over her, Helen pulled down her veil to conceal the bitter expression she was certain her daughters would notice.

'I shall not want . . .'

That was true. Financially she would be one of the richest women in Britain and indeed America if she chose to sell Mark's only true love, his business. In every other relationship he had been unfaithful. To her, to the children, probably even to his mistress as well.

Helen glanced over to her daughters, fresh-faced husbands at their side. The secret had been hardest to keep from them. It was difficult pretending to be heartbroken without being able to cry. How could she weep for a man who had betrayed her with a counterfeit marriage?

One of Mark's daughters gave a poignant reading she had chosen from Henry Scott Holland: 'Death is nothing at all, I have only slipped away into the next room. Whatever we were to each other, we still are.'

Helen gripped the hymnal, thinking, no, we're not.

'Let my name be spoken without the trace of a shadow on it. Why should I be out of mind because I am out of sight?'

Shadow? He was more like a big black cloud lowering over her.

The tribute followed, read by one of Mark's school friends, a man who had alcoholically stumbled to success year after year on British television. As he walked to the front, Helen noted with relief that his hands were hardly shaking, a symptom that had upset Mark at their last meeting.

Then the choir led the mourners to sing the hymn 'When the world and their love was young', which she and Mark had first heard sung by their daughters when as proud parents they were in the audience at a nursery school concert. At last Helen started to weep. One of her daughters passed her a handkerchief and as she dried her eyes, she wondered how she could explain that this first outpouring of emotion was not for her cheat of a husband but for herself.

It was her last date with her man and like all their meetings it was clandestine. She smiled to herself thinking what a stir it would cause if the congregation could see under the exterior to the white satin push-up bra with matching suspenders which were Mark's favourites. And as always when she was with him, she dispensed with panties. She was saying goodbye in the only way she was allowed.

She was conscious of the effect she had on the people around her in her austerely tailored dark blue suit, matching high-heeled shoes and tiny cloche hat with glints of gold. The colours she wore echoed the Temple-Smith colours and she was proud that Mark's choice of blue and gold had been her suggestion. Blue to match his eyes, she'd told him, and gold for success.

She cast a gaze over the elegantly-dressed crowd, but the faces were unfamiliar, though she recognised one or two from by-line pictures in glossy magazines. Nobody here was aware of her relationship with Mark, she was sure of it. It was ironic that having spent so much money with public relations companies to build up his image as a media tycoon he had had to hide behind dark glasses and false names when he was with her because he feared being recognised. But as he used to say, 'If you have something to hide, then hide it.'

She craned her head so she could see the front pew and the bowed head of Mark's widow, someone she could identify only from photographs. Alongside her were what were obviously his two grown-up daughters and their husbands. Helen's head was bowed and she was apparently praying. She wondered how grief-stricken the widow could be after reading Mark's letter and finding out about her existence and, worse, how generous Mark had been towards his mistress. In her place she would have felt venomous but her lawyer had assured her there was no way Helen could find out her identity. She shivered and hoped he was right.

If Helen ever did discover who she was, the financial arrangement between them would be put in jeopardy. Attending this service was dangerous but she had felt unable to go to the memorial service in New York and so needed to use this one to honour Mark's memory. She wanted to mount the podium and tell the congregation about the other side of the man they were here to remember, the things they used to do together, the places they visited, the house they shared, how good he was as a lover.

She missed Mark. His hands, his body, his mind. The enforced loneliness during her years as his mistress was nothing to this feeling of emptiness. Right now she could not envisage a situation where she would wish to have any other man look at her in that special way. But she was realistic. At her age, there would come a time when being alone was insupportable. At least she was starting afresh, in a different city. It had been one of the conditions of the settlement but she was sure it would prove to be the right place to make a new life for herself.

The last notes of the organ faded and the congregation began to move towards the aisles. The real purpose for many of them being here became clear. To see and be seen. To network, to fix up meetings and do lunch.

She had expected to bump into her ex-husband because he had known Mark and she was curious about how the years had dealt with him. Suddenly she glimpsed him. If he asked why she was here, she would have to make up some story about paying her respects to someone she had known in New York. He had matured well. Better tailoring and more careful grooming had combined to give him an air of attractive confidence. If she had stayed with him . . . she shook her head. No, she regretted nothing.

Now he was turning to survey the crowd. There was a certain look in his eye that stirred memories. She had forgotten how sexy he was. She tried not to think about that dreadful night when she had broken the news to him that she was leaving him but the images persisted. It had been the first time she had seen him cry. They had argued for hours. He kept asking, 'Why, why, why?' She had told him she had been too young to get married, that she needed to be free. All lies, of course. When a few weeks later he finally accepted that she did not love him any more, he had been too proud to plead for her to stay.

He had simply packed a suitcase and without saying a word had walked out of the house.

Of course he could have no idea that she had fallen in love with Mark Temple-Smith, that she could not wait to go to New York to be with him. She and Mark had decided it was better not to tell her husband that another man was involved in case he tried to discover who it was. If he thought that she merely wanted freedom to explore her personality he was more likely to accept her decision. And so it proved.

As the congregation crowded towards the exits, she thought this would be as good an opportunity as any to 'accidentally' bump into him. She could not resist finding out whether the old magic would still work on him.

Using her shoulder to edge forward, she delicately manoeuvred her way towards his tall frame and tugged at his sleeve.

He wheeled round.

'You,' he said, his face startled. 'You're the last person I expected to see.'

She was gratified to see a slight smile breaking out before he put up his guard.

'What brings you here?' he asked, a veneer of impassivity now in place.

'I read about it in *The Times* and thought I should pay my respects. Mark was kind to me in New York.'

She moved sideways to avoid being pushed by those intent on reaching the doors. He didn't catch what she said in the buzz of conversation around them and bent his lean body close towards her.

'I said,' she repeated, 'let's meet when it's less noisy. Perhaps dinner one evening?'

At that moment she became aware of a woman standing behind her, silently watching. His embarrassment was plain as he stuttered an introduction.

'This is Louise . . .'

He gestured towards the woman. 'My wife Georgina.'

Georgie looped her arm through Alistair's and said with a smile she hoped did not appear forced, 'If I'd read our magazines more thoroughly I'd probably know the etiquette of meeting a first wife.'

Alistair laughed nervously but Louise beamed radiantly at Georgie. 'All that's so long ago but now I'm back in London it'd be lovely to see you both. We must arrange it sometime.'

'Yes,' Georgie said promptly, 'we must,' thinking it would be a cold day in hell before she socialised with this woman, though a casual observer of the trio would scarcely have picked up any undercurrents, so seemingly relaxed was she.

When she and Alistair had first met, Louise's name would occasionally crop up and people would mention that she was 'quite good-looking'. But of course no one had been crass enough to describe the perfect features, the thick-lashed violet eyes and the dazzling smile. Despite her probing over the years, Alistair was incommunicative about his first wife. 'I can't remember much about the marriage now,' he would say, 'and I'd rather not talk about it.'

In the early days Georgie could not help searching for

photographs of the two of them, in an effort to dampen the intense curiosity she felt about the woman who had so dominated his life, but she could find none. Several times she had subtly tried to pump Rosemary about Alistair's emotional state after Louise walked out. His sister had been guarded but from the little she did say Georgie gathered that for some time Alistair, like most men in his situation, had hoped Louise would come back to him. And that the episode had left him distraught. Rosemary was adamant that Alistair had been blameless throughout his first marriage and had played little part in the break-up. But then Alistair could do no wrong in Rosemary's eyes. All the same, over the years Georgie had built up an image of Alistair's first wife as a callous woman who had left him so emotionally damaged that it took years to commit to another woman. But if a face was the mirror of the soul then she had been quite wrong. Louise was giving every appearance of being warm, amusing and good-humoured, and Georgie was ill-prepared to meet this vision.

She would be perfect, wouldn't she? And she would stand, as if by chance, exactly where a shaft of sunlight was shining through a stained glass window, creating a halo effect around that perfect blonde head. Watching Louise turn her spotlight on to Alistair, Georgie wondered how he could ever have recovered from losing this beauty. As Louise inclined her head gracefully, Georgie was struck by the thought that if someone made a sketch of her and Louise, she would be a straight line and Louise would be all curves.

Through Alistair's love and encouragement, Georgie had gradually built up her self-esteem, damaged by parents who were sparing in their praise. Alistair frequently commented how lucky he was to have found in her a woman who could captivate his mind as well as his body. The confidence their marriage instilled had been a great asset in her career, as she was fond of telling him. Would Mark Temple-Smith have promoted her to the post of publishing director, with all its staff and financial responsibilities, if she had not presented an air of complete self-belief? Mostly the veneer was safely in place though Alistair said he occasionally caught glimpses of the small girl inside the adult, whistling to keep up her courage.

Georgie willed him to smile at her, to show this woman that he belonged to her now. But Alistair did not pick up the vibes. What was he doing smiling at his first wife as if she were a treasured friend? And what had they been whispering to each other?

Mentally Georgie shook herself. Her insecurity and its cellmate, lack of confidence, were threatening to swamp her common sense. Nothing about Alistair justified this anxiety but her feeling of vulnerability would not disappear, it was there like a weevil burrowing away.

As Rosemary made her way through the crowds filing out of the church, she caught sight of a familiar figure on its way towards the door. Good God, it was Louise. What on earth was she doing here? She had a nerve, she'd only met Mark through Alistair, the husband she'd ditched.

Had Alistair seen her? Please God he hasn't, she thought. He had taken years to get over the hurt Louise had inflicted. And now, after eight years out of their lives, with not a word from her, here she was, perfectly turned out as usual. Rosemary was caught off guard by Louise's striking appearance. Of course she had always been attractive but maturity had given her a luminous beauty.

Louise was still ten yards away and Rosemary, anxious to avoid her, began to hurry in the opposite direction but her progress was hampered by the crush of mourners. When she at last reached the exterior gates of the church, a slender hand on her arm caused her to turn.

'How nice to see you again after all these years,' said Louise with a smile.

Rosemary coloured, feeling unaccountably embarrassed. 'Louise! What a surprise.' Her embarrassment increased as those violet-coloured eyes gazed at her steadily.

'I didn't know you had a connection with Mark Temple-Smith,' Louise said.

Rosemary gave a thin smile. 'Oh yes, I've been with his company for the past eighteen months.'

'Have you? Working for Alistair?'

'No, for Alistair's wife.'

'The last time I heard, you were with that auction house.'

'I loved that job but they were taken over and I was made redundant.'

'I'm sorry but do you like what you're doing now?'

Rosemary gave a deprecating shrug. 'It's a job.'

'Isn't it difficult working for a relative?' Louise was solicitous.

'Quite.' As soon as the word left her mouth, Rosemary regretted it.

'Do I gather you don't get on that well with the second Mrs Drummond?'

Rosemary ignored this. She was not going to provide Louise with fodder about Alistair's private life. Instead she said, 'You're the last person I expected to see here.'

'Well, I read the announcement in the paper and thought I'd pay my respects for old times' sake,' said Louise, turning her head to survey the crowd.

'That was good of you.' Rosemary tried to keep the sarcasm out of her voice. Louise had not changed. She always was a social climber. Most likely she was trying to get on the right side of some of the influential people here, rightly surmising that this would be a good place to make contacts.

'What are you doing back in London?' she asked, and as Louise raised her finely arched brows, Rosemary wondered why this woman always flustered her.

'Trying to negotiate premises for a new art gallery.'

'That's an expensive business,' said Rosemary, a chill in her voice.

'Yes, but I have an American backer. The money will be coming through in a couple of months' time and I'm looking for people to help me get started.' She paused. 'You had an interest in art, as I remember.'

Rosemary perked up. 'It's still one of my passions, a leftover from all those events I helped organise for Alistair when *Art World* started.'

'Perhaps I should get you to help me.'

This was the last thing Rosemary had expected and she was torn between showing enthusiasm and curtailing the conversation before Alistair saw her fraternising with his ex-wife. Still, this might provide the opportunity to leave Amalgamated. How she would love to do something worthwhile such as helping to establish new artists. It would be like the old days when, after his divorce, she and Alistair had spent hours trudging through galleries viewing the collections and trying to woo curators for the magazine.

Louise took a card out of her wallet. 'If you want to talk about it, here's my number.'

Rosemary glanced at the card before tucking it carefully into her coat pocket. 'I see you've reverted to your maiden name.'

Louise shrugged. 'Yes. A clean slate and all that. Anyway, I'll give you a ring at your office in a day or so to find out if you're interested. 'Bye for now.'

She was as assured as ever, thought Rosemary, and watched as the lissom shape walked across the flagstones past the press photographers who ignored the beautiful but unknown face.

Outside the church Margery Conlan moved towards the queue of people waiting for taxis. She was proud of herself for managing not to cry although tears had been very near. She did not want to convey the wrong impression about her relationship with her boss to either his widow or anyone else.

The fairly formal working partnership she'd had with Mark Temple-Smith had been her choice. In her previous job she had found informality led to the taking of liberties, not in a sexual sense but in the number of hours she was expected to work. Although Mark could be irascible and demanding, her work with him was rarely routine and never boring. It appeared as if working for Helen would be in the same mould, although with Mark she had never been allowed to travel outside the office.

Amidst the chattering, Margery heard a voice that reverberated in her memory. It took a moment or two to pin down where she had heard that deep tone before. She moved closer to the striking-looking woman giving instructions to a taxi driver. He appeared to be having trouble hearing her.

'No, you have it the wrong way round,' the woman was saying impatiently. 'I want to pick up something at Harrods before going to Fortnum's, not the other way round.'

Margery knew she had heard that voice before; only a few times, it was true, but she was certain she recognised that low timbre with its mid-Atlantic accent, particularly on the word 'wrong'.

As covertly as she could, Margery stared at the woman's features to ensure she would recognise the face again. Then the beauty climbed into the taxi, showing an attractive stretch of leg which had heads turning in her wake. Margery's eyes followed the taxi's slow progress until it disappeared into the busy traffic.

How incredible. This certainly wasn't the day to confide her suspicions to her boss. But what would Helen say when she told her, as she surely must, that she believed she had seen Mark's mistress at his memorial service?

In the taxi returning to the office, Alistair steeled himself for the inevitable questions from Georgie. It would have taken superhuman willpower for his second wife not to ask about his first. To be fair, if the position were reversed he would do the same. Nevertheless he was unprepared for Georgie's opening salvo.

'Why didn't you tell me she was so beautiful?'

He prevaricated. There had been no reason to describe his first wife's appearance and he had taken the precaution of throwing out all their wedding pictures and hoped that none had survived the cull and the various house moves.

'Beauty is in the eye of the beholder,' he teased, 'and after a time I didn't see it.' He stroked her delicate cheekbones. 'She's more of a Barbie doll. I prefer your looks.'

Despite his words, he had to admit to himself that when Louise had batted her eyes at him, for a moment he'd had a glimpse of her naked body, stretched beneath his on the counterpane, willing, wanting, waiting for him . . . He had felt a stirring of lust and had immediately been ashamed. Thank God his wife could not read his sewer of a mind, she would be so disappointed. How could he be so juvenile? And how could he forget how much Louise had hurt him? She had so destroyed his confidence and trust that he had kept his emotional distance from women for years until he had met Georgie. He told himself that what he had felt for Louise was nothing like the all-encompassing love he felt for Georgie.

'You don't think she was there as an excuse to see you again, do you?' Georgie's voice was deceptively innocent.

'Absolutely not. That was over a long time ago,' he said, taking her hand. 'You aren't bothered about her, are you?'

'It was a bit unsettling to meet her,' Georgie admitted. 'I wasn't expecting it.'

'Neither was I,' he said fervently.

'And I'm curious, I suppose. You've never talked to me about her in any depth.'

'Because it's over. She's not important to my life.' He tapped her knee for emphasis. 'Only women like to thrash around and examine every entrail of what's happened to them. Men don't. We just get on with our lives.'

She smiled at this. 'You mean you push problems aside, leave them to solve themselves.'

'Sometimes they do.'

The taxi stopped at traffic lights and Alistair played with her fingers. 'You already know how long Louise and I were together – by the way, it's a shorter time than you and I have known each other. OK, I was hurt for a time when we broke up but I got over it. That's basically it. All right?'

She rested her head briefly on his shoulder. 'All right,' she said.

He held on to her hand for the rest of the journey back to the office but his thoughts kept on straying back to that damned woman. Louise had always had the capacity to unsettle him.

Alistair had met her when he was covering a fashion show and she was one of the models. He had been immediately attracted to her pale beauty and had asked for her telephone number. She told him pertly that if he wanted it, he could discover it for himself. Liking the challenge, he had used his journalistic contacts to bribe a telephone supervisor to track down her ex-directory number.

A colleague had described Louise as a sex and shopping babe and had warned him off her. 'I've heard she notches up guys faster than a darts scoreboard,' he said.

'People always say that about girls as gorgeous as she is,' Alistair had retorted.

In those days Louise had had ambitions to be a world-class model. But she was not tall enough and decided that marriage provided an easier route to a pampered life than being confined to the unglamorous dressing rooms of designers. In one of those chances of fate, Alistair had been at the right stage of his life to settle down. Until then there had been too many models and junior actresses who had believed his sweet love words at night would be translated into cover photo sessions in the morning.

At first he had worried that Louise might be too young for him – she was only nineteen – but what his new lover lacked in the intellectual department she had made up for in the psychology of keeping a man happy. When at last she invited him to meet her parents, he discovered they had the kind of marriage he had only read about. They were devoted to each other and at that Sunday lunch, gazing at Louise across an antique table-cloth covered with homemade venison pie, he fell in love. Not only with Louise, but coming from a dysfunctional family as he did, also with her background, her parents and the stability they represented.

The end came with cruel suddenness. One day she was her pliable self, the next she was a distant stranger announcing that she did not love him any more, that she had been far too young to know her mind when they married. She wanted her freedom because domesticity would hamper her plans.

'What plans? I didn't know you had any.' To this day he remembered his bewilderment.

'Why would you know? You haven't asked. Nothing matters to you except work.'

Despite his questions and his many pleadings she had never offered any satisfactory explanation as to why she no longer wanted to be his wife and he still could not be sure there was not another man involved. With hindsight he strongly suspected there must have been. Why else would she have ended their marriage so suddenly and disappeared so completely? At first he had desperately tried to find her, but without success. Eventually he received a letter requesting a no-fault quickie divorce from a firm of solicitors based in New York and he assumed that was where she had set up home.

Since meeting Georgie he had given Louise no thought at all. If she had come back to live in London again, it was a nuisance, nothing more. He had more important things in his life to worry about than a disquieting ex-wife.

The sound of that voice troubled Margery for days. She felt guilty that she had not told Helen about it. But what would be the point of upsetting the widow when she seemed to be settling into her new job with gusto? It had been some time since Helen had raised the subject of Mark's mistress. Maybe it was better to let the matter rest until she had more positive information.

Nevertheless, while Helen was visiting Dublin to inspect the office and talk to Declan Geraghty, Margery could not resist using her time to scour the list of all those who had been at the memorial service. There was nobody on it that she couldn't account for. But that was hardly conclusive. Many people had turned up without informing her office and it had been impossible to monitor them all.

Margery decided to contact the photographers hired by the company to cover the comings and goings of the mourners and call in their contacts. There had also been several other freelance cameramen outside the church but their pictures were with various art editors of glossy magazines and newspaper supplements and would not be available for some time, if ever. Not for the first time, Margery was irritated by how unhelpful photographers could be when asked to give up their precious transparencies. It was as impossible as in America. The agencies had the business all sewn up.

It took hours but by the following day her desk was littered with contact prints delivered by messengers from those who had co-operated. Margery placed her magnifying glass over the tiny strips. Her task would have been easier if she had been able to put the pictures on computer but she thought it unwise. She did not want to alert anyone else as to what she was up to. After all, it was Helen's secret, not hers, and until she had permission to make inquiries, it was better to keep the entire quest under wraps.

Margery stretched her aching back and cursed her luck. She had been poring over these contacts for nearly an hour and there was no one remotely like the woman she could picture so vividly on any of them. With diminishing hope she examined one last strip of pictures.

Surely someone had taken a picture of that ridiculous hat, more suited to a cocktail party than a service of mourning? The woman had been exceptionally glamorous and would have provided an obvious target for the photographers so why wasn't there a picture of her?

She came to the end of the batch and had to admit defeat. Either the photographers were too distracted by the other celebrities or the woman had taken great care to avoid them. She laid down the magnifying glass with a mixture of disappointment and relief. If the woman had appeared in one of the pictures, she would have had to confess her suspicions to Helen and then her boss would have been compelled to seek out this woman. Margery put the contacts back into the envelopes ready for despatch back to the photographers, glad she would not be instrumental in reopening that particular can of worms.

Helen's daughters marvelled at how well she was handling her bereavement. 'I thought you'd fall apart,' was how the elder one put it, 'but it seems to have made you stronger. We're proud of you.'

Her daughters and sons-in-law returned to America a few days after the memorial service in London. Helen saw them off with mixed feelings. She would miss them, but at the same time it would be a relief not to have to watch herself so closely in their company. Their own grief at the loss of their father was painful to see, and made Helen feel even more of a fraud. But it reinforced her decision not to confide in anyone, even close friends, in case they unwittingly said something to the girls or their husbands. Above everything, Helen wanted to protect them from the knowledge of their father's perfidy.

National papers throughout the world had devoted space to Mark's life and achievements, in addition to covering the two memorial services. Now magazine pieces were beginning to appear, often mentioning what a fantastic, supportive family man he had been and attributing his success to his stable, emotionally-cushioned home life. In one article he was quoted as saying that although his multimillion-dollar estate in Greenwich set him apart from most of his readers, he understood the aspirations of the typical family man. To show his pride in his family values, he had placed both his daughters' weddings in *Town and Country*. God, thought Helen, how long would she have to endure reading such nonsense? Still to be faced were the luncheon with the Journalists' Guild of London and the Advertising Association awards. She felt a kinship with the Kennedy women. How they must have seethed at the eulogies given their husbands, knowing all the while the sleazy truth.

Plagued by visions of Mark's rented summer home in the Hamptons, Helen had driven out there one weekend shortly before her departure to London. She had paced up and down the main streets of the little coastal villages, staring at the women in the restaurants and antique shops. What did she hope to find? Someone who would come up to her and confess they had been having an affair with her husband? She was being absurd.

She mused ruefully that although she had a wide circle of friends and a loving family, there was only one person with whom she could now be truthful, a spinster of a certain age, who gave the impression of having emotions so under control it was hard to imagine her ever suffering the pangs of jealousy or lust.

One morning after her return from Dublin, Helen arrived in her office with dark circles under her eyes, testimony to another restless night. Margery was concerned. 'Have you been worrying about that woman again?' she asked. 'For your own sake you ought to put her out of your mind. After all, she can't hurt you now.'

Helen's laugh was sardonic. 'I wish it were that simple.'

'Yes, but you have to start walking up another avenue sometime,' said Margery sympathetically. 'You can't change what's past.'

'The thing that's driving me mad is that Mark's woman could be anyone,' Helen confided, 'absolutely anyone. She could be here in the office. She could be the first violinist at the Lincoln Centre, she could even be amongst our circle of friends, but they'd all deny it, wouldn't they? At first I thought I'd find it easy to pick her out, that I'd detect some vibrations, the way she was studying me, some guilty expression, anything. But of course it isn't like that.'

'I wish you'd start living your own life,' said Margery.

'If only I could. Do you think I want to live under the shadow of this woman?' Helen was so preoccupied with her thoughts that she did not notice the wariness in Margery's eyes. 'The worst thing is that every time I walk into a room I assess every woman in it, searching for one that might be Mark's type. I'm sure he travelled everywhere with her. She could be in New York, here in London, Rome, Dublin. I bring his name into every conversation, hoping to get a reaction from someone. But so far nothing.'

Initially Helen had been uncomfortable talking to people in the office, people like Alistair and Harry who had known her husband well. Part of her brain would be wondering whether their sympathy was tinged with guilt at being part of Mark's deceit. She had the feeling that it lessened her authority over them and this tended to make her insecure. To compensate she became more brusque, more curt in tone than the Helen they had known as Mark's wife. She had watched their faces while people talked of Mark's love of family and not once did she divine any hint that they were being ironic. She had come to the conclusion that they, too, had been deceived.

'I understand what you're going through,' said Margery, 'but you put on a good act.'

'Of course I do but imagine how it is, dealing with the fact that that woman knows everything about me but I know nothing about her. Margery, I have to find out who she is.'

Helen did not attempt to break the silence that followed and finally Margery said, 'I think I may have seen her.'

'What? You said you didn't know her, had never met her.'

'I don't, I haven't, and I wasn't going to worry you with it because I'm not sure I'm right.'

'Why didn't you tell me before?'

'I didn't want to upset you. And in any case I wondered what good it would do. You seemed to be getting on with life.'

'Where do you think you saw her?' asked Helen urgently.

'Outside the church after Mark's memorial service.'

Helen closed her eyes, hoping Margery could not see the flare of rage at the thought of the woman's audacity to dare to mingle with Mark's family and closest friends – at his memorial service, for God's sake.

'I certainly hadn't set eyes on her before,' Margery continued, 'but I can recognise a voice and I think I heard it again then.'

'Are you sure?' Helen asked, forcing herself to sound calm.

'Remember I told you that on a few occasions a woman called on Mark's private line while he was out and each time she'd say she'd dialled a wrong number?'

Helen nodded.

'It was a low voice, the accent was a mixture of English and New York, and the woman had a distinctive way of pronouncing certain words. When she was talking to the cab driver she used the same word as she had on the phone to me, "wrong", in a sort of sharp, peremptory way.'

'But you didn't recognise her face?'

'No, and I took a good look at her. It wasn't anyone I'd seen before. I watched her until the cab pulled away.'

'Would you recognise her again?'

'Definitely.'

Under the desk, Helen's hands were clenched. 'Describe her,' she said quietly.

'Very attractive, not all that tall, good figure, short blonde hair. She was wearing a dark blue velvet suit with a little matching hat. You must have noticed her.'

'There were an awful lot of people around that day

and I wasn't in a state to pay attention to strangers. Was she with anybody?'

'No, but afterwards I did try and find out who she was. I took the liberty of calling in all the photographs taken that day but she wasn't in any of them.'

Helen's frustration spilled over. 'For God's sake, somebody must know her. How can we find out?'

The two women sat in thought for a while then Margery looked up. 'What if I were to describe her to an artist? If he could make a reasonably accurate likeness we could show it to one or two people who were at the service.'

'How would we explain why we needed to do that?'

Margery smiled. 'We don't. If I'm asked, I'll put on my don't-mess-with-me secretary face. Not many people push their luck when I do that.'

'I can well believe it,' said Helen wryly. 'But we don't want a scandal in the company right now.'

'Since neither of us is going to tell anybody why we want to identify this woman, how can there be a scandal?'

Slowly Helen nodded.

# Chapter Nine

If Disney had designed a French mountain village, Mougins would be it with its faded sign of La Poste on the fourteenth-century building, the undulating cobbled streets faced with ochre-coloured stone and little caves converted into antique shops, wine cellars or shops selling Provençal tablewear.

At the top of the hill was the village square where gourmet restaurants festooned with scallops of fairy lights were to be found, as well as the Mairie with its constantly-changing exhibitions of the works of local artists. Every chair at the pavement cafes gave a grand-stand view of the comings and goings of jet-set million-aires who parked their yachts at Port Vauban in Antibes, and of the scurrying locals clutching their six-franc freshly-baked baguettes which had to be eaten that day or they would go stale.

Alistair and Georgie arrived straight off the early evening plane having spent much of the flight studying tomes on the subject of infertility. They intended to spend most of the weekend prone so they decided not to hire a car. A taxi took them through the winding narrow streets and they stared in wonder at the medieval world they were entering. To their left the lights of Grasse were visible as a carpet of twinkling dots below.

They had always liked visiting the south of France when they were attending the film festival but then they had been obliged to stay on the coast. As it turned out, the choice of Mougins for their baby-making weekend was inspired. The village had been taken over for the evening by an American software company as a reward for its top international sales force. A generous supply of dollars had brought a host of acrobats, jugglers, accordionists and violinists, drummers and flag-throwers, magicians and fire-eaters in black and gold velvet doublets. It did not matter if, like Georgie and Alistair, the visitors did not have the badge and requisite carnation buttonhole of company employees. The show, under clear warm skies, was open to all. Every cafe had a special menu and the tables were full with tourists and software employees who ordered freely, happy in the knowledge that the company would foot their bills.

Alistair and Georgie had decided on a small family-run hotel in the bougainvillaea-covered hills overlooking the square. Their bedroom was like a floral bower. The bed had a painted wicker headboard and was covered with a beautiful antique quilt. The tiny bathroom could have come straight out of a canvas of an Impressionist painting, tiled as it was in faded cobalt and ochre.

Alistair had brought with him two mobile phones, one to be charged, the other to take the all-important call from Helen, which would tell him he was one of those she wanted to interview. They tried not to let this subject dominate their conversations but inevitably it was on both their minds.

By eight thirty they were showered, dressed and had joined the throng in the square where they compared prices and dishes on the menus posted outside every restaurant by French law, each one more inventive than the last. As a violinist played 'La Mer', battle flags were hurled into the air like arrows, speeding to earth with frightening force, to be caught by members of the local band with gracious twirls of the wrist. Along with the rest, Georgie and Alistair joined in the appreciative applause as the teenage flag-thrower and his troop of girl drummers concentrated on the rituals followed for centuries by their forefathers.

Alistair and Georgie eventually settled on Redmonds restaurant because its 185 franc four-course menu included crayfish, ravioli and guinea fowl which Alistair had tasted only once before but had never forgotten, a perfect rack of lamb followed by a soup of orange sorbet and berries.

Over a bottle of the local rosé, Alistair watched Georgie's transfixed face as an acrobat did a pretend fall at her feet.

He reached across the table and took her hand. 'This is going to work,' he said, 'I know it. I've never seen you more relaxed.'

Her face lit up, her eyes bright with contentment. 'Can it get better than this?' She gestured round the square.

'The atmosphere, the music, the air, the food and you.'

'Thanks for putting me last,' he joked, dunking a slice of homemade bread into the melted Camembert dip.

She flicked her napkin at him. 'Punishment for taking two days to phone me after we first met.'

'It took me that long to get over your cooking,' he shot back.

'It was a mistake to experiment with recipes for a new man. I'll never do it again.'

'No, you won't. Because there won't be one.'

Initially Georgie had been reluctant to entertain a blind date but when asked by mutual friends to choose her ideal guest from a group photograph in *UK Press Gazette*, she had picked out the tallest, most attractive of the group. Discovering he was indeed the man already invited, she had quickly changed her mind, though her only knowledge of him was through his reputation in the industry.

'You'll like him,' promised the friend. 'Though beware, he's a great flirt.'

They had clicked at once, for apart from having jobs in the same business, they had a matching sense of humour and quickly found they could use verbal shorthand with each other.

That first night she had attempted a courageous menu, particularly for someone who spent less time in the kitchen than most of her contemporaries. Some perverse aspect of her character compelled her to cook the meal herself despite past cack-handed culinary experience. But Georgie had wanted to impress her guest.

'That meal is imprinted on my mind.' There was a wicked glint in Alistair's eyes. 'I admired your idea of spearing the fish on to skewers made from rosemary twigs.' His mouth twitched at the memory. 'Ingenious, although they nearly choked me.'

Georgie gave a grin. 'The meal couldn't have been so bad, you still married me.'

'Only to prevent you from poisoning anyone else.'

This time the napkin came flying over the table, narrowly missing his wine glass. They both laughed.

'One of the reasons I love you, Georgie, is that you never give up.'

As a divorcee Alistair had been one of the most eligible bachelors in London. While his business life prospered, his love life was erratic, consisting mainly of short erotic liaisons, but as soon as any woman showed signs of wanting more from him she was dispatched. But at the time of Georgie's disastrous meal, two years after his wife had left him, Alistair had grown weary of small talk and clinging women and had recently made a pact with himself to abandon casual flings. The timing, probably the most important aspect of any relationship as they happily agreed later, was perfect.

When Alistair plunged into matrimony with Georgie, he respected the fact that she was as career-orientated and ambitious as he was. This proved no barrier between them, even when she demurred at his suggestion that at his age he would like them to start a family immediately. She wanted to wait a couple of years, she said. Well, that time was over and sitting in a mountainside village in France,

Alistair hoped that an exciting chapter in their lives was about to begin both personally and professionally.

He raised his glass. 'You're the nicest thing that ever happened to me, Mrs Drummond.'

'Ditto, Mr Drummond.' Alistair took a coin from his pocket to throw into the cap of a strolling magician. 'Let's make a start on our dynasty.'

Arm in arm they walked back to the hotel. Outside the bedroom he suddenly swept her into his arms and carried her into the room, dropping her gently on to the bed. The laughter stopped as they began to kiss, long, deep, unhurried kisses, and started to undress one another, removing each garment slowly, one item at a time.

Gazing directly into her eyes, Alistair began to caress Georgie, whispering into her ear, 'I adore your body. I can't wait to make love to you.' He began to describe all the parts he planned to kiss and exactly what he intended doing to her. It always had the immediate effect of arousing Georgie.

Leisurely, his lips traced a trail across her shoulders, down her back, sensuously round to her nipples. Her hands stroked his muscular body, snaking round his firm buttocks to his flat stomach and downwards. Alistair began caressing her inner thighs.

By now Georgie was impatient. 'Darling, I want you. I want you, now,' a command he happily obeyed.

When their bodies merged, he held back until she shuddered in excitement before groaning her name as he reached his own orgasm.

Over the course of the weekend, mindful of the task in hand and wanting to increase the odds, they continued to work with a will, pausing now and then to sample freshly-baked croissants for breakfast, salade niçoise lunches and grilled red mullet dinners or to sunbathe by the pool in the lush, handkerchief-sized garden so that their skins took on a golden glow.

Reality intruded into this most sensuous of weekends only occasionally when they caught sight of the ever-glowing red light on Alistair's worldwide mobile perched in the corner of their bedroom.

It never rang.

The British trade press continued to snipe at Helen's decision to take over her husband's position. The idea that a housewife would dare assume command of a multimillion-pound organisation affronted media analysts and financial journalists alike. Since the death of Amalgamated's charismatic founder the company appeared to be rudderless, they wrote. Scurrilous rumours, later corrected, of debts to printers had one or two commentators suggesting that if this was the case, the company would undoubtedly attract predators.

Helen had taken the precaution of inviting her two major creditors to lunch the moment these stories began to appear, assuring them that their bills would be paid on time as usual, that the management was in safe hands and that a major appointment was to be announced soon. There would, she assured them, be no sell-off.

Then, in New York, one of the top editors was

poached, the first senior journalist to be lost to the company for several years. And when a London editor also decided to leave, the gossip columnists gave the tale extra prominence, especially when that editor took two of her top staff with her.

Each morning Helen found herself measuring her performance, evaluating how she had coped the day before with her new life. Was she standing up to the men in the company? Was she agreeing too easily with advertisers? She was not used to this pressure, not since the early days, and it was wearing.

After many years of accepting her status as a helper rather than a commander, she was still unsure of herself when she had to walk into a room to address a gathering of critical Suits. She was acutely conscious that only her majority shareholding protected her position. But she was determined to prove her mettle and exhibit the attributes that had helped the company at the beginning.

Her life now was a learning process, one in which she could not afford to make mistakes. She enjoyed the buzz of being back in the business but with it came fear. There was more to lose now. When she and Mark had started, they had nothing, it was fun and they could make their mistakes in private. Blunders in those days had not cost much. Now everything she did was under the microscope of media analysts who, like everyone else, expected her to fail. And there was no Mark at her elbow to advise or consult as in the old days.

And the business had changed. Everyone appeared so damned young. Many of the women arrived in the office wearing those ultra high heels which Helen privately thought of as 'sitting shoes'. Yet they kept them on all day in the office and afterwards when they went out too, no doubt. It made her more conscious of her age.

It was all so complex. Rival companies, poised to take advantage of what they saw was a vulnerable time for the company, were choosing this moment to announce expansion plans. It was no coincidence that they were trumpeting new titles, often advancing the launch to take advantage of Amalgamated's perceived vulnerability. They used the opportunity to fold the dead wood, old titles that were missed by no one except a dwindling band of ageing readers.

Helen had assured the staff that nothing in the Amalgamated pipeline would be halted. She had been tempted to lead one of the regular brainstorming ideas sessions initially instigated by Mark but her courage had failed her. It was a hurdle too far; she still had too much Greenwich, Connecticut, rather than Greenwich Village in her veins.

The first time she had to address a formal meeting at the Confederation of British Industry she had been so full of terror she thought her knees would give way as she walked into the conference room. But when she started speaking, there was not a tremor in her voice and no hint of nervousness in her manner to alert her watchful audience that she was not equal to the task. She had read somewhere that in every woman there was an instinctive actress, and she concluded it was probably true.

In fact this miracle of appearing to be in control was due to her increasing hatred towards Mark. Each day his treachery grew in her mind as she remembered more and more occasions when he had put his family second to the business or his wretched mistress.

Margery had wasted no time in trying to track down the woman whose voice she remembered. With the help of the art editor of *Visage*, they found an artist who took less than an hour to translate her description of the woman's features, her shape and outfit on to his sketch-pad.

'That's pretty good,' said Margery when he had drawn in the finishing touches, 'but the jacket was closer fitting and the hat was tilted more to the right. And could we have another go at the cheekbones?'

This proved more difficult and after several attempts Margery gave up trying to get a totally accurate portrait.

'This isn't bad, at least it gives an idea of what she was like,' she said, showing the sketch to Helen. There was a heavy silence while Helen scrutinised it. She felt a quickening of excitement. At last she had a small advantage. The thrill of cornering this woman when she thought she was safe from discovery would be extremely satisfying. At last she would be in control. The hunter.

'What do you have in mind now?' she asked Margery.

'I'll show it to one or two editors here. I'm hoping that if the women don't remember the suit, the men might remember the body.'

This was not the only problem with which Helen was grappling. The other was the appointment of her new chief executive. She was aware that her top teams were floating, their innovative ideas needed a new guiding hand. Moreover, her financial controllers had recommended that she should consider expanding the London end next year. If she accepted this, it would mean Europe would be even more important in the over-all company structure. The interviews she had already conducted in New York had gone well though only Ned Mastrianni had made it to the final short list. But she was not going to hurry. There was no point in being pushed into making the wrong choice. Though she would heed advice from Giles and Harry on the appointments committee, she had decided the final choice would be hers and hers alone.

Despite opposition from her board, Helen had gone ahead and hired a head-hunter to trawl the British market for candidates. When she was presented with their list of the cream of the UK's top television, advertising and media executives, there was one surprise inclusion.

'Georgina Luckhurst.' She pointed at the dossier with an elegantly manicured fingernail. 'She's married to Alistair Drummond. That's quite a complication. Is there any point in having her on the list?'

# Chapter Ten

Rosemary was curious about Louise's plans. Boredom with her job at Amalgamated had made the mention of a job in a new gallery extremely tempting.

She wanted to find something to fill her life. Many of her weekends and evenings were free though she took care to keep this secret from everyone. Friendships with men had rarely developed beyond the pecking-a-goodnight-kiss stage. Her only serious affair had been with a man who turned out to be homosexual. She had been fond of John but still did not comprehend what people meant by falling in love, the longing, the worry and the apparent ecstasy of it. She had only been able to watch and sympathise with Alistair's grief when Louise had walked out. To her, love meant loss, the loss of her parents and the loss of Alistair when he married first Louise, then Georgina. At least Louise had never put her career ahead of her husband, which was Rosemary's main complaint against her present sister-in-law.

As keen as she was to try the job in the gallery, Rosemary still could not bring herself to ring Louise, out of loyalty to Alistair. So a few days after their meeting she was gratified when in the middle of a hectic morning in the office, Louise phoned and breezily suggested dinner the next night.

Rosemary felt momentarily uncomfortable but Alistair had mentioned that he and Georgie had met Louise and had talked, apparently amicably, and had even discussed having dinner together. If Alistair could overlook the past, why shouldn't she?

She accepted Louise's invitation and they settled on a small restaurant near Bond Street where Louise was inspecting premises.

When she arrived at the restaurant she found her hostess at the window table in animated conversation with a waiter. Louise waved when she caught sight of Rosemary hovering at the door. Rosemary had taken more than an hour to choose which skirt to wear with which top, knowing that Louise would appear as though she had just come off the catwalk. The understated elegance of Louise's black velvet trouser suit spelt Knightsbridge boutique and probably had taken only a minute or two to select from her wardrobe. But then if you had a size ten figure and an apparently generous budget it was easier to achieve the kind of look which attracted the attention of the proprietor, as the waiter turned out to be.

Having discussed first the decor and then the menu, it was not long before Rosemary found herself being coaxed to talk about her life and career. So what if Louise was skilful at feigning interest, it was a novelty to talk about herself for a change. She down-played her unhappiness at Amalgamated, feeling it would be a mistake to allow eagerness for a new job to show. She would proceed cautiously and try to demonstrate to Louise how valuable her skills could be to the gallery.

Both women declined starters, though Rosemary longed to order an aubergine smothered in ricotta cheese. She settled, like Louise, on a grilled Dover sole on the bone. When Louise asked for a small portion of spinach without butter, Rosemary's resolve cracked and she called the waiter back. 'I'll have butter on mine, and a few boiled potatoes, please.'

'I haven't eaten a potato for years,' said Louise with a smile. 'Could I pinch one of yours?'

'I remember you doing that at Sunday lunch once,' said Rosemary and both smiled at the memory, relieving some of the tension between them.

Just when Rosemary was wondering when she would mention the gallery, Louise said quietly, 'I thought you might not talk to me again, after the divorce.'

Rosemary was silent. Louise was right, she had vowed never to speak to her again.

'Alistair and I both realise we should put the past behind us,' Louise went on. 'I'd like you and me to be friends. What do you say?' She put out her hand, giving Rosemary no option but to shake it.

'Why don't we have coffee at my place?' Louise asked when they had eaten. 'You might like to see the plans my architect drew up for the gallery.' She asked for the bill and then commented, 'London's changed so much.

There's a real buzz about the place now.'

'Where've you been then?' Rosemary asked.

'Where haven't I been?' she replied vaguely. 'I'll tell you about it sometime but I'm far more interested in discussing the art gallery. I'd like your help with it.'

A picture flashed into Rosemary's mind of how this woman could change her future. She'd be transformed into a smartly turned-out version of herself, greeting elegantly-dressed clients in a room filled with paintings. She would be a somebody, not simply an anonymous cog in an office. She would work hard, do her homework on the artists, perhaps she would attend art history classes. She would set about becoming indispensable. Louise would quickly find out her true worth.

But all she murmured was, 'I'd be pleased to do whatever I can.'

The women walked to Melford Court, a Regency house converted into six flats. The entrance hall was decorated in a bold navy blue. It retained what appeared to be the original cornices and there were expensive urns of greenery lining the walls. A uniformed porter greeted Louise warmly and fussed about calling the mirrored and mahogany lift. Louise must have done well to be able to afford this place, thought Rosemary.

The flat reminded her of the one Louise had shared with Alistair. The curtains were of apricot cream silk, swathed to set off the floor-to-ceiling windows. A pair of matching sofas in pale brocade dominated the room and in the corner Rosemary glimpsed a highly polished escritoire displaying several silver frames of Louise at various stages of her career. No man or children evident, Rosemary noticed at once.

The coffee was an expensive blend and the china was fine and fragile. Louise took only a couple of sips before moving over to the escritoire to pull out a sheaf of architect's drawings.

'You're the first person to see these.' She looked Rosemary in the eye. 'I'm trusting you with this because I want you to understand how serious I am about the project.'

Rosemary was surprised by Louise's openness. But there was still not a word about her personal life, where and with whom she had spent the past eight years. As the atmosphere between them appeared to be relaxed, Rosemary risked a personal question. 'You know, I've always been puzzled about why your marriage broke up without any of us realising what was happening.'

Louise regarded her thoughtfully, her blonde hair glowing in the lamplight. 'I was a young, stupid woman.' She shook her head. 'Not woman, child. Believe me, I've regretted my actions a million times over.'

Rosemary was surprised by the admission and began to feel better about accepting her hospitality.

'How's that company of Alistair's doing?' Louise asked suddenly.

'Fine, I think, but everything's going to change now that Helen Temple-Smith's in charge.'

'Yes, Mark's wife . . .'

'The word is Alistair will make chief executive here and might even take over in New York eventually.'

'I imagine he'd do well there. But would Georgina want to leave London? New York's such a different place to work.'

'I don't know. She'll do what's best for her, I've no doubt.' Rosemary could not keep the note of asperity out of her voice. 'Sorry, I shouldn't be talking to you like this.'

'Don't worry. You can be frank with me. If we're going to work together we have to have some degree of trust. I'm never going to say anything to anyone.'

*If we're going to work together.* That must mean Louise was serious about the job offer. Rosemary felt happier than she'd been for months.

Louise tilted her head inquiringly. 'Tell me about Alistair. You said some rather intriguing things at the memorial service.'

Rosemary felt uncomfortable. Had she been indiscreet about her brother's marriage? But she needed to bond with Louise. She leaned back on the sofa and said, 'The trouble is, Georgie's too ambitious. Alistair is very anxious for them to have a child but all she seems interested in is her job. She shouldn't have married Alistair if all she wanted was to be a career woman.'

'I wouldn't have thought Alistair was happy with that situation.'

'I'm positive he isn't. You know, on the day of their marriage, I had a strong premonition that Alistair wouldn't see his life out with that woman and I bet I'm proved right.'

'Poor Alistair.' With that, Louise stood up.

Rosemary, taking the hint, followed suit and Louise guided her towards the door.

'I'd like your input on a wish list of artists we might represent,' said Louise.

'That does sound exciting,' said Rosemary, shrugging on her coat. 'I'd certainly like to get in on the ground floor of something like this.'

'It's going to take several months to organise everything so I can't offer you anything formally until all the details like the lease are sorted out.'

'That's all right.'

As Rosemary walked to the lift, she could hardly believe how excited she felt. Louise had opened up possibilities of a new life she could never have envisaged a week ago. This woman was going to be very useful to her.

Louise washed the china by hand, a chore she usually left for her daily but the woman was rather clumsy. As she rinsed, she daydreamed about a rather farfetched scenario for her future.

What if she became close to Alistair, using Rosemary and the art gallery as an excuse? And what if Alistair was given the job in London and was eventually transferred to New York? If by some chance she again became Mrs Alistair Drummond, she would end up as the wife of the chairman of Amalgamated after all. Louise gave a broad smile. Same title, different man. It was a pity Mark wasn't alive to appreciate the irony of the situation.

Was it such an outlandish dream? The marriage had to be very rocky with this job rivalry and there was still that chemistry between her and Alistair. She could not have mistaken the frisson between them after the memorial service, could she? She was not surprised by it, remembering how obsessed he had been about her in the old days. Often when she had been watching television or reading a book she would glance up to find him gazing at her face.

If Alistair wanted a mother for his children, that was another challenge altogether. The pay-off from Mark's estate ensured she would have time to concentrate on netting Alistair without the constraints a career would impose, unlike his wife. What if she found the opportunity to convince him she had changed, that all she wanted now was to settle down and raise a family? If a baby wasn't a priority for Georgina, wouldn't that be her trump card?

But as Louise put the china away, she scolded herself. This was dangerous nonsense. Alistair and Georgina might be having trouble now but it was probably only temporary. As soon as the job of chief executive was settled they'd resume their marriage amicably, she had little doubt. She had never had any difficulty attracting men so why dream about another woman's husband?

Georgie and Alistair had been going to Ella's bistro since they were married. They lived round the corner from it and they used it frequently because Georgie did not have time or inclination to cook and there was no problem about drinking and driving.

It was like eating in a spacious farmhouse kitchen. Every table held a candle, a dish of home-roasted nuts and Ella's olives marinated in garlic and lime juice. Ancient prints of Moscow and St Petersburg lined the dusky chocolate-coloured walls – though Ella in fact came from Bury St Edmunds, Suffolk. A marmalade tabby stretched in front of an open fire to complete the rural scene in the midst of urban Kensington.

The moment they appeared in the doorway, Georgie and Alistair were enveloped in a warm embrace.

'Dahlink,' the pseudo-Russian accent rang out across the red-tiled hallway. 'Your usual table is free. I bring wine. Right away.'

Alistair was looking forward to one of Ella's good bottles of burgundy with dinner. He had come to appreciate fine wine since he had started earning a good salary. One of the treats he and Georgie allowed themselves was an annual trip to a French vineyard near Bordeaux to select cases for the company's executive dining room. And it was a rare event if they did not buy extra for their private use.

'I said you shouldn't worry that Helen hadn't contacted you yet,' commented Georgie, studying the menu. 'Where are you having lunch with her?'

'The Savoy, although Harry couldn't wait to tell me he's invited her there too. For dinner.'

'That's smart of him. Most people are too inhibited to ask her out at night, thinking she'll be too busy.'

'He's an operator, isn't he?'

'And Esme's learned to put up or shut up.'

'Poor Esme.'

'That's one thing she isn't. She's so rich whatever happens Harry won't leave her.'

'Poor Harry.'

They exchanged amused glances and the exuberant Ella arrived to pour the wine and wait for Alistair to taste then, as usual, wax lyrical over the bouquet.

When she had taken their orders, Georgie picked up a bread stick and asked, 'How is Helen these days? I've hardly seen her since she arrived.'

'I've tried to see her a couple of times but it's funny, every time I try and find out how she's getting along, she won't discuss anything to do with Mark.'

'It would be much better if she could open up.'

Steaming plates of aromatic chicken were brought to their table by a waiter.

'I would guess that my lunch tomorrow is just a preliminary.'

'But you must have a good chance of getting the job.'

Alistair picked up his knife and fork. 'Let's say I'm cautiously optimistic but I'm not taking anything for granted. It'll be up to me to convince her I'm the best one for the job. So start the brainstorming, do your worst.'

Over their favourite meal of chicken Kiev, Georgie began to prepare him for Helen's inquisition. She interrogated him with the kind of tough questions Helen would be primed to ask: the future of the magazine industry in Britain, America and Europe; how the company could use information technology to improve profits; what opportunities still remained for tie-ups with television.

'Thank God you're not doing the interview,' said Alistair. 'You're lethal.'

'Helen's going to want to prove she's as good a man as Mark.'

'I know. Those City editors have maddened her.'

'Remember how furious we were at those articles advising that people would make money by investing in our rivals because Amalgamated was weakened? Well, multiply that ten times and I bet that's where Helen starts from.'

Alistair found himself reflecting how helpful and supportive Georgie was being. She had focused his mind on what was important, had helped him refine his ideas and had analysed the strengths and weaknesses of the probable candidates against him. It was a good thing she was on his side, he would hate to think of any other candidate getting this kind of help.

# Chapter Eleven

When Georgie arrived in the office the following morning, she was puzzled by a memo from Helen requesting to see her that afternoon immediately after her lunch with Alistair.

'Why on earth does she want to have tea with me?' she asked Alistair. 'And at the Savoy? I could have gone down the corridor to her office.'

'I think we could see it as an encouraging sign.'

'How do you work that out?'

'I reckon she wants to find out how you'd react to my appointment,' he replied. 'She might be worried that you'll leave if I'm your boss. You wouldn't, would you?'

'Not in the beginning, perhaps never, but that's something we can sort out when you get the job. In the meantime,' Georgie laughed, 'I'll tell her what a wonderful person you are.'

'Remember the old saying that if you think you're overdoing it, you're just beginning to get through,' said Alistair.

Georgie wished him luck. Once Alistair was in place,

she would concentrate on how she was going to handle his elevated position. Perhaps she should consider moving jobs, seek a media consultancy away from Amalgamated so there would be no embarrassment with the staff coming up against the boss's wife. But that was for the future. Now she had to get herself together for the meeting with Helen.

Georgie had seen too many of her colleagues paying Helen Temple-Smith the barest lip-service at various functions before zoning in on her husband and she had always tried to redress the balance of their apparent discourtesy. But it was often difficult to strike up a rapport with a woman who had kept herself carefully in the background, apparently content with the role of mother of two daughters. Through Alistair, Georgie was well acquainted with the folklore of Helen's involvement in the formation of the company but by the time she joined Amalgamated, Helen was simply the wife of the chairman. Now she had metamorphosed into the woman who signed the cheques.

When Georgie was shown in to the suite at the Savoy, she could detect no hint of lack of confidence in Helen's manner, in spite of the bad press. She thought Helen looked several pounds lighter, which suited her. Indeed she appeared altogether sharper and prettier than when they had last met. Helen Temple-Smith had never made the best-dressed lists in New York but in spite of a reputation for parsimony, Mark was known to be proud of the bills his wife ran up at places like Ralph Lauren and Bill Blass.

Helen must be nudging the middle fifties, Georgie reckoned, but today, wearing a soft wool navy suit, she looked years younger. Had she succumbed to the knife? It was hard to tell. Georgie reproached herself for allowing her mind to drift away from the subject at hand. She ought to be concentrating on promoting Alistair's qualities.

Helen, for her part, was studying Georgie with equal interest as she took a seat on the velvet-covered sofa in the suite rented specially for the interviews at the Savoy. Margery had suggested this so as to avoid spreading gossip and insecurity internally and speculation and innuendo externally.

The head-hunters had more than justified their exorbitant fees. They had been impressively thorough and as Helen had read their report, she had begun to understand why those who uncovered the secrets held the power.

The two external candidates they had initially favoured had fallen by the wayside, one because his contract would be too expensive to terminate, the other because of a secret predilection for hard drugs. The head-hunters had suggested two others merited further consideration, plus Georgina Luckhurst. Helen was not sure. She hardly knew the young woman and her husband was Alistair Drummond, the front runner. But the report on Georgina said that unlike many people on the creative side she also had a sound commercial head on her shoulders. Well, she would see.

Earlier, her lunch with Alistair had confirmed her opinion that he was eminently well-qualified for the job. She had always liked him and in the early days his editorial expertise had been a good counterpoint to Mark's commercial flair. Helen admired Alistair and respected his talent but she was determined to be meticulous in her research before making up her mind. Maybe she was being unfair but she thought of Alistair as Mark's protégé. And Helen wanted one of her own. Also the head-hunters had doubts about his ability to run a major business. He was fine with editorial people but they questioned whether he paid enough attention to other less glamorous but vital aspects of the job like the balance sheet.

After her lunch with Alistair she was also left puzzling over that remark he'd made about his wife after she'd told him she was considering Georgina for the job. Alistair had the reputation of being an equable and fair-minded man and they had been chatting casually. Nevertheless he could not have survived in their world by being a pussycat and Helen could not make up her mind whether Alistair was being ruthless or merely indiscreet.

Certainly it would be easier to make a judgement about Georgina's suitability before the young woman found out she was a potential rival to her husband. She would wait until the right moment before revealing her intentions.

Helen had been impressed with Georgie's CV as detailed by the head-hunters. 'Good degree in English from Manchester University. Joined BDH Advertising, lasted eight months. Then went backwards, took up a traineeship at Fenton's. Had been publishing director for three years at the time of the merger but,' the report added cautiously, 'she's been with Amalgamated for only two years which might prove difficult within the company.'

Helen settled herself back into the Art Deco grey sofa. The long shades in the room were lined with pink silk which cast a peach glow and flattered skin tones. She felt more comfortable talking to people in these surroundings than sitting behind a desk. She had been intrigued to discover Britain's young Prime Minister had the same preference when conducting interviews.

Georgina's grey wool suit, worn without adornment, must have cost a great deal of money. Like her husband Helen approved of rather than resented this, though it was their money which had paid for it. Georgina was the kind of woman who had helped Helen's business to prosper, unlike the scheming parasite who had latched on to Mark.

There was a lot at stake and Helen would be relieved when she could share the decision-making when the right person was at the helm. Mark had always made clear that Alistair was his preferred successor, a view shared by most of the board. But Mark was not calling the shots any more. How furious he would be if he was gazing down at her. Or was it up? Helen grinned mischievously then sipped her mineral water. Time to find out what this young woman was made of.

She had decided to talk about herself initially, in the hope that this would break down the barriers that were usually present in formal interviews.

'You know, after Mark died I thought I would collapse in a heap,' she confided.

Georgina nodded sympathetically.

'But I've surprised myself. I've realised how eager I was to please Mark. Most of the time I sublimated my own personality. Mark had such high standards that I became afraid of making mistakes. Even when he protested, I would insist that he choose where we go on holiday and where the children should be educated. I lost so much self-confidence I would even try to draw him into picking the menus for dinner parties. Can you imagine?'

'Mark was lucky to have a foil for his ideas rather than an adversary,' said Georgie.

Helen hesitated, wondering if she was being too personal but she needed to draw Georgina out. 'And do you see that in your own marriage?' she asked.

Georgina shifted in her seat. 'Yes, it's quite difficult sometimes, we're both competitive.' There was a pause before she went on, 'The first year after the merger was quite hard. I tried not to disagree with Alistair publicly and I took my cue from him. At work he treats me as a colleague who has to prove her point, in the same way as I do him. Generally I think we balance it out quite well.'

Helen wondered how much competition their marriage could take but that was not her problem. 'It's a pretty big step being turned into an entrepreneur at my time of life,' she confessed. 'If you were me, where would you start? What would you concentrate on?'

From Georgie's startled expression, it was clear that whatever she expected from the meeting, it wasn't this. But she recovered well.

'I think I'd try to break down the barriers between the commercial and editorial people.'

Helen raised inquiring eyebrows.

'I've recently clinched a deal that's been good for the company,' Georgina continued, 'but it's caused an enormous upset in the advertising department.'

'Why?'

'Because I'm treading on their territory. You've probably heard that Glamour Inc is bringing its upmarket range to Britain. I've been working with Leonard Berger, the UK boss. I've known him for years and we hatched up an idea for a forty-page sponsored supplement.' Georgina wondered where this was leading. When would Helen start to sound her out about Alistair?

'That sounds like a real coup,' said Helen.

'Well, I hope so because it'll pay editorial costs for a couple of months. Unfortunately the advertising people are spitting tin tacks because I persuaded Leonard to let editorial handle the supplement completely, not them.'

'You mean the company hasn't insisted on the usual contract with five mentions on each spread? That's a first if I ever heard one.' The supplement would have an 'advertisement value equivalent', meaning the company's commercial approach would be more subtle, it would not look like a straightforward pitch. The subtle approach was highly prized by editors.

'Leonard agreed with me that an editorial approach will work better with our kind of readers.'

'But how did you deal with Leonard's agency?'

'That was tricky. I expected them to be furious so before the news got out I went to the agency's boss to explain the thinking behind the storyline.'

'Smart.'

'The agency boss wasn't thrilled of course, but at least he saw the sense of it. The ads he places with his other accounts won't be affected.'

Helen was impressed. This was a clever deal. Sponsorship was the way forward in advertisement revenue terms; the magazines of the future might have two or three partworks attached and if they looked attractive this would be an extra selling point to readers. It would also offer sizeable savings, giving the company the freedom to spread these savings around, on cover prices, editorial budgets, whatever was the priority. It would give them the edge.

So far Georgina had given little impression that she saw herself as a candidate. Helen was convinced that Georgina was there to act as Alistair's standard-bearer. Was she the tail to Alistair's kite or could she fly alone? Certainly she had earned the company a nice, fat profit and was beginning to show the calibre needed to head the European operation. Helen appreciated that women were still the outsiders in big business, statistically as well as emotionally. Women accounted for fewer than two per cent of top appointments. She had never taken a stand on women's issues, but the reaction to her taking over Mark's job had sharpened her awareness of, and her impatience with, male presumptions.

Now was the time to test this young executive's mettle. 'I've heard encouraging things about you,' she said deliberately, 'and I'm minded to include you on the short list.'

Georgina put down her cup sharply. 'That would be a wonderful opportunity.'

'Do you think you're made of the right stuff?'

The younger woman did not answer immediately, seeming to collect her thoughts. Finally she said, 'Yes, I think I am. I've had a great many ideas about how the business should develop in the future and I'd love the chance to see them put into practice.'

'Steady on,' said Helen, smiling. 'There's a way to go yet.'

'Of course, of course.' Georgie ran her hands through her hair. 'When I came here this is the last thing I expected.'

'I've promised my board that they'll be fully consulted, but we'd pick up some kudos from the industry if we did choose a woman. It'd negate the criticism that Amalgamated, like other publishing companies, hasn't promoted females to positions of real power.' She gave a short laugh. 'Mark used to say it was only because we never found a woman able to make the grade.' Helen leaned forward. 'I'll put your name forward, Georgina. Let's see how you measure up. In the first instance I'd like you to prepare a presentation to make to the appointments committee, preparatory to the final interviews.'

'Who'll be on that committee?'

'Naturally I'll chair it,' said Helen, 'but I want it to be small, only a couple of members of the British board, Giles and Harry. Will they present a problem?'

Georgina seemed to digest this information then she shook her head.

One question troubled Helen. If this young woman was entrusted with the job, could she handle having her husband under her command? Could he? Would their marriage be strong enough to cope?

'How do you think your being on the short list will affect Alistair?'

The question hung in the air and it was hard to read Georgina's expression. Eventually she said, perhaps a mite too heartily, Helen thought, 'Of course he'll be pleased but, like me, he'll be surprised.' She gave a short laugh. 'Very.'

'Yes, he was,' said Helen carefully, her eyes never leaving Georgina's face. 'Surprised, I mean. I told him over lunch.'

Georgina looked puzzled. 'Alistair didn't mention that.'

'No, I asked him to hold fire until I'd seen you,' said Helen reassuringly. 'I didn't want you to suspect when we met that you were being sounded out. But I must be frank and tell you that one of the problems with your candidature is that I understand from Alistair that you and he are serious about starting a family as soon as possible.'

Georgina's cheeks reddened but she said nothing.

Alistair had certainly been indiscreet, thought Helen, noting Georgina's discomfiture. She went on, 'So I suppose the question I need to ask you is, are you at a point in your life when becoming chief executive of Amalgamated would conflict with your wish to have a baby?'

Georgina was about to reply but Helen forestalled her. 'Before you answer, may I be permitted to give you some advice? Don't make the mistake I did. Once you change from the woman Alistair married, you operate on a different level. I'm not saying it'll be worse but you'll be perceived in a different light, not necessarily one you'll like.'

'Alistair and I have an equal marriage.'

'Yes, but that might alter when you have children. Naturally I don't intend to tell you how to run your life but you may want to consider postponing trying for a family at least for a few weeks until the decision about the job is made.'

Georgie understood immediately. Amalgamated had to be seen to be flourishing under Helen's stewardship and if she was successful in getting the job, she would be Helen's creature, moulded from the start to think of the company first and foremost.

'Of course we're only in the middle of our interviews but let's take a possible scenario,' Helen continued. 'Say you get the job. After a year or so, during which you'll work harder than you've ever done before, you'll have made your plans and placed your people into position. That would be the time to think about pregnancy. It would be much easier to manage both strands of your life with some experience of the job behind you.'

'That sounds sensible,' said Georgina swiftly.

'You may need time to think this over and talk to Alistair,' said Helen, watching Georgie closely. 'It's a big decision.'

'I don't think that will be necessary,' said Georgie giving her a huge smile. 'It's very flattering to be considered for such an important job. You've opened up opportunities I never knew existed an hour ago.'

'I take it then that you wish to be included on the short list?'

The answer was immediate. 'Absolutely.'

On her way out of the hotel, Georgie could hardly contain her elation. To be considered for one of the best jobs in publishing. On the world stage. It was almost too much to grasp. Of course it was doubtful she would get it but it was heady stuff to be considered in such talented company.

It was late afternoon and she decided to go straight home to wait for Alistair. There was only one blot on the sunny horizon. Why had Alistair felt the need to tell Helen about their plans for a baby? If it had come from anyone else she would think he was trying to scupper her chances. But then, he knew Helen so well. Perhaps it had just slipped out while they were chatting. Nevertheless, Georgie needed to hear his reasoning for such an extraordinary indiscretion.

She walked away from the group of Japanese tourists

waiting outside the hotel for taxis and made her way into the Strand. She flagged down a black cab and sat back, trying to avoid the thought that was pressuring her. Alistair. Her husband. Now her rival.

Whenever Georgie had a major problem to solve, she liked to lie in a hot scented tub to mull over possible solutions. It rarely failed to work. So when she returned to the flat she went straight to the bathroom ignoring the pile of mail on the mahogany table. That could wait. So could dinner. She needed time to think right now.

It took only a few minutes to fill the claw-footed tub with steaming water laced with a sensuous dollop of lavender and essential oil of bergamot. Breathing in the perfume, she tried to think objectively about what Alistair had said. On the face of it, it was treacherous. Helen had been quite precise. Alistair had only volunteered this information when he had been told that his wife was in the running. She hated herself for thinking of him in this way. Perhaps because he was desperate for a baby, it was uppermost in his mind and it had made him franker than usual. But it was hard to imagine someone as streetwise as he was blurting out information like that. Friends like Josephine knew she was trying to conceive but telling the boss, that was different.

Georgie slid further down the bath. These were seditious thoughts. This was Alistair. Her lover. Her best friend, the arch proponent of women's promotion within the organisation. Alistair was surely the last man on earth to hold old-fashioned views about women and work.

Well, this situation between them would certainly be a test of his liberal views.

She was battling with perceptions here. A man telling his employer that he and his wife were trying to start a family was an aside. Nothing would change in his job or career path. But a woman revealing the same thing signalled something completely different. She was virtually saying she would be out of commission for several months, therefore putting her promotion on hold. Implicit would be that if there were nanny problems or the child was ill, they would have first call on her. How would Alistair feel if he had to postpone his ambitions for a family for the sake of a promotion? He'd be as disappointed as she was now. For some reason this had not occurred to him. That was what she was fighting against.

Georgie began to imagine what life would be like as Amalgamated's chief executive and felt a surge of excitement, congratulating herself for having got this far. Undoubtedly the appointment of a woman to such a high-profile job would garner useful publicity for the organisation and she would regard herself as a standard-bearer for other females in the workplace. Flexi-time and job sharing for working mothers had not been a success in terms of profitability so far. Yes, that would be something substantial she could tackle. And more. She would give priority to franchising magazines. Publishers in other countries had shown interest in buying the licence to print in their own language, using much of Amalgamated's original material. One or two of their titles would also translate easily into short television series slotted into a daytime show, such as *This Morning*. Some of their titles were under-exploited assets; they could bring in healthy revenue without the need for too much extra investment.

The steamy atmosphere was beginning to relax her muscles, the tension was slowly slipping away. She heard Alistair's key in the latch and the thud of his briefcase as it hit the parquet floor. 'Where are you?' his voice sang out.

Georgie levered herself up and called, 'In the bath.'

She heard him emptying his pockets, going through his routine of taking off his jacket and walking through to the kitchen. When she heard the fridge door opening and closing, followed by a cupboard door, then a clink, she resigned herself to waiting. She knew he was unable to react to news, however trivial or important, until he had wound down.

Eventually he appeared in the bathroom doorway bearing two glasses of white wine so cold that the glasses were covered in vapour.

'What's new?' he asked, loosening his tie. The question usually signalled the start of a debriefing session about what had happened that day.

'You first. How did you get on with Helen?'

'It went well, I think.' He handed her a glass and gave her a kiss. 'How about you?'

'Same.' She took a sip. 'OK, you first.'

'I was impressed with Helen, she'd done her homework. I don't think she's going to be a cipher.' He drank some wine. 'She asked me for my ideas for the company, all the things we discussed. That brainstorming we did was a great help.'

Georgie turned on the tap for more hot water. 'Who are you up against?' she asked, keeping her voice neutral.

'She didn't mention names but she did say she was seeing several people.'

'Did my name crop up?'

He put down his glass. 'Ah. So she told you she was thinking about putting you on the short list.' When Georgie nodded, he raised his glass and smiled delightedly. 'Congratulations. She made me swear not to say anything until she'd discussed it with you. And as I wasn't sure if she'd changed her mind, I thought I'd better not say anything until you did.'

Georgie put her glass on the window ledge and climbed out of the bath.

'It's bold of Helen to give you a chance,' Alistair continued, 'but you're worth it, darling. Well done.'

As she put on her robe, he peered at her anxiously. 'What's the matter?' He followed her into the bedroom and sat on the side of the bed while she towelled her hair. 'Have I said something wrong?'

'Why did you tell her I was trying to get pregnant?' Georgie tried not to sound confrontational but Alistair seemed uneasy.

'But that's what we're trying to do, aren't we?' When she did not answer he added hastily, 'And anyway I only mentioned we were trying.'

Georgie tried to stifle her pique. 'She's not going to

hand this job over to a woman who could be pregnant in the next few months, is she?'

'Darling, I'm sorry. I shouldn't have told her but we were talking about her girls and she asked when we were going to start a family. I mentioned it was something we were thinking about. It was as casual as that.'

'She seemed to think it was more definite.'

'Come on, she's looking for an excuse in advance.'

'What do you mean by that?'

'I mean you're wonderful, you're great at your job but Amalgamated's never picked a woman for a top job, has it? No one in publishing has. Helen's only in place because she has the majority shareholding.'

'So you don't think I've got a hope.'

'Honestly? No, I don't. It's a credit to you that you've got as far as you have but in the next few years things are going to get tougher, negotiations will get harder. Men are more experienced to deal with all of that.'

'Now you sound like all the rest of them.' Fiercely she opened a drawer, took out her underwear and began putting on a pair of knickers.

He watched her. 'I hate it when we quarrel,' he said unhappily. 'Why are you getting dressed? I thought the plan was to stay in tonight and have another try.'

Georgie sat down on the bed without replying. Her lips were trembling. Alistair walked over and stroked her cheek and gently wiped the tears that were beginning to trickle down her cheeks.

'Darling, don't be upset. I hate you being unhappy. I'm sorry if you think I've kiboshed you but what I want most of all in the world is to have a baby with you, someone who's a continuation of us, someone who'll carry on our names, someone else we can love and cherish.' He took her in his arms. 'I thought that was what you wanted too.'

'I do but . . .' She decided against being too candid. In the past they had always been able to compromise over any disagreement about the minor things which inevitably cropped up at work or at home. But this was a life-changing decision and for the first time she experienced a tremor of real fear. The big job was not reality, this was.

Alistair had undressed and was in bed, watching her intently.

'You're probably right about the job,' she said quietly. She had been vain to think that Helen would prefer her above all the others, especially Alistair. And in any case, she did want a child. What was the point in waiting?

At her words his face visibly relaxed. He held out his arms and she climbed into bed, nestling her body into his, reaching for his lips before moving her mouth across his shoulders. As she trailed her fingernails back and forwards across his nipples, he groaned and her hands inched slowly downwards, caressing his skin. Urgently he enfolded her and the familiar feel and touch of him entering her body aroused a response which delighted him with its fervour and intensity.

After the moment of climax, she opened her eyes to see him examining her face. 'I love you, my darling,' he said softly.

'Ditto.'

It was several moments before, reluctantly, they separated and as they lay side by side in companionable silence she was reminded of how happy she had been since she'd met him. And how much she loved him.

# Chapter Twelve

A tap on Alistair's office door the next day heralded the arrival of Harry, as dapper as ever and full of self-importance.

'Helen's asked me to sit in on the appointments committee,' he said proudly.

'Who else is on it?'

'Besides Helen, only Giles.'

Finance and circulation, the two mainstays of any magazine business. It made sense, thought Alistair.

Then Harry brandished a fax which he brought out from behind his back. 'This should interest you, old boy.' He handed it over and Alistair saw it was stamped confidential and showed the list of candidates drawn up by the head-hunters. Georgie's name was not among them. Alistair checked the date. That would explain it. The memo was dated two weeks before Helen's meeting with Georgie at the Savoy so she must have been a last-minute addition.

He stared speculatively at Harry. 'Where did this come from?'

'I don't want to give you all my jewels at once.' Harry grinned. 'Let's just say it entered my radar.'

Alistair did not altogether trust the circulation director but he decided to confide in him. It might backfire but as a member of the appointments board Harry would know the final short list soon enough.

'There's one name missing,' he said. 'Helen's also asked Georgina to pitch.'

To his credit Harry managed to rein in his surprise, though not his derision. 'Helen's obviously menopausal,' he said. 'Only explanation for it, old boy. If this fashion for pushing women to the front continues, where's it going to lead? What would we men be used for? We'd be obsolete apart from being used as walking sperm banks.'

Alistair was about to protest when Harry added quickly, 'Not that I'm saying anything against Georgina in particular. In fact her magazines have had unexpectedly high revenues, mainly because they're the lifestyle ones. Surely Helen knows that's only because of the upturn in the economy?'

Alistair stared morosely in front of him.

'And another thing,' Harry went on, 'your wife's only been here five minutes. Let's face it, against you, what chance does she have?'

Still Alistair said nothing.

'Helen's being mischievous,' Harry concluded. 'She must know she's putting you in a monstrous position. I thought she was a fan of yours.'

'I'm not comfortable with it,' Alistair admitted.

'Helen's being contentious. Maybe she's trying to unsettle you to gauge how much you want the job.'

'I don't believe Helen's like that,' Alistair protested.

'No, but the head-hunters might be. I don't want to cause more trouble between you and Georgie,' Harry paused, 'but if I were you, I'd keep your wife in the dark about your ideas and plans for the company.'

Alistair scowled and Harry added hastily, 'Just to be on the safe side.' He walked to the door, hesitated and turned round. 'Are you free for dinner tonight?'

Surprised, Alistair asked why.

'I'd like to have a chat, away from the office. I think you'll find it interesting, old boy.'

Slowly Alistair nodded.

There was an unspoken agreement in the Drummond household that nothing contentious was discussed in the mornings when time was at a premium. This morning Georgie had hurriedly eaten her muesli, fruit and yoghurt breakfast but she was planning to allow time this evening to organise a special dinner for the two of them. They were in the habit of only having a snack at night so it would be an agreeable surprise for Alistair and it would give them time to relax and discuss the problem of babies and jobs quietly and, she hoped, without rancour.

Georgie spent a day in which personal problems hardly figured as she battled with the myriad complexities thrown up by her editors, advertising managers and the accountant who had niggled on about one of the magazines exceeding its editorial budget too early in the first quarter. She'd had to tread a fine line between placating the money man and staying loyal to her hard-working staff although she had asked the editor to ensure the second quarter balanced the books.

It was nearly seven o'clock before she could free herself to rush home and set the table. Alistair always expressed pleasure when he saw what she could create with a few napkins, some silver and a handful of flowers. She drove her regular caterer demented to provide Alistair's favourite canard à l'orange at short notice because she did not want to take the chance of plundering the freezer. She had never lived down the hilarity caused when she had taken a pie out of the freezer for unexpected supper guests to find, as she was serving it, that it was apple instead of steak and kidney pie. The incident had fuelled her reputation as an unfortunate cook.

Georgie put the dish in the oven and was cutting off the stalks from the weekend's flowers – underwater, as her gardening editor advised, so that no air locks developed – before transferring them to a cut-glass vase when Alistair called to say he would be home late. He was having a meal with Harry.

'I meant to mention it when I dropped into your office this morning but that advertising problem drove it out of my head.'

Georgie made no mention of her special preparations, nor did she ask why he should want to meet

Harry after working hours. But she was disappointed that her plans were wrecked and when the delectable smell of the gourmet meal filled the flat, she decided it would be a pity not to share it with someone and reached for the phone. Josephine was about to put Luke to bed and was delighted at the prospect of having company and a top-of-the-range meal brought along by her friend.

When Georgie walked through Josephine's kitchen with the casserole dish, she felt as though she was seeing her friend's flat for the first time. Why had she never noticed the welter of infant paraphernalia around the place? A carrycot in the hall, the high chair at the table, the playpen in the sitting room. She supposed that Josephine had usually tidied away all this stuff before previous visits.

'Alistair's missing a great supper,' said Josephine, lifting the casserole lid. 'You don't usually go to so much trouble midweek. What's so special about tonight?'

'We had a misunderstanding last night,' said Georgie. 'This was supposed to make up.'

'It's unusual for you to have a row, what caused it?'

Georgie instinctively hesitated, but she knew she could trust Josephine. 'This is in confidence but Helen has put me on the short list.'

Josephine's eyebrows shot up. 'Wow. I'm surprised. That's incredible. Well done.' She regarded Georgie thoughtfully. 'How's Alistair taking the news?'

'In the circumstances, fine, but he was rather indiscreet

with Helen.' And she explained about Alistair's gaffe.

'It's a pity he was so frank but in a way I can understand him saying it. He's always got on well with Helen.'

'And he's obsessed about having a baby,' said Georgie. 'He notices the passing of time more than I do and Mark's death has made it much worse.'

'Anyway, it's thrilling that you're actually on the short list. It's a miracle.'

Georgie took a deep breath. 'But I need to be sensible. It'll never happen. In fact, I'm thinking about asking Helen to withdraw my name.'

'Why on earth would you do that?'

'Because to be honest I haven't got a chance. Alistair thinks I'm only there for PC reasons.'

'Maybe he's right, but use it to your advantage. If you're on the list you're on the list. Have faith in yourself, for goodness' sake. I thought you were a disciple of positive thinking. You'll never forgive yourself if you don't at least try.'

'There are too many problems.'

'What problems?'

'Say by a miracle I did get the job. I'd be Alistair's boss.'

'So? If he got the job he'd be your boss. Would you have a problem with that?'

'No, I don't think so. But it's different.'

'How?'

'It's a man-woman thing. I don't know, it's just different. On the surface he says the right things but I'm aware all the time that he really doesn't like the idea of my being considered for the job.'

'Alistair's a grown-up guy. He can adapt. Isn't he a great promoter of women's talent? And I predict that if you're the lucky one, when he gets over the shock he'll be delighted and proud.'

'Well, it won't come to that.'

'Not if you pull out now. And by the way, if you do, I can't see you'd have a great future at Amalgamated,' said Josephine firmly. 'Helen will hardly think this is the action of a go-getter. And word will quickly get round the business that you're not a serious player.'

Georgie had not allowed herself to think this far but she could see her friend was right.

'You owe it to yourself to have a try,' Josephine insisted. 'All that hard work over so many years, you deserve this chance.'

'Maybe you're right,' said Georgie slowly. 'I'm going to have to do some serious thinking.'

Alistair pottered around the kitchen, poured himself a half-measure of malt and began humming. A memory of their love-making last night flashed into his mind and a smile crossed his face. It had been memorable, wonderful, completely obliterating the disagreement they'd had about the job interview.

Although he hadn't admitted it to Georgie, he had immediately regretted making the casual remark to Helen about their plans to start a family. No boss would want to know that one of her top people was going to be out of action, for however short a time. It was a private matter between husband and wife.

He wandered into his study and leaned back in his leather chair, a birthday present from his wife a couple of years earlier. As he waited for her, he nursed the amber liquid, warming the contents between his cupped hands, and after a while he poured out another measure for Georgie to toast his success with Harry. Judging by the state of the kitchen, some major culinary event had been planned. Their beautiful table had been laid with his collection of antique glass and their best cutlery.

But he did not worry. One of the things he loved about Georgie was that she did not bear grudges.

It was well after eleven when he heard her footsteps in the hall. He raced to the door to give her a bear hug. 'Where've you been?' Without waiting for a reply he drew her into the living room. 'Sit down and listen to some interesting news.'

'What?' she asked.

'Harry's decided to back me.'

'Good heavens, I never thought he was one of your fans.'

'He's not. Helen's asked him to sit on the committee interviewing for the job so he'll be immensely useful. Trouble is, I don't trust him. He's up to something but I can't figure out what it is right now. My guess is he's scanned the short list and feels it's curtains for his career if I don't get the job.'

'Did he say anything about me being on it?'

Alistair was momentarily flustered. Why should he be when she was going to withdraw her name? He said with a smile, 'I didn't mention it because Helen told me she wanted the names on the list kept confidential at this stage. Anyway, you know old Harry, life president of the British Blokes Society. He'd think Helen put you there only as window-dressing.'

'It couldn't possibly be for any ability I might have, could it?'

'Come on, even Harry would recognise you wouldn't be considered if you weren't one of the best in the business. No, this all came about because as far as he's concerned I'm the best of a bad bunch.' Alistair leaned back and half-closed his eyes. 'I may also have given the impression that he'd become my deputy.'

'Harry?' Her voice was hostile. 'Deputy? You didn't even consider me?'

Alistair was embarrassed. It had not crossed his mind. 'You're far too valuable in your present job,' he said lamely.

Georgie's eyes narrowed. 'It's all settled, is it?'

'No, it isn't, and anyway you gave me the impression last night that you'd made a choice between a big new job and having a baby and you were going to back out.'

A flicker of annoyance passed over Georgie's face. 'You were mistaken,' she said levelly and walked out of the door into their bedroom.

Alistair was genuinely baffled. An issue he'd thought had been solved amicably, indeed lovingly, the night before had suddenly been resurrected. He stood up and followed her. Georgie was sitting on her side of the bed and he settled down opposite her.

'I don't understand, darling, last night—'

'Last night I was still undecided.'

'Then what changed your mind?'

'The mention of that toad Harry.'

Alistair threw back his head and laughed. 'You could eat him for breakfast,' he said. 'Is that what this is all about? Forget Harry, he isn't important, a baby is.'

'I couldn't agree more and it's why I'd like us to wait until we know who's going to get the job. Can't you understand that?'

Alistair shook his head. 'There's always going to be something in the way, some reason why it would be better to wait. But we can't wait. Well, I can't.' He leaned towards her. 'Georgie, you're gorgeous, I'm gorgeous, we'll make beautiful children together.' He smiled at her. 'But I don't want to be the only sixty-year-old in the playground.'

'Come on, Alistair, I'm asking you for a little time, a few weeks, that's all.'

'Maybe you're fooling yourself,' he said, allowing his exasperation to show. 'Maybe you're using this so-called job opportunity as an excuse not to have a baby at all.' Her face registered such shock that he regretted the words as soon as they were uttered. 'I'm sorry but I've never known you like this, Georgie. We've always been able to sort everything out.'

'We've never had to face a problem like this before,'

she said hotly. 'You're asking me to sacrifice too much. OK, I'll probably be unsuccessful but I want to give it my best shot. Even if I can't become chief executive, I could be your deputy.'

Keep calm, he admonished himself. 'Do you think, honestly now, you could tackle a job like that when you're pregnant or the mother of a very young child?'

'Don't evade.'

Alistair's eyes slid away from hers. 'I haven't got the job yet.'

'That's all I need to know.' She stood up and folded her arms across her chest. 'Alistair, I've now made up my mind. I intend to let my name go forward.'

It was the first time Georgie had ever had to make a choice between her own wishes and those of Alistair's. They stared at each other, separated physically by the distance of their double bed but emotionally by centuries of prejudice.

'So,' he said slowly, 'tomorrow you intend going into the office as my rival?'

'Yes, I'm afraid so.'

Alistair awoke early. Unusually for him he had slept fitfully and woke up feeling disgruntled. For the life of him he couldn't see how he and Georgie were going to resolve this. Both of them had entrenched positions from which it was difficult for either to shift.

He had to admit that he had felt stirrings of resentment towards Georgie now that she'd definitely thrown her hat into the ring. This unpalatable fact gave rise to a difficult question. Was his commitment to equality so fragile that he couldn't cope with the idea of a wife who could match his abilities? He assured himself his main concern was to save her from unrealistic notions. Amalgamated would not consider a woman as chief of their European operation and he had to make Georgie realise it before she was rejected and before it damaged their relationship any further. God knows it wasn't an equal playing field but he hadn't made the rules.

Alistair began to allow himself some positive thoughts. Once he had clinched the job he could work out a compromise where she could have a baby but maintain her status within the company. Perhaps he could consider making her his deputy, if he could square that with Harry. He would have a bigger budget and his seniority would ensure that her work schedule could be as flexible as she liked. He hated upsetting Georgie and this was creating precisely the situation which might sidetrack them from their priority.

In the bathroom Georgie stepped into the bath, hoping the hot water would relax her taut body. She'd had such a miserable night lying in their bed without Alistair's comforting body close to hers. Her mind had raced over the events of yesterday. By dawn, still sleepless, she had not worked out how to reconcile their different agendas. Of course, if she had already conceived, there would be no dilemma.

The jarring thought flitted across her mind that perhaps, as Alistair had said, she was indeed seizing the possibility of promotion as a way of avoiding pregnancy altogether. Could it be that in truth she did not want to feel dependent on Alistair by becoming pregnant?

She leaned back, promising herself another two minutes maximum in the water. She heard the click of the door handle and Alistair appeared clutching the *Financial Times* and the business sections of the broadsheets.

'I'm sorry about last night,' he said. 'I'm sorry you're upset but you have to face facts.'

'Thank you for your apology,' she kept her voice ultra polite, 'but do you think it's wise to continue last night's argument?'

'I know you think I'm being unfair but take a look at these,' he waved the papers in the air. 'There isn't a mention in any of these stories of one woman heading up a company like ours.'

'That's because men keep us out.'

He gave an exaggerated sigh.

'We'll forget about British Airways, the Pearson group, those women in the City, shall we?' she asked sarcastically.

He dropped the papers into the soapy water, where they lay in a sodden mass over her toes. She rose hastily and stepped out of the bath. 'Alistair, what on earth's got into you?'

Without replying he passed her a bath sheet. She wrapped it round her shoulders, as if to erect a barrier between them. But Alistair seemed not to pick up the hint. He put his arms round her and pulled her close.

'Darling, I'm not trying to make you angry,' he said.

'All I want to do is stop you getting your hopes up. We could be squandering valuable time because Helen has taken some politically correct advice from a head-hunter who probably doesn't believe a woman will be chosen either.' He kissed the top of her head. 'If we have a daughter she'll probably have an easier time than her mother.'

'With the right man to back her, I'm sure she will,' said Georgina tartly.

When Alistair arrived at the office he discovered that Helen had changed her schedule. She wanted to continue, as her secretary described it, 'further discussions with the Dublin office'. That could mean only one thing. Another candidate was holding her attention. His spirits, already low, plunged.

His mood was not improved when, after concluding a lengthy and complicated phone call involving an expensive book deal, his secretary told him, 'Georgina wants you to ring. She can't make the party tonight.'

'Right,' he said brusquely and punched the direct dial button on his intercom. When he heard Georgie's voice, he took a deep breath but could not stop his anger showing. 'Why are you crying off? You know how important this evening is.'

There was a short silence.

'Please take that tone out of your voice,' she said pleasantly. 'As I told your secretary I hate to let you down but I'm not strictly necessary tonight and I have some important work to finish.'

'More important than helping me host this party?' *Art World* was their most prestigious magazine, his brain-child. It had been slavishly copied in America where it had also been a success. He had dreamed up the idea, launched it, edited it and watched it joyfully over its ten years of life. It was the nearest thing to an offspring he had and many of the New York executives and their spouses were making an excuse to come over for the party.

When Mark had been alive the milestone anniversaries of his magazines had been the high spots of the company's calendar. Alistair had to replicate that tonight for the newspaper diarists, the City, their rivals, and not least for the company wives who liked to visit the theatre and the shops while their men indulged in their favourite occupation, sitting around plotting. As Helen was spending more time than expected in London since Mark's death it did not take the highly-charged antennae of the US board to work out that this year's tenth anniversary celebration was worth a priority visit. They were likely to be disappointed, however. Helen apparently intended remaining in Dublin for another day.

'It was quite clear for months that this was a command performance,' said Alistair, tapping his desk irritably. 'What's cropped up that you can't put off?'

A slight pause and then she said, 'I want to get on with my presentation. It's going to mean a lot of work.'

Alistair stared at the ceiling, feeling irritated and exasperated. But he replied mildly, 'I have to do mine too.'

'Yes, but you've had more time to think about it and prepare.'

'Couldn't you break away for an hour?'

'I really can't, Alistair. I've so much to do. I have to delve into all the financial details of the past ten years. I have to get some of them from the archives. And I'm having to nag figures out of advertising. You don't need me there, Alistair. You'll have plenty of support.'

'Really? Helen's not going either.' His hand gripped the receiver. 'It doesn't make any difference, I suppose, that I've always backed you whenever you asked for it.'

'Only when it didn't conflict with anything else.'

Alistair hardly ever lost his temper, priding himself on invariably being able to appreciate the other person's point of view, even if he did not agree with it. But Georgie's remark provoked such a surge of rage that he slammed down the receiver so hard the casing nearly cracked.

The unfairness of it. Being chosen for the short list had changed Georgie. She was becoming more self-centred, more selfish. Only the other day he had changed all his arrangements because she needed him to attend that balls-achingly boring dinner with some of her major advertisers. How outrageous for her to say he did it only when it suited him. Was that the kind of partner she thought he was?

Well, he would go to the party tonight and show everyone there that he was the best front guy for Amalgamated. He would have a bloody good time. And he wouldn't hurry home.

★ ★ ★

Outside Georgie's office Rosemary walked softly away from the door, having heard every word of Georgie's end of the conversation with her brother. She felt exultant. If Georgie didn't want the invitation to the *Art World* party, she knew someone who did.

# Chapter Thirteen

Alistair believed a good party was like an orchestra coming together under the baton of a great conductor. And this one had all the hallmarks of being a brilliant success. He paused at the entrance to the ballroom of the Gladstone Hotel and listened to the deep, throaty roar from the throng of guests. He could feel the heat emanating from the constant movement of three hundred people eating canapés, drinking champagne, laughing and talking.

He recognised major players from the art world, some of whom were regular sponsors of exhibitions organised by his magazine. Virtually every major British and Continental artist, architect or sculptor was in this room, together with their wife, mistress or agent. Many of the painters or sculptors had been unknown when *Art World* first started. This was the specialist magazine that had discovered them and had explained their works to a wider public. In a few cases the publicity had turned them into world-famous names with millionaire bank balances. A smattering of actors, playwrights and politicians, so-called gossip fodder, supplemented the guest list. This party was the place to be seen in the capital tonight.

Alistair noticed with satisfaction that centre stage was the Prime Minister's wife talking to the magazine's current editor. Close by was a book critic who looked as if he wanted to interrupt. Alistair hoped he would keep his sarcastic tongue in check for once then heaved a sigh of relief when he saw that the critic was in fact diverting himself by tracing adept fingers down the bare back of Amalgamated's newest fashion recruit. A flock of angular models, clad in dresses that would be unforgiving on other women, were outnumbered by advertisers, as ever the lifeblood of Amalgamated's oldest magazine, indeed of all their titles.

Alistair had been impressed when the caterers had suggested using Picasso's blue period, Gainsborough's Blue Boy and Monet's blue lilies at Giverny as a theme for the decor, the food and their waiters' uniform. Jasper John would have been proud of the canapés, toast fingers topped with black and red caviar and crème fraîche in a Stars and Stripes pattern. Miniature hamburgers and bruschettas, like the ones made famous by Lichtenstein's comic-style paintings, were being devoured alongside tiny cups of Campbell's tomato soup, chosen as an act of homage to Andy Warhol.

Although he smiled frequently, made conversation animatedly and sipped champagne thirstily, Alistair felt downcast. This was an important evening and the person he most wanted to share it with had refused to attend.

★　★　★

In her office Georgie was trying hard to concentrate on the most important document of her career. But too often she found herself staring sadly out of the window across the courtyard that the building encircled.

They had never before put down the phone on each other. Why had he been infuriated by her comment? Alistair was very obliging but she was only being honest when she said that he did so only when it didn't conflict with more important things, like preparing an urgent paper for the board. They both knew there were always some priorities so why be upset when she pointed it out? If he hadn't slammed down the phone, she would have softened the explanation. But she was damned if she would phone him again to apologise. Apologise for being truthful?

It was the mention of the presentation that was behind all this. If she had lied and used another excuse, he would have accepted it. If he didn't think she had a chance of succeeding, why was he so discomfited? Did he think she presented some sort of threat? Georgie shook her head impatiently. No, it wasn't that. Like all men, he did not want to be thwarted. He expected her, in the true tradition of dutiful wife, to accept his version of their future together. The trouble was, it didn't conform to her version.

She tried to discipline herself to concentrate on the figures for the business plan but she was making little progress. If she wanted to mend bridges, there was only one course of action; swallow her pride and join him at the *Art World* anniversary party. Tomorrow she would somehow have to find time, however difficult, to work on the presentation document.

She abandoned the computer and went to spruce herself up. She would arrive at the party when it was winding down but at least she could try and get Alistair away on his own for a quiet meal on neutral ground. That might be difficult as he was the host but after what had happened between them she was certain he would accept her olive branch.

Georgie rehearsed her first words to him. 'I come in peace,' she would say. He'd grin, give her a quick kiss and she would entice him away. Then over a meal she'd say that she loved him very much and that she did want his baby. Later. She needed him to understand that she had as much right to pitch for the job as he did. He was a reasonable man and she was confident he would see her point of view.

When Louise walked into the crowded ballroom, it took her only a couple of minutes to pick out Alistair's distinctive frame, his blond mane easily visible in the crowd. She zig-zagged her way towards him until finally she reached his small group and stood quietly at his elbow until his companion indicated her presence.

'Louise!' he said, surprised, then immediately turned to his companion. 'Michael, this is Louise . . .'

'Palmer,' she supplied quickly. 'Louise Palmer. How do you do.'

Alistair did not appear overjoyed to see her but she

disregarded him, turning instead to his companion whose face broke into a smile. Louise began to relax. She had not met many men who could resist her charms when she made an effort. The appreciative stare of the doorman as he pulled open the revolving doors of the hotel and the openly lascivious stares of a group of Arabs in the lobby gave her all the confidence she needed. She had wondered whether the strapless peach chiffon was a touch outré for a cocktail party but she was glad she had decided to risk it. In Britain money was important but those who mattered, particularly in the art world, gave you an entree only when the introduction came from the right people. People like Alistair. This was his world and she wanted to be part of it. Alistair was liked and trusted, she needed his expertise, his contacts and, above all, his ability to sell her gallery to agents and their exalted clients.

Slowly Alistair's colleagues drifted away, and he swivelled to face her. 'You turn up in some very unexpected places.' It was hard to tell what he was thinking.

Louise tilted her face up at him and gave what Mark used to call her one-thousand-kilowatt smile.

'I didn't gatecrash. Here's my official invitation.' She opened her bag and pulled out the card.

He frowned. 'How did you get one of those?'

'I have my ways,' she replied, accepting a fluted glass from a waiter who was handing round champagne at a costly rate. She found his ill humour stimulating. It had been an effective ploy of Mark's, to pretend to be irritated with her when he wanted her to woo him into a good humour.

She glanced around the crowded ballroom. 'I don't recognise a soul here.'

'I'm not surprised. Since your day, most people have left. I'm about the only senior editorial person still on the payroll.'

'Just as well. We don't want people gossiping about you flirting with your ex-wife, do we?'

'I'm not flirting, I simply want to know what you're doing here.'

'Don't be grumpy. Introduce me to the editor of your gorgeous art magazine,' she said, surveying the room.

'Why should I do that?'

'Because I'm going to be such a famous art gallery owner, darling, you'll be pleased to be seen with me. And as Louise Palmer I won't be known as one of your appendages,' she smiled roguishly, 'which might work against me.'

'I don't think so. Whatever you set your heart on you always get.'

So there was still some animosity there. That was better than being indifferent. She sipped her champagne and gazed steadily up at him.

It used to be easy to rouse Alistair sexually in the old days and Louise moved imperceptibly so that her unencumbered breasts brushed his arm. He stepped back with an involuntary movement. Ah, she thought, it still works.

The taxi drew up in front of the Gladstone Hotel and Georgie got out. She had changed into a simple silk suit, kept in her office cupboard for occasions like this. It was fashionable enough but somehow it did not give her the kind of lift she needed to face the elegant crowd invited to what the *Daily Mail*'s gossip column had described as the party of the season. But as she walked towards the babble coming from the chandeliered ballroom, she felt optimistic about her mission. She was sure they could sort out this nonsense and return to normal. She paused at the door, surveying the crowd, trying to pick out Alistair. Yes, there he was, looking relaxed and smiling.

With a jolt, she saw Louise. What was she doing here? This was strictly an invitation-only event and only one person had control over the guest list. Alistair.

At his side, Louise was patting his arm with what Georgie thought was a proprietorial gesture. She was only about five feet four inches tall but she seemed to put all the rest of the guests in the ballroom into shadow.

With an effort Georgie rearranged her features, took a deep breath and moved towards the pair. Alistair was bending his head towards Louise, listening intently, as he had done at the memorial service. As she came closer, Georgie overheard Louise saying, '. . . and I really do regret the past so very much.'

Georgie's mouth was dry and she prayed her expression did not reflect the consternation she felt. Taking great care not to look in Louise's direction, she touched Alistair's arm. He swivelled round and his face lit up. 'Darling,' he said and bent to kiss her. Georgie was happy to oblige, not on the cheek which was their habit in public but straight on his lips. A message to Louise certainly, but equally a message to him.

'So you finally got away,' he said, beckoning a waiter. Always the diplomat, he did not seem perturbed at seeing his first wife alongside his second. Again.

'You remember Louise.' It was not a question.

'Of course, how are you?' Georgie turned towards the exquisite image and forced a smile.

'Very well,' replied Louise. 'It's a great party. Alistair made such a witty speech.'

God, she was flawless. Glossed lips, flossed teeth and tossed hair. Georgie was conscious that her own make-up had been hastily re-applied in the inadequate glow of a five-watt bulb when the cab stopped at the traffic lights. She had forgotten the stiletto shoes she kept for this kind of after-work occasion. They were still in her desk drawer and these low-heeled suede pumps were chic but lacked glamour.

'I'm sorry I wasn't here for your speech,' Georgie said quietly to her husband.

'You didn't miss much,' he replied modestly. In fact he was an accomplished speaker. He always spoke off the cuff, using as a memory prompt only a small card bearing names of people to thank. He had the kind of cultured voice which gave him an air of authority without sounding affected. When asked the secret of his skill as a speaker, he replied, only half-jokingly, 'Simple. If you haven't struck oil after thirty seconds, stop boring and sit down.'

Georgie noticed a world-renowned French sculptor hovering. She raised an eyebrow at Alistair and moved her eyes in the direction of the artist. Dutifully Alistair turned, to be enveloped in an embrace by the Frenchman who had made his name coating buildings in cellophane.

After two double kisses, the artist and Alistair began talking volubly in his native language. Georgie confidently joined in, being fluent in French. She was aware of Louise listening in silence and was relieved to see that after a while the slim figure stepped back and melted into the crowd.

When the artist had moved on, Alistair touched Georgie's shoulder. 'Thank you for coming. You look whacked, I bet all you wanted to do was go home.'

Georgie felt a flush of annoyance. It did her ego no favours to be reminded how tired she appeared but she recognised he was expressing concern, albeit tactlessly, and she made a determined effort to enter into the spirit of the evening.

After nearly an hour, when her legs seemed to be unconnected to her body, Georgie could not face the idea of dinner and whispered to Alistair, 'Do you think we can go now?'

He was about to answer when one of his prime advertisers tapped his shoulder, wanting a few private words, and she saw he was stuck. While she waited, Georgie examined the thinning crowd, searching for one face in particular. Louise was nowhere to be seen. Good.

At last Alistair was free and Georgie, drooping with exhaustion, told him she was desperate to go home. He frowned. 'I have to take a few people to dinner. Can't you come? I'd really appreciate it.'

'Alistair, I've been up since six.'

'I know, working on your presentation,' he said blandly.

'And other things.'

'Some of the Americans coming to dinner are pretty influential. I'd have thought you wanted a chance to shine.' He grinned. 'I don't want to take unfair advantage.'

'Thanks, but I don't think I could stay awake, I'm dead beat.' She could not bear the idea of going out where the conversation was likely to be in at least three languages.

'All right, but if you are disappearing, can I suggest you do it as swiftly as possible. I'll make your excuses.' He leaned over and putting his face close to hers whispered, 'I wish you'd make the effort. You know I would back you if things were reversed.'

And without waiting for a reply he moved towards two of his dinner guests, linking arms with a husband and wife who had moved their agency from an atelier in Nantes to a penthouse on Fifth Avenue with *Art World*'s help.

Dismayed, Georgie turned abruptly, threading her way through the crowd towards the heavy doors of the ballroom. Thank God Louise had disappeared before she did. Exhausted as she was, the way she felt about that woman she could not have left Alistair alone at the party. It wasn't that she didn't trust him, she didn't trust Louise.

As she made her way swiftly through the reception

area, she saw no sign of the woman. Thankfully there was a row of taxis at the kerbside and Georgie hurled into the back seat of one.

As soon as Georgie's taxi had disappeared, a phone booth door opened and after a rapid glance in the mirror to check her make-up, Louise Palmer strolled back to the ballroom.

The nimble fingers flew over the computer keys in Georgie's office. It was in darkness apart from the glow of the monitor. Familiar with the layout of the room, the operator had long ago discovered that the door key was secreted in the drawer of a desk in the reception area.

Damn. The password to allow access to the computer had been changed. The operator tried every combination connected with the couple – their marriage date, Georgie's birthday, Alistair's birthday, the day of the Fenton takeover, the licence number of both their cars, even Georgie's middle name. None of them worked.

It was coming close to the limit of half an hour when the security officer would do his rounds. Though the operator was a fixture around the place it was stupid to draw attention to oneself. If this didn't work, Harry would be extremely pissed off. He needed to know what was in this presentation. But how to find the bloody password? People always used figures or numbers that were easy to remember and had relevance to their own lives. Didn't the Drummonds once own a cat in the early days of their marriage? Reluctantly they had given the animal to the little girl in the next street because they were out so much, but what was it called? Ah yes, Angus. Unfortunately the name did not yield access. The operator was about to switch off the computer in disgust when the hand paused. Of course, the cat's name was an abbreviation of angostura, a joke about Alistair's fondness for gin and bitters. With happy certainty the letters A N G O S were keyed in and instantly the screen came alive and offered up its files.

The following morning the only voice to be heard in the Drummond household was that of John Humphrys giving some Cabinet minister grief. The antagonism on the radio was matched in the kitchen as Georgie and Alistair separately prepared their fast-track breakfasts. Both believed they had right on their side.

Georgie was painfully aware that Alistair was still annoyed because she had not gone to the dinner. He made it obvious by every movement of his body. She had been asleep by the time he had come home but had woken up briefly to look at the clock. This morning she was showered and dressed before he appeared in the kitchen.

She was very keen to know how Louise had managed to inveigle an invitation to the party, especially since Alistair had commented how rigorously he was having to ration the tickets. But she was not going to be the first to mention the bloody woman's name.

When they had politely skirted each other twice at the fridge door, Georgie decided she had to speak because she could not stand the tension.

'You didn't get in till late,' she said. It had been two thirty-eight.

'One o'clock or thereabouts isn't that late to entertain important guests.'

She wondered why he had bothered to lie about the time of his return home. 'Important guests? Your old mates, more like.'

'Oh yes? I love taking out people like Ned Mastrianni's right-hand guy and his cohorts. By the way, they asked where you were.'

'What did you say?'

'I covered for you, I didn't say you were knackered, if that's what you're worried about.'

'So who else was there?'

'The usual suspects, few of whom spoke English.' He smiled. 'Franco and Henri did that vodka-testing duel again. I bet they have the mother of hangovers this morning.'

Georgie went to the hob to pour herself another cup of coffee. Alistair packed his briefcase. He gave her a cursory kiss on the cheek and made for the door.

'You off so soon?' she asked, irritated that she hadn't been able to raise the worry on her mind.

'Yes, I'm in a rush. See you in the office,' he said cheerily.

How had Louise obtained an invitation and why was she at the party? It could only be to see Alistair again. Georgina had the unwelcome thought that the first Mrs Drummond gave every impression that sex was for recreation not procreation, whereas for Alistair their love life was dominated not by eroticism and rapture but temperature and ovulation cycles. Though both agreed it was necessary and hopefully temporary, Georgie was conscious that, apart from that exciting interlude in the executive cloakroom and in Mougins, all too frequently this timetable blunted inventiveness. How could there be any mystery, any allure when you had ringed the dates to have sex many weeks in advance?

Recalling Alistair's amused face as he had gazed down at Louise, Georgie shivered. Had he always regarded her as second best? She instantly reprimanded herself for being so melodramatic. There might have been a time when Alistair was mourning Louise but he was well over her by the time he had met her. She was worn out, that was why she was feeling vulnerable. Of course Alistair loved her.

Nevertheless, preoccupied and troubled, she set off for work.

She was finishing off a memo to her advertising manager when a smiling face appeared at her office door.

'You look like you're trying to solve the problems of the world,' said Josephine. 'And failing.'

Georgie leaned back in her chair. 'Come in. I could do with some cheering up,' she said. It wasn't long before she was describing the events of the previous night to a sympathetic ear. 'And you should've seen the way he was lapping up the attention. He was staring at her like a mesmerised ferret. Jo, she's stunning. Her skin's like a peach. I couldn't see a single blemish and believe me I was searching.'

'I can't believe I'm hearing this. You know Alistair's mad about you. A long time ago we used to say he'd flirt with dirt but from the instant he met you, you've never had a moment's worry, have you?'

Impatiently Georgie shook her head. 'But don't you see, with any other woman, he was in the driving seat. Not with Louise. She's the only woman who's ditched him. She's unfinished business. Seeing her again couldn't have happened at a worse time. We're going through a down phase.'

'You two have the best marriage of anyone I know. You'll get through this.'

'I suppose you're right.' Georgie was anxious not to appear paranoid. But then Josephine hadn't set eyes on the first Mrs Drummond.

The sight of Margery Conlan, the widow's extra ear, as she had come to be known, walking into their offices caused a flutter amongst the staff. The reason for her tour of the departments seemed a little odd, but nobody had the temerity to question her.

The first three to be asked if they could identify the woman in the drawing were plainly eager to be of assistance but could not help. It was only when Margery widened her search to include the fashion departments that she had some success.

'Definitely Chanel,' pronounced one of the fashion editors who was on her way out but stopped to examine the sketch. 'I saw it at the Paris collections. Costs an arm and a leg, of course, but from the reaction of the buyers, they thought it would be a winner.'

The fashion editor had not been at the memorial service but she was certain she had seen the woman somewhere. Margery tried to contain her impatience as the woman dredged her memory to think where.

'Sorry,' she said finally. 'I'll go through my diary, maybe it'll jog my memory.'

'Can you do it now?' said Margery firmly, making it clear this was not a request.

'I can't, I'm already late for a show. It'll take me a little time,' she opened her bag to show Margery a bulging Filofax, 'but I'll get back to you as soon as I can,' and rushed through the door.

Margery had to be satisfied with that but, true to her word, a couple of hours later the fashion editor rang from a designer's showroom.

'I can't be certain,' she said, raising her voice over the noise, 'but she's the same shape and hairstyle as a woman who was at the *Art World* party.'

What on earth was she doing there? thought Margery. There was only one way to find out and she went round to Alistair's office but there was no sign of him. Disappointed, she set off for the third floor. Maybe the *Art World* editor could help.

He remembered the woman well. 'Delightful person. We had a long talk. I thought she was a model at first but she's searching for gallery premises in Mayfair. She says she'll invite me to the opening when she signs a lease.'

Margery smiled. 'Good. Do you know her name?' She

held her breath but the editor shook his head regretfully.

'I'm sorry, I don't. I've a great memory for faces, especially one like hers, but I'm lousy on names.' He turned to his secretary, showing her the sketch. 'Any ideas?'

'Sorry, no,' said the young woman in clipped tones.

'We must know who she is, for God's sake,' snapped the editor. 'It was our party, after all.'

'We can't look her up on the guest list because you can't remember her name,' said his secretary unhelpfully.

He sighed then brightened. 'Maybe she gave me a card. Hang on. I usually put them in my diary.'

'Sometimes, if we're lucky,' muttered the secretary, turning back to her computer.

The editor began rummaging around his desk. 'Now what have we here?' He fished out a pocket diary and began flicking through the pages. 'I can't be sure but . . . ah, here's the night of the party. And here it is,' he said with a triumphant glance at his secretary's rigid back. He looked at the card. 'Charles Bilsky, no, that's not her. Hang on.'

Margery tried to contain her impatience.

'What do you know, I made a note to send her some back copies.'

'If you can find her card,' floated the comment from his secretary.

'Anyway, here's her surname, right here. "Send BCs", that's back copies, "to . . . something Palmer". I'm pretty sure that's right. The initial is,' he squinted, 'I. Or maybe L.' He grinned. 'I'd had quite a lot of champers that night.'

Margery was impervious to his boyish charm. 'But you don't know where her card is?'

'It's here all right,' he gestured to an overflowing desk. 'We'll keep searching.' He turned to his secretary. 'Won't we, sweetheart?'

She scowled.

The editor gave Margery a sly look. 'If you find her number before I do, will you let me have it?'

Margery retraced her steps to Helen's office. Something Palmer. And she was negotiating premises for an art gallery in central London. Well, she thought, she wouldn't tell Helen yet but surely any investigator could find the missing pieces of the jigsaw from that information?

# Chapter Fourteen

Immersed in compiling facts, figures, concepts and projects, the cornerstone of her presentation, Georgie tried to shut out her personal problems. She only partly succeeded. At the oddest times, when she was waiting for figures to appear on the computer screen or trying to forecast advertising revenue, her mind would wander and she would try to make sense of the past few days. How the hell had she and Alistair drifted into this downward spiral in such a short time?

At home, things appeared normal on the surface. They talked, smiled, watched the same television shows. But both were aware they weren't together in the way they used to be. For the first time, Georgie filtered her thoughts before she spoke to him, hesitating before discussing Amalgamated Magazines and their jobs. She stuck to non-contentious subjects like the difficulties with the car park and the new computer system. Alistair seemed only too happy to avoid tricky subjects and of course neither mentioned Louise or the short list.

Georgie had been accustomed to using Alistair as her

sounding board and she missed that aspect of their relationship. She resolved to shake off her lethargy by trying to do something positive. What she needed were pointers on how to impress on the interview panel that she was not the token woman candidate but a substantial contender.

She turned to Susan Merrill, an executive coach whom she had met a year before while attending a seminar. Susan trained high-fliers in blue-chip corporations on how they could be more effective. She claimed to be able to turn any company mouse into a lion, given the right conditions.

Georgie's request appealed to the American guru.

'The reason American women are more successful in getting to the top,' she advised, 'is that they're taught that any belief that doesn't lead towards success is a lie. So let go of any negative thoughts and focus on why you would be a great chief executive for your organisation.'

Georgie was guided through the most effective ways she could make a powerful impression on Helen and the interview panel, and after the session she floated home on a cloud of optimism.

An interview panel could apparently make up its mind within six seconds of the applicant walking through the door so she opened her wardrobe to choose an outfit for the big day. After discarding several black suits, she decided on a bottle-green two-piece suit, a colour that denoted trustworthiness and competence, according to Susan Merrill. It had brought admiring comments at last week's editorial presentation to advertisers held at the Ritz.

Georgie's body was in good shape although she did not have time for a regular exercise routine. Running up and down the stairs all day long to see her staff rather than using the lifts had paid dividends. And she was careful about what she ate, bingeing only when her oestrogen level collapsed. She fingered the shoulder-length hair that aroused Alistair so much, especially when it fell on his shoulders as they made love. It was beginning to look tousled. She picked up the phone and made an appointment with her hair stylist. It was time for a new image.

That afternoon as she watched the tendrils of hair falling to the salon floor, Georgie had a twinge of anxiety. She had lived with her hair at more or less the same length since she had met Alistair. What would he think of this jaw-length bob? It danced when she made the slightest movement and it made her feel wonderful. And wasn't she following Susan's advice to make her own decisions and stop worrying about their effect on others? Even a husband?

When Georgie returned to the office, the reaction to the radical change in her hairstyle was instantaneous. The girls in the outer office were very complimentary and her secretary, who rarely volunteered personal remarks, also approved.

Georgie felt energised and purposeful. She called a meeting of all the editors in her group, and gave her secretary a long list of people she wanted to speak to as soon as possible. They included the head of Helena Rubinstein in New York, the advertising chief of BMW in Stuttgart and the boss of the Parisian publishing company she had been wooing for weeks. The French company was considering a deal to franchise spin-offs from several of her titles. It would mean forming a new joint imprint which could create endless merchandising opportunities. Being busy exhilarated her.

By the end of the working day, Georgie had chased up a list of ideas from her staff and was working on an enticing project which, if she was lucky, would come to fruition in time to include in her business plan. She had achieved a great deal in a short time and was glad she had overcome her cynicism and booked the session with Susan Merrill. This new-found optimism alone made it worthwhile.

She was wrestling with the profitability of *Visage*, a magazine devoted to beauty, when Alistair appeared carrying two coffees. He grinned at her and said, 'Like your new hairdo, missus.'

His visit could not have come at a better time and Georgie began discussing *Visage*'s problem almost as soon as he sat down.

'The editor and her staff feel a sword is hanging over their heads, not good for morale especially at a time like this. And as you know, worry expands to other magazines.'

Alistair nodded and flicked through the copy on her desk, hot off the press. 'It's good,' he said.

'And it's well-established but it needs more pages. But

more pages means more paper and higher print costs, and look at these figures.'

He came over to stand closely behind her, studying the screen. 'What about trying a fresh layout, busier, more boxes?' He leaned across, touching her shoulder, and switched to the layout design screen and began swiftly moving the mouse. 'Something like this.'

As the layout unfolded, the possibilities became apparent and Georgie was excited by them. She began to amend his ideas, suggesting a slightly different format and type style. They had a robust discussion about the appearance of the cover, scribbling on yellow pads, comparing them with the screen, changing, moving – their differences totally forgotten in the heat of their creativity.

Couldn't it always be like this, whatever happened about the job?

They were so relaxed with each other. Of course they were sticking to business. She had been very careful not to make one personal remark and neither had he. But it was great to laugh and talk freely with him, even if it was confined to magazines.

It had been a good day.

Louise's elation, in contrast, had evaporated. How could she have been mistaken? How could she have misread the signs at the party? Still no phone call from Alistair.

She had chosen the body-hugging peach silk dress because it always got results. When she had inveigled herself into the dinner after the party by chatting up an

Italian sculptor, she had positioned herself in Alistair's eyeline. Not next to him, which would be far too obvious, but opposite, where the dress could do its work.

Across the long, narrow table she had noticed his eyes sweeping across her, regularly, like the beam from a lighthouse. As he turned to talk to someone on his right, his gaze would seek her out on the way there and again when he turned back to his neighbour on the left. She had got through to him, she knew she had.

So why didn't the bastard phone? Louise was not used to being ignored by men. Maybe the current Mrs Drummond had a stronger hold on him than was apparent that night. She could hardly be described as beautiful, certainly not in her league, but that implied Alistair had fallen for her personality rather than her appearance, which could be more difficult to deal with.

Alistair intrigued her. Yes, she needed his help to establish an art gallery but that was only part of it. He had matured into someone substantial, reminding her of Mark in many ways, his *savoir faire*, his confidence, his intelligence, his humour.

Rosemary had said her brother's marriage was fraying at the edges. Perhaps it was time to tweak the threads. If she pulled hard enough, maybe she could unravel it entirely.

The last person in the world Georgie expected to receive a phone call from that afternoon was Alistair's first wife.

When her secretary announced that Louise Palmer wanted to speak to her, her heart started racing. She could think of no reason why this woman would want to talk to her and her first instinct was to pretend to be out. Then she reproved herself for being a coward and told her secretary to put the call through. She had to admit she was curious to know why Louise was phoning.

She picked up the receiver and said a composed, 'Hello.'

'Georgina,' the voice was throaty, a hint of a smile behind it, 'I know you must be surprised to hear from me but I wondered if you and Alistair would like to come to one of my dinners to launch my art gallery.'

'Art gallery?'

'Yes, it's at the earliest of stages,' said Louise lightly, 'and I know you're very busy but I'd very much like you both to come.'

'I'm not sure . . .'

'I hope you're not going to let ancient history get in the way.'

'Certainly not,' said Georgie carefully. She was damned if she was going to let this woman know how disconcerted she was.

'After all, Alistair and I were married in another lifetime. It doesn't mean we can't all be friends, does it?'

'Of course not,' said Georgie in her politest tone. 'The problem is our diary is pretty jam-packed. When is this dinner?'

'Any Wednesday during the next three months,' said Louise, sounding amused.

Damn. Only the Pope and the Prime Minister were booked up that far ahead.

'May I let you know?' parried Georgie.

'Of course,' said Louise. 'I hope you'll be able to come. The art world's a village so I know I'll be running into Alistair now and then but I'd love to see you both.'

Georgie did not know how to respond to this and as she hesitated Louise went on, 'May I be candid? Although the gallery will be quite small, I do want it to be successful and . . . oh dear, this is difficult. I'm worried that Alistair won't be able to help me because of you. That's why I want us to meet.'

'Well, send the invitation,' said Georgie pleasantly.

'The dinner will be at my flat, so much cosier than any restaurant, don't you think? It isn't far from you.'

So she knows where we live, thought Georgie.

'It's in Melford Court, number five.'

Very Georgian. Very over-priced. Very near.

'I'll see what we can do,' answered Georgie with a note of finality in her voice.

'Fine. I've already mentioned it to Alistair.'

'At the *Art World* party?'

'No, at the dinner afterwards at Antonia's.'

Georgie went very still. Alistair had not told her Louise was at the dinner, and he had not told her it was in an exclusive, dimly-lit nightclub.

She knew she was being unwise but she couldn't help saying, 'Alistair's so busy with his job it'll be difficult for him to help you. I'd advise you to concentrate on your other contacts instead.'

After a pause, Louise said softly, 'You have no intention of coming to my dinner, do you?'

When Georgie made no answer Louise said, 'Let me give you some advice. I know Alistair and if I were in your position and had to choose between a job and a baby, I know which one would make him happier.'

Georgie slammed down the phone, seething. She walked quickly to Alistair's office and knocked once. She opened the door then had to adopt a bland expression when she saw a roomful of people staring at her.

That was the problem with working together, one wrong word or glance could lead to a buzz of gossip throughout the building.

'Can I have a word, please?' she said, trying to sound unhurried.

As his colleagues rose to leave, Alistair held up a hand. 'No, you carry on. I'll be back in a minute.' He took Georgie's arm and guided her into the interview room where they could be guaranteed some privacy.

'What's up?' he asked, closing the door.

'Why did you discuss our private business with Louise?'

'What the hell are you on about?'

'She's been on the phone giving me advice on how to run our marriage, if you please.'

Alistair appeared bewildered. 'Louise phoned you?'

'Her excuse was to ask us to dinner but really she wanted to tell me she knew intimate details of our life. She wanted to humiliate me.'

'I don't know anything about this,' said Alistair, shaking his head.

'She said she talked to you.'

'Sure, at the memorial service. And at the *Art World* party. You were there both times.'

'How did she get an invitation to that party?'

'I have absolutely no idea.' When Georgie frowned he added quickly, 'It certainly wasn't from me. We've never talked about anything personal.'

'She says the two of you had dinner afterwards.'

'No, we didn't. At least . . .'

'Yes?'

'It was hardly the romantic meal your imagination has no doubt conjured up. There were twelve others present.'

'Why didn't you tell me she was there?' she asked.

'It was the dinner you didn't want to come to, remember? Did you want me to wake you up and tell you the guest list and the menu?'

'But why haven't you said anything about her since? I wondered why you got home so late.'

'You didn't leave that party till gone eleven and it took us another half an hour to round everyone up and you know how busy it is at Antonia's.'

'You danced with her?'

'Don't be silly. Nobody danced.'

'Who asked her to dinner?'

'I think one of the French did.'

'She doesn't speak their language. Oh, silly me. Of course. They speak hers.'

'Don't make cheap remarks, it doesn't suit you.'

'What happened after I left that party?'

Alistair folded his arms and faced her square on. 'I have a room full of people waiting for me, I have three calls I need to make to Paris before they go home but you insist I tell you about a stupid dinner at which nothing happened which concerned you or our marriage.'

Georgie caught sight of her face in one of the gold-framed mirrors. God, she looked grim. She tried to relax her features.

Sounding irritated, Alistair began to recite in a monotone the precise timetable of events after she had left the hotel. It made Georgie realise how devious Louise had been. She had been convinced that Louise had left the hotel. Where had she been hiding?

'You're making all this fuss about Louise and I didn't even sit next to her,' Alistair continued. 'So even if I had wanted to, which I don't, I didn't have the opportunity to discuss our marriage with her.'

Georgie's voice, low yet forceful, came at him like an Exocet missile. 'Then how the hell does she know we've had rows about having a baby?'

He stared at her. 'She doesn't.'

'She does.'

'Not from me.'

'Who else could have told her?'

'I don't know. If you'd bothered to come to the dinner, we wouldn't be having this row,' said Alistair hotly. 'And why didn't you come? Because nowadays you don't think of anything else but that cursed job. Not about having a baby, not how you can back me up, not how I want my wife with me on these sort of occasions, nothing. Only your ambition.'

219

'The best line of defence is always to attack.'

'Ever since you were put on the short list you've become impossible to live with.'

'I suppose you'd prefer to go home to someone like Louise.'

'I think you've said enough,' he retorted and walked out, slamming the door.

Harry ordered up a couple of glasses of Chablis for himself and his companion before settling into one of the booths that lined the room of the basement wine bar.

His colleague's tone was anxious. 'It's not good. Alistair's too far in front. I think we're wasting our time.'

'Toughen up,' said Harry. 'None of that defeatist talk from you.'

'Not defeatist, realistic. Ned's candidature was always a long shot, let's face it.'

'I don't agree. I've done a lot of lobbying and several people have pledged their support,' said Harry.

'Name them.'

Harry reeled off three names.

'Minnows.' The tone was scathing.

'All right but I've only started. Remember, I'll have the chance to push things Ned's way on the interview panel.' Harry lifted his glass and frowned. 'We need to make trouble between Alistair and Georgie.'

'Why?' asked his companion.

'If you're fighting a battle on only one front, you've more chance of winning it than if you're fighting on two.'

'I don't think we'll be able to manage that. How can we control their relationship?'

'It's not as difficult as you think. Remember those figures we found on Georgina's computer?'

'The reduction in paper costs? What about them?'

'She's such a precise little cat, I wondered if she'd done any more work on the overall costs. So I listened to more of the last tape.'

'And who suggested placing that bug in Georgie's office?'

'Yes, and who said it'd be difficult to run the company from a prison cell?' He laughed mirthlessly and continued, 'It's been pretty useless so far. If I hear Rosemary gush to her about Alistair one more time I'll puke. Anyway, I've come up with something. Remember the Fenton takeover included everything except their printing offshoot?'

'What of it?'

'On the tape I heard clever little Georgina having a cosy chat with her old boss. Roger Fenton's not only re-equipped his old printing works, he's spent all that lovely merger money on two more. One company's in France, the other's in Spain.'

'Why hasn't there been any publicity about it?'

'Georgina asked him the same question. He told her he's kept it under wraps and wants to surprise everyone, mainly the City, with a great comeback. He's been hiding behind a holding group and he has other people to negotiate for him.'

'So?'

'So by the time our printing contracts have expired, Fenton's presses will all be bedded in, ready for action. If Madam switches a few magazines or any new launch to Fenton now, he's promised to undercut whatever printing costs his rivals come up with by at least ten per cent.'

'Smart move on Fenton's part. If he helps his old protégée get the job, his company's in pole position for more contracts from us.'

'Exactly.' Harry sipped the wine. 'God, this is terrible stuff. Anyway, our Georgina was being very canny on the phone. She dangled a non-exec directorship in front of him and he loved the idea.'

His companion was impressed. 'She'll make this print reduction one of the main planks of her presentation and it'll go down bloody well. There's nothing they love more than creatives who are also good with money.'

Harry smirked. 'So wouldn't it irritate her if Alistair happened to come up with the same idea with the same firm?'

Whenever Harry wished to de-stabilise someone, he would make a judicious phone call at lunchtime when they were bound to be out wining and dining. Forecasts of a major drop in circulation for their magazine, criticism of a cover picture from the buyer of a huge supermarket chain or a complaint about the current issue from a leading wholesaler would be left on their desks to await their return. It would unsettle the executives far more than hearing it direct, when they could ask pertinent questions. They would worry, too, about how many others in the department had seen the message.

Today Harry had been busy. After obtaining the name of a certain executive working at the Fenton company, Harry used his mobile to phone Alistair's office at 1.40 p.m. precisely, certain that the call would be taken by a secretary. Lowering his voice an octave, he introduced himself as Greg Streeter, sales manager for Roger Fenton. He outlined the proposal he had gleaned from the bugged phone conversation and suggested to the secretary that this might be something Alistair would like to discuss further. He left the main Fenton switchboard number and his name.

It took only a short time to discover the ploy had worked. An elated Alistair came round later that afternoon to tell him how Fenton's had rung him up out of the blue offering the possibility of a cut-price printing contract.

'It seems a dynamite deal,' said Alistair. 'They're prepared to pare down to the bone to get new business. I'm going to give the sales manager a ring and ask for the deal to be put in writing.'

Yes, but I suggest you keep this under your hat,' said Harry. 'Save it for your presentation. It could be the clincher for the job.'

'No, saving this amount of cash for the company is more important than my pitch. We need to move fast on this one. I'm telling Helen right now.'

Harry did not argue. If Helen heard about the Fenton deal first from Alistair that would put Georgina in an embarrassing situation to say the least when she made it a major part of her presentation. There would be fire-works all along the line.

When Alistair described the deal to Helen, she was quick to congratulate him.

'This could make a useful difference to our bottom line. And it's natural justice in a way that Roger Fenton is going to do well out of Amalgamated. I always thought Mark took advantage of him when his cash flow problems erupted,' she said.

At that moment her secretary buzzed through. 'Miss Luckhurst asks if you have a minute to discuss the memo.'

'What memo?'

'I put it on your desk about an hour ago.'

'I haven't had a chance to read it. Ask her to come in anyway,' said Helen, picking up the memo and scanning the first few lines.

There was a tap on the door and Georgie entered.

'How extraordinary, have you two been doing some pillow talk?' asked Helen.

The pair exchanged puzzled glances.

'Alistair came in to tell me about a printing deal with Roger Fenton and you, Georgina, have sent me this memo on exactly the same subject.'

Georgie sat down and turned to Alistair. 'Who told you about this?'

'Greg Streeter, Fenton's sales director, phoned me.'

'How could he? Roger and I worked it out in confidence. No one else knew about it.'

'However we got it,' said Helen, 'it's great for the

company.' She gave a little laugh. 'If this works out, our profits will go up considerably.' She scanned Georgie's carefully-worked out figures. 'Impressive.'

This was not the time to argue. Georgie quickly realised that it would be Helen's reputation which would profit most and it did not matter to her who had come up with the idea.

As they emerged from Helen's office, Alistair caught Georgie's arm. 'I'm sure there's some logical explanation.'

'There must be.'

'Maybe Fenton's are so keen to do a deal they're using both of us.'

'I don't buy that. Roger Fenton is a very particular man. If he says it's secret, it is.' She strode determinedly down the corridor.

'Then why did they phone me?' he called out to her retreating back.

'Why indeed?' muttered Georgie, but he missed that. There was something odd about this and she was going to get to the bottom of it.

Georgie did not return to the flat until late. It was a wet, chilly night, all the parking spaces in their street had been taken and she was obliged to put the car in the next street. However many umbrellas she kept in the car, there was never one there when it was needed and by the time she reached home she was drenched.

She stripped off and was towelling her hair vigorously when Alistair came into the bedroom.

'Darling,' he said, concerned, 'you're so late. I thought you were coming home straight from work. Why didn't you phone? I would have picked you up.'

She bent over to pull out a tracksuit. He moved behind her, cradling her buttocks in his hands. 'You're not in a hurry to eat, are you?'

Instead of answering, Georgie bent down lower. He was hard against her and he took the movement of her body as encouragement. But she was scrabbling in her handbag and abruptly stood up and flung a small white matchbox-sized object on to the bed.

He straightened abruptly and peered at it. 'What is that, some kind of transmitter? Where did you find it?'

'I phoned Roger Fenton. He couldn't understand how our deal had got out and he suggested I had my office swept for bugs.'

'And this is what you found?' He picked it up to examine it more closely.

'Just think,' said Georgie, her eyes as hard as industrial diamonds, 'that little thing can pick up every word of a private conversation I had last week.'

'You're not suggesting . . . Are you accusing me?'

'Of course not but it's so strange. The sales manager swears he didn't phone you. You phoned him.'

'In that case someone left a message in his name.'

'Alistair—'

'Unless you think I'm lying, that I did plant a bug in your office to steal your ideas. Maybe you believe I do this all the time. Have you checked there isn't a bug under your pillow in case you talk in your sleep?'

Georgie sagged on to the bed. 'I hate all this.'

He sat down next to her. 'I'm telling the truth, you have to believe me.'

'I do,' she said softly and he put his arm round her. 'You're tired and you're still wet.' He stroked her damp hair. 'I think you need some pasta inside you and some wine.' She nodded and he added, 'It works for Italians.'

Georgie tried to smile.

'Friends?' he asked.

She nodded but inside gnawing at her were a lot of unanswered questions.

The following day the surveillance expert was engaged to sweep the executive suite of offices. Nothing was discovered. But an itemised record of telephone calls supplied by Fenton's confirmed the sales director's version of events. Alistair could not explain this.

'I can only tell you the truth,' he told Georgie.

'It doesn't add up.'

He hesitated. 'There can be only one explanation. I've been set up, no doubt about it. Both of us have. But by whom?'

They stared at each other then Georgie gave a heavy sigh. 'Who had the most to profit by embarrassing me with Helen?'

Alistair raised his eyebrows. 'You do believe me, don't you?'

'Yes . . . oh, I don't know what to believe any more.'

Alistair contemplated her thoughtfully then stood up. 'Rosemary's asked us to supper tonight but I think it'd be best if I go alone. And as I need to drink I shall probably stay the night.'

'Why?' she asked, startled.

'Because I find your confidence in my innocence somewhat under-whelming. Being apart might concentrate our minds. In any case, you're going to Milan first thing, aren't you?'

This was the first time Alistair had suggested a need to be apart. Hurt pride made her lash out. 'All right, if that's what you want. Stay at your sister's place. After all, you won't have to make excuses or lie to her about what you've been doing or where you've been, will you?'

Alistair shook his head and Georgie marched back to her office. As her anger subsided, she was left with a feeling of bleakness and the distinct impression that a seminal moment had been reached in her marriage.

Lately she had been telling herself that the situation in which they found themselves was a short-term difficulty. However much the executive coach had bolstered her confidence, in her heart Georgie was convinced there was no possibility of her being successful. What was troubling her now was whether things had gone too far. Would she and Alistair ever return to how they had been before, regardless of who got the job? In the past they had always been able to reason, to talk things through. Slamming down phones, shouting, walking away in the middle of an argument was not their style.

Could she leave it like that? Their marriage was the best thing in her life. She had to believe it could be good again. She was appalled that Alistair was, for the first time, spending a night away from her by choice. When travelling on business he made great efforts to get back even when it meant a late flight. Staying at his sister's flat would only deepen the chasm between them.

Quickly she walked across the corridor to his office but the room was in darkness. Could he have gone home to pick up his overnight things? If so, she might catch him there. She must persuade him that the way to solve their problems was to talk them over, not to disappear to his sister's.

When she rushed into the flat, there was a faint glimmer of light coming from underneath the bathroom door, visible from the hall. Georgie called out his name and hurried towards the light but the bathroom was empty. Worse, his shaving kit and toothbrush were gone and his dressing-room wardrobe door was half open with shirts in disarray. He must have been very upset to leave in such a hurry.

As usual his mobile was switched off. These days he preferred to use it only for outgoing calls. Should she drive round to Rosemary's place in south London? She dialled Rosemary's number but the answer machine cut in after two rings and Georgie groaned, remembering they had arranged to go out for dinner.

She needed him to know she had been trying to contact him and that their quarrel should be patched up now before it festered. It was a very personal message to leave on a tape but she felt she had to do it.

She took a deep breath. 'Alistair, I love you,' she said, trying to steady the tremor in her voice. 'I don't want us to fight like this. Being apart is no solution. Don't you think we should talk things over? Please phone me at home.'

She settled back to wait for his call.

Rosemary was just leaving her flat to drive to the restaurant and turned back at the sound of the phone ringing. She was about to pick it up when she identified Georgie's number coming up on the dial. She hesitated then listened intently to the emotionally-charged message. When the call ended, she leaned over and pressed the erase button before switching off the machine.

Alistair should never have married a career woman, thought Rosemary as she drove to the restaurant. Patently they wanted different things from life. The longer Alistair was apart from Georgie, the more likely it was that he would realise he was better off without her. Rosemary knew she was taking a chance in not mentioning the message because Georgina might ask why he had not rung her back. But answer machines had been known to go wrong and no one could prove she had been in the flat to hear it.

She was not being unfair, Alistair was deeply unhappy about Georgie being on that short list and he had made it perfectly clear that he did not want to be in competition with his wife. If Georgie was committed to her marriage, why didn't she withdraw her name? Had the woman no loyalty to Alistair?

He was such a steadfast soul he would want to stick to his vows. But didn't he deserve better? Rosemary couldn't see why he should spend the rest of his life compromising. He wouldn't if she could help it, and Louise could be a useful catalyst to help this estrangement become more permanent.

Georgie gave Rosemary the impression that she believed Alistair still carried a torch for Louise. She didn't think Georgie was right. Louise's motives for wanting to meet Alistair seemed straightforward enough. On the face of it, wanting his help to put the art gallery on the map sounded perfectly reasonable and Louise had made a point of saying that her marriage to Alistair was so far in the past that it had no relevance now. This had the ring of truth. Certainly Rosemary doubted if her brother would allow himself to be controlled by his first wife again. It had cost him too dear. But it would be easy enough to fuel Georgie's jealousy.

# Chapter Fifteen

The trip to Milan involved an overnight stay at the world-famous Villa de Teatro. The hotel had a five-star rating in the Michelin guide and was renowned for its fountain-filled gardens and its statuary. Outsiders would have been surprised by the lack of enthusiasm shown by Georgie and Josephine at having to attend an event at such a legendary watering hole.

Both had tried to find a valid excuse not to accept. The pressure to keep to punishing new printing schedules meant there was little spare time for non-essentials. The idea of joining an international gathering at the invitation of a major domestic appliance manufacturer to talk about hot spins and crease guard cycles with other editors was low on their wish list of how to spend a day and a half in Italy, even in such luxurious surroundings.

They had toyed with the idea of sending substitutes but the domestic appliance manufacturer had made it clear the invitations were strictly personal. As his company had spent millions of lire on buying advertising space across Amalgamated's titles, he expected the publishing director and her senior editor to attend so Georgie and Josephine had reluctantly decided that this was not a matter for debate.

But they were vexed to discover that the reception was held not in the famous garden but in an over-heated, over-decorated room which didn't have a single window. Georgina's head was buzzing from the previous night's sleeplessness waiting for the call from Alistair which never came, the plane journey at dawn, and the tobacco haze from the enthusiastic Italian smokers. Idly she watched a waiter hurry to a corner of the room. Maybe, like her, he wanted to find some breathing space. She saw him press a large switch, whereupon, to an outburst of applause from the crowd, one entire tapestry-covered wall in the room slowly descended into the floor to reveal the other section of the room.

It was vast and in the centre was a three-hundred-foot table covered in a gold brocade cloth woven, their host proudly boasted, in Tuscany, without a single seam. The room was lit entirely by candles in wrought-iron chandeliers and through the large picture windows, open to the soft early evening breeze, they could see part of the renowned gardens.

Each guest was served a white truffle en-croute, followed by lobster with a puree of potatoes shaped into nests containing Beluga caviar. Delicate canoes of spun sugar holding a portion of wild strawberries were served for pudding. When the doyenne of the American contingent complained that to serve both truffles and caviar was excessive in one meal, a male journalist from Paris snapped, 'That's like complaining about having two orgasms in a row.'

Once the spectacular firework displays had subsided and they had paid their elaborate farewells to their host, Josephine turned to Georgie and said, 'After all this is over I have to find some way of making their bloody washing machines interesting.'

When she suggested a nightcap, Georgie at first demurred, for despite the glittering surroundings, her mood had not lifted. But this was one of the times when she needed to talk to a woman who had only her best interests at heart.

The pair made for the deserted bar where they found two comfortable leather armchairs in the furthest corner of the room and ordered camomile tea. Although Georgie was desperate to plunge straight into talk of her problems, she allowed Josephine several minutes to air her concerns. She was thinking of hiring a male nanny. At four Luke was starting to be interested in playing football and surrounded as he was by women – his mother, grandmother, aunts and cousins – Josephine was beginning to think he needed a male role model.

'I'm prattling on, sorry,' she said at last. 'You're looking worn out.'

'I'm not getting much sleep these days,' said Georgina wearily. 'Things are a bit rough between me and Alistair.'

'I'm sorry, Georgie, I wish there was something I could do. But I'm convinced you'll get through it.'

'I'm not sure we can,' said Georgie gravely and began

telling her friend about the incident involving the Fenton print deal.

'Come on, you're getting carried away, of course Alistair can't have had anything to do with that. You've been spoiled, you know. All marriages go through rough patches.'

'Especially when there's someone waiting to pick up the pieces.'

'Please, don't start with that first wife business again.' Josephine was impatient. 'You can't believe there's anything going on between her and Alistair.'

'Can't I? He lied to me about seeing her for dinner,' and Georgie recounted their row after the *Art World* party.

Josephine's expression changed. 'Are you sure you're not making too much of this?'

'I don't know but if she's making herself available, is it beyond the realms of possibility that he would take what she's offering?'

'That's quite a leap.'

'Whenever Louise's name crops up, I always imagine the worst,' said Georgie. 'She's a man's woman, that one. Knows exactly what to do, what to say.'

'Alistair wouldn't throw away everything you two have.'

'A week ago I would have agreed with you. Today I'm not at all sure.'

In Rosemary's spare room Alistair loosened his tie and sat down on the bed. His sister rarely had people to stay and although she had made an effort, placing fresh flowers at his bedside, the place had an unlived-in air. He sighed, thinking of his own comfortable, welcoming familiar bedroom at home, his lovely wife, invariably reading, and, when he appeared, instantly throwing her papers to the floor.

He was unnerved by the conversation he'd had with his sister the night before in the restaurant. It had started over the pasta. He had pushed away his plate almost untouched.

'You must eat,' she fussed. 'You need to stay strong.'

Alistair grimaced. 'That's what you used to tell me when I was a kid.'

Rosemary put her hand over his. 'You'll never be alone while I'm around. I promised Dad I'd always take care of you and I will. Even if you and Georgie don't get back together again, I'll be here.'

'Come off it, Rosie. It's not the end. You don't really think that, do you?' Despite himself, Alistair was alarmed.

'I've never lied to you,' Rosemary answered quietly, 'and I'm not going to start now.' She started twisting her hands, something she always did when she felt stressed. 'You and Georgie want different things from life, darling.'

'I used not to think so.'

'You're ready to settle down and have a family and she hasn't reached that stage yet. And now with this job . . .' She shrugged. 'It's unfair.'

Alistair put his head in his hands. 'I want a baby but

that's only one part of it. I love Georgie, I can't imagine living without her.'

'If two people want to patch things up, of course they can,' said Rosemary. 'All I'm saying is to be careful that the marriage you go back to is the kind you want.'

Well, he thought now, the only kind of marriage he wanted was with Georgie. He toyed with a slip of paper bearing her contact number in Milan. He'd never felt less like sleeping. What the hell was happening to them? And how could it have occurred so fast?

He and Georgie had never quarrelled like this before. The last straw was the bugging business. She said she believed he had nothing to do with it but she wasn't behaving as if she did. He'd always thought there ought to be courtesy in marriage. It would take a great deal to forget her distrust of him. But he had to admit to himself that at least one thing was true, his attitude to her inclusion on the short list was hostile, however much he had tried to disguise it. He should not have been so frank about her being considered just because she was a woman. How would he have felt to be told that it was not his ability but his gender that had ensured his selection? In retrospect what he should have done was to have waited until she was bumped off the list and then commiserated with her. The fault lay with Helen. She had fed Georgie ideas that she could be a major player in the firm.

Alistair could not bear the thought of another night without making an effort to heal the breach. He picked up the phone and dialled the number in Milan.

'Georgie? It's me? Did I wake you?'

'It doesn't matter.' Her voice sounded sleepy.

There was a silence and Alistair found himself unable to think of the best way to start. Finally he managed the most banal of remarks. 'How's the hotel?'

'Fine.'

'Is Gianni looking after you?'

'He's away, his wife gave birth to their third this morning.'

Another silence. She was the one who had started it all but she wasn't going to make it easy for him.

'Don't you think we ought to talk about things?' he managed eventually.

'Of course, I've already suggested that.'

'When did you do that?'

'Last night. I left a message on Rosemary's machine.'

'I didn't get it.'

There was no sound for a moment, then she said, 'I'm not surprised she didn't tell you. Haven't you realised your sister is jealous of me?'

'Of course I have and I'm sorry about how she deals with it.'

'I try and ignore the little digs but it's quite difficult sometimes.'

'I'm sorry about that but you have to make allowances. She's always been jealous of anyone who's been near me.'

'That's understandable,' she said promptly. 'So am I.'

Thank God, it was going to be all right. 'Darling,' he said, 'I hate it when we fight.'

'Me too,' she said with a catch in her voice. 'I'm sorry I practically called you a liar over that bugging business. But I was bloody angry and I didn't know what to believe.'

He heard a heavy sigh and said quickly, 'And I'm sorry I wasn't totally frank about Louise being at the dinner. Georgie, you know she means nothing to me.'

'But it's not only about Louise, is it?' Her voice was stronger now. 'I'm worried we have different views on how our lives should go forward.'

Alistair's hand tightened on the receiver. 'I love you. Isn't that enough to solve things, find a compromise?'

'That's easy to say, Alistair.'

'All right, you go first. Tell me what you want.'

'It's not what I want, that's the problem. We both have to want it.'

'I'm trying to understand, Georgie. For God's sake meet me halfway. What exactly do you want?'

'It's the baby business. I don't think I'm being unreasonable to want to postpone all that until the job decision is made. You've told me in no uncertain terms that you disagree. Tell me, how do we resolve that one?'

'You have to look at this in the longer term and decide what's important.'

'There you are, we go round in circles.'

He could hear the sound of her breathing while each waited for the other to speak. He broke the long pause. 'Georgie, I want things to be good between us again. And if that's what makes you happy then I'll have to go along with it.'

'Are you sure? There's no point if you're going to resent it.'

'I'm not but I am compromising. All I want is your word that we'll try for a baby the minute the job decision's made.' Ouch, thought Alistair, once again he had made it clear he didn't think she stood a chance. Luckily Georgie did not react.

'All right,' she said slowly, 'as long as I don't get the job. But you know that means we'll have to take precautions until then.'

'I can't quarrel with that. But take note, when you're knackered because we've been overdoing it, I'll remind you of that.'

'Beast,' she laughed. 'Can you meet me at the airport tomorrow evening?'

'Absolutely.' His voice was completely different. 'I'll count the hours, the minutes, the seconds.'

Her voice also lightened. 'I'm no good being bad friends with you.'

'Good night, friend.'

'Goodnight, I love you.'

'Ditto.'

That night Mr and Mrs Drummond both had their best night's sleep for a week.

When Georgie emerged from Customs at Heathrow's Terminal One the following morning, Alistair was there to present her with a peace offering. Not flowers, not chocolates, but a large bag from the chemist. Invited to peek inside, she counted several packets of assorted condoms.

'When I make a promise,' his eyes had a wicked glint, 'I keep it. That should take care of tonight.'

Georgie squeezed his arm and smiled affectionately.

'I've had quite an educational morning,' he added. 'Condoms would make a great feature. I had no idea there were this many different colours and sizes. You can even get them ribbed. And flavoured.'

'Maybe we've been missing something.'

'Not for long.'

When they reached home, Georgie found a new computer work station set up in the spare room. Alistair had organised it through an IT expert from the office.

'I'll be able to work in here while you have the study,' he explained. 'That'll save us arguing about whose turn it is at the keyboard and it'll give us more R and R together.'

Georgie put her arms round him, conscious that both of them had been shaken out of their complacency. They had been too close to several disintegrating marriages not to heed the warning signs. In their different ways, they were determined that having looked over the edge of the precipice, they would return to the sunlit uplands.

'You mean go out?' she said. 'As in movies, museums, walks in the park?'

'Call me old-fashioned but isn't that what we used to do at weekends?'

'I'm glad we've both been thinking along the same lines. Come along, I want you to see what I brought from Milan, the world's best sweatshirt for you and something else as well.'

She led him into the kitchen where two large brown carrier bags and a package were resting on the table. Alistair was admiring the electric blue sweatshirt when Georgie picked up one of the carriers and swung it from side to side under his nose. He inhaled the pungent aromas appreciatively.

'That smells so . . . Italian. I'm impressed that you took the time to buy all this. I know how frantic those trips are.'

'I wanted to make you pleased that we're back to normal again.'

Alistair put down the sweatshirt. 'I am,' he said gently. 'More than pleased.'

'Should we have some ground rules?' she asked.

'All right, you first.'

'No, you.'

'OK,' he said. 'We don't mention jobs, interviews, presentations or widows.'

'Agreed. And no talking about babies, calendars and time's winged chariot.'

'Agreed. Now, what have we here?' He peered inside the carrier. 'Ah, smoked salmon.'

'Wild, I'll have you know, not farmed,' said Georgie, pulling a selection of olive and onion-flavoured breads from the other bag.

'Truffles,' he put each package on the table, 'smoked duck, cheeses, hmmn. That smell, it's wonderful . . .'

'Someday,' said Georgie, 'I'd like you to look at me the way you're looking at those cheeses.'

'Wear the same stockings for a few weeks and I will.'

'What a Romeo you are.'

They grinned at each other and Alistair moved over and nuzzled her neck. 'If ever you were beginning to think that you weren't my number one priority, you were wrong.'

They were almost shy with each other, like first-time lovers as they kissed unhurriedly, lightly, luxuriating in the feeling that they were about to make love for pleasure and for mutual support rather than to conceive.

Alistair tilted her face and their kisses became more urgent, more prolonged. When they could breathe again, he murmured, 'I've had hours to think about exactly what I want to do with you . . .'

There was a way he gazed at her when he was aroused, as if his eyes were fuelling lasers between them. That look made Georgie shiver with the sheer power, excitement and sensuousness of it.

He led her out of the kitchen, his eyes never once leaving hers. They had made love in every room in the flat though never in the hall and when he made it clear that this was as far as he was taking her, she gave an appreciative half-smile.

He could see the swell of her breasts under her thin blouse and he tore off his tie and undid his top shirt buttons and pulled her roughly towards him. Effortlessly they began to undress one another, no tugging at zips or clasps, movements rapid and dexterous, as they kissed with deep thrusts of their tongues.

She ran her fingers through his thick hair and feverishly licked the hollow between his neck and chest and nibbled his ears. He cupped her breasts in his hands, his lips moving downwards to her nipples, working the same magic on her with his tongue and teeth, and teasing her nipples with feather-light fingertips until they stood taut and erect.

He whispered hoarsely, 'I want to touch you all over, I want to be inside you . . . I want to kiss you here . . . and,' he went lower, 'here . . .' lower still, 'and definitely here . . .'

He was about to enter her when she pulled away gently, her hand reaching out for a packet of condoms lying at her side. For a moment he hesitated then groaned, 'Hurry.'

Impatiently she undid the wrapper and helped him put it on. He lay back and as she sat astride him, his hands caressed her breasts. The rhythm of their movements was perfectly attuned and they reached the climax together.

Afterwards, exhausted and exhilarated, Alistair gently stroked her bare limbs, telling her how perfect their lovemaking had been, how desirable she was. She in turn told him how great a lover he was and they both said how much they loved each other.

Their exertions had made them ravenous, so they abandoned their clothes in the hallway and returned to the kitchen, still naked, and sampled the delights of the food Georgie had brought, all washed down with a superb bottle of wine. When they were sated, Alistair started stacking plates into the dishwasher.

'I don't want you over-tired. That was only the beginning,' he leered at her so comically that she laughed.

'Alistair,' she said, 'I wish . . .'

'You wish what, my poppet?'

'I wish . . . you'd leave those and come to bed.'

He closed the dishwasher instantly. 'OK. Whatever you say. From now on, I'm going to make it my business to see you have everything you want, when you want it.'

'That's very, very dangerous talk.'

'I know,' he said happily, following her into the bedroom. 'Do with me what you will, woman. I'm yours to command.'

'Actually all I want to do is sleep.'

'Fine. Whatever you want. In fact, you name it and I'll get it from the far corners—'

'Alistair?'

'Yes, my love?'

'Shurrup.'

'Whatever you say.'

If anyone noticed that both publishing directors were late for work the following morning, they did not comment. But those around them did gossip that the atmosphere in the office was brighter. Perhaps Georgina should go to Milan more often.

As soon as Helen was given the hand-delivered package and glimpsed the emerald-green folder that was the hallmark of the investigators' stationery, she ordered Margery to hold all her calls.

She had personally given the investigator all the information gleaned by Margery about the woman at the memorial service and had requested this report be given priority because she did not want Margery to ask any more questions around the office.

Quickly she opened the folder. There it was, on the first page. Louise Palmer. She had the whore's name at last.

Helen was exultant. It was only eleven in the morning and usually she made it a habit never to drink alone but she went to the corner cabinet, opened it and hastily poured herself a double brandy.

The investigator had managed to snatch a photograph without the subject knowing. Helen put on her glasses and carefully examined the six-by-four of the young woman emerging from a smart-looking block of flats in Mayfair.

So this was Louise Palmer. She was breathtaking to look at, even in this grainy print. If Helen had had to pick a woman that Mark would find bewitching, she would have chosen Louise Palmer. In the early days when they were looking for models for fashion spreads, she could always pick out the women Mark would ultimately favour. Invariably they'd be wide-eyed, full-lipped, with large breasts on a slender body.

Helen buzzed Margery's internal phone. 'They've tracked her down,' she said triumphantly and gave her Louise's name and full address. 'You know what to do now, don't you?'

'Leave it to me.' Margery's voice was loud and clear.

Helen turned back to the folder. The investigator had completed the job in record time but his report was nevertheless thorough. She flicked through the pages.

Louise Palmer apparently lived alone and spent much of her time inspecting premises for an art gallery she proposed opening. There was another photograph of Louise walking into a shop with a prominent 'To Let' sign above the door.

Where had Louise Palmer met Mark?

The answer was on the second page of the document, which carried a photostat of a marriage certificate. The revelation came like an electric shock. The certificate stated that the bride's name was Louise Palmer and the groom was *Alistair Drummond.*

Helen shielded her eyes, trying to make sense of this. Alistair's first wife was Mark's mistress? How could that be? As far as she could remember, she and Louise had never met. In the early days, Amalgamated's executives worked round the clock and had no time for social niceties like getting acquainted with company wives. Helen was sure she would remember meeting a woman who looked like this. It must have been Alistair who had introduced Louise to Mark.

Helen scanned the dates in the investigator's report. The bitch had been making up to Mark behind Alistair's back. The liaison had started while Louise was still living with Alistair and just before Mark moved the family to New York. Alistair couldn't have suspected his part in the failure of his marriage or surely he wouldn't have gone on working for him.

My God, Mark had been taking a chance. To snatch the wife of one of his senior executives, to take her with him to New York, to keep her in a centrally-situated apartment and travel around the world with her in tow were acts of such brazenness, Helen wondered whether Mark had ever been capable of loyalty to anyone. Had she ever really known the man she'd married all those years ago?

A disturbing thought intruded. What if Alistair did know about the affair and Mark had bulldozed him into silence? No, she could not believe that. Alistair was not the kind of man to step aside in that way, especially when his best friend had cuckolded him. It was inconceivable that he was part of the deceit. Not Alistair. Helen recalled how, along with everyone else in the office, she had tried her best to comfort a bewildered Alistair after Louise had left him. He had given no impression that he knew another man was involved. 'I thought we were so happy,' he had told her. 'I had no idea she wanted something else from life. She feels she married too young. It's my fault, I pressurised her, I loved her so much.'

Helen took another mouthful of brandy. The woman must have flown straight to New York to be with Mark. But that did not matter now.

She cleared her diary for the day and considered what to do with this new-found knowledge. Should she tell Alistair now that his first wife was a liar and a cheat? Not unless she was forced to. Her instinct was not to inflict further misery on him, especially at the moment.

She put on her glasses to study Louise's features once more. So this was the woman who, in a couple of weeks,

was due to be richly rewarded with the finest of diamonds. But what kind of woman would choose to stay in
the background as a mistress for so many years? To
share a half-life when her lover had opted to stay with
his family?

She had to find out.

She picked up the phone and, before dialling, keyed in
141 to withhold her own number. A woman's melodic
voice answered and Helen put down the phone at once,
heart thumping.

# Chapter Sixteen

Alistair was a people person, relying on his personality, experience and charisma to sell the package. In the three-year plan which the board had requested from all the candidates, he had used broad brush strokes to paint a future which contained a skilful balance of the innovative and what a conservative company would accept. True, there were the obligatory diagrams, bar charts and exciting headlines but they were secondary.

In contrast, it was attention to detail that was one of Georgie's strongest points. Her unending tapping away at her computer, long after he had switched off his machine, irritated him, however much he tried to control it. Though Georgie had assured Alistair she believed he had nothing to do with the bug found in her office, he noticed that whenever she worked in the study, she was scrupulous about not leaving any paper in the waste bin, no files were left lying around, and she had taken to locking her small filing cabinet. Alistair found it depressing. Once upon a time their lives had been relatively uncomplicated and rivalry was something that featured only in other people's lives.

This was why, on a crisp Sunday morning before the final interview, he was looking forward to blowing away the cobwebs and forgetting the bloody job on a visit to the country.

This was not any old visit. He and Georgie had been sent one of the most envied invitations in London, to Lord Watersham's party, usually a byword for gossip, style and outrageous behaviour. As well as being a peer of the realm, Piers Watersham was chairman of one of the two major television conglomerates and his annual day out brought together movers and shakers from showbusiness, politics and commerce. Watersham and his family, unlike many of the British aristocracy, prided themselves on their high IQ and expected no less from their guests.

The Drummonds were regulars on the list and though they were 'off duty' they would invariably uncover some high-octane information which would help one of their magazines. Word of an exciting new novel which would end up as a play in the West End or a Hollywood film, a TV company being taken over, or some political rumour meant they were never bored at this gathering.

Newspapers carried pieces by writers who pretended to sneer at the event, which usually started at mid-day and ended at midnight, but all of them cherished the hope that one day they, too, would receive the embossed card that simply stated, 'Piers Watersham. At Home' and the date. Enclosed was a map and the departure times of two large, air-conditioned coaches to transport guests to and from the Sussex mansion. There were always bets on how many empty bottles of champagne the driver removed on arrival at the enormous Palladian-style home which commanded views of the Downs from every one of its ten bedrooms. Those who preferred to travel from Victoria in two special trains hired by his lordship would be entertained by a jazz band en route to put guests into the party mood.

The annual event always had a theme. One year guests had to dress as their favourite character in literature and were encouraged to speak in the style of their hero or heroine. Another year they were required to resemble chess pieces and their efforts at responding as queens, knights or pawns provided many a diary piece in the following day's newspapers.

This time everyone had been asked to base themselves on their favourite film legend. Alistair and Georgie had decided on Katharine Hepburn and a rather tall, thinner Spencer Tracy. They had hired their outfits from Berman's the theatrical costumiers and had found time to learn a few lines of the best dialogue from one of the starry couple's most famous films.

Judging by the sound of tapping from the study, Georgie had still not started to dress. It was clear they would miss the first train and Alistair was at his most diplomatic as he tried to ensure they caught the second. But Georgie looked dejected.

'Alistair, I'm really sorry but I've still got so much to finalise for the presentation. I don't think I can go.'

'Come on, darling, don't say that. It won't take you

long to slip into the costume.'

'It isn't as simple as that,' sighed Georgie. 'That nineteen forties hairdo is quite complicated. I just haven't the time to do it. You go without me.'

'Spencer Tracy without Katharine Hepburn? Unheard of. We both need a break and I won't go without you.'

With some reluctance Georgie capitulated. By the time she declared herself ready after battling with her hair combs, they only just managed to catch the second train and only because it had been delayed for a member of the royal family.

Piers's party was not held in his house but in three barns on the estate. Built in the mid 1900s, the buildings were big, high and wide, and led into each other. In one was a swimming pool with wave machine and other requisite boys' toys, a snooker table and juke box. It had a sound system that could, and did, blast his lordship's favourite music, Wagner's *Götter-dämmerung*, countywide. The second barn was for children and had every known piece of inventive play equipment. The third barn was pure party-time. It was lit by halogen spots, fairy lights and flickering candles. Situated around a professionally-sprung dance floor were small tables covered by damask cloths ready for three hundred of the cream of society from Britain, Europe and America.

By the time Alistair and Georgie arrived, a game of boules was taking place in the garden and the couple was dragooned into taking part. Amid much laughter they were placed in the side which included a son of the Queen, a Cabinet minister, and one of America's top newscasters and his child bride. There was a great deal of good-natured cheating before the teams floated in to lunch. Dozens of trestle tables, set outdoors under the trees, were laden with the Sussex version of a Tuscan feast. Whatever the party theme, the food always comprised salamis and assorted olives in large wooden bowls, pasta and chicken dishes, platters for vegetarians, and rosemary and onion infused breads. Italian wines, cheeses and fresh fruit were arranged on separate tables. The guests sat in large rattan chairs or on tartan rugs laid out on the grass, and an orchestra played everything from Mozart to Andrew Lloyd Webber.

After lunch, several of the guests stretched out on the grass and had a snooze. Others, including Georgie and Alistair, rowed out on the lake. Georgie lay back, watching her husband's strong arm muscles as he rhythmically plied the oars. She was glad he had insisted they came. It was an idyllic, peaceful interlude.

At dinner each table was laid for twelve. Alistair was placed next to an up-and-coming French actress who was in England to perfect her accent. Georgie, across from him, was seated beside one of London's most successful art dealers, a man who had helped Piers amass his collection of Impressionist paintings. The actress, Georgie noted without any pangs of jealousy, was flirting outrageously with Alistair. Georgie was used to his receiving this kind of attention. He was an attractive man, he had a rare combination of good looks, intelligence and plain damn niceness. She congratulated herself for marrying him.

She was enjoying herself; she only wished she had the means to take advantage of the insider information the art dealer was freely divulging. Then he said something that switched on a thousand-kilowatt current in her stomach.

Carefully she laid down her fork. Apparently he had been one of the guests that had gone to Antonia's after the *Art World* party and had sat next to a beauty, who turned out to be Louise Palmer.

'She told me how delighted she was that she's managed to rope in Alistair for her new art gallery. He certainly could make a difference to the launch.'

Georgie forced herself to comment, with a smile, 'Alistair likes to help where he can.'

The man carried on, obviously unaware that Louise had once been married to Alistair and oblivious of the effect his words were having on his fellow guest. Georgie began to probe gently but it was evident that that was the extent of his knowledge of Louise's plans.

Why shouldn't the publishing director of an influential art magazine help a new gallery? It was perfectly legitimate. Then why had a cloud settled on her, dampening her spirits and ruining her appetite? Because not only had Alistair failed to mention his ex-wife's visit to the nightclub, he had not said anything about helping her.

The train journey back to Paddington late that

Sunday evening was made in near silence. Georgie made no mention of the art dealer's disclosure. She was sensible enough to recognise that she was in danger of destroying something precious unless she made an effort to control her pangs of jealousy and insecurity.

Alistair pronounced himself spent with the effort of translating French all night. The party had offered a temporary respite from the tension of waiting for the interviews but at least, he thought, the end was in sight. Arguments about the future, the nervousness around the office and the continuous gossiping about them would soon be over. Tomorrow the decision would be made, life could revert to normal and they could get back to trying for a baby.

Georgie was feeling as apprehensive as Alistair about the events of the next day, although by now she had convinced herself that her inclusion was a mere formality. Alistair would be appointed and it might be better for both of them if she left the company. She loved working at Amalgamated but undoubtedly it would be difficult with her husband as boss. However, she would wait until he had settled into the new job before making a final decision.

All the same, she could not help wondering whether the interviews tomorrow would mark the end of their conflict or merely the beginning.

A chink of light filtered through the bedroom curtains and played on Georgie's face. She blinked and squinted at the clock. Damn, only five o'clock. She lay there, listening enviously to Alistair's slow, regular breathing. Since her teens Georgie had been prone to insomnia and had learned to judge the time within an hour by the lightening sky.

Experience had taught her it was little use getting up to make tea, or read or listen to the radio. Nothing worked. Sometimes she drifted back into slumber but she had ceased to worry about her bouts of sleeplessness since they did not seem to affect her activities. She had come to the conclusion she needed less sleep than most people. She watched Alistair for a moment, his hair unruly, looking a fraction of his age, marvelling that nothing seemed to disturb his rest. She had spent much of the night rehearsing responses to possible questions the board might put to her and wondering whether the outfit she had selected would send the correct signals.

Georgie slipped quietly out of bed and went into the bathroom. She turned on the shower, closing the glass door to drown out the sound although they often joked that Alistair would qualify for the gold medal in any sleep Olympics.

As she stepped out from behind the glass cabinet and reached for one of their extra large bath sheets bought on a trip to America, a hand appeared round the door, holding a mug of tea.

'How are you this morning, my treasure?' asked Alistair, his face alight. He stretched. 'Didn't sleep a wink.'

'I noticed you were lying there all night pretending to be asleep. It was great acting,' said Georgie, taking her tea through to the bedroom.

'Impersonating a log of wood is skilled work,' said Alistair gravely, taking the top off the toothpaste tube.

While he was in the bathroom, Georgie decided to make a proper breakfast for a change. She squeezed oranges and pierced a couple of free-range eggs for boiling. By the time Alistair appeared, the table was laid, the toast was wrapped in a napkin and coffee was already poured.

'Thank you. I'm impressed you had the time,' he said, smiling.

'I'm a woman, I can do everything.'

He began buttering his toast. 'Whatever happens today, we're not going to allow any job to come between us again, agreed?'

'Definitely.'

'We'll compromise whenever there's a problem.'

'There won't be and after this the baby's back on the agenda.'

'Darling, thank you for saying that.' Alistair leaned over to kiss her. 'And may the best man win,' he said, smiling.

The appointments committee was scheduled to make its decision that day. It was always going to be a difficult session, and in the event it took all afternoon. The candidates would have to wait until the morning to hear the verdict.

Courtesy and good business practice demanded that all the candidates be informed of the board's decision before the appointment was made public. Helen decided to break the news to each candidate individually, after which they would leave through another door to avoid any possibility of their meeting the next person. They were also requested to keep the news confidential until the official announcement later that day.

Georgie was the first to be summoned to the inner sanctum. She had prepared herself for disappointment, having convinced herself that this board would find it too difficult to go against company tradition and appoint a female.

She took a deep breath and pushed open the heavy oak door to the boardroom. A sober-faced Helen, sitting alone at the board table, motioned her to sit opposite.

'I want to tell you how we arrived at our decision,' she said.

Ah-hah, the gentle let-down.

'In selecting a new chief executive for London, our main concern has been to safeguard the future of this company in Britain and Europe. In the wake of Mark's death we need someone to guide us through these challenging times, someone with vision, talent and flair, someone with exceptional experience.'

Must be Alistair, thought Georgie. My past experience was with another company, they've known him far longer. They can't possibly value my skills as highly as his.

'We were lucky that we had such exceptional candidates,

each one of you well able to do the job.'

For God's sake, Helen, Georgie screamed silently, I can take it, put me out of my misery, please.

Helen studied her notes. 'Declan's strengths are in distribution and marketing,' she said. 'Alistair is unsurpassed in editorial skills. He also has a talent for exploiting the market gap for new titles . . .'

That's what the job's about and he's got it. Georgie forced a weak smile and nodded. But Helen was still talking. '. . . but what swayed the board in your favour was . . .'

Georgie's eyes widened. 'What swayed the board in your favour'? Had she misheard?

It had been a close fought battle, thought Helen, watching the shock on Georgina's face give way to delight and excitement.

After lengthy and heated wrangling Giles had still held out. 'In my opinion we need someone who knows what they're doing,' he insisted, 'someone like Alistair.'

'Alistair has fine qualities,' said Helen.

'So has Ned Mastrianni,' said Harry.

'But Georgina is the perfect fusion of finder, minder and grinder,' she said firmly.

Giles raised his eyebrows. 'Some of our senior employees will have difficulty reporting to a woman.'

Like all of you, thought Helen. You've surrounded yourselves with submissive females, wives, secretaries, mistresses no doubt. It was time that archaic attitude was well and truly ditched.

'Georgina will be able to win them over,' Helen stated.

'But she'll most surely take time out to have a baby,' said Giles. 'They all do.'

'We can't make that an issue, it's against the law,' warned Harry with a humourless grimace. 'We're supposed to regard everyone these days as genderless, nothing between their legs.'

Helen gave him a frosty look. 'Georgina has assured me that should she be successful, this job will be her priority and that she will postpone starting a baby for at least two years.'

'That's what they all say,' said Giles. 'I still think Alistair's our best option.'

Helen was at her most authoritative. 'I believe she means what she says.' Was Giles championing Alistair's cause as the best route to a consultancy after the New York job ended? He'd often told her the last thing he wanted, as a widower, was banishment to his Hampshire acres.

'You'll give her the job even if it means Alistair will resign?'

'I don't think he will. He'll stay to support his wife.'

'Ned Mastrianni would make a good compromise candidate, then we can keep both Georgina and Alistair,' said Harry.

Ignoring this suggestion, Helen made her final pitch. She would impose her choice if she had to, but persuasion would be preferable.

'There are two main candidates here,' she said. 'Although Alistair is closer to my heart, Georgina's view of magazines is closer to my head.' She surveyed their impassive faces. 'My instinct has served this company well in the past. I want to ask you to trust my gut feeling again.'

The vote was carried, though Giles wanted it noted he was endorsing Georgina Luckhurst's appointment only in the interests of board unity.

'Gentlemen,' said Helen proudly, 'today we have made publishing history.'

No, Georgie realised, she had not misheard.

'. . . but what swayed the board in your favour was that in addition to editorial skills you have a vision for our company which is daring but feasible.'

In all this long, miserable time of waiting, Georgie had not dared to hope for success. But even while she had printed the final draft of her presentation, she had had a sense of how exciting it would be to have the power to put these projects into practice, see them evolve, grow, succeed. Now she was fighting the impulse to jump up and down and squeal with childish delight but Helen was watching her reactions and she had to force herself to show the restraint compatible with her new role as head of a multimillion-pound company.

Her joy was closely followed by a pang of intense regret for Alistair. How would he react to the news that the board had passed him over – in favour of his wife?

'I'm sad that it was Mark's death that created this

vacancy,' Georgie said quietly, 'but I'm pleased my ideas gave you the confidence to appoint me. I intend to make them as successful as I know they can be.'

Helen regarded her warmly. 'The decision to appoint you was unanimous and the board of Amalgamated Magazines has great pleasure in formally offering you the post of chief executive in London.' She held out her hand. 'Congratulations.'

Georgie had never wavered from wanting the job and until that moment had not dared to believe it would happen. The job was hers but was she up to it? Of course she was. Wasn't she as well-qualified as her rivals? Hadn't she the conviction that her ideas for evolving the company would be successful?

The board had made a bold choice. They had confidence in her and she would prove them right. Never again would she allow her uncertainty to show.

'Thank you,' Georgie smiled and shook Helen's hand. 'I'll make sure you'll never regret your decision.'

'I won't pretend that there wasn't opposition. Understandably there were anxieties that you might get pregnant. But I assured them they had no need to worry on that score. I was right, wasn't I?'

Georgie nodded, with more assurance than she felt, thinking of Alistair.

'I shall see the other candidates now, starting, of course, with Alistair. I confess I'm not looking forward to it. How do you think he'll take it?'

'He'll be bitterly disappointed but I believe we can rely on his commitment to the company.' Georgie hesitated for a moment, weighing up whether to offer to break the news herself. But that would be usurping the chairman's role and she had better start thinking like a chief executive rather than a wife.

Abstractedly Helen plucked out the stem of a drooping cyclamen from the array of pink-hued plants adorning her glass-topped coffee table. Alistair would be in her office in ten minutes and she needed to marshal her thoughts.

She stretched her arms and caught a glimpse of herself in the cheval mirror. God, how she'd changed since Mark's death. In every area she was altered. Apart from her body being in better shape because she was always on the go these days, her memory had sharpened. Not long ago she would have had to write down every little thing. That simply wasn't practical in her current situation, and she had surprised herself how good her memory was when she was forced to exercise it.

Over the weeks her top management teams' attitude towards her had subtly changed from barely disguised scepticism to benign tolerance and now to dawning respect. Lately they had begun to seek her out, and it wasn't always sycophancy; they were genuinely listening to her suggestions.

Helen was enjoying herself. She had become an independent woman. The umbilical cord between her and Mark had been cut and she loved having the power to make things happen. It was highly aphrodisiacal. Until today.

How to tell one of your most valuable employees who had been a staunch ally through many dramatic events that you had rejected him for the job he had coveted for many years? It was for the good of the company, but that didn't stop her feeling guilty. She wondered if Mark had experienced the same apprehension before a task like this. Helen doubted it. Once men were convinced they had made the right decision they seemed to be able to detach their personal emotions from their business life in a way that she had not managed so far. Mark had been able to sever his emotions altogether, she thought sourly.

The buzzer went, indicating the next appointment was waiting.

Scrunching up the cyclamen stem, she threw it into the wastepaper basket. Well, she had better get on with it.

When Alistair was seated in front of her, she realised there was no way she could couch this tactfully.

'I'm sorry to disappoint you,' she said without preamble, 'but you haven't been successful. We've appointed Georgina.'

Alistair's face remained impassive but she noticed his hands clenching. The measure of a man was how he took bad news and on that score Alistair rated highly. Helen had never admired him more.

After what seemed an age, he asked slowly, 'May I know the reasons?'

'Her overall vision for the company, some of her plans . . .' Helen faltered. 'It was a very difficult decision. We had to choose between conquering new territory with Georgina or your preference, which was to build on what we have.'

Alistair made no response and Helen went on, 'I know how hard this must be for you but I don't want you to leave the company.' Her eyes held his. 'I need you to be part of the team.'

Alistair stood up. 'I have to think, I can't decide anything now. You must see I'm placed in an impossible position. God, Helen, Georgina will be my boss.'

This was a discouraging reaction. Despite his rhetoric, Alistair seemed to have the same blinkered attitude as some others in the company (and they were not all male). With his impeccable reputation for promoting female talent she had not thought he would respond like this. She had asked all the candidates how they would react to not being successful and Alistair, in particular, had assured her that he would be happy to continue to serve whoever was appointed.

'I'm surprised by your attitude. At the interview—'

'I know what I said but I never really believed she'd get the job. I don't see how that can work. God knows it's going to be difficult enough to deal with at home.'

'Mark would be most upset if he could hear this conversation,' she said sadly.

Alistair made no reply to this so Helen produced her ace card. 'I'd like to offer you the position of executive in charge of all magazine launches for the group, to report directly to me,' she said, smiling. 'It's a key position in the company.'

Alistair appeared to soften. 'Helen, you've always

been good to me. I remember in the old days how much confidence you had in me. Mark made no secret how much he valued your opinion and obviously I don't want to walk away from all I've helped to build.'

At least he hadn't turned the job down, but neither had he accepted it.

'Please consider my offer,' Helen urged. 'If not for my sake, then in Mark's memory. You'll be travelling a great deal, you'll be out from under Georgina's feet.'

He remained silent.

'Will you at least promise me that you won't do anything in a hurry?'

Alistair seemed to be struggling to find the right words.

'Why don't you take a break from all of this?' she went on, sensing that he was weakening. 'You haven't had a holiday for some time. It'll give you the opportunity to think.'

'That sounds appealing,' said Alistair slowly. 'I could do with a few days in the sun just at the moment.'

Helen felt optimistic. Once Alistair had overcome his shock she was sure he would stay and give his support to Georgina.

The contrast between the gloom of his staff and the excitement in Georgie's office was so marked Alistair could hardly bring himself to cross the threshold of her secretary's den. He could hear Josephine's voice from the corridor.

'I'm making up to the new boss right from the start,'

she was saying. Then there was the unmistakable explosion of a champagne cork.

Alistair pushed open the door to find his wife surrounded by acolytes toasting her success. She caught sight of him at once and raced across to usher him into the room, but he noticed that her eyes were anxious.

'I'm so proud of you,' he said, pleased that he could be sincere about that at least, and planted a kiss on her cheek.

'Thank you,' she said, relieved. 'I hoped you'd be happy for me.'

He picked up a glass of champagne and put his arm round her shoulders. Gazing at their expectant faces, Josephine among them, he decided the only thing to do was make a short speech to nail the evident embarrassment.

To applause and cheers, he flourished the glass in the air and said, 'I give you a toast to the cleverest, most talented employee in the company. To our new chief executive.' There was little point in trying to avoid voicing what they were undoubtedly thinking, so he added cheerfully, 'And a toast to me, who had the good sense to marry her.'

He heard relief in their laughter and as they clinked glasses, Georgie whispered in his ear, 'Thank you, darling.'

After a while, Georgie said something to Josephine who began to usher out the excited staff. At last Alistair and Georgie were alone.

They smiled at each other and Georgie hugged him

269

tightly. 'I know how you must be feeling.'

'It hasn't really hit me yet.' Again he was being truthful. After his emotionally bruising talk with Helen, he had tried not to think about the ramifications of his wife's appointment. 'I'm disappointed, of course I am,' he said, 'but the decision's been made and I can't argue with it.' He smiled at her. 'At least they chose an editorial person rather than a bean counter. And I'd much rather you got the job than any of the others.'

'I'll need your help,' she said tentatively. 'There's so much to do.'

'You'll be great at it,' he said, 'just don't let anyone, especially the men, think you'll be a soft touch. Start off as an Ayatollah and soften up if you need to later.'

They separated hastily as Georgie's secretary came in to deposit a vase containing an enormous bunch of white roses, then retreated embarrassed.

'And we'll be OK?' asked Georgie.

'Of course we will,' he said, hoping it was true.

'I'm not going to let this job wreck what we have,' she said firmly.

Then it hit him. How the hell was he going to be able to make love to his boss? And what about their plans for a family? He'd readily agreed to wait because he'd been damned sure he would get the job. But now, what would happen about starting a baby?

'It might be better for you if I leave . . .'

'No,' she said quickly. 'You said you'd be able to cope.'

'I can. It's just that . . .'

'That you can't,' she said dully.

'I didn't mean that. I need time to adapt, that's all. Don't worry, we'll be fine.'

When Alistair left her office, Georgie was full of misgivings. Alistair was trying, she could see that, but she could also see that behind his brave façade he was not voicing his obvious foreboding, as he did not want to spoil her moment of triumph.

# *Chapter Seventeen*

Now that the new chief executive had been appointed, Helen decided she would wait no longer to confront the woman who had dominated her thoughts since her husband's death.

Despite her nervousness she felt a sense of excitement as she was driven to Louise Palmer's flat. She was clear about what she wanted to achieve from the encounter – to force an admission from Louise that she was Mark's mistress, and to tell her in no uncertain terms there would be no diamonds and damn the consequences. She would have to give her name to gain entrance. Would Louise Palmer agree to see her? If she were Mark's mistress, she would want to find out what his widow wanted. She had decided not to mention Alistair's name. He was an irrelevant complication at this juncture.

By the time the car pulled up outside the converted Regency mansion, Helen was wiping her hands nervously with a handkerchief. There was still time to back off. It would be easy enough to ask the driver to take her home. No one need know about Louise Palmer. Once they had met, she would start something that could escalate beyond her control. She had a sudden picture of how it would all look to Mark if he could see her.

Helen stared up at the imposing frontage in one of the most expensive parts of London. Her money was paying for this and the thought propelled her out of the car.

With a trembling hand she pressed the intercom buzzer at the entrance. It was answered almost at once.

'Who is it?'

'Helen Temple-Smith.'

Louise froze and held the intercom receiver for several seconds. How had Helen Temple-Smith found out her name and where she lived? More importantly, why had she come? Louise took a deep breath to calm herself. Maybe she was jumping to conclusions. Maybe the reason for this visit had nothing to do with her relationship with Mark. Somehow Louise doubted it. But she needed to know, and Mark's widow was obviously not going to tell her standing on the doorstep.

'Take the lift to the fifth floor,' she said into the intercom. 'I'm the first door on the left.'

How should she play this? Dumb, she decided. The widow would have to make all the running.

Her reflection in the mirror showed a white, strained expression and she tried to relax. She must give the impression of someone completely guilt-free if she was to bluff her way out. After all, Helen couldn't possibly have proof of what she had been to Mark. They had been so careful. They had never been found out.

As Louise heard the whine of the lift she wrapped her cream silk peignoir, one of Mark's favourites, tighter round her, trying to hide her bra-less breasts. At the sound of the bell, she hurried to the front door.

'I'm Louise Palmer, how do you do?'

The snatched picture certainly did not do justice to the perfect complexion and that curvaceous body, thought Helen. She forced herself to touch the cool hand briefly.

'I've read about you in the *Daily Mail*,' Louise gushed. 'It's wonderful what you've done, taking over all those magazines. Of course your business is a complete mystery to me, I just buy the magazines.'

So this was how the bitch was going to play it. Helen seethed with rage. This woman had been with Mark to conferences all over the world. She had shared his bed and would have been privy to many of his plans and secrets. After eight years with him she would understand the publishing world almost as well as she herself did.

'I hope this isn't inconvenient,' Helen said quietly. 'I wanted a quick word with you while I'm in London.'

'I can't imagine why – unless it's to do with the gallery I'm planning to open. Perhaps you saw that piece in the *Express*. Anyway, do come in. I'm afraid you'll have to excuse the chaos. I wasn't expecting visitors.' Louise ushered her into the sitting room. 'I'll make us some coffee,' she said, and disappeared into the kitchen.

A few minutes later she returned bearing a tray. 'I read about your husband's tragic death.' She looked sorrowfully at Helen. 'I'm very sorry for your loss.' Louise's brow was unclouded, her wide eyes showed no vestige of guilt. For a moment Helen wondered wildly whether she had made a mistake. One thing was sure, Margery had seen her at the memorial service and had recognised her in the photos snatched by the investigator. She would start with that.

'I can't help thinking I've seen you before,' she said blandly. 'It couldn't have been at my husband's memorial service, could it?'

'No, I wasn't there,' said Louise, a puzzled frown wrinkling her lovely face. 'I didn't know there was one. When was it?'

Helen told her the date.

'I was out of the country.'

Helen experienced a surge of relief at this lie. This was the right woman. She leaned back, feeling less anxious, and looked round at the rich furnishings, the cut-glass decanters, the Persian rugs on the gleaming floors and the exquisite coffee service. Mark's money had paid for all of this. Her money. It stiffened her resolve to punish this woman for what she had stolen.

Louise poured the coffee and handed over the milk jug. Helen set it down purposefully and gazed steadily at her. It seemed to unsettle Louise; she began to prattle.

'You've come at a very good time. I always love,' the voice was almost a trill, 'a cup of coffee at this time of the morning. Now tell me, why did you want to see me?'

'It's not about your gallery,' said Helen, pushing the coffee aside.

'Then what?' Louise jumped up suddenly and began

fiddling with a thermostat near the light switch. She seemed rattled, Helen thought with satisfaction.

'I haven't been able to get this darn temperature right,' Louise said quickly. 'It's either too hot or too cold. Brits don't seem to be able to get central heating to work properly in these old houses. Not like in New York.' She stopped, seeming embarrassed.

'Oh yes, you lived there, didn't you?' Helen inclined her head slightly, like a falcon waiting for its prey to settle. 'Which part of New York?'

Louise came back and sank on to the sofa, appearing more composed. 'I was always on the move,' she said brightly. 'If it wasn't the rent, the maintenance charges were sky-rocketing. New York's getting very expensive.'

'I think so too. That's one of the things we have in common.'

Louise gave a half-smile. 'What else do we have in common?'

Helen couldn't resist replying, 'My husband, Mark Temple-Smith.'

Louise's reaction was expected. 'I never met him,' she said calmly.

Her brazen poise incensed Helen but she forced her voice to remain impassive. 'You were my husband's mistress. For the last eight years.' She felt as though she was standing in a witness box, giving testimony to a presiding judge.

'I don't know who told you that but you're making a terrible mistake. I warn you not to repeat it.'

A liar would go to the wire rather than admit guilt,

thought Helen. It was time to try some tactical lying of her own.

'Mark needed someone to cover up for him in the office,' she said levelly, 'a confidante he could rely on to disguise his expenses when he was traipsing around the world with you. That woman now works for me and she has given me dates, places and exactly how much he spent on you.'

The face in front of her showed no sign of apprehension.

'I'm sure all that you're saying is true. But it's not me.'

'I have the evidence,' Helen bluffed. 'My colleague produced your address in New York and the Hamptons. I have proof of your living there with my husband. How do you think I found out your name, or this address in London?'

'That's nonsense. I don't know why you're troubling me with this. I want you to leave. Now.' Louise stood up and made for the door.

'I'm not finished. Don't you want to hear what I discovered was in a bank in Liechtenstein?'

That stopped Louise in her tracks and she turned round.

'Diamonds, held in a numbered account.' Helen watched Louise's face transform from that of a glowing, innocent-looking young woman to a tense neurotic with neck cords straining and fingers clenched tightly by her sides.

'What diamonds? What account? I know nothing about them.'

Helen decided to end the charade. 'No more lies,' she rapped, and with a feeling of power she recited the account number. She wasn't clear how Paul Wallis in New York had obtained the name of the bank, let alone the account number. She hadn't asked, and he didn't say.

Louise appeared to shrivel. She struggled for words. 'Please believe me,' she said finally. 'We did try to stop, many times, but we couldn't.'

'Couldn't? You mean wouldn't.'

'It wasn't like that. We loved each other.'

Helen did not dignify this with a reply. If Mark had been so in love, wouldn't he have left his wife and family and married Louise? Nevertheless, just hearing the words caused her pain. The anger of the last few months spilled out. 'I'm damned if I'll let you get a penny from Mark's estate.'

'You can't do anything about that.' Louise seemed to have gathered strength. 'My lawyer says the agreement Mark signed is watertight.'

'But Mark's dead. I'll dispute it.'

'Then I'll take you to court.'

'Go ahead. I don't give a damn who knows about you and Mark.' Helen was rewarded by a flash of concern on Louise's face.

'I don't believe you mean that,' said Louise. 'What about your daughters?'

'That's my problem. You never let them worry you when you were screwing their father.' Helen's dearest wish was to be able to give in to her primeval instincts and rake her nails across that flawless complexion.

'Whatever he promised, Mark never had any intention of making a life with you.' Helen's tone was withering. 'He understood very well that all you were concerned about was money.'

Red blotches were appearing on Louise's neck and Helen felt an upsurge of satisfaction.

'That's not true,' Louise retorted. 'He wanted to provide for my future, to pay me for what I gave up to be with him. It was my insurance.'

Although Louise was younger and more beautiful, at that moment Helen felt superior. She gathered up her coat. 'Insurance, you say.' She smiled. 'Well, consider the premiums cancelled.'

Alone in her flat, Louise lit a cigarette and paced the floor restlessly. Helen was threatening to spoil all her plans. Without money from the diamonds she would not be able to rebuild her life, but she had no intention of returning to a salaried existence. Nor was she prepared to give up her privileged lifestyle.

Quickly she dialled the number of her American attorney. He listened silently to her account of the intimidating exchange.

'She's bluffing,' he said as soon as he had finished. 'We've crawled all over that contract. She could go public but she can't get out of handing over those two parcels of diamonds. You won't have broken the terms of the contract. My advice is not to worry, sit tight and let me handle any flak.'

It was a slow news day and the announcement of Georgina Luckhurst's elevation made a page of London's *Evening Standard*, with an unflattering picture of her taken at the launch of a new title a few months previously. Georgie always thought pictures showing a person with a drink in their hand made them look like a lush, though hers had been mineral water.

After that her phone rang ceaselessly with requests for interviews and she and Helen agreed to fix a photo call. Helen's advice was that Alistair should not attend, and when Georgie sounded him out, he'd said to her, 'I wouldn't be there normally, so why should I go just because I'm your husband? You want them to concentrate on the job, not your personal life.'

'Some hope,' she'd said ruefully, knowing that the newspapers would home in on how she'd vanquished her husband.

The photo call was arranged for late afternoon and Georgie faced the photographers and reporters with a mixture of elation and apprehension. Despite the short notice, the boardroom was packed with journalists from both the business sections of the morning papers and the tabloids, as well as two television stations.

Editors undoubtedly thought the announcement of a major female appointment to such a senior position made useful feature material. It was an added bonus that Georgina would be her husband's boss. Their questions bordered on the offensive, focusing on the rivalry between husband and wife rather than her suitability for the job.

'Why do you think Amalgamated appointed a woman?' asked one woman who appeared not to have washed her hair for a week.

'I hope it's because I'm the best person for the job,' replied Georgie.

'What does your husband say? Didn't he expect to get the job?' These questions came from an ageing hack in a much-creased tweed jacket.

'Naturally he was disappointed but he's pleased for me.'

'Where is he now?' The business reporter from the *Daily Mail* was as impeccably dressed as ever.

'Working.'

'Shouldn't he be with you, showing how pleased he is?' asked a ferret-faced reporter from a mass-circulation tabloid. He seemed to put quote marks round the word 'pleased'.

'He fully backs the decision the board has made.'

'Why did they choose you over him?' The tabloid hound would not let go.

Careful, thought Georgie, they want to rubbish Alistair. 'You'd have to ask the board. You can't expect me to list my many fine qualities,' and she laughed with the rest of the room.

'Isn't it going to be difficult being his boss?' he pressed. Were the other reporters going to leave it all to this one?

'Not at all,' she said, hoping she sounded more confident than she felt.

'Who's going to be the boss in bed?' The hack

appeared to be enjoying himself.

Georgie lifted an eyebrow and keeping her face impassive said, 'Are there any more relevant questions?'

To her relief, a woman from BBC's Radio 4 obliged. 'What makes you think you are qualified to run a multimillion-pound business?'

'In what way am I not qualified?' asked Georgie without heat. 'If being in the magazine business for ten years doing everything from sub-editing to overseeing advertising, distribution, printing, editorial and launching several successful titles isn't qualification enough, what is?'

Helen nodded approvingly and the woman journalist moved her tape recorder closer to the dais. 'Do you think you got this job because you're a woman?'

'That's naive, if you don't mind me saying so. Do you really think our company would entrust itself to someone simply for politically correct reasons? That's insulting to women and certainly I wouldn't have accepted the job on those terms.'

After the press conference, Georgie tried to phone Alistair to tell him how it had gone but he was out, and as usual he had switched off his mobile. Alistair's secretary was in a dither because she could not contact her boss. Helen had organised a celebratory dinner at the Ivy and wanted all senior staff to be there. The secretary told Georgie that she had left the information about the dinner on Alistair's message service.

There was still no sign of him when Georgie began to dress for dinner. She worried that he would not have time to change, and wished they didn't have to go out tonight. But as guest of honour she could hardly have told Helen that she would have preferred the event to be on another night. That what she wanted most right now was to be alone with her husband. At least they would be able to talk on the way to the restaurant. She needed to assure herself of his support or how could she enjoy her success?

It was not often that Alistair took refuge in alcohol but right now he was sitting in a dimly-lit cellar bar several miles away from Amalgamated's office, nursing a Bushmills. Beside him, Harry did a tour of the optics drinking – blends, malts and bourbons.

Alistair contemplated his drink. How many times did you get passed over for the job of your dreams, one that was half-promised to you? And how many times did you discover that you were a hypocrite? A hundred-per-cent, solid gold hypocrite. It was all very well making the right noises when you imagined the situation. It was quite different when faced with the reality of having your wife as the boss. He'd always thought he was some liberal, able to treat men and women equally, happy to promote women. But now that Georgie had landed the one job he wanted, he found he could not cope with it. How could it not change the balance of their relationship?

And he resented the brutal way Helen had delivered the blow. She hadn't bothered to soft soap him, she'd simply come right out with it. He had been too stunned to say a word. When he had walked in, he had expected to come out as the winner. There had been no preparation.

Harry had offered to come with him to this bar to help drown his sorrows but he had only succeeded in making him more depressed.

'They've made a big mistake, old boy. I spoke up for you. But there was no moving Helen. I've said it once and I'll say it again. Georgie got the job because the widow thinks it'll bring good publicity.'

'The decision's made,' said Alistair, attempting to curtail Harry's diatribe.

Harry raised his glass. 'First today,' he said, 'with this hand.' He took a deep swig. 'Mind you, they'll keep on trying to pretend her appointment has nothing to do with gender when we all know she wouldn't have clinched this job if she wasn't female.'

'Steady on,' said Alistair. 'Georgie's got a good head on her shoulders.'

'Maybe, but if I were you, old boy, I'd stick around. I give her three months before they ask you to take over.'

Alistair made no reply and stared into his glass. Maybe Harry was right. Maybe it was because it was a woman's turn.

Georgie certainly wouldn't want to get pregnant now, not with all these new responsibilities. He cradled his head in his hands, oblivious of the stares of the others at the bar. This was not the marriage he wanted. He wanted a baby. His and Georgie's baby.

Well, he was damned if he was going to be turfed into a side turning by Helen. No, despite his promise to

285

consider the job she'd offered, his instinct was to walk out and build a career elsewhere. He felt hurt, humiliated and despondent but if his marriage was to survive, of one thing he was certain. He could not work in his wife's shadow.

At some level Georgie was able to stand outside of herself and admire the façade of this laughing, confident, animated woman, waving her champagne glass. She greeted Helen and her colleagues at the Ivy with vivacity, responding to their congratulations with the broadest of smiles. This woman was a winner, clinching one of the four major appointments in Britain's publishing world. No doubt about it, she had done exceptionally well. The buzz was that within three years she could be running the show in New York. This was not the anxious woman who was unable to shift her position facing the door, waiting for a tall, distinguished figure to stride in.

It was time to take their seats for dinner and still there was no sign of Alistair. When a mortified Georgie gave Helen some lame excuse about Alistair being delayed and perhaps not being able to make it, Helen motioned to a waiter to take away the cutlery and the empty chair.

As Georgie watched the waiter remove the setting, and walk out of the room, chair aloft, she could not help thinking that it symbolised Alistair's removal from an important part of her life.

Harry watched Alistair leave the bar but made no move

to follow. Going home to his wife had even less appeal than normal because his chances of escape had narrowed after the decision in that board room.

Ned had accused him of not giving his candidature sufficient support when it mattered, and if truth be told, Harry agreed with him. Of course he had tried but when Giles and, more importantly, Helen, were so solidly against Ned getting the job, it wouldn't have been in Harry's best interests to nail his colours to the Mastrianni shirt.

Georgina's appointment was a blow that even now was difficult to comprehend, let alone accept. When he could see that Helen's mind was made up he had to go along with it but my God he didn't like Georgina and he was sure the feeling was mutual.

For all his plotting and scheming his future prospects at Amalgamated seemed pretty dim.

Harry ordered yet another one for the road.

Unaware that his wife was being fêted by the company, Alistair decided it was time to put a brave face on his disappointment and return home.

To his surprise the flat was in darkness. There was no note on the kitchen table, nor was she at the office. He tried Josephine's number but the baby-sitter said she would be home late. For once, he did try to retrieve his messages on the mobile, but the battery was flat.

Georgie must have gone out to celebrate with her colleagues. Why hadn't she told him? Deflated, Alistair thought of his sister. She had always had a cool head and he needed to talk over his problems with someone rational. This was an evening he did not want to spend alone. He ordered a cab to take him to south London. It might anyway be better to sort things out in his own head before tackling the problems with Georgie.

Rosemary was not alone. As he stood in the doorway of her flat, he saw the silhouette of a blonde head leaning against the sofa and stared at his sister in dismay.

'Sorry,' he said quietly, 'I didn't know you had visitors. I'll come back.'

Rosemary took him firmly by the arm and steered him through the door. 'Come in,' she said, her expression full of sympathy. 'I know what you're going through. It's so unfair.'

He resisted her attempts to lead him into the living room. 'I don't want to meet anyone right now.'

'Don't worry. You know my visitor. It's Louise.'

'What's she doing here?' he asked, surprised.

'We're discussing a project. She's offered me a job in her art gallery. I'm going to leave the company.' Rosemary smiled brightly. 'I suppose you'll be off too.'

'Probably.'

'I guessed as much as soon as I heard the news. I'm sure you're right. But you shouldn't be on your own now. Come in and have a drink.'

Alistair shook his head. 'No thanks. I've had enough. I need to get back.'

'They're all out celebrating. Didn't you know?'

He shook his head. 'I don't feel much like talking in any case.'

'Not even to me?' Louise appeared in the hallway. 'Come and sit down. You shouldn't go home to an empty house, not tonight.'

Reluctantly Alistair gave in, and before he could protest, Louise poured him a stiff whisky, with a thimbleful of water. 'Isn't that exactly how you used to like it?' she asked, patting the sofa.

He sat between her and Rosemary and drank absentmindedly. In fact, the whisky was strangely comforting, topping up the few he had had earlier. But he remained clear-headed enough to avoid discussing himself and Georgie in front of Louise. Deftly he steered the conversation away from his problems by asking questions about Louise's art gallery and Rosemary's part in it.

'It sounds like the sort of opportunity you've been waiting for, Rosie,' he said. 'If I stay at Amalgamated I'll help you all I can.'

'I can't bear the thought of your leaving the company. We need you there, don't we, Rosemary?' Louise butted in.

So that was it. Louise wanted his contacts to get her business up and running. Well, he would see what he could do. Say what you like about Louise, she had never been his rival, never even been ambitious, come to think of it. The whisky was sweetening his memory.

It was late when he glanced at his watch, rose from the sofa and stretched. 'I think I'd better get home.'

'I'll give you a lift,' said Louise quickly. 'My car's right outside and I haven't had anything to drink.'

'No, that's not necessary. I can get a taxi.'

'At this time of night? Not easily,' said Rosemary. 'This isn't Kensington, you know.'

'You'd be doing me a favour,' said Louise. 'I hate driving around London late at night by myself.'

For a moment Alistair wondered if Louise was making a play for him. He nearly laughed out loud. What had he to offer? It was a ridiculous idea. He was the ex-star of Amalgamated, pushed to the sidelines by his wife.

He dozed off in the front seat of Louise's Five Series BMW as they sped through the rain-spattered streets of the capital. He was roused by a gentle shake and groggily he tried to get his bearings.

'Where are we?'

'Outside my flat. I don't think your wife would appreciate seeing you in this state, do you? You need some strong black coffee.'

She brushed his protests aside and in truth he agreed with her.

Louise's sofa was seductively comfortable and when she raised his feet up on to the cushions, he made no effort to resist. Out of the fog that was his brain, he heard sounds of her movements in the kitchen but as he sank lower into the cushions, he found he was unable to keep his eyes open.

There was no feeling of victory, no sensation of triumph or success. Two hours after the celebrations, Georgie's only emotions were emptiness and frustration. Neither Helen nor anyone else had believed her paltry excuse why Alistair had not turned up. She could see it written on their faces: it was a case of sour grapes.

All night Georgie had been hoping that, however late, he still might make it. Not for a moment, not even at the height of the toasts, listening to the laudatory words and the amusing poem someone had swiftly composed, was she able fully to enjoy the evening. Despite her best endeavours, her eyes kept sliding towards the doorway each time it opened, only to be disappointed.

By the time she arrived home, her anger was building. Unless Alistair had a damn good excuse, it was selfish of him to let her down. For her to take centre stage this evening had been something of a novelty and no one knew that better than Alistair. He would have known the company would organise something to mark her appointment and yet he had deliberately put himself out of contact and, worse, had not bothered to tell her. A few months ago she could not have imagined a situation where he would not have telephoned to let her know where he was.

Exhausted, she slumped into a chair and must have dozed off because it was nearly three thirty when she awoke from a fitful sleep. Maybe he hadn't noticed her sitting in the study. She rushed into the bedroom but the coverlet was unruffled, the bed had not been touched.

Where the hell was he? His secretary had mentioned something about him disappearing with Harry but she dared not phone Harry's home so late. Alistair certainly wouldn't have spent the night there. Maybe he had gone to Rosemary's flat. After a few seconds' deliberation, she decided she would risk phoning her sister-in-law. At least she might have an idea of his whereabouts.

Rosemary's voice, gruff and slurred by sleep, came down the line. 'Wassamatta? What time is it?'

'It's Georgie, I'm so sorry to wake you but I'm terribly worried. Alistair hasn't come home. Is he with you?'

Now Rosemary did not sound sleepy at all. 'No, he's not here but he did pop in earlier.'

'When he left, where did he say he was going?'

'Home.'

'Do you think he's had an accident? Should I phone the police?' asked Georgie, her voice rising in alarm.

'No, no, don't do that. I'm sure he's OK.'

'What sort of state was he in? People thought he'd gone drinking with Harry.'

'Yes, he did appear to have had one or two. But he was fine when he left here, and that was hours ago. He must have gone to a club or something.'

A club? That was so unlike Alistair. There was nothing more she could usefully say to her sister-in-law except to apologise for disturbing her. She put down the phone and sank on to the bed, her head in her hands.

Alistair must be drowning his sorrows somewhere. When faced with the reality of her being his boss, he could not hack it. But this wasn't the Alistair she lived with, the man who happily gave interviews extolling the virtues of equality.

She was determined to stay awake and try and reassure him. Maybe this would be a good time to remind him of the person he used to be. She went over to the cabinet and pulled out a video labelled *News Time* and settled down on the sofa to watch it. She pressed the play button on the remote control and the screen filled with a studio shot of BBC2's leading killer shark who led the current affairs programme. He was just finishing off his kebabbing of the Foreign Secretary, an encounter so ferocious that the smell of singeing flesh virtually emanated from the set. The interviewer then swivelled to camera two.

This was it. Georgie could remember the interview as if it were yesterday. Herself and Alistair, a fêted couple.

'And now, to marriages and mergers. Four years ago two publishing houses were joined in a dynastic union when publishing director Georgina Luckhurst married Alistair Drummond, also a publishing director but of a rival group.' The screen switched to footage of their wedding. The dark-haired bride, wearing a sheath of chic silk, was laughing up at the tall, jubilant-looking bridegroom.

How carefree we were then, thought Georgie ruefully as the interviewer went on, 'Today their companies announced they are to merge.' The anchorman tilted his head to one side and turned a quizzical gaze on Georgina and Alistair sitting beside him. 'Already there is speculation about which magazines will survive and which heads will roll. Is it going to be yours, Mr Drummond?'

Alistair laughed, handsome and seemingly self-assured. 'No,' he said. 'And it won't be Georgina's either.'

'But your magazines have a bigger circulation,' said

the interviewer, turning to face Georgina.

She smiled and said, 'That shouldn't be the only criterion.'

Hadn't she sounded unsure of herself? She would do better now. She had wanted to comment that profits mattered as much but Alistair got in first. 'But it's profits that count and my group does very well there.'

'Ah, so there is rivalry?'

'You bet,' said Georgie quickly.

'Keeps us on our toes,' smiled Alistair.

'But, Miss Luckhurst, the possibility exists,' persisted the interviewer, 'that because his company merged with yours he may become your boss.'

'I don't see a problem with that,' said Georgina with a smile.

The interviewer bared his teeth at Alistair. 'And what if the reverse happened? What if she leapfrogged over you and became your boss?'

On the sofa Georgie leaned forward. 'I want to work with people who are the best at what they do,' said Alistair firmly and with apparent sincerity. 'I'd have absolutely no problem with my wife as my boss.' The screen filled with a close-up of his face and Georgie zapped the button to freeze the picture.

For a few seconds she stared at her husband's smiling image and said quietly to the screen, 'Liar.'

She ejected the tape and sat for a while, gazing sightlessly at the blank television screen. There was no question of being able to sleep so she drew a bath and set out her clothes. It wasn't yet five o'clock but she might as well go to the office and start her new job. Work would be her salvation. She felt too tired to drive so she ordered a cab on the firm's account.

Half an hour later the flat's intercom buzzed. 'Morning, Miss Luckhurst. Taxi here.' The cabbie's voice was loud and cheery. 'You're off early,' he said when she appeared. He turned from the steering wheel to study her for a second or two. 'You and Mr Drummond OK?' He was one of the regular drivers and had often picked them up, separately or together.

'Yes, thanks. I have a difficult problem to sort out,' she said, hoping he would take the hint and stop talking.

No such luck. 'Ever notice how fast the pace is these days?' he asked companionably, shifting into first gear and moving off. 'We're all doing more but are we really accomplishing anything?'

Oh God, a philosopher at this time of the morning.

While the cabbie chattered on, Georgie tried to marshal her thoughts. It was no use castigating Alistair when he finally appeared. In her new job it would take all her tact, guile and love to keep him from feeling emasculated. How was she going to deal with him now that she was his boss? One tactic would be to try and involve him in all aspects of her job. Would that appear patronising? Georgie sighed. How many women had found themselves in such a sensitive situation?

The radio in the cab began squawking information about upcoming jobs. The world and its mother seemed to want to go to airports, rail stations or the Eurostar link at Waterloo.

'Would you mind turning off that noise?' she asked. 'I need to concentrate.'

'Sorry, love. Have to keep it switched on so they can give me details of my next job.'

Georgie sighed and closed her eyes, trying to ignore the burblings between the controller and his cabbies.

'Terminal Four job. Anybody on the road to Heathrow?' There was a crackle of static and a voice responded, 'Four nine three here. Can do in ten minutes.'

'Right. Here's the pick-up address.'

There was more crackling and Georgie found herself irritated. Why the hell didn't they get that sorted? There was less interference between NASA and moon-walkers than there was here in London.

'Anybody in the Mayfair area? Melford Court,' came the controller's voice again.

Georgie straightened. Where had she heard that address before? For a minute her mind went blank, then it came to her. Wasn't that the block of flats where Louise Palmer was living? Yes, she was sure Louise had mentioned it when issuing that invitation to dinner. She remembered thinking how much money Louise must have to live there.

'Wake up, you lot,' said the voice. 'Who's near Melford Court. Urgent.'

'I can be there in about four minutes,' came another voice, reciting his number.

'OK. Pick-up's name is Drummond, Mister,' continued the controller.

My God, that was Alistair.

Georgie gazed out the window, her hands tightly clenched, trying to think clearly. That's why he hadn't come home. He'd been with Louise all night. Rosemary had been trying to fob her off with that story about a club. Come to think of it, she had sounded evasive. But she would cover up for her brother.

The thought of him spending the night with Louise was unbearable. If he was trying to bolster his wounded ego by seeking solace with his first wife, he was playing a highly dangerous game with their marriage.

But she mustn't jump to conclusions. Part of her wanted to believe there had been some mistake. But as if to mock her, the taxi supervisor's voice came through again loud and clear. 'That job's on the Amalgamated Magazines account,' it boomed. 'Press bell for flat number five, he'll come straight down.'

'On my way,' came the disembodied voice.

Disconsolately Georgie stared ahead and noticed the driver observing her through his rear-view mirror. With a rapid movement he leaned over and switched off the radio.

Alistair crept quietly into the flat, head pounding and a God-awful taste in his mouth. He tiptoed into their bedroom to find the bed already made and Georgie gone.

He was feeling bloody guilty and wanted to tell her the truth. It wasn't so awful. He hadn't meant to stay out all night but nothing had happened. Louise had been kind, that was all.

He had a clear picture of a coffee cup in front of him

on the table, then nothing. A few hours later he had woken up on the sofa, fully dressed apart from his tie and shoes, feeling dreadful. He had not set eyes on Louise before he went downstairs to wait for the taxi to take him home.

Then he realised that his story, though true, sounded thin. And God knows, after the *Art World* party Georgie was already hivey about Louise. Perhaps it would be wiser not to say where he spent the night. It would be asking a great deal of his wife to believe that nothing had happened between him and his ex.

Alistair hated the idea of deceiving Georgie but this was not a time for honesty. There were many fences to mend and what would he achieve by telling the truth? He did not want to hurt her and as he had done nothing to be ashamed of, what was the harm in telling her he had spent the night at his sister's flat?

Georgie appeared calm enough when he walked into her office an hour or so later and he decided to try and take control of the situation from the start. He kissed her pale cheek, something they avoided in the office but he thought it was a good tactic.

'I'm sorry I missed your party,' he said. 'Did it go well?'

'Yes. Where were you?'

'I was out drinking with Harry, then I went to Rosemary's flat. She told me about your dinner but by then it was too late. I'm sorry I didn't phone to say what happened.'

'And what did happen?' Her voice was cool.

'I was so tired I must have passed out on Rosie's sofa. I hope you weren't worried.'

'The first time you've stayed out all night? And you hope I wasn't worried?'

He felt ashamed. Of course she had worried. He should have telephoned, at least.

'Darling, I'm very sorry.' He went round the desk and tried to put his arms round her. But she pushed him away. 'I said I'm sorry.'

She ignored this. 'I know where you spent last night and it wasn't with Rosemary,' she said, gazing directly at him.

His heart sank.

'You were with Louise.'

'I did go to Rosemary's,' he said defensively, 'and by chance Louise was there. She gave me a lift home but I went in for a black coffee and fell asleep. On the sofa. I swear nothing happened. Honestly.'

'Honestly?' she repeated, her tone withering.

Alistair felt a surge of anger. 'How dare you imply that I think so little of our marriage that I would risk it by sleeping with Louise? I'm surrounded by some of the most beautiful women in the world, I'm on first-name terms with supermodels and actresses. Do you think I couldn't fuck them if I wanted to? I don't do it because I love you.'

'But Louise is different, isn't she?'

'For the last time, I did not sleep with that woman. Why can't you accept my word?' Alistair was seething.

Georgie met him head on. 'Because I can't trust you any more. You lied to me about her after the party and you lied about last night.'

'Don't do this to us, Georgie. Don't say things you'll regret.'

She seemed not to hear him. 'I want you out of the flat. Today.'

A couple of hours later Louise had a phone call from Rosemary in the office. She had to hold the receiver tightly to her ear because Rosemary was whispering. 'I have to be quick. Alistair's asked if he can stay with me. He and Georgie have separated.'

'Is it serious?'

'Seems to be.'

'What happened?'

'Alistair didn't say. He's upset of course but I think he must realise things can't go on like this. He's going away for a few days.'

'Oh?' said Louise. 'Where?'

'Boca Raton, Florida.'

'Thanks, Rosemary.'

Louise replaced the phone thoughtfully. It had started as a game, trying to see what effect she could have on her former husband. She needed his help to start the gallery. But now? After Helen's visit, Louise had done some serious thinking. She wanted security and commitment; since Mark's death those were qualities she had come to prize. Alistair could provide both.

Yes, the gallery was important to her but there was far

more to it than that. She did not care that Alistair had been passed over for the top job, that he would not take Mark's place in New York. It wasn't power or position that made her want to snare Alistair. Nor was it money; she was wealthy in her own right now, and she had been reassured that the widow could not take it from her. What mattered now was not to be some secret lover tucked away out of sight but to be on someone's arm as his wife. Official. For the one thing Mark's death had taught her was that wives always won.

Last night she had tiptoed round Alistair as he lay asleep on her sofa, to stare at his sleeping features. As she traced a finger over his soft, relaxed mouth, she felt a moment of tenderness.

Louise admired what Alistair had become. Maturity had made him more attractive and his talent would always command a top salary. She would enjoy being his wife as well as being the owner of a successful gallery.

She remembered how protective he had been when they were married, how safe she had felt being with a man who always put her first. He would look after her, like Mark did. It would not be difficult to make Alistair fall in love with her again.

# Chapter Eighteen

Over the next few days, Georgie found herself on a steep learning curve. There were so many appointments pencilled into her desk diary, it was not possible to see a white space. When her secretary suggested cancelling one or two meetings, Georgie refused, saying she needed to enthuse as many people as she could with her ideas for the company, but she felt she was tap-dancing and juggling at the same time.

She was battling with deep-rooted perceptions. There was no doubt that the media viewed her appointment with scepticism and forecast rough times ahead for Amalgamated. The flak in the City pages had affected staff morale and there were rumours of one or two high-profile walk-outs. To counteract the negative publicity, Georgie brought forward two launches. This had the desired effect of creating a buzz on the editorial and advertising floors. And she was planning internal promotions, several long overdue, in her opinion.

From time to time, Josephine would peer anxiously round the office door. But Georgie turned down her invitations to supper or even a cup of coffee.

In the office she hinted to the staff that Alistair was away on a secret buying trip on Helen's behalf. She could not bring herself to tell them the truth, although most people seemed to guess something was wrong, judging by the way conversation ceased whenever she approached. His name would crop up in the normal course of events but it was as if he had dropped out of their orbit. Helen's secretary had told her where he was and she remembered the place very well. They had spent one of their most relaxed, most loving holidays there, about two years ago.

She had shown him the door, but she did not want to believe their marriage was over. Now he was at their special hotel without her, he would have time to think things through. When he returned, she would ask him to work with her to repair their marriage.

Flying backwards in time, Alistair arrived in Boca Raton in the mid-afternoon. Before unpacking he sat, depressed, on his balcony, watching the mesmeric motion of the sea and the palm trees bending gently in unison like bowing courtiers. Along the sunny Florida sands was where half the fashion shoots for European magazines started life.

His decision to come here had been greatly influenced by the thought that Georgie would be told where he had fled. Perhaps she would fly over for the weekend, and then they would find a route out of this impasse.

Twice a year he and Georgie tried to build in a trip to

America for an infusion of Yankee creativity as part of a work-cum-holiday. They would have cocktails with advertisers and public relations friends, dinner with writers and photographers, and the occasional lunch with model agency owners before heading off to Aspen for a few days' skiing if the season was right, or a couple of days in Florida for the sunshine or the Napa valley vineyards for an indulgent day sampling the excellent wines.

Going to the USA was like acquiring an intravenous adrenalin drip. Alistair was stimulated by their television, their magazines, their books, even their dull-looking newspapers. He never failed to return home revitalised by new ideas. But without Georgie, America did not work its magic.

Alistair decided he could not face dinner at one of the splendid restaurants. He opted instead for the very best that room service had to offer. Caviar and a half-bottle of Dom Perignon for starters, followed by a Caesar salad. But, sitting alone in his suite, he found little enjoyment in the meal.

He reflected on how strange he had found walking into the empty flat yesterday to scrabble about for last summer's swimming trunks and to locate his lightweight clothes. Packing together, suggesting to each other what to take, shouting out reminders to cancel the papers was how their holidays usually started. He sighed, wondering if he should take the initiative and phone Georgie.

The events of the last few days had left him feeling drained. The fact was, he could not envisage day-to-day life with his wife in charge of the company and of him. He had a decent enough reputation in the business; he would start again in a different company. Not with a rival publisher, that might be difficult for Georgie. Perhaps with an advertising agency or a television station. Those were the ideas he would work on when he returned.

Louise was no threat to his wife, never had been. He still loved Georgie. Although she'd told him to leave the flat, he was sure when she'd had time to simmer down, she'd change her mind. He did not regard his marriage as being over. Far from it.

Alistair did some calculations. It would be lunchtime in England. What would Georgie be doing? He resisted the impulse to phone for only an instant and quickly dialled their flat. No answer. He rang off before his own voice on the answering machine clicked in. If she were anxious about him, she could dial the number recall service. Hearing the number was unavailable, would she guess it was a transatlantic call? Maybe not.

That night he dreamt he was roller-skating down the office hallway, searching for Georgie but she was nowhere to be found. By the time he awoke it was too late to phone again and he spent a lazy day by the pool flipping through the dozens of magazines he'd bought at a convenience store called 'If We Don't Stock It, You Don't Need It'. He barely registered the women relaxing on sun loungers around him, their lithe, firm bodies every shade of skin, from pale cream to mahogany. He'd done the model-actress-or-whatever routine and was happy to have left that frantic period of his life behind.

After twenty-four hours, despite the luxury of the Hotel Del Mar, the sun's warmth and the tempting food, Alistair was miserable. Georgie was never far from his thoughts and he hated being without her. He was used to being part of a couple and what he wanted most in life was to be Georgie's husband. He pictured her face as she gazed at him after lovemaking. She always looked at him with such tenderness that he felt secure, emotionally cradled, filled with confidence. She was so good for his ego, making him feel he could achieve anything. He could visualise her messy, wet hair as she stepped from the shower, Georgie laughing, Georgie sad, Georgie brisk, Georgie sentimental. She was special and he loved her. Maybe when he got back he could persuade her to come away with him for a couple of days, to talk and sort things out.

It was 7 a.m. in England when he dialled their home number. It rang several times and he was bracing himself to leave a message on the answer machine when he heard her breathless voice.

'Oh, hello,' she said warily when he greeted her. Thank God she did not sound angry. 'I was on my way out.'

'It doesn't matter,' he lied. 'I can speak to you tomorrow.'

'No, no, carry on. I have a few minutes.'

'I wanted to straighten things out between us. I know you think I slept with Louise. I did not. It's important to me you believe that.'

She did not make any comment.

'I wish you were here with me. Do you know where I am?'

'Margery Conlan told me.'

'Remember when we were last here?'

'Yes,' she said quietly.

'Georgie, I can't believe it's over between us. I just can't.' How could he convince her that he still loved her? That he was desperate for their marriage to survive? 'Darling, let's try again, please. I was pig-headed to rush over here. Shall I catch the next plane back?' Alistair held his breath, waiting for her reply. Would she give him any hope? He could tell by her breathing she was about to speak when there was a knock at the door of his suite so loud it was audible down the line to London.

'What's that?' she asked.

'It's the middle of the night here and there's someone at the door, would you believe.'

'Room service?' inquired Georgie, sounding amused.

'Not for me,' said Alistair. 'There must be some mistake. I want to—'

The knock was repeated more insistently and she said, 'No point in ignoring it, better sort it out. I have to go anyway.'

'No, please wait. This won't take a second, don't hang up,' he pleaded, sounding to his ears more than a little desperate. He marched to the door, tightening the belt of his towelling robe. Who the hell could it be at this time of night? He flung open the door and his face tightened. Standing there, in a shiny black PVC mackintosh and

308

high-heeled patent shoes was a smiling Louise. He barred her way, trying to make her stay outside, but she pushed past him.

Frantically he put his finger to his lips and indicated he was on the phone. She nodded and stood silently in the middle of the room.

'I'm back,' he stuttered as he picked up the receiver. He glared at Louise and turned his back on her. Surely she'd take the hint and leave him to finish his phone call in private.

'Who was that?'

'Someone not too steady on his feet trying to find his room,' he lied, conscious that the hairs on his neck were beginning to stand up. He glanced over his shoulder at Louise and his eyes widened. She was undoing the buttons of her coat.

Concentrate, concentrate. 'I think we need to talk face to face,' he said desperately, gesticulating at Louise to leave the room.

Georgie said something but Alistair missed it.

'Alistair, are you still there?' she asked sharply.

'Sorry, yes, of course.' He sounded distracted to his own ears.

'What's going on there?' Georgie said sharply.

'Nothing, nothing. What were you saying?' He watched in mounting panic as Louise slid her coat off her shoulders and let it drop to the floor. She stood motionless, wearing only a tiny sprigged blue and white bra and sheer black hold-up stockings.

The carpet was the safest thing to look at.

There was an exasperated sigh from across the Atlantic. 'This doesn't sound like a good time to discuss something as important as our marriage,' Georgie said. 'Why did you run away after I got the job?'

'I didn't run away,' he said quietly. 'A second's thought might have told you that I'd had a bloody big shock and I needed a break. My God, that job's made you insensitive.' He regretted the words as soon as he said them but the image of his first wife doing a striptease here in his bedroom had momentarily driven out the vision of his second thousands of miles away at home.

Georgie's voice hardened. 'And you're a selfish shit.' The phone went dead.

Alistair did not replace the receiver immediately. When he did, he felt Louise's now naked body press up close to his. He stepped away from her but she moved with him and he could feel the softness of her body through his robe. She took his head in her hands and pulled it down so her lips were close to his ear.

'Let me help you to forget,' she whispered.

'No,' he muttered thickly. 'I can't.'

Her hands began reaching insistently underneath his white towelling robe and when he tried to turn away, she quickly untied the belt. 'Remember how I used to be able to arouse you in seconds.' Louise's voice was husky. 'Look what's happening now. You can't resist me, can you?'

'Stop that,' was all Alistair could manage.

'It's too late for that,' she said, opening his mouth gently with her tongue. Her hands were caressing his loins and, finding no resistance, she guided his responsive body towards hers.

It was only seconds later that his robe joined the PVC coat on the floor. Alistair made a feeble attempt to disentangle himself but by this time the President of the United States could have burst into the room and he would not have been able to control the urgent demands of his body.

But immediately after he reached climax, he found himself saying, 'No, no, no.'

Louise was amused. 'That's a change from yes, yes, yes.'

Cursing himself for his weakness, Alistair made his way to the bathroom. How had he allowed this to happen? He had the willpower of a gnat. Had he given Louise any encouragement? No. The image of Georgie's dark eyes came into his mind. It must never happen again. He had always been faithful to Georgie. This was just one lapse, and in extraordinary circumstances.

Alistair came out of the bathroom and studied the figure sprawled drowsily across the bed. He drew in his breath. Still rosy from their lovemaking, her tousled hair spilling across the pillow, tanned skin and soft curves framed by the white sheets, Louise was every man's fantasy. Of course he was physically attracted to such a woman. Few men could resist someone like her, especially when she was making such a determined effort. But he was overcome by guilt. He had just committed adultery with the one woman in the world who made his wife feel insecure. He would have to ensure Louise's silence. And get rid of her fast. It would be no use trying to reassure Georgie that for him the magic was not rekindled, that his body had regarded it as physical release. He intended to spend the next day or so quietly by himself devising a plan of action to get Georgie back. For that he needed Louise to leave, immediately.

Alistair shook Louise's shoulder gently. Her eyelids opened and she focused her almond-shaped eyes on his face. She gave a slow, satisfied smile. 'That was wonderful,' she purred.

'Yes, well, it won't happen again. I'm a married man.'

She smiled coquettishly at him. 'For now.'

'For always,' he said firmly, taking her hand and pulling her up from the bed. 'I think we can be grown-up about it and see it for what it was.'

'Are you telling me you didn't enjoy it?'

'I'm telling you it's over.'

Louise's eyebrows lifted in surprise and her mouth pursed but she recovered well. 'I could really help you, you know. You've gone through a bad time. You're a highly talented, desirable guy and I bet I could restore your confidence. Helen's made a mistake about the job.' She slipped from his grip and lay back on the bed. He could not help noticing the undulation of her breasts as she stretched an arm on to the pillow above her head.

He shook himself mentally. 'You're catching the next plane to London,' he told her, 'so we're going to have to say goodbye now. Louise, I'm sure I don't need to say this to you but for both our sakes I hope we can keep this little incident quiet. I don't want Georgie to find out.'

Louise gave him a gaze he'd once found captivating. 'I'll be happy to promise that. But there's a price.'

Alistair frowned. 'Don't play games.'

'I'm deadly serious. I won't tell your wife if you agree to make love to me one more time.'

'Absolutely not. I can't.'

'Oh, I think you can.'

Georgie bitterly regretted what she'd said. Was calling her husband a selfish shit the way to get him back? And she wanted him back. She missed his physical presence, not so much the sex as the hugs and cuddles for which there was positively no substitute. She scrutinised their bedroom with an unhappy eye. Where were the discarded socks, the tennis gear that was never put away after their Thursday night game? She missed the look in his eye that said 'I love you above anything else in this entire world'.

As soon as it was light over there she would phone him. Agony aunts in her own magazines would advise a cooler approach, a slightly longer wait, but she did not want the marriage simply to trickle away. She should have encouraged him to fly home, as he had suggested. What had she gained by snapping at him?

A few hours later she picked up the phone and before she lost courage quickly dialled the hotel number.

'Good morning, Hotel Del Mar in golden Florida. This is Dee-Dee, how may I help you?'

Georgie suppressed a smile. American telephone operators were a breed apart. 'I'm trying to contact Mr Alistair Drummond.'

'One moment please, ma'am.'

As she waited to be connected, Georgie was conscious of her heart thumping so fiercely she had to take a deep breath to steady herself. What would she say? She must try and make her voice light, not to give the impression that she was tense.

At last the receiver was picked up and Georgie heard a throaty laugh and then an amused voice drawled, 'Hello?'

Georgie's throat constricted. She recognised those distinctive tones at once.

'Hello?' The woman was more peremptory this time. 'Anybody there?' After the briefest of pauses, during which Georgie thought she heard the sound of a shower in the background, the connection was broken.

Georgie sat on the side of her bed, staring into space, shaken.

Images of Alistair's naked body entwined with Louise's came unbidden into her mind and she felt a stab of jealousy as intense as if a serrated knife was pirouetting in her chest.

How long had the affair been going on? Despite their bitter quarrel, she'd hoped he had been telling the truth that nothing had happened between them the night he stayed at Louise's flat. And now, to discover that she was with him in Florida. They must have planned this sneaky assignation together. And he had taken her to their special hotel. How could he be so callous?

For the first time Georgie faced the prospect that reconciliation was out of the question.

Sex with Louise had been amazing, no other word for it, thought Alistair as he packed his suitcase. But after the second time he'd had a disturbing vision of Georgie's face immediately after climax. It was a helluva passion killer but Louise had not seemed to notice anything.

Since her dramatic re-entry into his life he had come to realise that he had always viewed their marriage too rosily. When he thought about their life together he recalled it had been a succession of spats followed by marathon sex sessions. She used to find rows exhilarating and some of their best lovemaking sessions had happened after quarrels. But at least that technique would not work with him any more. He had been living with a grown-up since then.

Louise had left an hour ago but not before he had made it clear to her that there would be no more assignations. She appeared to accept that he meant what he said. In fact, she had given no indication last night that sex with him was anything more than a pleasant distraction. She said she had been wanting an excuse to escape the dreary London weather and when Rosemary had told her where he was, on impulse she had booked herself a flight to keep him company. Thereafter she had confined her conversation to business. Despite himself, he had been interested to hear the details concerning the purchase of her gallery, her plans for finance, and her ideas for exhibitions. This was going to be manageable, he had thought. Louise just wanted to make use of his contacts to establish herself in the art world. As ever, promoting herself was her primary motive – though her attempt to join him while he was in the shower this morning made him realise he would be wise not to relax his guard with her.

The water was pounding his shoulders and he was shampooing his hair when the shower door had opened and a pair of hands had enfolded his body and begun caressing his stomach.

He had tried to slip out of her grasp. 'Stop that. I thought we'd reached an understanding.'

'We certainly have,' she said playfully. 'Turn round and let me see if there's a present for me.'

He had shrugged her off firmly and ordered her out of the shower, and with a laugh she had obeyed.

Alistair was certain he would not have found enduring happiness with Louise. If they'd had children their relationship might have survived but now he regarded her disappearance soon after their marriage as fortuitous. He could see clearly that it had been her rejection of him which had kept her memory vivid in those unhappy years following the divorce.

Suddenly he had a craving to hear the sound of Georgie's voice. Their last conversation had been scratchy by any standards and he felt a great need to start the healing process. He would not let Georgie slip away from him without a fight.

She answered the phone immediately but before he could launch into an apology for his boorish behaviour over the last few days she disconcerted him by snapping, 'Isn't Mrs Drummond with you?'

'What are you talking about?' he said, alarmed. 'You're Mrs Drummond.'

'Silly me, I meant Mrs Drummond the first.'

How the hell had she found out? 'I don't know—'

'Alistair,' she interrupted angrily, 'you can take me for lots of things, but don't take me for a fool. I know you're there with Louise.'

Alistair decided this was not the time for evasion. 'She's not here any more and it's not what you think. It wasn't planned, I didn't know she was coming.'

Georgie ignored this. 'How long have you been consoling yourself with her?'

'I haven't. Nothing happened in London, I didn't sleep with her then.'

'Then?' The word hit him like a bullet.

'Georgie, I'm sorry. She really did turn up out of the blue.'

'Poor boy, and you didn't feel able to tell her to push off? You had to sleep with her, did you?'

'I was feeling bloody miserable and you and I had just had that big fight—'

'And you think that's a good excuse to fuck your first wife,' she interrupted. 'In our hotel.'

He was silent.

'At least I should thank you for not telling me another lie.'

'I can understand how you feel,' said Alistair desperately.

'Can you now?'

He winced at the sarcasm in her voice. 'I don't think it's a good idea to talk about this on the phone,' he said quickly.

'Alistair, I don't ever want to talk to you about Louise.' She paused. 'Or about anything else. In case I haven't made myself completely clear, our marriage is over.'

# *Chapter Nineteen*

Georgie felt numb, as if someone had injected an anaesthetic drug into her veins, deadening her mind, her body, her emotions. As ever in times of crisis, she took refuge in work. She forced herself to push personal matters to one side and immersed herself in a maze of meetings, video conferences and business lunches. Her activities stretched the working day until late into the evening so that at home she had energy only for a quick shower before falling into bed.

When her mind was less occupied with work, everything reminded her of him. Driving home she would pass the wine bar on the corner where they first met, the cinema where he had sat so close she couldn't concentrate on the film at all, and the florists where now and then he would buy her flowers. When she switched on the late-night news, she would remember how they would lie in bed and make comments about the newscaster.

Whatever she was doing, Alistair kept intruding, the way he threw back his head and shouted with laughter, the way he coaxed her out of a black mood when she was tired or out of sorts with the world. She could not bring herself to acknowledge that her marriage, that solid edifice she had relied upon and trusted, was a sham. But had he flown back immediately to plead his case when she'd caught him out in adultery? No, he had not. He preferred to remain in Florida with Louise.

Georgie was filled with a mixture of rage, bitterness and despair, and an overwhelming certainty that however fulfilling her career, she would find it impossible to overcome this feeling of emptiness. She had no motivation to socialise or confide in friends. She saw no point in responding to messages on her home answering machine inviting her to dinner or the theatre with couples who had no idea what was going on in her marriage.

The flat was unbearably lonely and her rare periods of leisure were spent, meals forgotten, poring over budget plans, manuscripts and suggestions from staff. Some of the ideas needed careful research and Georgie was grateful to be able to spend time on them. But there were too many anguished moments when she was tortured by the image of Alistair whispering the same sweet words of endearment to Louise that he had whispered to her, giving her those same tender kisses, bringing her to the pitch of excitement with the same caresses.

Georgie's jealousy was so acute that the snatch of a love song made her wince, seeing a couple entwined in each other's arms at a bus stop made her turn away. When she arrived home, she would switch to the movie channel, subconsciously searching for a weepie in an effort to release her pent-up emotions. The 1950s film *The Last Time I Saw Paris* in which Elizabeth Taylor died of consumption in the rain started a paroxysm of weeping that went on long after the film was finished.

She tried to convince herself that a man who could jeopardise a basically secure marriage the way Alistair had was not a man with whom she wanted to share the rest of her life. But here in their flat she found thinking about creating some kind of existence without him almost impossible. Her marriage was over and she ought to find somewhere new to live. They had made love so many times in this room, she could almost feel the weight of his body on hers. If she closed her eyes, she could smell the soap he liked using, and feel the droplets of water from his face when they made love after a shower. Yes, she definitely had to leave this place.

Exercise was supposed to lift one's spirits by releasing endorphins, but in her case it did not happen. Walking was a disaster. It gave her too much time to think and work-outs at the gym did not provide her with the buzz that used to accompany every sweat-soaked session.

Although few knew of their split, those around her seemed careful not to mention Alistair's name. The newspaper stories about her promotion and Alistair's position had made them tactful. Georgie had been too raw to discuss what had happened with anyone but finally, desperate to talk, she asked Josephine if she could spare a few minutes for a coffee outside the office.

Sitting at a wrought-iron table at a pavement cafe, oblivious of the sunshine and the people walking past,

Georgie told her friend what had happened in Florida.

'Oh, Georgie, I'm sorry. I thought you two were welded for ever.' Josephine squeezed her arm. 'I always thought your suspicions about him and Louise were paranoid nonsense but you must have been right all the time.'

'It's probably been going on for ages. I've been such a fool.'

'The shit. You know what I think? The guy's found the best way to punish you for getting his job. Fucking the one woman you couldn't forgive him for.'

It was unlike Josephine to be this critical and for a second Georgie wanted to defend her husband. But she suppressed the urge.

'It's over, Jo, it really is this time.'

'I'll never forgive him for hurting you like this,' said Josephine fiercely.

'I'll never be able to trust him again.'

'I don't blame you. You shouldn't allow him back in the flat,' said Josephine.

'I don't see how I can stop him when he returns from Florida.'

'If I were you, I'd change the locks. You don't want him taking her there while you're out, do you?' Josephine was caustic. 'Drinking out of your cups or, worse, making love in your bed?'

Georgie shook her head. 'Alistair wouldn't do that.'

'Wouldn't he?' Josephine gave her a pitying glance. 'You didn't think he'd take Louise to Florida.'

Slowly Georgie stirred her coffee and Josephine asked,

'Are you going to be all right?'

'I've been better. I feel, there's no other word for it, bereaved.'

'I know what you're going through.'

'Do you?' Georgie's pale face was strained.

'It's as if you have barbed wire all twisted up inside, tearing at your organs.'

'That's about it.'

'You have to learn to grow round the wire so it can't hurt any more. When that happens maybe you can begin to live again.'

'I can't imagine getting back to normal.'

'Give it time. You're doing all the right things, keeping busy, keeping away from him.'

Georgie smiled wanly. 'The only good thing to come out of this mess is that I've lost seven pounds and rediscovered my cheekbones.'

'See? Every cloud . . .' Josephine warmed her hands round her cup. 'You won't be able to admit it to yourself yet but there are a few advantages to being an independent woman.'

'I suppose. At least I have total control over the duvet.'

'And the TV zapper. One of mine used to drive me mad channel surfing.'

'Alistair's always so bloody cheerful in the mornings. At least I don't have to talk now.'

'Be grateful he didn't leave wet towels on the bed.'

'But he did,' and for the first time since hearing Louise's hated voice in that hotel suite, Georgie's face lit up with a genuine smile.

★ ★ ★

Harry was surprised to receive a call from Ned Mastrianni. Their last encounter, following Georgina's appointment, had been full of recriminations, and Harry had been told in plain language that he was lacking in the balls department. Yet now Ned's tone was friendly, as if nothing had happened.

'I've had some time to think,' Ned was saying, 'and I'm of the opinion that our options are still open in spite of the adverse conditions.'

'I see,' said Harry, masking his surprise.

Ned lowered his voice. 'I believe the more we can make trouble for the other party the better our prospects in future, though the time scale will be slightly longer than anticipated. Hold the thought that it's not over yet, not by a long way.'

'I'm pleased you think that way,' said Harry. 'As it happens, there is some information that I can use.'

'Good. Keep the pressure up and I think things could turn our way pretty quickly. Keep me posted.'

Harry replaced the receiver feeling less wretched. If Ned was still willing to have a go, then he was worth supporting. In any case at Harry's age other high-level jobs were hardly plentiful and when Georgina reorganised the company he'd be lucky to be put in charge of ordering the stationery. He picked up the phone and pressed an internal number.

'Meet me outside Sotheby's in ten minutes.' His voice was brisk. 'Yes, of course it's important.'

Shortly afterwards, Harry and his spy were squeezed

together in the phone booth outside Sotheby's in Bond Street making a call that could not be traced back to any itemised bill.

Like many national newspapers it was a long time before his call was dealt with and he asked to be put through to the news desk. Harry tutted in annoyance. What a way to run a business. His company had a policy of picking up calls after five seconds. Of course it meant hiring extra switchboard staff but he had won this particular battle against Giles Beamish and he was proud that they had maintained their record.

'News editor, please . . . No, the name's not important. I have information I'm sure will interest your paper . . . No, I won't speak to anyone else . . . No, you can't ring me back. I'll wait.'

A few seconds elapsed before Harry gave a nod to his companion to indicate that the person he wanted had come on the line.

'News editor? Good. I thought you'd like to know that the new chief at Amalgamated, Georgina Luckhurst, and her husband Alistair Drummond have split up.'

Harry listened to a question.

'You're damned right it's because of the job. He's brassed off that she was put in over his head and now she's trying to push him out of the company.' He nodded into the phone. 'Yes, I thought you could make something of that.' He put down the phone.

'What's that going to achieve?' asked his companion, pushing open the door.

'It'll be a nine-minute wonder but the more we can

destabilise Georgina, the better. She's only on trial and her reign is closely allied with Helen's. I want Helen to get out of the business and take Georgina with her.'

'I have to admire your perseverance.'

'Ned says there's still a lot of play for.' He punched his fist into his palm. 'Dammit, we're not going to sit back and let those pussies ruin our plans.'

Georgie managed to slip into the office through the car park entrance, avoiding the photographer who was door-stepping the front of the building. So much, she thought, for the agreements after Princess Diana's death not to hound people.

The receptionist gave her a sympathetic smile as she ran up the stairs. Breathlessly she greeted her secretary who came into her office a few seconds later with a cup of freshly-brewed coffee.

'I think you need this,' she said.

'Golden Couple Split' was the lead story on page five of the *Daily Chronicle*, followed by a feature written at speed by their top woman writer: 'Should you sacrifice a job for love?' The copy suggested a resounding 'No', underlined by the hastily-culled vox pops. There were quotations from the usual rent-a-mouths, notably B and C list celebrities desperate to have their name in print and remind casting agents that they were still alive.

'Who talked to the papers?' Georgie wondered out loud.

'Our press office has been trying to find out all morning,' replied her secretary. 'No luck so far but they say it must be somebody inside. And Helen has asked if you'd stop by, please.'

Georgie sipped the coffee, asking herself who could gain from telling the world that she and Alistair had split? She couldn't believe Alistair had told anyone and the question tormented her. Quite a few egos had been wounded when she was made chief executive. But how would this make things better for them? She could understand if it was a story about her competence, but her marriage?

Undoubtedly Helen would be upset that two of her top executives appeared to be at war. She still fostered hopes that Alistair would remain at Amalgamated, and naturally she would be worried about how their problems would affect their performance at work.

When Georgie went in to see her, Helen pointed at the newspaper. 'I was sorry to read this. I hope it's only temporary.'

'I'm afraid I can't answer that yet.'

'Is there anything I can do? Speak to him?'

Georgie shook her head vehemently. 'I may not want the marriage to end but if I'm realistic things may have gone too far. I don't know if we can straighten this out.'

'That's a great pity but I hope it won't affect the two of you working together.'

Georgie had rehearsed her answer. 'We'll try our best of course, but we may not have to for long. Alistair will probably leave.'

'I wouldn't be too sure of that,' Helen replied. 'I've

offered him the job as head of magazine launches and he's considering it.'

Georgie frowned, momentarily diverted from her personal problems. This was an important appointment and as the new boss she should have been consulted about it. The job of chief executive was more than just a rubber stamp for Helen's commandments. Awkward as it was, she had to take a stand now.

'Helen, I understand that the board tried to avoid a potentially embarrassing complication when they chose me over Alistair but I'm a little surprised you made the offer without waiting to talk it over with me.'

'Point taken,' said Helen mildly.

'Why didn't you mention it to me before?'

'Well, we needed to give him some incentive to stay with us. One or two people felt he might leave, as you did. I made the offer when I told him we had decided to appoint you chief executive. There was no time to discuss it with you and having made him the offer, there was nothing to talk about really.'

It sounded reasonable but nevertheless Georgie felt excluded. Would they have done this to a new chief executive if he had been male?

'I should have been given the chance to persuade him to stay,' she said without heat. 'It would have reinforced my authority. As you know, I want to rationalise the two divisions. We've been talking about it for long enough and it's my priority. I would have wanted to discuss whether this was something which would interest him more than magazine launches.'

'Alistair's still chewing over my offer so it may not be too late,' said Helen. 'It's whether or not he stays which is important. It would be a disaster for this company if we allowed Alistair to leave. I had to move fast.'

'I understand that.' Georgie was unable to keep a note of steel from her voice. This was her first disagreement with Helen and she was conscious that she had to persuade her that a chief executive must be allowed to lead. 'But you must realise that unless I have a free hand in staffing arrangements, however senior, my job will be impossible.'

Helen nodded and said, 'Yes, you're right.' But she did not elaborate and Georgie left the suite feeling deflated.

Was Helen going to delegate any power? Despite her fine words when she was appointed, Georgie was beginning to wonder about her. Did Helen think she could be fobbed off with a title, an enlarged office and a driver at her disposal? If so, she was in for a surprise.

Georgie accepted that despite the publicity and kudos her appointment had brought the company, there would be no mercy shown if they felt she wasn't up to scratch. Did they want to keep Alistair on ice, to be on hand if she failed? She wanted a chance to operate in her own way before she was judged.

When she returned to her office, she summoned the press officer to draft a press release for the media. It quoted her as saying that her marriage was a private matter and she categorically denied that she and Alistair were considering divorce. It wasn't a lie, neither of them had mentioned divorce. When the press officer suggested they conclude by stating that Mr Drummond fully supported his wife's appointment as chief executive, she nodded her assent, thinking that Alistair would hardly go public to deny it.

# Chapter Twenty

In the vast ballroom, the clinking of cutlery and glasses stopped when the toast mistress asked for silence and began reading short citations to the cream of British professional women attending this year's Women Of Our Times dinner. As each name was announced, the applause eddied and flowed, accompanied by cries of 'Well done'. Eight women were being honoured this evening, including a nun who had survived an especially violent African massacre, a nurse who had saved three mothers in labour when they were caught in a hospital brawl, and a teacher who had led thirty four-year-olds from a blazing classroom on the second floor of a school. They were followed by Britain's first female bishop, and then the head of a global industrial firm who, unbeknown to her audience, had only yesterday escaped a boardroom putsch. She received only quiet approbation from the guests although she had probably witnessed more blood on the walls than those preceding her.

Then the toast mistress called for silence and recited

the final name on the list. 'Georgina Luckhurst, the new chief executive of Amalgamated Magazines, the first woman to head a major magazine publishing company in Britain – indeed in the world.'

The room erupted. That morning's newspaper stories had reported Georgie's marriage break-up and the professional women there who knew that for their gender success always had a price reacted in the traditional way. Hands that had once sported wedding rings banged on the table. Some guests used their feet to beat out a tattoo of sisterly support. Once again it had been shown that men could not cope with being married to women in the fast lane, who then overtook them.

The events of the last few days suddenly hit Georgie. She had been too numb and too scared to show any emotion publicly. But now, with all these women, friends and strangers alike, extending their warmth and encouragement, she had to fight down a desire to weep.

She was aware that those in their twenties and early thirties thought she was their heroine. But in the faces of the older women she saw sympathy. How many of them had sacrificed their relationships to have a successful career?

The event was being photographed as well as televised and Georgie knew she must accept this accolade looking like a winner. Helen and all those who had competed for the job would be watching. She lifted her chin, praying that the moisture in her eyes would appear to be tears of delight.

Almost blinded by the flash bulbs, Georgie made a

short but gracious acceptance speech, paying tribute to her company for having faith in her abilities. To more applause, she sat down.

'Quite a reception,' said a voice and Georgie turned to the guest seated on her left. Frances Hammond was one of the organisers of the event and had spent much of her spare time during the year working on this one evening. She was a senior partner in a law firm, a spare-looking grey-haired woman in her late fifties, expensively but neatly dressed, someone who did not draw attention to herself.

'Yes, I'm quite overwhelmed,' admitted Georgie.

They talked about how Amalgamated's employees were reacting to her promotion and then Frances Hammond said sympathetically, 'I was sorry to read about your marriage problems.'

'That article was a bit premature and I've issued a denial. I'm damned if I'm going to allow newspapers to take control of my life.'

'I know what you're going through,' said Frances. 'My break-up wasn't in the public domain like yours, thank goodness, but my husband left me for another woman. Of course I divorced him immediately.'

Georgina hesitated for a moment. 'You were right,' then she added, 'weren't you?'

'Was I? Twelve years later I'm not so sure. I realised not too long afterwards that he didn't want to be with this woman and I still had feelings for him.' Frances stared into the distance, her fingers crumbling a small breadstick. 'But I stuck to my guns. "He done me wrong", as they say, and he had to be punished. But,' she turned an unhappy face to Georgie, 'I was punished equally.'

'There's another woman in my case too,' admitted Georgie.

'If you two still love each other, you should consider whether you can get over that. Only you can decide whether your marriage is worth saving. That's all you should be thinking about now. Nothing else and nobody else should be involved.' She gave a smile, 'Certainly not lawyers.'

Georgie smiled wryly. 'We can't have it all, can we?'

'There's often a price to pay, weighing up a glamorous but demanding job against a lonely private life.'

Frances's words struck home. Georgie could not banish her feelings of emptiness and desolation. Was it good to get to the top of the mighty slope only to find that you were up there alone? She would tell herself many times that Louise was welcome to Alistair but it did not stop her missing the feel of his arms round her before they settled down to sleep and the way he used to gaze at her sometimes when she caught him unawares, a look of such love and warmth that she felt treasured. She used to try to project herself into the future and imagine them as parents, even grandparents. It would fill her with anticipation, not trepidation, because what she wanted from her marriage was a soul mate in every sense. And the plans they had made. That cottage near the sea because they both loved water, the garden they were going to create, the trees they would plant, and of course the babies they would have. The images were so powerful she fought hard to keep control.

People in the ballroom were preparing to leave and she and Frances Hammond stood up as well.

'I'm interfering in your private business,' said the lawyer, 'but I don't apologise for it.'

'You don't have to,' smiled Georgie. 'You've given me a lot to think about.'

'I'm glad. Talking is always good although it keeps lawyers out of business,' said Frances. 'Of course, if you need my professional services,' she proffered a business card, 'I'd be more than willing but I hope I don't hear from you.'

As Georgie made her way towards the exit, her mood somehow seemed a little lighter and she hoped it would last.

Alistair disembarked from the Florida plane at London Heathrow trying to feel resolute about saving his marriage. In his pocket was a letter to Georgie he'd spent days composing and most of the flight honing, trying to get every phrase right. He desperately wanted to make her understand that he had not pursued Louise, that she had followed him to Florida without any encouragement from him. He had no intention of seeing her again. What he wanted most in the world, he said in his letter to Georgie, was to love and care for her, if she would give him another chance. He was painfully aware of how much he had lost, how much they had together and how proud he was of her. If she had any affection left for him, would she please at least give him some hope. He ended the letter with a postscript that he would wait by the phone all night.

He intended to be staying with Rosemary but decided he would make a detour and collect some clothes from home first.

On the way through the arrivals lounge to the taxi rank he bought a newspaper to read on the way. He was about half an hour from home when he read the media section and saw a reference to a story the previous day about their marriage break-up being officially denied. Alistair read the brief statement three times. He felt a surge of hope, but then reminded himself that it was probably a diplomatic move to appease Helen. Still, it could be a delaying tactic, a sign that Georgie was ready to consider talking about their differences.

This small spark of optimism burned brightly as he entered their block of flats and fumbled for his keys.

'Haven't seen you around for a while, sir,' said the porter walking before him towards the lift.

'No, I've been in the States.'

'I didn't think you'd got that tan around here,' the porter replied and pressed the call button. 'The weather's been something chronic.'

The smell of lavender wax filled the air and Alistair felt a surge of regret as he gazed round at the lobby with its Persian carpet and extravagant arrangement of fresh flowers delivered every Monday morning. He had missed this place, it was inextricably bound up with his life with Georgie.

He remembered how painstakingly they had collected pieces of furniture for their flat, wandering round antique shops locally and on weekend excursions a little further afield. They were proud of the home they had created together.

Impatiently Alistair decided to give up waiting for the lift and began bounding up to the second floor. Fingering the letter in his pocket, he wondered how Georgie was dealing with her new job. He missed the gossip, the action and the laughs.

Arriving at the door of their flat, he put the key in the lock but it wouldn't turn. Strange. Maybe he had inserted the wrong key. He took it out of the lock and examined it carefully. No, it was the right one. He tried again. Still no go.

Without much conviction he made a third attempt but the lock did not yield. Then he changed keys and tried the Yale lock below, again with no success. He jerked the key out and sank down, his back against his own front door, unable to come to terms with what had clearly happened.

Damping down his anger, Alistair closed his eyes. Georgie had changed both locks. How could she? This was still his home. That denial she had given to the paper was obviously a public relations exercise. Presumably she thought the break-up would be bad for the company image.

Alistair took the envelope from his pocket, ripped it open and tore the letter into pieces which he stuffed back into his jacket. Then he scrawled on the back of the envelope, 'How do you expect me to get my stuff?'

The swift descent of the lift reflected Alistair's spirits. He strode out of the building without acknowledging the farewell salute from the porter. He paused a moment on the pavement, glancing up at the sky, which was grey. Why hadn't he noticed before how drab and colourless this street had become?

As he walked towards his car, he had an image of how structured his life had been before Georgie's elevation. He'd had a brilliant career, a fabulous wife and a fulfilling private life. Now he was searching for a job, he'd had a bust-up with his wife and he couldn't even gain entrance to his own bloody flat.

When Rosemary got home that evening Alistair was still in a state. She had barely taken her coat off before he told her about being locked out of his own home.

'I don't know what she's up to.' He flourished the newspaper. 'This denies we're splitting up and then she does something like that. What's she said to you?'

'She hasn't talked to me, Alistair.'

No, of course not, thought Alistair. Georgie and his sister were not exactly close. 'I think I'll tell Helen I need some more time,' he said dejectedly. 'I want to avoid going to the office. I'll see what other jobs are available. But I'd be grateful if you could ask Georgie tomorrow when I can get my belongings.'

'Of course I will,' said Rosemary. 'But why is she doing this?'

Alistair felt uncomfortable but he would rather his sister heard what happened from him than Georgie.

'Louise followed me to Florida,' he told her.

Rosemary appeared discomfited. 'I'm sorry, Alistair. That was my fault. I told her where you were.'

'You weren't to know she would be so brazen. I asked her to leave almost immediately, but we did have a fling,' he said self-consciously.

'Oh dear, you're not getting involved, are you? I'd hate to think she was going to hurt you again.'

'Don't worry, she won't,' he said grimly. 'It was a moment of weakness. I've made sure she understands it will never happen again.'


The next day Rosemary was still at work well beyond her usual time, as she had been several days this week. Georgie expected everyone to work the hours she did. Rosemary often said to herself that she would be pleased to do that if only her pay packet matched that of her boss. That woman had not even suggested a rise and she had so demoralised her staff that Rosemary was the only one who had dared mention it. When she had brought up the subject with that bitchy secretary of hers, she had said, 'All in good time. She'll get round to it. And anyway she's not in charge of pay rises.' Huh. As if she believed that.

'Rosemary.' The voice made her start. Hurriedly she forced a smile as Georgie's PA handed her a sheaf of papers. 'Could you input these as soon as possible, please. Georgie needs them for a breakfast meeting tomorrow. I have to leave now so could you take in what you've done?'

With a sigh, Rosemary turned back to the computer. How irritating. Everything was always urgent with Georgie.

When she had a print-out, tentatively she knocked on Georgie's door. Georgie did not welcome interruptions these days.

'I'm told you wanted these figures now.'

To her surprise, Georgie flashed her a smile. 'Come in, it's good to see you.' She gave the papers a cursory glance. 'Thank you for these,' she said, placing them on the cluttered desk before sitting back. 'How are things?'

This was not a query about her health, thought Rosemary. She was trying to find out about Alistair.

'Fine,' she said blandly.

'I've noticed you've been working late these past few nights. I'm sorry, there's so much to get through. I hope it hasn't been difficult, especially if you have to cook for Alistair when you get home.'

'I don't have to cater for Alistair. He's quite at home in the kitchen.' He's had to be, thought Rosemary.

'Alistair's lucky having someone like you to talk things over with.' Georgie walked round the desk and perched on top. 'I met someone recently who advised me not to let go of the marriage too easily. She said we should talk it through before making an irrevocable decision. What do you think, Rosie?'

Careful now, thought Rosemary. 'Well, he was very upset about your changing the locks.'

Georgie bit her lip. 'I shouldn't have done that but I thought—'

'Alistair asked me to find out when you'll be out so the porter can let him in to get his stuff.'

'I see.' Georgie's face was impassive now. 'I take it from that he feels the time for talking is past.'

'I wouldn't say that,' said Rosemary cautiously. 'But he does think this break is a good idea.'

'I'm sure he does,' said Georgie. She got up and sat behind her desk again.

She's desperate to ask about Louise, thought Rosemary, but of course she's far too high and mighty to come right out with it. Her own attitude towards Louise was ambivalent. She didn't want Alistair hurt again but she and Louise were setting up the art gallery together. If she proved her worth in the gallery and Alistair and Louise did get back together, she would not be pushed to the sidelines in the couple's private life as she had been by Georgie. If it came to a choice, she reckoned Louise was the one to back.

Georgie began to rearrange some papers on her desk. 'Perhaps I'd better start thinking about a divorce,' she said suddenly.

God, she had actually mentioned the D word, thought Rosemary. This was progress. 'Whatever you decide, I'm sure he'd want everything to be amicable,' she said. 'After all, there's no reason why you two should quarrel any more and as there aren't any children, it needn't be a drawn-out affair.'

'You're right, we need to get on with our lives. Besides, Louise might have been the catalyst but she didn't break up our marriage. It's much more complex than that.' She sighed and stood up. 'Ah well, suppose I'd better get back to work. By the way, did you get those European figures for me?'

'They've been promised for tomorrow,' said Rosemary. In fact, she'd forgotten to chase them up. The bloody woman can't even switch off when she's asking about Alistair, she thought as she left the room. The sooner he's out of that marriage the better.

# *Chapter Twenty-One*

A Machiavellian plan had been fermenting in Helen's mind, something of which in other circumstances Mark would have approved. Mark may have been less than perfect as a husband and father but as a manipulator of events in business he was matchless.

Helen had reviewed the details of the plan with Margery Conlan dozens of times. It would work perfectly except for one snag. Both of them were at least fifteen years too old when judged by the date of birth on the official papers.

'We have to involve someone else,' Helen pronounced. 'Someone of the right age and someone we can trust.'

'You have someone in mind.' It was not a question.

'I wouldn't even consider it otherwise,' replied Helen. 'Georgina Luckhurst.'

'Little close to home, isn't she?' said Margery cautiously. 'She'll have to know everything.'

'It's a pity and I wouldn't involve her if we could get round this some other way but we can't.'

'Are you sure we can rely on her discretion?'

'I'm certain of it. Another plus is that we'd be keeping it in the family, so to speak.'

'We're treading on dangerous ground. She'd have something on you.'

'I'll have to take that risk.'

Margery was thoughtful. After a moment she said calmly, 'Of course you gave her the job. That would be reason enough to help us. But I'm still not happy about involving anyone else.'

'I agree it's not ideal but what's the alternative?' When Margery remained silent she said, 'Ask Georgina to come and see me.'

A short while later, watching her chief executive walk towards her desk, her face alert, Helen's resolve faltered. Was she right to burden this young woman with more complications in her life?

She was growing to admire the way Georgina handled herself. If one of her daughters decided to follow them into the business, she would hope that she would behave like her new chief executive. She had taken over the reins of power with such authority and graciousness that she had not aroused any antagonism amongst the staff that Helen could detect. It was early days but the omens were promising. And Georgina had become much more relaxed with her.

Helen opened her office safe and extracted Mark's letter. 'I haven't called you in here because of business,' she said, handing Georgie the letter. 'This is personal and once you've read it you'll understand why I'm asking complete secrecy from you.'

Georgina's eyes were wary as she began reading and after a short time the silence in the room was broken only by the sound of a swift intake of breath. Georgina looked up. 'Helen, how terrible for you to find out in this way.'

'Read it to the end.'

Eventually Georgina put the pages down on the desk. 'Why did you want me to know about this?'

'Because in spite of Mark's best efforts I've found out who the woman is.' Georgina leaned forward expectantly and Helen took a deep breath. 'My husband's mistress was Alistair's first wife. Louise Palmer.'

Georgina sat back abruptly. 'Louise . . . and Mark? That's not possible.'

'Oh yes it is. The affair started while she was married and when she walked out on Alistair she went to be with Mark right under my nose in New York. And as this letter makes clear, it lasted until the day he died.'

Georgie shook her head and placed a hand over her eyes. 'I can't really take it in,' she said. 'You're sure about this?'

'I confronted her and she admitted it.'

Georgie seemed unable to speak and Helen went to the cabinet and poured her a glass of water. 'If you're shocked, imagine how I felt.'

Georgie took the water gratefully and drank deeply. 'I didn't want to tell you before but history's repeating itself. Alistair and I . . . well, I'm afraid our marriage is definitely over.'

'I'm very sorry,' said Helen sadly.

'Alistair has left me for Louise.'

'What!' Helen's jaw dropped. 'He's gone back to Louise? I never thought that someone like Alistair would make the same mistake twice.' She burned with anger against Mark's destructive mistress.

Georgie went on, 'Ever since Louise came back she's tried to get close to Alistair. She made a play for him at the memorial service. I could see the signs but he convinced me I was imagining things and maybe I was, on his part.' Her voice faltered. 'He didn't come to my celebration party because he was with her.'

'What an idiot the man is. He deserves all he gets with that woman.'

'My sentiments exactly,' said Georgie fiercely. 'It's not as if he doesn't know what he's in for but he's so obsessed with her he doesn't seem to care what she did to him in the past.'

'That one doesn't seem to care who she hurts, does she?'

'No, she doesn't,' said Georgie. 'I wish there was some way . . .' She stopped.

'To pay her back? I'm glad you said that,' Helen's face softened, 'because that's exactly what you and I are going to do, Georgina.'

A week later Helen and Georgie nervously approached the stately-looking building in Vaduz, grateful to have the bulky figure of the lawyer with them. He had been chosen from the hundreds available in Liechtenstein, selected on the simple premise that as a one-partner practice he would be more hungry for the commission than larger companies. And apparently he had conducted business with this bank before. If he suspected they were hiding something, he did not say so. That way he could profess ignorance should anything go wrong.

Helen was confident nothing would go wrong. The first lot of diamonds was due to be handed over today. The bank wouldn't be suspicious, there was no reason why they should be. The documents that would authorise the release of the diamonds were in the lawyer's briefcase. They would bear the closest scrutiny, Helen was sure. And it had been easy for Paul Wallis, ostensibly on a flying visit to London, to make an appointment with Louise for this morning to discuss the possible financing of her gallery. Apparently Louise had done her best to try and postpone the meeting, saying she had urgent business that day, but he was adamant that it was his only window available. Helen had gambled that Louise would abide by Mark's often-expressed dictum always to use other people's money to finance your projects. By the time she discovered Paul was not going to show up, she and Georgina would have completed their business.

On the flight out they had discussed how to behave during the ordeal ahead. According to a behavioural psychologist who occasionally contributed articles to one of Amalgamated's magazines, the biggest giveaway that you had told a lie was to touch your face, usually to rub your nose or ear. Experienced interviewers were trained to spot this at once. Another was to stare too directly into someone's eyes. And talking too much, making lengthy explanations, was also a pointer that something might be amiss.

As Helen and Georgie walked into the coolness of the bank's marbled entrance hall, each took a few deep breaths to steady their nerves. Without delay they were guided courteously into a small, panelled meeting room, whose expensive furnishings, Helen noticed, had been allowed to become slightly worn.

An official entered the room, dressed in smart blazer and flannels. He smiled warily. 'Madame Palmer, welcome to the bank.' He took Georgina's hand and she introduced Helen as her financial adviser, as they had planned. As Helen returned his smile, she was aware of being studied closely and was in no doubt that this official would be assiduous in checking their credentials.

He and the lawyer exchanged informal greetings; clearly they knew each other well, which ought to work in their favour.

A soft tap on the door heralded the arrival of coffee. Helen refused charmingly, saying she had recently had some at her hotel. In truth she could not have trusted her hands to hold a cup steadily. Georgina also refused.

The women sat back as a signal to the lawyer that he should proceed. In line with the advice they had received they had agreed that the less they said the better.

'My clients have to return to the UK immediately,' said the lawyer, 'and I have assured them we can be very swift when we want to.'

'*Certainement*,' said the official but he did not take his sharp gaze from Georgina's face. She seemed remarkably composed under his scrutiny, thought Helen.

'These are the documents you need,' continued the lawyer, taking out of his briefcase a passport giving slightly amended details of Louise Palmer and showing Georgina's photograph, and the letter of introduction, ostensibly signed by Mark.

Slowly, achingly slowly, the bank official carefully inspected the documents. Helen thought irritably that he had had time to read them three times and still he was bent over them. Then she chastised herself. She mustn't show impatience; relax and breathe evenly – as Georgina was doing.

'This seems in order,' said the official after another few anxious moments. 'Now, Madame,' he said, turning to Georgina, 'I need the special code you have been given.'

'MTS dash 22 dash 6554,' said Georgie in a firm voice and silently Helen gave thanks to Paul Wallis.

There was another lengthy pause while the official's gaze went from the passport to Georgie and back again, then he crossed his legs and leaned back in his chair. Helen's heart sank. Now what?

'I must tell you an amusing story,' he said. Helen gritted her teeth. 'One of our rivals, not us, I'm happy to say, was suspicious about a woman who came in, just like you, Madame,' he smiled at Georgie, 'wanting access to her safety deposit box. But the bank was not completely convinced. In such circumstances the police are called as a matter of course. She was immediately put into prison where she remained for no less than three weeks before she was able to contact someone to verify her story. She turned out to be the sister of the president of, well, a prominent country.'

Why the hell was he telling them this? thought Helen.

'Rather drastic, don't you think?' Georgie said coolly.

'Not at all, Madame. Our bank's reputation, our country's income, depend on absolute confidence in our system. We must not make even one mistake and if it means someone loses their liberty temporarily to ensure that does not happen,' he shrugged, 'so be it.'

There was a pause, then he opened a drawer and took out a document. 'So let us proceed. Do you confirm that you are Louise Palmer as stated in this document?' He indicated the letter of introduction.

'Yes. I do,' said Georgie.

'Thank you. Please sign it here.'

Helen noted admiringly that Georgie did so with a flourish.

'This is a legally-binding document and your signature will now be witnessed by your lawyer.'

'Of course.'

When this was done, the bank official passed the document he had taken from his desk to Georgie and said formally, 'This certifies that I have checked all the required codes and account numbers. Please sign here and here.'

Georgie did so.

'Do you wish us to discontinue your rental agreement on the safety deposit box?' he asked, addressing Georgie.

She looked at Helen, who shook her head. 'We shall

not be removing anything for the moment so my client wishes to retain your service.'

They were taken to the safe deposit vault where they were shown into another private room. The bank official, accompanied by an attendant, carried in the safety deposit box. The attendant turned the key in the lock and there was a click as the lid sprang up.

'Press that buzzer on the wall when you have finished and we will return,' said the official before both men left.

Georgie stood aside as with thudding heart Helen opened the lid.

Inside the box was an envelope, which she put into her handbag, and a small packet wrapped in black velvet. She removed the velvet to reveal a folded square of stiff white paper.

Cautiously she unfolded the paper and shook out the contents on to the black velvet. The most stunning, luminous diamonds she had seen in her life lay before her.

Beside her, Georgina was silent. They had agreed that whatever the temptation they would say nothing during the entire operation. Helen glanced at her watch. She must waste no time if they wanted to make the flight.

Three minutes later she had re-wrapped the package and satisfied herself that everything was in order. She buzzed the officials, they made their farewells and the lawyer drove them swiftly to the airport to catch their flight to Zurich.

In the glass-encased first-class lounge at Zurich airport,

Helen waited while Georgina freshened up in the cloak-room. She took out the envelope she had found in the deposit box. It appeared to be a letter Mark had written to his mistress in the event of his death.

'If only things had been different,' she read, 'we could have been together all the time. I would have been proud to have had you by my side, my darling, as my wife. That could not be, but please know that I loved you and I would never have left you. You meant so much to me, more than you will ever know, more than words can ever say.'

Did that sound like someone who loved his wife? Hadn't he written almost the same words to her? Hadn't he gone to great lengths to convince her that not once had he ever considered leaving her? The two-timing bastard. What was the truth? Helen did not know and today, she thought happily, she didn't care.

Sitting back Helen began to feel so euphoric she could have flown back to London without benefit of a plane. They had done it. In spite of the hazards, Operation Revenge had been completely successful. She could not wait to tell Margery. All it had taken, she thought wryly, was nerve. Nerve and money, mountains of the stuff, but she had not begrudged one single penny. Margery had located the company who had provided the forged pass-port, and arranged payment in cash, half in advance, half on completion. She had been careful to disguise her identity but both women were aware that the firm had the facilities to track them down should they need to. If the job was ever traced back, it could mean a jail sentence for all of them, including Georgina. Helen had had to gamble that nothing would go wrong. And it hadn't, thanks largely to Paul Wallis who had furnished her with both an exact copy of the document of introduction giving the account number, and with the pre-arranged code.

When Georgie returned from the cloakroom, two glasses of chilled champagne were waiting on the table.

'I thought we could congratulate ourselves on a job well done,' said Helen, handing her a glass. 'I want to thank you for helping me.'

'There's no need for that. It was a pleasure. Believe me, getting the better of Louise gave me as much satisfaction as it gave you.'

Helen had a wicked glint in her eyes. 'I must say I'm enjoying this sweet moment of revenge.'

'So am I, but there's one thing puzzling me. How are you going to stop her picking up the second package of diamonds in two years' time? Especially since it's in another bank and you don't know which one.'

'Yet,' smiled Helen. 'I've plenty of time to decide on a strategy, and, believe me, I will. That woman will not profit from Mark's death.'

'I've been wondering,' said Georgie, 'have you decided what you're going to do with the diamonds?'

'You bet,' smiled Helen. 'I'll sell them and put the money in trust for my grandchildren.'

They clinked glasses and contentedly sipped the vintage champagne.

'Do you know what I'm focusing my mind on?'

Georgie said after a while. 'I'm following Louise into that bank in Vaduz, I'm seeing her entering the building . . .'

Helen entered into the spirit of it. 'Let's assume she isn't immediately arrested for impersonation and fraud and that she's managed to charm that stiff-lipped bank official and convince him she's the real Louise Palmer.'

Georgie nodded. 'He's taking her down to the vault and putting his key into the lock of the deposit box.'

Helen's eyes were dancing. 'She's really pleased with herself. Another man, another conquest. Now she opens the packet of diamonds. How her heart is thumping. How excited she is as she runs those beautiful stones through her fingers . . .'

The call for first-class passengers to board the London flight interrupted their happy fantasising.

'She'll be bloody lucky to get near the diamonds,' said Georgie as she followed Helen to the exit. 'That bank official made it quite clear what they do with impostors.'

'If she does,' said Helen, 'the sweetest part of the revenge is that she might suspect it was me there today, but she'll never be able to prove it.' She took Georgina's arm. 'Perhaps she'll think Mark double-crossed her. That would really please me because then her memories will be soured. Just like mine.'

The business with the jewellery had been a nightmare for Louise. The bank had been difficult but after two hours she was able to satisfy them that she was who she said she was. They were so devastated that they had not detected the forgeries that they had been putty in her hands.

Her heart had leapt when she was told that the false Louise Palmer had not wanted to take anything from the safety deposit box. And when she saw the beautiful stones, Louise did not stop to wonder why they were still there. She simply scooped them up and made her way back to the airport.

The following day she was calm and confident as she waited for the valuation. The diamonds would be of the highest quality because that's what she expected from Mark. Louise had already arranged with a London jeweller, renowned for its integrity in dealings with wealthy clients, for the stones to be valued.

The jeweller came back in such a short time that Louise knew something was amiss.

'Is this some sort of joke?' he asked coldly.

She stared at him.

'You intimated these were high-carat diamonds but they are zircons. Good quality zircons, I give you that, but did you think you could fool me, Madam? I, who have been in the diamond business since I was a boy and my father before me? Pah.'

The stones were worthless.

Her first thought was that Mark had duped her. But it didn't make sense. Zircons could not buy her silence, which is what he said he wanted above all else. Besides, she was as sure as she could be that Mark had loved her and would not play such a spiteful trick.

In panic she had telephoned her lawyer in New York. 'Somebody's impersonated me,' she said wildly, and recounted the saga. 'It can only be his bloody widow,' she concluded. 'That so-called banker who didn't turn up makes sense now. I had to catch a later plane, which gave her time to switch the diamonds.'

'That's as maybe but proving it is another matter.'

'Don't they have security cameras? Can't they take fingerprints?'

'You signed a document confirming that the contents of the security box were intact.'

'I'm not a diamond expert, that's what I thought at the time.'

'The bank will be desperate to save face. They will insist they went through all the procedures and were satisfied that the woman gave the correct information.'

'I'll sue them.'

'They will wave that document in front of a judge and that will be that. Save your money.'

'How did she get the right account number and the code?'

'No one will ever tell.'

'For God's sake, there must be something you can do to help me. Without those diamonds I'm practically penniless. It was Helen, I tell you. I know it.'

'You have suspicions but no proof. Those banks only survive if their security systems are foolproof. They'll never admit a mistake and they sure won't allow one client to jeopardise their reputation.'

'But what am I going to do?' she asked, a question to which the lawyer had no answer.

Despondently she reviewed her future. Without the

substantial cushion provided by Mark's bequest, there could be no art gallery, no Mayfair flat, little socialising, little else.

Mark's death had been devastating but it had made her determined to follow her own path. Art had been her great comfort in the days she spent waiting for him. At one stage she had practically lived in the Guggenheim Museum. She had taken their art history course and immersed herself in the colours and techniques of great artists. Planning her art gallery with the architect, discussing design elements with the interior decorator had provided her with the happiest of times since Mark's death. To have these highly paid specialists paying such attention to her suggestions and to have the power to make decisions had changed her from a passive mistress into a confident businesswoman. And lately she had been finding that several hours had gone by without her thinking about Mark. There was no doubt that having such an absorbing interest had helped her cope with her bereavement.

And now, having signed a lease for an expensive property in Bond Street, all her plans were in danger from Mark's widow. Louise's jaw tightened as she thought of a triumphant Helen Temple-Smith. She remembered the widow's last words as she swept out of the flat, 'Consider the premiums cancelled.'

She was damned if she was going to allow that woman to dictate how she, Louise Palmer, could live her life. She would not abandon plans for the gallery. There must be a way to save it and if it meant her secret would be made public, so be it.

# Chapter Twenty-Two

A couple of days after returning from Zurich, Georgie asked Josephine if she was free to come round for a few minutes after work. She was delighted.

'Hi, stranger,' she said, as usual arriving breathless from running up the stairs to the flat. 'I was beginning to think that now you're top dog you didn't have time for us minions.' One glimpse of Georgie's strained face and she ceased her chatter. 'What the hell's the matter?'

'I'm eleven days late.'

Josephine paused for a moment. 'You've always been able to set the calendar by your cycle.'

'I know. I'm not going to get worked up about it,' said Georgie, filling the kettle. 'After all the things that have happened to me lately my body's probably out of kilter. That could happen, couldn't it?'

Josephine looked doubtful. 'Possible, I suppose. How d'you feel?'

'Worn out, stressed, bloody miserable but I don't feel pregnant. But then how would I know? I've never been bloody pregnant.'

'Why don't you find out?'

'If you saw my schedule, you'd know. All I ever think about is magazines, who prints them and who reads them.'

Josephine, ever practical, said, 'I'll go right now to the all-night chemist for a testing kit. You phone my home and say I'm going to be late.'

Georgie gazed at her gratefully. 'Thanks. Get two kits, might as well make sure.'

'OK, as long as you remember this when I want a salary increase,' she laughed, putting on her coat. 'I'll be as quick as I can.'

On her return, they read the instructions carefully.

'It says here that you'll know within two minutes,' said Josephine. 'If it turns pink it's positive, if it's blue there's another reason for being late and maybe you should see a doctor.'

Georgie padded to the bathroom and re-read the instructions. It was important to obtain accurate results. She faithfully followed the directions and then, too strung up to do anything else, sat on the edge of the bath examining her damson-red toenails while the chemicals in the test determined her condition.

After two minutes she examined the square in the centre of the testing stick on both tests. The colours were the same.

Outside, Josephine waited. At last, Georgie emerged, holding the small wooden sticks.

'If you want my opinion, they are very definitely pink,' said Josephine.

Georgie nodded.

'So you could be pregnant,' Josephine went on. 'On the other hand, the tests could both be wrong and you could simply be late.'

'Thanks for that deeply authoritative view.'

'It's unlikely that both tests are wrong. Georgie, you'd better accept that you're probably pregnant.'

The two women sat and stared at each other. After a while Josephine said quietly, 'Am I pleased for you?'

Georgie's hands played across her taut stomach. The thought of a new life developing in there was awesome. Pregnancy did seem the most likely explanation. Was it her imagination or did her breasts seem fuller, more tender?

'Jo, I'm scared.'

Josephine was brusque. 'It's only pre-baby nerves. You'll have the baby, you'll organise yourself, it'll be fine.'

'Will I? It couldn't happen at a worse time.'

Josephine gave this some thought. 'It's invariably the worst time for everyone. When do you think it happened?'

'Soon after Milan.'

'I thought you'd reached an agreement . . .' said Josephine delicately.

'We did, but once or twice . . . you know how it is. I thought it was safe.'

Josephine did some rapid calculations. 'That's about the right timing.' She looked at Georgie's stricken face. 'You know you'll have to tell Alistair.'

'I can't,' said Georgie dismally. 'I don't want to. If he knows I'm expecting his baby he'll feel he has to come back to me and I don't want him on those terms.'

'He does have the right to know.' Josephine's tone was gentle.

'Didn't he forfeit that right by sleeping with another woman?' asked Georgie belligerently. 'In any case, my priority here is my career. I need to buy time and keep it secret.'

'So you're not going to tell Helen.'

'Are you crazy? I don't want to kibosh my chances before being certain this isn't a false alarm. If I wait a couple of months I'll have had a chance to prove myself and it'll be easier for Helen to accept the situation.'

Josephine hesitated. 'Keeping it secret may not be quite as easy as you think.'

'Why not?'

'There's a little matter of morning sickness. You may be luckier than me, I was sick from day one. And boy, it's hard to disguise.'

'What am I going to do?'

'If you feel nauseous in the morning you'll have to work at home and it might be better to institute that right away. Say you need thinking time away from the phones.'

'Do you think I can justify that?'

'You're the new boss, you can make the rules. And what's the alternative? Believe me, you have to keep out of sight when you feel like that.'

'Oh, Josephine,' wailed Georgie, 'what a mess.'

★ ★ ★

Josephine hesitated, her hand on the receiver. Did she have the right to tell Harry that Georgie was pregnant? It could mean curtains for Georgie's career, but wasn't that Harry's plan? And hadn't she been his accomplice, if not willing, at least compliant all this time?

Josephine put aside her scruples and dialled Harry's number.

Predictably he was thrilled with the news. 'Capital, capital,' he chortled. 'Now all we have to do is tell Helen. Why don't you arrange to see her right away?'

'I absolutely refuse,' Josephine said vehemently. 'Why is it always me that has to do the dirty work?'

'OK, I'll do it if you feel that strongly. But, angel face, we're on the home straight. Helen will be furious. Yes, Georgina's on the way out and who else can step into the breach? Alistair is still considering his future and he's unlikely to forgive Helen for passing him over last time round. Ned Mastrianni is out of the running – Helen made it clear to the appointments committee that she can't stand the man. OK, Helen might see me as a stopgap. But I'll work my balls off to prove to her what I can do for this company. And I can do a lot. You know that. And when I do,' he paused for effect, 'that's when you'll get what you deserve.'

After Harry Ferguson had left her office, Helen went into the bathroom and leaned against the door, taking deep breaths to clear her mind.

Her nightmare had just come true. The constant

refrain of the board, Giles in particular, repeated itself in her mind. It was foolhardy giving this kind of job to a woman of child-bearing age, sooner or later the job would be abandoned while the woman took maternity leave. Once the child was born, her mind would be only half on the job.

Harry had been unable to keep the triumph out of his face when he had told her about Georgie's pregnancy. He was such a toad, saying that if Georgie needed time away and with Alistair still undecided about where his future lay, she could be assured of his full support.

Helen could understand why Georgie had kept the pregnancy a secret from her. After virtually telling her she had no chance of doing the job properly if she had a baby, how could she blame her?

It had all been going so well. Georgie's plans for the future had begun to excite the entire board. One or two had told Helen privately that they were pleased she had cajoled them into accepting Georgie. Helen had been gratified, and remembered thinking that this was only the beginning. Now it looked as if it was the beginning of the end.

Her reputation was inextricably linked with Georgie's and she hit the edge of the washbasin so hard that her hand stung. As she rubbed her aching palm, an idea occurred to her that was so manipulative she tried to dismiss it. Then the image of a circle of contemptuous faces round the boardroom table surfaced. How they would gloat. And would they not be right? If her most significant decision proved to be a mistake, how could she expect them to trust her in future?

Georgie had to be persuaded not to have this baby. Helen wasn't sure she had the veniality to follow her survival instincts in the same way a man would. A strong bond had formed between herself and Georgie since the diamonds. But there was no alternative. She had to steel herself to put business before friendship.

It was fortuitous that later in the day she and Georgie were booked to see the managing director of Timpneys, Britain's most prestigious health hydro, to finalise details of a venture suggested by Georgina on her first day in charge.

'It's not time effective to try and persuade advertisers to spend money in one title,' Georgie had told the board. 'The big spenders need to be given a broader vision of our reach.'

Timpneys was undertaking an immense expansion programme and needed to broadcast the fact to its international clientele. In exchange for a multimillion-pound contract over two years, Amalgamated would provide advertisements, supplements and editorial promotions across four target titles. Georgie had offered them decor features in the upmarket interior design magazine, fashion spreads set in the grandeur of the refurbished reception rooms in their designer clothes magazine, stress-buster articles in a health title, and low-fat, elegant cookery recipes to be published by their market leader, a magazine with a covetable circulation of three million AB female readers. The managing director of Timpneys had been highly impressed and had, as he said, made the quickest decision of his career. Today was to be the signing of the lucrative contract.

Helen and Georgie arrived at Timpneys in the rolling Hertfordshire countryside separately but within fifteen minutes of each other. The contract was signed and all was smiles with the spa's executives. 'If you don't have to rush back to London, ladies,' said the managing director over a glass of champagne, 'feel free to try out any of the services. Can I tempt you to a facial, or our marvellous new steam cabinets? They're the most advanced in Europe, great for de-toxing.'

Georgie, who had been somewhat subdued in what had been a noisy gathering, was starting to shake her head when Helen intervened quickly. This was the opportunity to talk to her protégée away from the office.

'Yes, we'd love to.'

'I'm sorry, Helen,' said Georgie, 'I can't spare the time. I must get back to the office.'

'No, Georgie, I must insist on exercising my proprietorial authority. Men play golf during office hours and it would be a sin to go back without trying that amazing swimming pool.'

The managing director was enthusiastic. 'We can kit you out with swimsuits and I'll put the hairdresser and beauty salon at your disposal.'

'Thanks very much,' Helen laughed. 'Tell them to be on red alert for me. These days I need everything they can throw at me.'

'Helen, I don't want to be a killjoy but . . .'

Helen waved a hand airily. 'You heard the man. It's our duty. To the company. To the readers. Come on.'

The pool was indeed breathtaking. It was enclosed in a thirty-foot-high glasshouse, full of exotic foliage, with a view of the Hertfordshire hills in the distance. It was heated to a satisfying eighty-eight degrees. They had the place to themselves and Georgie had to admit to Helen that she was glad they had stayed.

As they were towelling themselves dry, Helen said, 'Why don't we travel back together? You could send your driver away.'

'Of course,' replied Georgie, following her to the hair salon.

An hour later Helen's dark green Bentley was wending its way down the tree-lined driveway towards the London motorway.

Helen pressed the button which activated the window between themselves and the driver and waited. Would Georgie take this opportunity to confess she was pregnant? It soon became apparent that she would not.

'You've got quite a schedule for the next month,' Helen said. 'You're going to be in three continents in the space of about a fortnight. But without a husband,' she paused, 'or a baby or any other distractions you'll be able to give the job one hundred per cent.'

'A baby would certainly be difficult to fit into my schedule,' said Georgie distractedly.

'Not difficult,' said Helen firmly. 'Impossible. Happily you don't have that to contend with so don't let's even think about it.' She looked out at the countryside speeding past the window. 'With any luck, Alistair will come to his senses. Or you might meet someone else.'

'I don't think so. I'll never trust another man.'

'Certainly you will, you're still young. It's when you reach my age that it gets difficult.' She sat back wearily, deliberately avoiding Georgie's stricken face. 'Let's be grateful you and Alistair don't have a family. The situation would be much worse.'

The rest of the journey passed in silence, the greenery of the countryside giving way to the familiar rows of suburban housing on the outskirts of London. Helen hunched down unhappily into the leather upholstery. Had she said enough to make Georgie understand that having this baby would do irreparable harm to her career? Harry had told her that Alistair did not know about the pregnancy. That should make her task easier.

This was what business made you do, kill or be killed. Only a masculine mind could have given voice to the views she had just expressed in the full knowledge of how it would affect Georgie. But dammit, she was acting for the good of the company. She had to behave like a man and that also meant not having a guilty conscience afterwards.

Well, her work was done. Now she had to leave the decision to her new chief executive.

# Chapter Twenty-Three

Craving nothing more than a good night's sleep, Alistair was dismayed when he opened the door to Rosemary's flat just before midnight to see all the lights blazing.

Oh shit. He was in no mood to talk to anyone. He had spent the day, as he had each day since returning to London, discussing possible jobs. This evening it had been done over a tedious dinner with an advertising chief whose mood had not been enhanced by the cocaine he had clearly been sniffing on his numerous trips to the gents. Alistair had hoped his sister would be fast asleep by now.

The door to the living room was wide open but there was no sign of Rosemary. Thank God, she must have grown tired of waiting up for him. He snapped off the light and there was an immediate cry of, 'Hey, what do you think you're doing?'

Startled, he turned on the light again and saw Louise stretched out on the sofa. Damn the woman, what on earth was she doing here? He had not contacted her since Florida and as he hadn't heard from her he had assumed she accepted that their brief fling was over.

'Where's my sister?' he asked warily.

'She had to go out but she said to tell you she'll be back soon.'

He felt irritated but he couldn't just ignore her and disappear to bed, so he offered her a drink. He was thankful when she refused.

'I'm sorry to come here uninvited,' Louise disentangled herself from the cushions and smoothed her skirt, 'but I couldn't help myself. I've something wonderful to tell you.'

Good God, tears were welling in her eyes. What was she up to now?

'I'm so very happy, Alistair.'

'About what?' he asked impatiently, wondering where on earth Rosemary had gone at this time of night.

'I'm pregnant. I'm going to have a baby. That is, we're going to have a baby.'

'We?' he repeated, wondering what kind of joke she was playing.

'Isn't that wonderful? Alistair, say you're pleased, darling.'

What on earth was she talking about? Hadn't she assured him that contraception was 'all taken care of'?

'You're pregnant and I'm the father?' He repeated the words without expression and she nodded happily. 'How sure are you?'

'That I'm pregnant? Darling, as sure as I can be. I had a test this afternoon and it was positive. Isn't that thrilling?'

Alistair couldn't believe it. He and Georgie had been trying for months without success, and now Louise pronounced herself pregnant after such a brief encounter.

She gave an enchanting smile. 'You know how big the baby is right now?' She put up her little finger and pressed the nail. 'This big. It's a miracle. It's a sign that we belong to each other. We should never have parted. It was all my fault. But now I can give you something you've always wanted, I'll make up for the hurt.' She moved round the sofa towards him. 'Oh, Alistair. This is the most exciting day of my entire life. I hope it's a boy. Or a girl. I don't mind, do you?' She put her arms round him.

He pulled himself away and ran his hand through his hair distractedly. 'I need time to think.'

'What's there to think about?' asked Louise, a slight frown appearing on her brow. 'In about eight months' time we're going to have our own baby. If it's a boy I want to name him after your father. I always loved him.'

'Just a minute,' said Alistair. 'I hate to ask this delicate question but how can you be so sure it's mine?'

Louise blinked and again her lovely eyes filled with tears. Alistair felt growing apprehension. Surely she couldn't do that to order.

'I am sure,' said Louise, reaching for her handbag for a small square of handkerchief and dabbing her eyes. 'Very sure. I've been with no one else since . . . the man I was involved with went back to his wife six months ago.'

Alistair said nothing.

'I'm so positive it's yours that I'm willing to have a

DNA test as soon as the baby is born.' Leaning towards him she added urgently, 'Tell me you believe me when I say you're the father.'

Alistair felt intensely uncomfortable but to prevent those welling tears overflowing he said hastily, 'All right, I believe you.'

Another deliberate dab. 'I'm so glad because if we're going to be together we need trust.'

Together?

She saw the expression in his eyes. 'Darling, I want the very best for this child and that means two parents living happily under one roof.'

'Louise,' he said carefully, 'can I remind you I'm still married.'

Louise opened her eyes wide. 'But that's not a problem. Rosemary says Georgina wants a divorce.'

'She and I haven't discussed anything about a divorce,' said Alistair, annoyed.

'Well, that's what she told Rosemary.'

Alistair was still. 'Georgie told my sister she wanted a divorce?'

'Yes. You can ask Rosemary when she comes home. So you see? There's no obstacle.'

'To what?'

'My dearest wish is that you and I should remarry so that our child can be born legitimate.'

'Louise, I can't believe you're springing this news on me and then expect some kind of immediate decision. Divorce, remarriage,' he snapped his fingers, 'just like that. Well, I'm sorry, I can't make such major decisions instantly. They need to be thought out because they affect many lives.'

'Alistair,' said Louise quietly, 'as far as I'm concerned, this baby was conceived in love. I don't intend to force you to do anything you don't want to do. But I tell you now that I want my baby to have a mother and a father.'

'And the baby will have that,' he said quietly. 'I won't let you down on that score. You won't want for anything, either of you.'

'I'm not talking about financial support, Alistair. Do you want your name on the birth certificate?'

He squirmed. 'If it's my baby of course I do.'

'Then I have the right to expect the baby to have your name.'

'I have no objection to that,' said Alistair quickly. 'In fact I would welcome it.'

'But if the child has your name, you have to be committed to it.'

'I will be committed, very much so.'

'But will you also be committed to me?'

He could not answer and after a few seconds she went on, 'After living in America all those years, I have no support system in this country. If you're not willing to commit to me as well as to our child, I've no choice but to go back to New York. I have friends there who will help me.'

He shifted uncomfortably. 'But I'll help with everything.'

'Everything short of marriage,' she said.

'Yes, I'm afraid so.'

'I'm sorry, darling, that's not good enough.'

Helplessly he could think of nothing to say.

She had no such constraints. 'It's all or nothing with me,' she said. 'I don't want a live-in lover. Our child needs, and I need, a father and a husband living with us twenty-four hours a day, every day of the year. Not some fly-by-night relationship with access weekends, fitting us into your schedule when you can.' She softened. 'I realise what a shock it is to you. Believe me, it's the last thing I planned and I still can't understand how it happened. But I'm happy it did, very happy. And I think that whatever you say, you are too.' Louise paused, waiting for a response.

Alistair remained silent, his face pale and restrained.

'If you don't feel you can commit yourself fully,' Louise said softly, 'I won't allow you to play any part in the child's upbringing. It's up to you, Alistair.'

It was an hour past the time she was due to go to the office but Georgie was marooned in the bathroom. She had tried all the natural remedies but nothing worked.

How on earth could she function feeling like this? She staggered to the phone and asked her secretary to switch her first two meetings to the afternoon. Then she went to lie down on the bed, a cold compress on her forehead. If this was going to be her life for the next eight months, she would shoot herself.

She dozed off. It was mid-morning when she woke. And to her surprise she felt human again. Quickly she dressed and phoned the office to say she was on her way.

On her electronic organiser she had about fifty items that required attention but as the taxi dodged in and out of the traffic lanes, she found she could not concentrate on work.

Her breasts ached, another reminder of the pregnancy which linked her inextricably to Alistair. She tried to justify her decision to keep the knowledge from him. If it made him want a reconciliation for the sake of the child, that was no basis for a solid future together. Particularly when she had no idea how important Louise was in his life. But did she have the right to keep him in ignorance? And for how long did she intend to do so? She had wrestled with this long enough. It was time to face up to what deep down she knew was right. Alistair had to know.

When Georgie walked into her office her secretary was all smiles. 'Your husband phoned. He'd like to see you as soon as you can manage it.'

As this was his first call since she had taken over, it had apparently caused comment in the office. Odd, that it should come just when she had made up her mind to ask to see him to break her news.

'Ring Harry and say I'll see him later,' she said. 'Then ask Alistair if he'd like to come along now.' Harry would not be pleased. This was the second time she had postponed their meeting. But what the hell. She would not be able to concentrate until she had told Alistair.

Was there time to freshen her lipstick? She darted into the cloakroom adjoining her office and blessed the audacity of a former colleague who had to fight the bean counters to justify the cost of a personal cloakroom when the lavish executive suite was only a year old. She wondered how Giles had squared this extravagance with his Scrooge-like personality.

There was a tap on the door. 'Your next appointment has arrived,' said her secretary and for a second there was absolute silence as she and Alistair stared at each other. He looked strained but she motioned him into an easy chair.

'This new office suits you,' he said eventually.

Georgie quickly skirted the desk and sat down in another easy chair. 'Thanks. It's amazing how easily you can get used to all this.' And she waved a hand at the specially commissioned art that adorned the walls. 'I've had it tickled up a bit since Giles went to America,' she said, gesturing towards the leather buttoned sofa which was big enough to sleep in and matched the chairs on which they were sitting.

'I bet,' he said, and she felt a moment of awkwardness, wondering whether she had been tactless. After all, he had expected this to be his.

'Coffee? Tea?' Her voice sounded disembodied.

'Nothing, thank you.'

She was relieved. She did not want to explain she had given up anything with caffeine in it because it made her feel queasy. She would tell him about that afterwards.

Alistair was clenching and unclenching his hands. 'I think we have things to discuss,' he blurted.

Georgie leaned towards him. 'Yes, I wanted to talk to

you and if you hadn't asked for this meeting, I would have.'

'All right. You first.'

'No, you.' She gave a faint smile. This was the way they had always dealt with each other, insisting that the other had the more interesting news. 'But if it's about work I'll go first.'

'No, it's not about the job.' He was silent for a moment. 'I really want to settle things between us.'

'So do I,' said Georgie quickly.

'It's time. We can't go on like this, in limbo, for much longer.'

'I couldn't agree more because—'

'I suppose it was inevitable we would reach this point,' he interrupted, sighing heavily. 'You'll find out soon enough but it's better you hear it from me.'

This didn't sound like the conversation she had envisaged. Her fingers were gripped tightly in her lap.

'There's no easy way of telling you this. Louise is pregnant.'

Georgie's face drained of colour. Her every instinct was to flee, go anywhere, be anywhere except here facing a grim-faced Alistair.

'It's my baby,' he said so quietly she had to strain to hear.

With a great effort of will, she said, 'Are you sure it's yours?'

He frowned. 'I wouldn't be here if I wasn't.'

'What are you going to do?'

'Louise wants me to marry her.'

'And will you?'

'You and I weren't ever going to get back together again. You called me in today to ask for a divorce, didn't you?'

Georgie wanted to cry out, 'No, no, no,' but she didn't. He seemed so sure their marriage was over. What would he do if he knew she was also pregnant? Would he abandon Louise for her? She cut off that thought abruptly. If he could forgive what Louise had done to him and take her back, then he had to be crazy about her. In the circumstances it was better for him to think that she wanted a divorce. She supposed it was better for her in the long run. She had always thought of his ex-wife as unfinished business. How right she had been.

Alistair leaned towards her and involuntarily she flinched back.

He straightened. 'This must be a shock,' he said. 'It was to me. However much I wanted to be a father, this isn't the way I wanted it to be. It's important to me you believe that.'

She could not trust herself to speak. What she most wanted was to place her hand over his mouth to stop him talking.

He ran his hand through his hair. 'I have a baby to think about now, responsibilities. We both need to get on with our lives. Don't you agree?'

Georgie focused all her attention on the door leading to her cloakroom and concentrated on how quickly she could bolt for it.

'Georgie?'

She moistened her dry lips and finally found her voice. 'I'll see a divorce lawyer right away. You won't have any trouble from me.'

He appeared grateful. 'I knew you'd take it like this. I wish . . . well, what's the point of wishing?'

She cleared her throat. 'You must be excited about the baby.'

'I am. It's the only thing in this whole business which makes some sense. I still can't believe it.' He shook his head and they sat in silence for a few seconds. Then he got up. 'I'm sorry, Georgie, this is tough for us both. But it's a little easier for me knowing that you want a divorce.'

She stood up beside him. Why didn't he leave now? He'd said what he'd come to say.

'I don't think . . . well, a clean break would be best. I mean with the company as well. I'm sure you'd agree with that.'

Georgie nodded mutely, overwhelmed by words unsaid, feelings unexpressed.

'I'll give Helen my formal resignation,' he said, appearing more composed.

She acknowledged this with a curt nod.

'Well, goodbye then.' He leaned forward to kiss her on the cheek but she stepped back quickly.

After he had closed the door, Georgie willed herself to wait until she was sure he had left her outer office before allowing the tears to flow.

Helen paced up and down her spacious office as she waited for Alistair to arrive.

The image of Georgie's ashen face when she told her that she and Alistair had agreed to divorce would stay with her for a long time.

One thing puzzled her. Alistair was not rich so why was Louise setting her sights on her first husband? There might have been a reason when he was the hot favourite for the top job. Then Louise could have become the first lady of Amalgamated, a role she had shadowed for so long. But the job had gone to Georgina so what was Louise Palmer's game plan now?

Whatever it was, she intended to scupper it. If Louise wanted Alistair, she would make sure she would not have him.

It did occur to her that by breaking up Alistair and Louise she might open the door to a reconciliation between him and Georgie, in which case Georgie would most likely keep the baby. Well, that would be a pity but she was not irreplaceable. Helen hoped it would not come to that. She had grown fond of Georgie. It was unlikely anyway. Georgie had been too hurt.

Alistair was in a despondent mood as he made his way to Helen's office. His marriage to the only woman he had truly loved was over and he could see no way of repairing the rift. He had nothing to keep him here now. No wife. And in a few minutes when he saw Helen, no job. The baby was all he had to cling to. But he had no intention of marrying Louise and he would make her understand that a marriage based on blackmail was bound to fail. He did not take seriously her threat to move back to America, not when she had just signed a lease for the art gallery, something she seemed passionate about. He would insist on playing a large part in the child's life, which would mean seeing Louise often. He sighed. Maybe that was his penance, a sacrifice he would have to make for the sake of enabling his child to have a secure and stable upbringing.

He walked into Helen's office, overcome by a wave of nostalgia. He understood this company so well. His relationship with Mark had become far more than employer and employee. It had been almost symbiotic, a partnership of minds envied by many people in the media. Over the years he had been offered many incentives to leave but he had been totally loyal, not only to the company but also to Mark.

Who would have thought his career at Amalgamated would end like this? Whatever he did next it could not be as exciting and challenging.

Helen seemed unsurprised by his news. 'Georgina told me you had separated and I'm sorry to hear it. Is there no chance you might get together again?'

'I fear not.'

'Why not give it more time? Stay with the company for, say, another six months before deciding you have to leave. If you want to put your marriage back together again, it might be the answer.'

'No, it wouldn't be fair to Georgina.'

'Why not? I would have thought it eminently fair to her.'

'It won't be.' She looked at him inquiringly and he

burst out, 'I didn't want to tell you but, oh hell, the reason I can't come back to work here concerns . . . Louise, my first wife.'

Helen's face was difficult to read. 'How long has this been going on?'

His hackles rose at her intrusion into his private life. 'I don't think that's relevant. It's personal.'

'Believe me, I have a good reason for asking,' she said, more quietly. 'I'm not prying.'

'A few weeks.'

'No time at all.'

'It does seem sudden but Louise and I are hardly strangers.'

'Before you say anything more, there's something I want to show you.' She reached into her handbag. 'I was hoping that you wouldn't need to know about this,' she handed him Mark's letter, 'but I think under the circumstances I ought to share my secret with you.'

Only the noise of far-away telephones disturbed the silence as he read the letter. Helen went over to the walnut cabinet, took out a decanter of brandy and poured out two stiff measures.

Finally, Alistair laid the pages down and said, 'Helen, this must have been terrible for you.'

'It was.'

Alistair could hardly take in the extent of Mark's deceit. Despite their close working relationship over many years, he had never suspected for a second that his friend and mentor had been leading a double life.

'Do you know who she is?'

Helen walked to the window and Alistair could not see her face. 'Yes, I do,' she said. 'The woman who was fucking my husband for eight years was your ex-wife. Louise Palmer.'

Helen turned round to face Alistair, his face ashen. 'She didn't tell you?'

'No, she did not,' he managed to say. 'But it can't be true. Louise barely knew Mark. She only met him once or twice many years ago when we were first married.'

Helen slowly shook her head. 'I could give you every cough and spit of their affair.' She opened the top drawer of her desk and pulled out a sheaf of papers. 'Receipts, travel agents' documents, flight passenger lists. They were very careful to cover their tracks, but once I found out her name, it wasn't difficult to match her movements with his. Take a look at this bill. Remember when Amalgamated took over La Residencia in Mallorca for our top advertisers? Two days later, another ticket was issued. Note the date. It doesn't take a genius to work out that only weeks after you married her, your wife was sleeping with my husband. They were together eight years. He was on his way to see her in the Hamptons when he died.'

Alistair was motionless.

'The bills tell the same story month after month, year in, year out. See for yourself. Every time he took a trip, who went with him? Louise Palmer.'

'I just can't believe all this,' Alistair said, slowly leafing through the papers.

'I went to see her in Melford Court, bought, I've no

doubt, with Mark's money. She didn't try and brazen it out for long. I had too much information on her.'

Alistair put his head in his hands.

'She's never told you about what she did after she left you?'

He shook his head.

'She certainly lived the high life. First class all the way. On my money, with my husband.' Helen sat down suddenly, looking tired. 'She had the impudence to come to London several times during those years. They must have lain in bed and laughed at us, thinking how clever they were.'

Alistair's face was pale. 'I trusted Mark.'

'So did I.' Helen watched him anxiously. 'What are you going to do?'

'It's worse than you can imagine. Louise is expecting my child.'

For a moment Helen did not react and miserably Alistair stood up and made his way towards the door.

'Wait, Alistair. I've something more to say.' Her voice was commanding and he hesitated in the doorway.

'Don't put your happiness in that woman's hands. And don't believe a word of what she tells you. She's been taught by an expert to lie before breakfast, lunch and dinner.'

# Chapter Twenty-Four

Play-acting was something at which Louise was skilled. Over the last eight years she'd had to gauge Mark's mood instantly. His first few words would usually give her the clue as to how he wanted their time to be choreographed. If he wanted her to be a party girl, she would open the champagne and start undressing. If he needed a more sober ambience, to discuss work or simply relax in front of the television, she would put on her cashmere robe and serve supper on a tray.

Now the new man in her life wanted her to be pregnant. Louise would give every impression she was. Soon she would complain about feeling queasy in the mornings and tell him of the tenderness in her breasts. What a pity she would have to lay off cigarettes while he was around. She regretted having to take such desperate measures but it was the only way she could think of to guarantee her security in the face of what Helen Temple-Smith had done.

The morning she had been due to collect the diamonds, her plans had been going so well. The gallery was on track. Alistair had recommended a useful property broker who had found the perfect site and she had signed the lease. Now thanks to Helen Temple-Smith everything had fallen apart.

Alistair would provide a very satisfactory way out of her difficulties. She could not get out of the lease, she had checked, but Alistair was on first-name terms with people who might give her gallery financial backing. There was not much time to spare. She'd have to step up the pace.

It was better for her that Alistair had decided to resign from Amalgamated. Helen would certainly try to poison his mind about her but Louise had already prepared her story.

She left the door ajar after Alistair buzzed through on the intercom and returned to the living room which she had carefully prepared to create the perfect atmosphere for a new mother-to-be. The room was filled with lavender-scented candles, there was a large bowl of sweet-smelling potpourri bought from Harrods that afternoon and Louise lay on the sofa, listening to the Amadeus Quartet.

She gazed at Alistair dreamily as he stood in the doorway. He had to be the answer to her problems. But instead of smiling at her, he switched on the overhead light, strode over to the stereo and cut off the Amadeus Quartet mid quaver.

'Darling, what's the matter?' she asked in some alarm. 'Have you had a bad day? I'm trying to think tranquil thoughts for our baby.'

'Louise, be quiet. It's time for the truth.'

Startled by his harshness, she sat up. 'Alistair, why are you looking at me like that?'

'I met someone from your past, someone who had interesting things to say about you.'

'Really?' she said cautiously.

'You did pretty well in New York.'

That bloody Helen, she thought immediately.

'These and those,' Alistair touched the pearls at her ears and throat, 'don't come cheap.' He pulled up a chair. 'We've never really talked about your days in New York.' He was sitting so close, she could see the slow rise and fall of his chest.

'Before we do that, don't you want a beer?' She made to stand up.

He shook his head. 'No, I want a few answers,' he said coldly.

'Ask whatever you like.' God, he was frosty. She'd have to use all her skills.

'You told me your apartment was on 84th and Fifth. How did you earn the big bucks to be able to afford that?'

This was going to be easy. 'I was lucky,' she said with a smile. 'Some friends went off to Hong Kong and needed a house-sitter. I paid them a nominal amount.' If only she could get him to kiss her, she would be able to divert him. She uncrossed her legs and leaned towards him. 'You haven't even kissed me hello,' she pouted.

He ignored this. 'And the man in your life? What was his name?'

'Darling, what's brought this on? Can't we carry on with this over supper?'

'He was married.'

'It's not something I'm proud of, but yes, I told you he was.'

'How long did it last?'

Louise pretended to think. 'He went back to his wife after two years. But why are you talking about this? It's all in the past. What's important now is us and our baby.'

'There can be no "us", Louise, unless you're honest with me.'

'But I have been honest. How often do you want me to apologise for the past? I thought you'd accepted that was the old Louise, selfish, uncaring. Now all I want is a stable life. A husband, a home, a family.' She ran a pale hand over her stomach. 'What have I done to make you doubt me now?'

It was such a skilful blend of truth and fiction she almost believed it herself. But, oh God, it wasn't working, for he snapped, 'There's no point in pretending any more. I've just come from seeing Helen and she's told me all about you and Mark.'

There was a long silence while she stared at him, weighing up the damage Helen had done. This needed very careful handling.

'I'm sorry you had to find out from her. I was going to tell you but I was waiting for the right time. Alistair, surely you of all people could understand that I didn't want to risk losing you again.' Would he go for that?

This was a fragile moment, but then his face softened slightly and Louise allowed herself to relax a fraction.

'I suppose I don't blame you for not telling me,' he said.

Men, they were so malleable. Why did women say they had trouble trying to be their equal? She didn't find it difficult. Indeed, mostly she felt superior to them.

Alistair leaned back with an odd expression on his face. 'I could do with that beer now.'

As she came back from the fridge carrying the bottle, she said tenderly, 'I've never loved anyone the way I love you now. Can't you understand that?' She passed him the bottle-opener. 'I was lonely over there and I suppose I was vulnerable. I contacted Mark as a way of making friends and he was kind to me.' She shrugged. 'Things went on from there.'

Alistair slammed the bottle down on the table. 'Liar!' His face was contorted. 'I gave you the chance to tell the truth but you're incapable of that. I happen to know you started the affair with Mark right under my nose, soon after you were married to me, living under my roof, pretending to be my devoted wife.'

'It wasn't like that.' Louise's voice was panic-stricken.

'Yes, it was,' Alistair said with contempt. 'You went with him to Mallorca when we were living together, before he went to New York. I've seen the bills. And the rental agreement for the place in the Hamptons and the apartment in New York, not to mention the rest.' He waved his arms to indicate the flat. 'Helen said you were a liar. What else have you lied about?'

'Nothing,' she whispered. She had to stop him walking out. She'd make damn sure she soon would be pregnant if only she could get him to stay.

Alistair gestured towards the potpourri and the scented candles. 'All this is a charade, isn't it? You knew how much I wanted a child and you used it in the most cynical way to trap me.'

'I didn't.' Louise was near to tears. 'I am pregnant, I really am.'

'Then let's prove it. Now. We can go and see a gynaecologist friend of mine and have you tested right this minute. I presume you'd be willing to do that? After all, if it's true you don't have anything to worry about, do you?'

He had caught her unawares and she could not meet his gaze.

'Stop playing games, Louise,' he said more gently. 'Don't take me for such a fool. Tell me the truth. You owe me that.'

Louise took a deep breath. She had only one chance and she had to make the most of it. 'When I met you again I made up my mind to use you like Mark used me. To set up the art gallery. You knew everyone, I needed you and you wouldn't have helped me because of the past. So I set out to trap you sexually. But something changed. I fell in love with you. Don't look sceptical. I didn't plan it that way, believe me.'

'Love?' His voice was bitter. 'You don't know the meaning of the word.'

'That's unfair, Alistair. In the beginning I admit I was

intrigued when I thought you would become head of Amalgamated. It was a game I was playing. I had this crazy idea that if we remarried I'd be able to get some sort of revenge on Helen.'

'What did she ever do to you?'

'She made Mark unhappy but he didn't want to leave the girls.'

'I don't believe that either but I'll let that pass. When I didn't get the job, why did you still hang around?'

'Because it didn't matter to me any more. I wanted you for yourself, not for money or power.'

'What a shame I can't believe anything you say any more.' He gave a wry smile. 'You're not pregnant, are you?'

Louise shook her head. 'No, sadly I'm not. But I do want children,' she went on rapidly, 'your children, Alistair. Please believe that.'

Alistair stared at her. It was impossible to tell what was going through his mind. Tentatively she reached out for his hand and when he made no attempt to withdraw it, she allowed herself to feel encouraged.

'I know I can make you happy, darling. Please give me another chance.'

The weather reflected Georgie's mood. When it was not raining, the clouds seemed to press on the grey ground beneath. The whole world seemed grey as she set off for her appointment with the gynaecologist.

Since her pregnancy had been confirmed, she had felt no elation about this baby, only dread and apprehension.

Helen's words at the health hydro came back to haunt her. How could she have a child at this stage in her career? How could she cope with a baby and a fourteen-hour day? Georgie well understood that these first months in the job would set the pace, would mark her style, put the seal on her appointment. As Helen had pointed out, her schedule was punishing. Only this morning she had had to rearrange her timetable to fit in with Helen's suggestion that she visit the holders of the franchise titles in Turkey and Rome.

At the moment Georgie felt she could not manage her own body, let alone a baby. She spent at least an hour every morning hanging over the bathroom basin. It was not the greatest start to an executive's day. By the late afternoon, when New York was on stream, she felt bone weary these days. Josephine had assured her this would pass but that was no consolation now. So far the only stamp she had put on her new role was to cancel and postpone meetings because she felt unwell.

What hellish fate to get pregnant at the same time as Alistair's first wife. All through its life her child would have a weekend father who shared his time with another child of exactly the same age, except the other child would have the advantage of living with both its parents. It would be difficult for any mother to compensate for that, never mind one who was going to have to travel and work as hard as she was. Georgie sighed.

She was certain that Alistair would not be difficult about maintenance but she had never had to depend on a man for money. She had always adhered to her granny's advice, 'Always be mistress of your own life,' and could not envisage a day when she would willingly place control of her financial needs in someone else's hands.

There was always the possibility that she could change her life, leave Amalgamated and become a freelance to give her more flexibility in her working life. But when she had discussed this with Josephine, her friend had sounded a warning.

'Your problem, like mine, is that we've gone too far up the ladder to find work that provides the necessary flexibility. You can get short-term contracts, sure, but they want you eighteen hours a day for three months to do a rush job and you can't put your child's life on hold. Besides, some editors don't want you around even in the wings because they see you as a threat. They think managing directors like having a spare editor around. The bastards think that by destabilising them, the editors will work harder, longer, better.'

Of course if she carried on earning this sort of salary, she could afford a properly trained nanny. But over the years, observing the experiences of her friends and writing features about the subject, Georgie had become convinced this arrangement was most successful when the nanny's influence was diluted by the presence of family and friends. Certainly this was true in Josephine's case. She had aunts and cousins nearby with children of the same age, who were constantly in and out of her home when she was at the office.

In her own case the nanny would have sole care of the baby and she would only see the child late at night and at weekends. Her frequent trips abroad could involve lengthy absences and she hated the idea of being a long-distance mother. Georgie remembered an interview in a recent issue of one of her magazines. In it, a woman MP who had just been elected had confessed how her child-minder kept a diary of her son's day for her. 'I can't read it without a pang,' she had told the writer. 'One entry said he was getting good at using a beaker and I thought, why haven't I seen this?' Georgie found that quote particularly heartbreaking.

Later on, her child would probably spend time at Alistair's home. At the thought of a smiling, victorious Louise playing with her child, Georgie crossed her arms protectively. Not my baby. Not with her.

When Georgie left the gynaecologist, she had an appointment at the abortion clinic on Monday. If she wanted it.

She didn't know what she wanted any more. All weekend her mind wrestled with her emotions, threatening to overwhelm her. She felt totally alone. If only she could share some of her anxieties. She had been pushing away the constant thought that Alistair had a right to know what she was planning and she knew she could no longer put off talking to him. Tentatively she picked up the phone to dial Rosemary's number.

She wasn't sure whether to be relieved or disappointed when the answering machine clicked in. She chose her words for the tape carefully.

'Alistair, it's Georgie.' Once she wouldn't have had to announce who she was. She swallowed. 'Could you please phone me as soon as possible? There is something we need to discuss, something important.'

# Chapter Twenty-Five

Every last piece of the jigsaw fitted. Luke clapped his hands and delightedly turned the box upside down. 'Again. Again,' he chortled.

Josephine gave a swift glance at her watch. It was only a few minutes past seven, she didn't have to leave for work yet. 'All right,' she smiled, 'once more.' Patiently she guided the chubby hand towards the corner pieces of Old Macdonald's Farm.

Their playtime was interrupted by the shrill ringing of the phone. Luke scampered towards it. He loved answering the phone; often the call would be for him – Mummy ringing from the office.

He seemed to recognise the voice and prattled happily into the receiver.

'Who is it, darling?' Josephine gently tried to wrest the phone from him. He resisted. He liked this game. In his short life Luke had chatted unconcernedly to the Home Secretary, the Transport Minister, Tom Reeves and other Hollywood stars, and Mark Temple-Smith. The parents among them had been patient but occasionally it had caused embarrassment.

This time it was Georgie, sounding agitated. 'What's up?' asked Josephine. 'I got your message when I got back last night but it was too late to ring.'

'I'm sorry you were away. I really needed to talk to you.'

'What's happened?'

'I saw Dr Bischoff on Saturday and I've decided this morning to be realistic about all this and have an abortion. I'm on my way to a clinic in Barnet.'

Josephine was appalled, and not only because this meant Georgie would stay in her job and all Harry's plotting would come to nothing. 'Georgie, you shouldn't do anything in a hurry. Come back and discuss it.'

'No point, Jo. I've thought about it from every angle and it's not fair on the baby.'

'Come on, you'd be a wonderful mother.'

'No, I wouldn't be. I've spent all weekend thinking about nothing else. I haven't slept, I haven't eaten, and I've come to the conclusion it's the right thing to do.'

'Babies don't come to order, you know,' said Josephine urgently. 'Have you taken that on board? When you're ready for it you may not be able to have one. You should know better than most.'

'I have to take that chance,' said Georgie. 'Every instinct is telling me no. Not now.'

'What can I say to change your mind?'

'Nothing.'

'What about Alistair?'

'I wanted to tell him and I left a message for him last

night to ring me. But there's been no word. I wish I didn't still love the bastard.'

'I think he needs to know that.'

'Absolutely not. He's forfeited that right. He's having a baby with Louise.

Josephine was horrified. 'I can't believe it.'

'It's true, and as far as I'm concerned, they're welcome to each other. He might come back to me if he knew about our baby, but it wouldn't be because he loves me.'

'I'm not sure you're right about that.'

'Well, I am.'

Think, think. There must be something else she could try. Luke began pulling at her trouser leg and Josephine lifted her toddler on to her knee. Suddenly he flung his arms round her neck and gave her a rapturous squeeze.

Josephine responded in kind and then said into the receiver, 'Luke's just given me one of his special hugs. If you don't have this baby, you'll never know what you're missing.'

'Oh, Josephine, please don't . . .' and the line went dead.

Alistair asked Rosemary to have a quiet early morning stroll with him around St James's Park. He said he felt stir crazy and if he did not do something active he would explode.

'I've totally fucked up my life,' he told her gloomily as they watched a squirrel inspecting a discarded bread roll. When Rosemary tried to protest, he said bitterly, 'Don't try and comfort me. I've lost everything I've ever wanted.'

'You'll get another job.'

'God, it isn't the job I'm talking about. It's Georgie. She's everything I wanted in a woman and because of my stupidity, my pig-headedness, I've lost her.'

'But I thought you and Louise were together now?'

'She was pretending all the time. She doesn't love me. She even lied about being pregnant. Can you believe that?'

'She lied?'

'She made it up to trap me into marrying her.'

'How could she be so cruel?'

'Easily. She's what's known as a mimophant. She has the sensitivity of a mimosa when it comes to her own feelings but those of an elephant when it comes to others.'

'She hasn't changed at all, has she?'

'No. She's still the same liar. And you'll hardly believe why she left me in the first place.'

Rosemary waited.

'She had an affair with Mark, soon after we married. And she went off with him to New York. She was his secret mistress right up until his accident.'

Rosemary gaped at Alistair.

'Yes, and that bitch has made me lose my wife.'

Guiltily Rosemary pushed away the memory of all she had done to create trouble between them, most recently erasing Georgie's message last night while Alistair was out. He had been out most of the weekend, in fact; she had hardly seen him and had assumed he was with Louise. 'Alistair, can't you tell Georgie all this, persuade her you've made a mistake?'

'No, it's too late. She wants a divorce and once Georgie's made up her mind, that's it. And who can blame her? I've been a bloody fool. I've done a lot of thinking this weekend,' Alistair continued. 'I can't get Georgie back and it's too painful being in the same city, going to functions in the hope that I'll bump into her. So I'm leaving, Rosie. Leaving the country.'

'Where are you going?'

'Don't know yet. But I'm going.'

'I want to come with you, I could—'

'No, I need to be on my own. I'm going to do some travelling first.' He stood still. 'Do you mind if I leave you here? I was on my way to see a travel agent across the park.'

Rosemary began to cry. 'All this is my fault.'

Alistair put his arms round her. 'Don't say that. Don't even think it. How could it be your fault?'

Rosemary said nothing. He must never know how hard she had worked to break up his marriage, how she had taken every opportunity to throw not only spanners but big monkey wrenches into the works. Erasing Georgie's messages, encouraging Louise to make a play for Alistair because it would serve her own interests, failing to tell him how much Georgie had wanted to meet, to talk. She had done all this because she knew what was best for her brother. Or so she had thought. She had not changed her mind about Georgie. Even now, she still believed Georgie was the wrong kind of woman to make Alistair happy in the long term. But he loved her.

Through her misery she heard Alistair say, 'Please stop crying, Rosie. I don't like to leave you like this.'

She managed to stem the tears. 'Please don't go, please. Georgie still loves you, I know she does.'

'You're kind to say that but I don't believe it and neither do you.'

'I do,' she insisted, trying to gain control over her tears. 'I really do.'

'I have to go now, darling. Hey, stop that. I won't be leaving until next week and when I go I'll stay in touch. I'll phone you regularly from wherever I am. You're the only real friend I have in the world. The only one I'll want to speak to.'

Rosemary groped in her handbag for a tissue and blew her nose.

He took her arm. 'You all right now?'

She nodded sadly and he leaned over to kiss her on the cheek. 'Dear Rosie, you've always been there for me.'

Rosemary watched his tall frame stride past the lake and head in the direction of Trafalgar Square. As she stared at his retreating figure, she thought miserably of how unhappy he was, and her own part in causing it. She hoped fervently she had not done him irreparable damage.

Rosemary could see her life stretching ahead in a melancholy procession of days at Amalgamated without even Alistair to temper the greyness. And no glamorous job at an art gallery either. If Louise could fake a pregnancy to try and trap Alistair, she could also fake a friendship. As far as Rosemary was concerned, Louise could return to the rat hole from which she had come.

Rosemary winced at the memory of how she had urged Louise to attend the *Art World* party behind Georgina's back, and how she had encouraged her to follow Alistair to Florida, knowing full well she wanted to snare him. And for what? A spurious job with an untrustworthy character. It was probably all a ruse in the first place to get close to Alistair and, more importantly, his contacts.

All her life she had convinced herself she was putting Alistair's interests before her own. It wasn't true. It was time to face up to the fact. She must let him go and start to rebuild her life without the crutch he had always provided.

Sitting there in St James's Park, she decided she would leave Amalgamated. She would move nearer the sea, and if necessary re-train. When she was younger she had dreamed of owning her own catering company. She had always been successful at organising every aspect of Alistair's dinner parties and she enjoyed cooking. Maybe, even at her age, somebody would give her a try. She would advertise when she was settled on the south coast.

But for now there was a great deal to repair between Alistair and Georgina. What was it Georgie had wanted to discuss when she left that message on the answer machine for Alistair last night? She had erased it then without much thought. If she could only get the couple to talk, perhaps even at this late stage it might stop Alistair from leaving the country. And if he stayed, maybe they could try and patch things up. It was worth a try.

She hurried to the nearest phone kiosk and spent several minutes trying to contact Georgie. She could not remember her mobile number but as it was still only eight o'clock, she tried her at the flat. After a number of rings, her sister-in-law's friendly announcement suggested the caller leave a number.

The sound of Georgie's voice triggered another bout of remorseful weeping and it was several seconds before Rosemary could leave her message. Who else would know Georgie's movements? Josephine Clarke. Rosemary did not have her home number but directory inquiries did.

After an immense effort to steady her choking voice, she said into Josephine's answer machine, 'This is urgent. I haven't been able to find Georgie but she needs to know that Alistair does not love Louise, he never has, and she's not having a baby, that was a lie. Alistair loves Georgie. But he's planning to leave the country. She has to stop him. Please, please tell her.'

Harry Ferguson cupped his hand over the receiver as his secretary walked into the room. He waved the young woman away impatiently and said quietly, 'Thanks for your advice over the last couple of weeks but I've lost, old boy. She's on her way to the abortion clinic.'

In New York Ned Mastrianni responded more loudly,

'I can't hear you. What's that you say?'

Harry sighed. 'I can't talk any louder. Georgina Luckhurst's getting rid of the kid.'

'You sure?'

'Yes, I am, and you know what that means, she's giving her career top priority. We haven't a prayer. We can't get her pushed out now so we may as well forget the whole thing.'

'Not so fast, my friend. Does that husband of hers know what she's doing?'

'No, he doesn't, but it doesn't matter because it's over between them. They're getting a divorce.'

'God, you Brits. I don't know how you fuckin' won the war. Find out when the op is scheduled and let Alistair know.'

'Didn't you hear? They've split up, it won't do any good.'

A heavy sigh came down the transatlantic wire. 'Listen, dumbo, it's still his kid, isn't it? He'll want to stop her. And that's what we want. If Georgina keeps the kid, she won't be able to juggle the same number of balls. And Helen'll be up shit creek. *Capice*?'

'I suppose it's worth a try.'

'Get to it.'

Harry's next call was to Josephine. He asked her to come to his office immediately.

When she appeared, he put forward Ned's idea as if he'd just thought of it himself.

'OK, this is what we're to do. We have to tell Alistair his chance of becoming a father depends on how quickly he can get his butt over to Barnet.'

'It's a minute to midnight and you're still scheming,' said Josephine, watching him with ill-disguised contempt. 'Don't you see, you've lost?'

'Excuse me, I'm not alone in this. Don't you mean we've lost?'

'I don't know why I let myself be talked into this stupid scheme. What's been the result of all this conniving and plotting? We're exactly where we were when we started.'

'We can still do it, Jo. If you want to be the top editorial honcho in this company, you need me in place. We're so close to winning. All we have to do is persuade her to have the baby. If we do that it'll be only a matter of weeks before she has to sod off out of the company. Helen will see to that.'

Josephine's expression of disdain had not altered. 'You don't get it, do you? Getting Alistair to talk to her won't work. She'll show him the door the minute he turns up.'

'Why would she do that to the father of her child?' asked Harry petulantly.

'Because, Mister-Know-It-All, if he says he wants a reconciliation now, Georgina knows it'll only be because she's pregnant. That won't be good enough for her.'

'Listen, if you want to be publishing director, give me solutions, not problems. You're supposed to be her friend, play on that, for God's sake. Say anything, do anything, but get the result we need.'

'I can't imagine why I was stupid enough to think you

could get me what I want. You've no idea what the hell's going on,' snapped Josephine.

Harry leaned back in his chair. 'Suppose you tell me.'

'Alistair won't go back to Georgie because he happens to be in love with Louise.'

Harry hid his surprise. 'When did this happen?'

'While you were playing your stupid games. And they've decided to get married because,' she paused before delivering the final salvo, 'they're having a baby.'

This time his mouth dropped open.

Josephine glared at him scornfully. 'Why didn't I see that underneath that smarmy smile and flashy suit was someone with a second-class job, a third-class life and a no-class mind? It's finished, Harry. You've lost.' With that, Josephine flung open the door and walked out, leaving her former co-conspirator staring at his hands.

Harry always believed the secret of his success in business was that he never acted until he was privy to every scrap of relevant information. It was only then that he would formulate his campaign of action.

He paced around the office. Josephine had sounded certain of her facts but he had to check them out. Marriage and a baby? Alistair had never even mentioned he was seeing his first wife again. Who could confirm this astounding story? He did not know Louise's address, God only knew where Alistair was, and he could not ask Georgie. But there was another person who might know. He opened the door and strode towards Rosemary's office.

She looked as if she had been crying but he had

enough problems of his own without burdening himself with anyone else's, so he ignored her obvious distress. He forced a smile. 'I've just heard the wonderful news.'

Her eyes were dull.

'About the baby?' he ventured.

'There is no baby,' she said miserably.

So Josephine had been wrong about that. 'I'm sorry to hear that, was it a miscarriage?'

Her mouth twisted. 'Yes. Of justice.'

What was the woman talking about? Harry did not understand and did not want to try. 'But they're still getting married, aren't they?' She appeared uncomprehending. What was the matter with her? 'Louise and Alistair,' he said tersely. 'Getting married?'

'They're not.'

No baby. No marriage. Harry spied a glimmer of light. Now he had to avert the abortion. He had to locate Alistair. Seating himself opposite Rosemary's desk, he leaned forward intently. 'Rosemary, there's something you don't know that I think you ought to.'

She showed no curiosity and seemed to be examining her fingernails.

'Pay attention,' he said more brusquely than he meant but it did make her look up at him. 'Georgina is pregnant.'

'It's not true. If Georgina was having a baby, Alistair would know.'

'She's kept the news from him because of Louise having his baby.'

'But she isn't.'

Harry tried to keep his patience. 'I know that. You and Alistair know that. But Georgina does not. In fact, she's already made the decision not to have the baby.'

Rosemary stared at him.

'She's going to have an abortion,' he said. 'This morning.'

Rosemary was aghast. 'Oh no, we can't let that happen,' she cried. 'Alistair still loves her.'

This was exactly what Harry wanted to hear. 'Then he has to tell her that.' He took out a pen and notepad and started writing. 'She's on her way to this abortion clinic right now. Get Alistair to stop her.'

Harry was pleased with his endeavours. His eyes glittered as he contemplated the prize within his grasp. If all went according to plan, Georgina would keep the baby and be eased out. And he would be in. Helen, desperate to save face, would act quickly. He was the perfect steady-as-she-goes replacement until things had calmed down. But after he had moved into that palatial office occupied by the chief executive of Amalgamated Magazines, they'd have to prise away his fingernails one by one from the desk before he'd leave.

Once he was in charge, how he would relish making Josephine pay for her insolence. He would give her the title of publishing director but not the power. He'd downgrade the position and cut her right out of the decision-making loop.

Now, how else could he repay her ill-disguised contempt for his abilities? How would she like it if Georgina found out about her double-dealing, hmn? Georgina was smart in most things but like many intelligent women she trusted people close to her. She would be horrified to learn about Josephine's betrayal. Ned would approve.

Harry checked the abortion clinic's telephone number and started dialling.


Alistair seemed to have disappeared. Rosemary's first call was to his secretary but she had no idea of his whereabouts. As always his mobile was switched off but the secretary promised to give him a message, though she warned Rosemary that he did not often come in these days.

When Rosemary stressed how important it was that she talk to her brother, the young woman said, 'When he had any free time, he usually visited an art gallery but I've no idea which one he'd choose now. Occasionally he'd go to the coffee shop downstairs and sometimes, especially if he had a problem, he'd mull it over during a work-out at the gym.'

The waitress in the coffee shop downstairs informed Rosemary that Alistair had not been in there for some time, so she made her way to the gym in Lamb's Passage. She pushed through the swing doors, ignoring the 'Men Only' sign, and swept straight past the startled receptionist.

In the main hall housing the fitness equipment she was relieved to see Alistair's familiar figure doing shoulder presses with an iron bar, sweat pouring off his torso. When he caught sight of her anxious face, he dropped the weights with a clang.

'What are you doing here?' he said, reaching for a towel to mop his face. 'What's happened?'

'You'd better prepare yourself for a shock.'

'Go on.'

'Georgie's pregnant.'

Alistair sank on to the bench. 'I don't believe it. Who told you?'

'Harry.'

'How the hell does he know?'

'I didn't think to ask but he was very sure of his facts. But that's not all. Georgie's on her way to an abortion clinic right now.'

'Oh my God.'

'Here's the address. Go after her and stop her doing something she'll always regret – that both of you would regret.'

# Chapter Twenty-Six

Georgie was feeling dry-mouthed, sick and terrified. She had taken the precaution of wearing a headscarf and kept on her dark glasses when she had arrived. Her picture had appeared often enough in print lately to make her worry that she might be recognised. Imagine what her detractors would do with ammunition like this.

The receptionist had encouraged her to take a taxi as they did not recommend driving for a few hours afterwards. Yet the gravel drive had been filled with top-of-the-range horsepower. Fruits of the labour of surgeons and anaesthetists, she assumed. Business must be brisk if they were all in attendance at such an early hour.

Beyond the floral wallpaper of the reception area, the ambience quickly became clinical. Within the hour Georgie had been undressed, jewellery put in the safe, nail varnish and make-up removed, her blood pressure checked and pronounced ready to be transferred to the theatre in a short while.

Georgina Luckhurst, newly promoted chief executive of Amalgamated Magazines, had her persona removed and became patient number 2174, identified only by her wristband. She was feeling bereft, completely alone in the world. No Alistair and no baby. The only fixture in her plummeting world was her career. She had to hang on to thoughts of that but at this moment it did not seem remotely like adequate compensation.

Of course, at thirty-three she could still have babies later. But if she went ahead she was taking the risk that conception might become more complicated, if there was to be a next time. As it was, she had read that one in six couples had difficulty conceiving. She doubted if babies could ever be fitted into a schedule. When would it ever be a better time for her?

Georgie tried unsuccessfully to distract herself by reading the papers as she waited for the anaesthetist to administer the pre-med. He was due in ten minutes.

As she lay there in the starched white hospital gown, feeling like an object rather than a person, Georgie watched the second hand on the clock above the door. It seemed to be racing round the dial.

Tick. Tick. The sound reverberated around the room. Then the telephone rang. It was Harry.

The elegant Georgian mansion with its vivid flowerbeds and box-edged lawns was far better cared for than its neighbours in the avenue. The London suburb was an archetypal picture of middle-class respectability, giving no hint of what business was conducted inside the mansion.

Josephine pulled up outside with a squeal of brakes

and dashed into the building. She had jumped every amber light in her anxiety to try a last-ditch attempt to dissuade Georgie from a course of action she was sure her friend would bitterly regret later. Thank God Georgie had agreed to see her when she had rung her from home, having walked out of the office in disgust and gone back to Kensington and Rosemary's message.

Josephine's conscience had been troubling her for weeks for playing that deceitful game with Harry. Why had she fooled herself into believing his phoney promises? The only way she could think of now to try and make amends was to give Georgie the message from Rosemary regarding Louise. It might make her hesitate about what she was about to do, or even lead to a reconciliation, although she doubted it. But it was worth a try, she owed that much to Georgie.

The reception area had been designed to give the impression of a country house, with faded chintz and aged leather sofas, glossy magazines on mahogany tables and elaborate arrangements of dried flowers everywhere.

Two receptionists, dressed in smartly tailored suits, greeted her warmly, giving the impression of working in a high-class spa. Yes, one of the receptionists told her, Miss Luckhurst would talk to her in the private room reserved for meetings. 'The anaesthetist is due to see her,' she added, 'so you can't stay long.'

When Josephine was ushered into the small anteroom, she found Georgie sitting in a buttoned armchair, waxen-faced and unsmiling.

'Thank God I'm not too late,' said Josephine, flinging

her arms round the unyielding figure.

'Sit down.' The tone was unaccustomedly sharp, the voice of a chief executive, not a friend.

Taken aback, Josephine pulled away. 'I know this is not the best time but—'

'You've been scheming behind my back with Harry Ferguson,' Georgie interrupted. The words were all the more deadly because they were spoken without heat.

Josephine sat down heavily. 'So he's phoned you. I'm not surprised the little shit's turned on me. We had a mega fight and I made sure he knew exactly what I thought of him. I was going to tell you about it.'

Georgie stared at her impassively. 'Why did you do it?'

Josephine gave a short laugh. 'Because Harry is the father of my son.'

'What?'

'It was a stupid fling, not much more than a one-night stand after a boozy dinner when we went on a think tank in France.' She saw the flicker of distaste that crossed Georgie's face. 'Don't think I haven't castigated myself for that a hundred times over. As for why I helped him,' Josephine ran a hand through her hair, 'Harry played on my insecurities. He went on and on about what a raw deal I'd been given. He offered to help me get promotion.'

Georgie sat unmoving, staring at her coldly.

'I don't expect you to understand,' Josephine went on nervously. 'Why should you? Harry wanted Ned Mastrianni to get the job so when he went back to America Harry would take over London. Then I'd be publishing director with a hefty salary hike.' She lifted her chin. 'Everything I did to get that promotion was so I could give Luke a secure future.'

Georgie's expression did not alter. 'I'd always understood that Mark offered you a bigger job and you turned it down.'

'Once, years ago, but I did expect to get the job of publishing director after the merger. When you were brought in over my head, I was jealous. My chances of promotion seemed to be over for good. The trouble was, I grew to like you.'

'But if you wanted me to fail why did you push me when I wanted to withdraw from the short list? It was you who made me think again. At every turn when I was having trouble with Alistair you kept me going. Why?'

'I meant every word. As a friend—'

'As a friend?' Georgie was withering. 'Is that why you caused such trouble between Alistair and me over that printing deal?'

'I regret that very much. That was when I realised I was in too deep but Harry's such a bastard. If I didn't toe the line he was going to let everyone know he was Luke's father. I was so ashamed of how it had happened . . .' Her voice trailed off, then became stronger. 'But I don't take back anything I said about the job. You owed it to yourself to try for it. But I admit it never occurred to me that you'd be successful.'

'I'm sorry you were disappointed.'

'I wasn't. Oh God, I'll never be able to make you understand how thrilled I was, in spite of Harry. But I didn't come here to get absolution for myself,' she said hurriedly. 'I know that's too late. I came because I wanted to tell you that Alistair's planning to leave the country. He doesn't love Louise, and she's not pregnant. Alistair loves you.'

'You know that, do you?' Georgie's voice was caustic.

'Yes, Rosemary left a message on my machine. She's been trying to get hold of you.'

'Rosemary?' Georgie's voice was scornful. 'I never believe anything she says.'

'She sounded genuine.'

Georgie made no response and Josephine stood up to leave. There was nothing more she could do.

'You'll have my letter of resignation when you get back to the office,' she said, picking up her handbag and avoiding Georgie's tense face.

This time Georgie did respond. 'Our friendship is over,' she said quietly, 'but as your employer I consider you an extremely experienced editor.'

'Thank you.' Josephine felt mortified by Georgie's generosity. 'Does that mean you could bear to give me a decent reference so I can find another job?'

Georgie ignored the question. 'I've been drawing up plans for a complete reorganisation. I had already made up my mind that Harry would not figure in the new scheme of things. I don't trust his business acumen and this disloyalty has only reinforced my decision to ask for his resignation. And,' Georgie continued, 'you're wrong in thinking I didn't consider you for promotion.'

'Then it's a pity I'm leaving.'

'Don't. Because I intend promoting you to publishing director.'

Josephine had expected anything but this. 'I don't understand. How could you work with me now?'

'You're good at your job. Why should the company lose you because of what's happened between us?'

Josephine opened her mouth to thank her but Georgie held up an imperious hand. 'Don't thank me, don't swear you'll work hard, don't say anything. It'll take me a long time to get over this betrayal and you'll be on trial in this new job. I'll give it six months to see if it's going to work.'

'Do you think you could ever forgive me?'

'I don't know.'

Josephine left her and walked out into the bright sunshine, a headache looming. She could hardly believe what had just happened. Promotion when she deserved to be fired. But instead of elation, she felt an overwhelming sense of deep shame.

Since learning about Louise's fake pregnancy, Alistair had done some serious thinking. It had focused his mind on what was important to him. When Louise had tried to get him to commit himself, it had made him realise that it was not just a child he wanted, but the woman. And that woman was Georgie.

His arrival at the clinic might make her change her mind about having the abortion, something which, he was positive, would haunt her for ever. He would do his best to convince her to keep their baby. God, he hoped he wouldn't be too late.

Then he had to set about making things right between them. First he would try and persuade her to give their marriage another chance. And not for the sake of the baby. He would do his best to woo her back. He would rent a flat near to hers and be on hand to see her whenever she wanted. If she decided to keep the baby, he would help, support and love them both. If things went well between them over a period of time . . . well, he didn't dare think that far ahead.

But he could not contemplate a life without her, and if that meant giving up the idea of having a family, then so be it. And he would stay with Amalgamated. He would work as part of her team and report directly to her, not to Helen. His stupid pride had ruled all his thinking. He had behaved in exactly the way he despised in people like Harry Ferguson. He had even let his pride use Louise as a sort of buffer when he thought Georgie wanted a divorce. It wasn't even Georgie herself who had told him that. It was Louise, quoting Rosemary, for God's sake. When he thought Louise was having his child, of course he had felt honour bound to look after her but he would never have been black-mailed into marriage. He bitterly regretted leaving Georgie with the impression that marriage to Louise was a possibility.

He couldn't bear to think his actions had pushed Georgie into having an abortion. God, how could he have been so wrong about everything? If he had encouraged and supported her, they wouldn't have ended up in this mess.

Few would have recognised the tall, dishevelled figure in a sweatshirt and jeans that hurried into the clinic's reception. Breathlessly Alistair cast about for someone to give him information. Ignoring the protests of the reception staff behind the counter, he raced through a door marked 'No admittance. Authorised personnel only'. Presumably it led to the wards and operating theatre.

At the far end of the corridor a noticeboard covered with miscellaneous pieces of paper caught his attention. On it was a list of that day's theatre admissions.

There it was, 'G. Luckhurst, Room 9', with the time scheduled for her operation. He checked his watch and groaned. He was ten minutes too late. Oh, Georgie, why didn't you tell me? Why didn't you at least give me the chance to show that I can change, that I made a terrible mistake? That I love you, I want to be with you, and I want our baby.

'Sir, sir, stop.' A security guard was racing towards him down the corridor.

'I need to see my wife,' he shouted back. His last hope, that the operation had been rescheduled or postponed, was dashed when he reached Room 9 and he saw the rumpled bedclothes. There were Georgie's belongings, clothes hanging in the wardrobe, her make-up bag on the locker, and as always she had brought with her all that morning's newspapers and a formidable batch of magazines.

'I'm afraid you'll have to leave, sir,' said the guard. The man was still trying to regain his breath after his sprint. 'This area is confined to patients only.'

'This is my wife's room.'

'You can't wait here, sir. I'll take you back to reception.'

'Just give me a minute, will you?'

The guard looked at Alistair's miserable face and hesitated.

Alistair sat down on the bed. He wanted to be here when she came out of the operating theatre, comfort her after the trauma, and beg her forgiveness. Then he had an uncomfortable vision of how it would appear to Georgie. Here was a man who professed to be in love with his wife but who scorned her efforts at trying to get the job of her dreams, who gave her no support, no encouragement, in fact actively worked against her, chipping away at her self-confidence. Yet in spite of that she had been strong enough to go ahead and impress Helen and the appointments board. She had landed the job fair and square. And she had deserved to win, some of her ideas were brilliant. More importantly, they would work. Then at the very time he should have congratulated her and vowed to help her, what did he do? He went off and fucked his first wife, the woman who had been the cause of so much apprehension to Georgie from the moment she reappeared in their lives.

If he were Georgie, regaining consciousness, seeing him at the bedside, he knew what he would do. Turn his face to the wall. He wasn't worthy of her love or her trust. He had hurt her too much. She would be better off without him. She would be a great success and he would only hold her back. And for his part, he would have to live with the result of his mistake for the rest of his life.

Head bowed, Alistair walked out of the clinic and made his way across the road towards the park. He had no idea where he was going and cared less. He took out a handkerchief and wiped it across his eyes.

# Chapter Twenty-Seven

Georgie had settled her bill and had gone to her room to pack her things. As she waited for a taxi, she ruefully surveyed the room in which she'd had such a painful encounter with her erstwhile friend only a short time before. She and Josephine had been close the last couple of years and she would miss her wise counsel. Now she wondered how objective her advice had been. Had Josephine always had a hidden agenda? It was an uncomfortable thought, all those shared confidences, all those revelations.

First Alistair then Josephine. What was it about her that attracted people who would betray her? It must be a flaw in her character which prevented her from being able to see them in their true colours. Could it be that she was so needy that she missed the warning signs? Certainly that was the case with Alistair.

The decision to cut Josephine out of her private life from now on had been made for her. But God knows she could appreciate the pressure she'd been under from Luke's father. At the start of this business hadn't she herself done the same thing with Alistair?

Tick. Tick.

The sound of that damned clock at the clinic would stay with her for ever. Lying in that small impersonal room, with the anaesthetist only minutes away from performing his job, Georgie had begun to ask herself some searching questions about her values, about what she was working for, about what she wanted for the future and, more seriously, whether she could abort a child for no other reason than that it was inconvenient. These questions kept buzzing around her head like a trapped wasp under a glass. If she had been ill or mentally unable to cope, that might have been a different matter, but patently she was not.

Georgie thought about the ephemeral nature of life. After Mark's death, Alistair had asked what legacy they would leave behind and had come to the conclusion it would be nothing really important. A few magazine titles, some awards, that was about it. Now she could choose to leave something far more tangible than those. A person, to continue her connection to being alive, to being a woman.

Tick. Tick.

And there was Alistair. Within her body was the new life which combined his genes with hers. Though she did not need to consult him from the legal point of view, didn't he have the moral, the biological right to have a say in whether or not his child lived?

So far her reasoning had been cerebral but what did her heart say? The answer came swiftly. Her baby wanted to live. Certainly she would be worried about the effects of her child having to share his time with the offspring of Alistair's new wife. Not for a moment did she believe what Rosemary had told Josephine concerning Louise. But a semi-detached father was better than no father at all and she was certain Alistair was capable of loving more than one child.

And she wouldn't be too proud to refuse any financial assistance if he offered. It was his baby too, she wanted him to have a part in its upbringing, and not only financially. It would be his responsibility to make time and effort to be a father to their child in every sense of the word.

Georgie had flung back the sheets and walked out of her room to find the surgeon and cancel the operation.

As the taxi pulled away from the clinic, Georgie began to give herself a pep talk. Hadn't she made extraordinary things happen in her life? Hadn't she taken enormous risks occasionally and hadn't things always turned out right eventually? She would have to make the next phase in her life work for her. Who said she and the baby couldn't manage? She had. Who had declared her life couldn't go forward in some different way? She had. If having an abortion was the kind of sacrifice needed to make it in a man's world, she was not prepared to make it. She wanted her life to add up to more than another set of profit forecasts.

Helen had made it clear that to make a success of her job she must have no diversions outside her work, especially in the vital first year. But why should she simply accept that Helen was right? Why shouldn't she be able to convince her that with the right kind of back-up the job would not suffer?

Georgie was a fighter, always had been, always would be. Her pale face regained some of its colour as she sat in the taxi, marshalling her arguments.

Where was it written in stone that meetings had to be at the end of the working day? Why couldn't they take place over working lunches instead? Why couldn't she do some of her thinking work at home? For God's sake, wasn't modern technology, like scanners, e-mail and modems, created to make life easier? And when she couldn't be with her baby she would pay for the best child care available. Most of the nannies who'd turned out to be unsuitable were young girls more interested in their social lives than caring for a small child. Why wouldn't they be? That's what youth was for. The answer wasn't to castigate all nannies but to seek out someone older, more of a grandmother figure. Wasn't that what had happened in earlier days? She needed to look for a nanny who could become part of the family rather than an employee. And however painful it was, she would have to talk to Alistair about what she was doing. She hadn't even managed to tell him she was pregnant, she thought guiltily. Because of Louise's pregnancy, probably nothing would change between them but at least she would have fulfilled her obligations to him.

Her mobile shrilled, making her jump. It was Helen.

'I've been told you're out of the office for the day. Where are you?'

'My plans have changed,' replied Georgie. 'I'm on the way back to the office. Can it wait?'

'No, I'm sorry.' Helen's voice was brisk. 'Margery and I are on our way to Heathrow Airport. We're off to New York. I have some loose ends to tie up. Georgina, I've made a couple of big decisions and I wanted you to be the first to know. I've decided to relocate.'

'The magazines?' She ought to have been consulted at the very least.

'No, no,' said Helen. 'Me. I've loved being back in London, I feel at home here. I've thought it through very carefully. I've nothing much to go back to and the girls have their own lives.'

'This is sudden, isn't it?'

'No, I've been thinking about it for weeks. Don't worry, it won't affect you because I'll still be concentrating on New York, only from a different base.'

Georgie didn't swallow this. Helen was not the kind of person who could be in the London office and not interfere, whatever promises she made. It didn't make sense to say she would run New York from Europe.

'Who'll do the day-to-day stuff over there?' she asked.

'That's the best part of it,' Helen replied. 'As you know, Giles is due to retire and I've chosen someone to replace him who'll be a good counterpoint to you. You may find it difficult at first to work with him . . .'

Georgie's heart did a leap. Alistair.

'. . . but I reckon after a period of adjustment it'll work well for the company. I want you to remember that.'

'I think I can guess who it is,' said Georgie faintly. 'Alistair.'

Helen coughed. 'No, no. It's Ned Mastrianni.'

For a moment Georgie bristled at the unfairness of the decision. The job should have gone to Alistair. But of course he didn't know America as well as Ned did. And to be truthful she would not have enjoyed the idea of him going off to work in America.

'But you don't like Ned,' she said.

'I don't have to like him,' retorted Helen. 'You and I know shits always prosper and Ned has the killer instincts I need, especially as I'm going to be over here. What's your reaction?'

Georgie gripped the receiver tightly. 'There's no bad blood between Ned and me,' she said. 'I'll do my best to get on with him but there's something I ought to tell you.'

'Yes?'

'Harry's been scheming with Ned to oust me and I'd already decided to get rid of Harry. I intended to discuss this with you first thing.'

'I'm not surprised. Harry finds it difficult enough to cope with me as the proprietor. As far as Ned is concerned, I've had some extremely frank chats with him and he accepts you're in sole charge here. I assure you he won't intercede on Harry's behalf if you sack him.' Helen laughed merrily. 'I've given him the title of deputy chairman. He's delighted and I've told him that after a couple of years I'll see whether he's ready to become chairman. I expect he's plotting already to cut down the wait.'

'What will you do then?'

Helen chortled. 'I'll still be around, as life president.'

'That's a relief. I'm not sure I would find it easy to report to Ned as chairman. I much prefer to work with you.' Georgie took a deep breath. This was not the way she had planned it but, 'I've something else I wanted to tell you about. There's no easy way of putting this, Helen, but I'm going to have a baby.'

There was no reaction.

'Of course I realise this is the worst of all possible times, both professionally and personally, but—'

'You're right about that.' The chill in Helen's voice upset Georgie. She had not expected Helen to be pleased but she thought they had developed enough of a friendship for her to be civil.

'Look, I know how much flak you took from the board on my behalf but I'm certain I can do the job with the child.'

Helen's response was blunt. 'No, you can't. I thought I made that clear.'

'I've thought it all out and I can.'

'I don't agree.'

'Sack me when the profits dip, not because of the baby.'

'You're putting me in an impossible position and I can't discuss this now, we've reached the terminal.'

Georgie had hoped not to resort to this, but in desperation she made her last throw. 'Helen, when you asked me to help you with the Louise business, I did. All I'm asking is that you give me a chance now.'

There was such a long silence, Georgie wondered if the connection had been broken but then she heard a sigh.

'You play a tough game. I never thought you'd use Vaduz as ammunition.'

'I'm sorry I needed to.'

'You've got balls, I give you that. OK, since you put it that way, you've got your chance. But I'm warning you, I'll be watching those profits closely.'

'You won't regret it. Thank you.'

'You're lucky I'm the majority shareholder and that I've decided to be a dictator and stop worrying about what other people think about me. Or my decisions. I'll see you when I get back.'

Helen switched off her mobile and lifted an eyebrow at Margery. 'That girl's toughened up. Did you hear how she put the bite on me?'

Margery nodded. 'I gathered from your conversation that she was not averse to using a bit of blackmail.'

Helen surprised herself by laughing. 'I know I should be furious but I can't help admiring her guts. Even though Alistair's left her, she's decided to go ahead and have the baby.'

'I applaud her courage, but it's going to be tough for her.'

'Right, and Georgina knows there'll be no concessions from me on that score.'

Margery smiled. 'That's just what Mark would have said.'

'I can see now why my dear husband loved going to the office each morning. It certainly gives you zest. You know, I was dreading telling Giles that he had to step down sooner rather than later, but that was another surprise. He was very sweet about it, said he understood my reasons and, get this, thought I'd made the right decisions. In any case he said he was looking forward to living in England again. New York doesn't suit him.'

'And it doesn't suit you, apparently,' said Margery, gazing sideways at her boss. 'I suppose this relocation wouldn't have anything to do with Paul Wallis being transferred to Dublin?'

'Just a coincidence.'

'Really? Then why did you spend those extra days there?'

'I was interviewing candidates, as you know, but then Paul came over to Dublin to give me details of the Liechtenstein business.'

'You didn't tell me that.'

'I wonder how he managed to get the account number and codes. I didn't even ask because he wouldn't have told me. If it ever came out . . .'

'Was he the reason you didn't come back for the *Art World* party?'

'That was naughty, wasn't it? So unlike me. But from now on I intend to please only one person. Myself. And after all those years of trying to second-guess Mark, I can't tell you what a great feeling it is. Finally, finally I'm in charge of myself.'

'And is Paul part of the new plan?'

'Probably not.' She gave a roguish smile. 'But who knows?'

As they waited for the driver to load the luggage Helen suddenly laughed. 'It's funny how things turn out. Life's pretty good for me now but,' she paused, 'I imagine poor Louise will find things tough.'

' "Poor" is right,' agreed Margery. 'Legally she can't get out of the lease she signed for that gallery and now she hasn't a backer, what's she to do?'

'Get a job?'

The idea of Louise job-hunting set them off again.

'What's she qualified for?' asked Margery sarcastically.

'Oh, I think she has a real talent. As a manicurist.'

The smiles remained as they checked in at Terminal Four and made their way towards the Concorde lounge.

Georgie sat back feeling exhausted after her conversation with Helen. She had achieved what she wanted but she felt nothing but sadness. She badly wanted to share this moment with Alistair. If Rosemary was to be believed, he intended to leave the country. Was he taking Louise with him? Probably. How long did he intend to remain abroad? In London he might have come round and spent time with the baby. Maybe, in time, they would have found something to salvage from their relationship. She was sure they could. But whatever Rosemary said, she was sure Louise and her baby were still on the scene. So it was senseless to daydream over something that could never happen.

The taxi was skirting the two-lane carriageway round

Totteridge Common, one of north London's biggest public parks, the venue for open-air concerts and the haunt of Sunday-morning football teams. Joggers, walkers and strollers could cross to the main arterial road via a diagonal short cut through the heart of the common.

The driver braked fiercely at a zebra crossing as a brown-blazered youngster broke away from a crocodile of schoolchildren and darted back to pick up a fallen exercise book.

The driver cursed. 'If I'd hurt him, who'd have been blamed? They don't teach them sense in school these days,' he said angrily over his shoulder.

Georgie was only half-listening. She had spotted a tall figure in sweatshirt and jeans on the path through the park. She blinked. He had the same build and colouring as Alistair but it couldn't be him, she told herself, not here in Barnet. Her imagination was playing tricks because she was thinking about him.

As the driver moved into gear, Georgie stared at the figure, walking slowly, head bent. The man was about two hundred yards away and she had trouble keeping track of him.

That blue sweatshirt. Didn't she recognise it? My God, it was the one she'd bought him in Milan. It was Alistair. There was no earthly reason for him to be in this remote part of the suburbs, except that it was where she was.

Georgie allowed herself to feel a small spark of hope and she leaned forward. 'Cabbie, pull over, please.'

# Best of Enemies

## Val Corbett, Joyce Hopkirk
## and Eve Pollard

Charlotte – 'Charlie' – Lockhart has it all: a devoted MP husband, Philip; an adorable toddler, Miranda; and an absorbing television career. But things aren't quite perfect. There's another woman in Philip's life: his ex-wife.

Five years after her divorce, Vanessa Lockhart would love to remarry. But dates are rare for fortysomething divorcées. At least she's close to her two girls, and she's made sure they know *exactly* how she feels about Charlie.

A rare face-to-face meeting between Charlie and Vanessa brings hostilities into the open. And there's worse to come. Someone is on the trail of a long-buried secret – a secret that could create scandalous headlines and destroy Philip's career. The slow torture of two families is about to begin . . .

'Kept me reading far too late into the night'
Maureen Lipman

'A page-turner . . . great fun' *The Times*

'Enjoyable blockbuster' *Sunday Times*

0 7472 4968 7

**HEADLINE**

# Splash

## Val Corbett, Joyce Hopkirk, Eve Pollard

'Bold, bubbly and deliciously bitchy. From three women who have seen and probably done it all'
Michael Dobbs, author of *House of Cards*

Katya, Liz and Joanna have been friends for years; closer even than sisters, they have always shared everything – except men. They have always supported each other on their way to the best jobs in a world dominated by men, acquiring the trappings and luxuries of authority that are the envy of other women. Nothing could drive them apart – or could it?

Now they're coping with new pressures. Katya is breaking all her own rules, for her new lover is married and she won't tell even her closest friends who it is. As the Television News Personality of the Year, Katya is a front page story waiting to happen – and the news, much more sensational than mere adultery, is beginning to break. It's just the story Liz needs for Page One to clinch her appointment as first woman editor of a British national daily newspaper. Their friend Joanna, editor of a glossy women's magazine, argues no story is worth destroying a friendship for – but how can Liz resist the splash of the year?

SPLASH is the story of power struggles between men and women, of unexpected love and the hurt of betrayal. Above all, it is the story of a friendship. No woman who has ever had – or been – a friend should miss it.

0 7472 4889 3

**HEADLINE**

*If you enjoyed this book here is a selection of other bestselling titles from Headline*